The History of Light Book 3:

THE BOOK OF SCENT

KEVIN HINCKER

THE HISTORY OF LIGHT

VOLUMES 1 THROUGH 5

THE SHADOW WAITING ON ITS THRONE

THE BOOK OF SCENT

THE HISTORY OF LIGHT BOOK 3

KEVIN HINCKER

CONTENTS

A WORD ABOUT THE CITY

Skysill Beach Master Plan

Skysill Beach is an art colony on the Southern California coast. It is stylish and quaint, wholly dedicated to taking money from tourists, and hosts a multitude of art galleries that *compel* shoppers to buy, using special ultraviolet paint. This is a town where ghosts and psychics and magic *light* are the pressing mysteries. Ringed by high coastal hills, resting in a bowl tilted toward the Pacific, it feels at once wild—filled with parks, pressed against the sea, separate from the outside world—and oppressively controlled. An unseen power oversees the painters of Skysill, who have lived for generations, trapped without knowing it, in a city they can never leave.

THE FIVE FAMILIES

~

1. **ASPECTU** *sight* [*The PAINTER*] *
2. **AUDITUS** *sound* [*The MUSICIAN*]
3. **SAPOR** *scent* [*The HUNTER*]
4. **NIDOR** *taste* [*The ALCHEMIST*]
5. **TACTUS** *touch* [*The DANCER*] *

* PRIME

THE THREE PSYCHIC PATHS

~

1. The offspring of either Prime and AUDITUS - <u>The Path Before</u>
2. The offspring of either Prime and NIDOR - <u>The Path Beneath</u>
3. The offspring of either Prime and SAPOR - <u>The Path Behind</u>

THE HIGHER COLORS

~

1. **choke** - *accumulation / dissipation*
2. **compulsion** - *attraction / repulsion*
3. **reason** - *transparency / obscurity*
4. **crush** - *large / small*
5. **farewell** - *beginnings / endings*
6. **wander** - *near / far*
7. **bleed** - *destruction*

CHAPTER
ONE

After Samantha appeared and shot me up through my skull I found myself going a little fast, with momentum carrying me up the flanks of a ghost mountain out of control, which in some way felt like a metaphor for my life. Though in exactly what way wasn't clear. I usually can't tell.

Below me spread the hamlet of Skysill Beach, crowding to the sand in its cup of coastal hills. And floating up with no control I came to a realization, because I had all that extra time: in the same way that all ghosts had become my responsibility because I was the only one who saw them, responsibility for this mountain would fall to me. And you could tell it was going to be a problem. It was going to be exclusively a me problem.

It towered over Skysill. It cast ultraviolet gloom on all our malls and our beach umbrellas and art galleries and stoplights. And I'm against gloom, which some people might be surprised to hear. I like a beach that's blazing bright which I can hide from in a bar. In the past avoiding beaches like that has given my life a simple kind of purpose.

Up through gloom I power lofted until, coming fast, I saw the peak. It pierced the stratosphere, where I was headed. The bare ghost stone of it streamed out in *dominion* banners across the sky, like pinnacle snow off Kilimanjaro, while sheets of bare stone plunged miles before piercing the distant tree line—or whatever that line is. What am I a botonist? I'm a psychic.

From that height, Skysill was just an urban fingerprint dusted onto the coast. The California shoreline dimmed north, toward Los Angeles, and south to Mexico, in haze and cloud trail. Above me as I rose the stars appeared.

I went higher until I came level with the stone needle tip of that mountain. Miles away but as clear as a junkie's conscience I saw it. Sheered off. A high, lonely platform. Out of that platform emerged a throne, carved from the peak itself, facing away from me.

And I shuddered. I felt again a foreknowledge of my oncoming death. And not in my usual drunken way of foreknowing things— like when is happy hour over—this was very specifically psychic and horrible.

The thing with foreknowledge, I suddenly found, was it seemed a much higher quality of knowledge than any of my other knowledge. And I just trusted it as the no-question truth: I would die on that ghost peak, touching the top of that throne, in three months' time.

Then I ran out of momentum, and back down I started, with no control of speed or destination which, again, probably a metaphor. The moment I changed direction there came a shimmery shake in the air and the entire ghost mountain vanished. I had a moment of vertigo being up so many miles without a mountain for stability.

I plunged, but it went pretty slow for a plunge—I could see it was going to take many boring minutes. It left me wondering, what do you do with psychic foreknowledge of your own death when nobody really thinks you're psychic? My first impulse was ignore the foreknowledge, but that didn't seem right. And what about this mountain? With this throne?

I'd seen it twice—just now, and the time Amy blew up Veronica's birdhouse. Two visions. So visions, ghosts, *dominion,* how anyone could doubt I was psychic at this point was beyond me. But a vision was a psychic thing I could ask Caroline about the next time she called, and that was a nice thought. In fact, thinking about Caroline felt like dopamine sugar rushing inside my head. I resolved to hurry down from the sky as fast as possible and go buy a phone.

But hurrying wasn't one of the speeds I had. Skysill widened out below me slowly as it approached, like a Google Earth animation of quaint shopping opportunities and lack of affordable housing, and a surprisingly high ghost population and murder rate. Which I was pretty sure were related to each other, by math. I mean I'm no murder expert but it seemed like an abnormal murder rate. Disproportionate stabbing numbers, at least.

Through my ghost feet, I finally saw the roof of Julian's California bungalow crypt, where my flesh body waited for me in Julian's studio gallery. On the walls where I'd left flesh me were masterpieces Julian had painted over the course of at least five hundred years, in between bouts of murdering people. Which said everything you needed to know about Julian: brilliant artist, violently insane, very, very old.

I knew Samantha was hanging around in the gallery below because if she'd left I'd already have been sucked back in my flesh. And I knew Veronica was still there because I heard her, a little tinny and distant, through my ghost connection to my flesh ears. And Veronica was irritating, but Samantha was the real problem. If Samantha planned to hang around, then before I could get my body back I'd have to puppet flesh me cross-eyed and kill this *storm.* And since that was as pleasant as swallowing lava I liked it only as a last resort.

As I floated the last few yards toward the roof I looked out at the coast. There I saw the paint store, Fenestram Color, and just behind that the house Amelia blew the roof off, which I'd escaped without injury because I'd been *Gray* and it's hard to touch me at all when I'm *Gray*. These days at least. I ghost-shuddered, remembering my recent greyscale days up Aliso Canyon. The things I remembered were...the *Gray* always has been a sensation junkie, but its cravings were getting much harder to satiate. This time I'd almost killed Amelia by almost letting her die without trying to help her.

The *Gray*, I thought, as the soles of my ghost feet slipped through the shingles, the *Gray* was getting too powerful. I'd need to be careful. Which wasn't one of my strengths. If Julian showed up here, now, in his gallery, I'd probably go *Gray,* I suddenly thought. And then who knows what kind of damage I'd do, or who I'd do it to?

Up to my knees now I heard Veronica's voice clearly. She was on the phone issuing commands in her favorite language, Standard Billionaire. I don't know why these people put up with it.

"—and I will also need to speak with Shay," I heard her command. "Yes. I will go to her if I must. If the Conclave is truly to be *tomorrow night* there is no time. Set a meeting with Willametta and say nothing of Asher or...*dominion.* And I—just a moment I have another call..."

A bird from a coastal oak took off and flew right through me. It was unsettling. Birds don't see ghosts either, I concluded. I'm the only one.

Up to my chest I slid, and now had only my head and shoulders outside the room. I heard Veronica's voice turn softer as she took the new call. It was still disturbing in a different way. Like a statue smiling.

"Hello dear," I heard her say, my chin slipping through the roof, "I have Asher with me, he's on the floor at my feet. Because he came to the store and insisted!" Her voice got less soft. "Because you were elsewhere and—no Amelia, stay where you are. I will take care of him. I promise, yes... because I'm *leaving as soon as possible* and you have other—Amelia do not—"

I heard Veronica growl. She'd been hung up on. My sister has a low tolerance for almost everything I've ever seen her deal with. It's an interesting sensation, hovering down through the roof of a house, in that there's no sensation, but some part of your brain expects a sensation. The addict part probably.

My head fell emerged down through the ceiling and I appeared inside the gallery and was once again shocked at the brilliance of the paintings. All the canvases here were Julian's—or Niccolo Filippi's since they were one person. It seemed impossible. At over five hundred years, Julian would be the oldest crack-head in history. But impossible or not I knew it was true. I know a forgery when I see one. And the canvases here were not forged—painted over the last five hundred years, yes, but the work of only one hand. Julian/Niccolo.

Veronica was dressed in white like an elegant butcher with her hands on her hips, and she stared down at flesh me. New Dwayne silently attended her. Samantha floated to the side pounding *light* through the room and staring at flesh me like the other two, though she had no choice. And in her hand she held nothing. No goblet. It looked like a trama hole. Flesh me himself lay on the floor, though I didn't remember leaving him on the floor. I hoped he hadn't tripped. If he kept smashing my face this way I'd need a safety mask.

He curled on his stomach, drooling, black hair sprayed all directions and stiff from hours asleep on Amelia's couch. He had stubble everywhere, which has always been my best look, but that's saying practically nothing. His eyes bleared open but didn't dart or drift at all because he was locked motionless. One shoe was untied. He looked like a very particular smell. Oh, flesh me. What a mess.

Veronica flipped back to her non-Amelia call. I listened from the ceiling.

"Are you there?" she demanded. "It was Amelia. Now. I need detailed information on the Tactus, where in Skysill they are staying, where in the city they go. Leander particularly. We will get Asher to the car somehow and transfer him to you at the store. This is exactly the same as what happened in Los Angeles—in the presence of a ghost, or what he claims is a ghost, he is awake but unresponsive. No, I prefer him this way. Go. I need my report on the Tactus!"

She pocketed her phone and sighed, and said to New Dwayne, "I suppose we must carry him."

I dislike being carried as a general rule, except by my favorite bouncers, so the idea of Veronica doing it and being subtly put off the whole time seemed insufferable, which is not a word I ever remember using before. And Samantha showed no signs of evaporating. So the time had come for me to merge my bodies.

I kicked down. I left my ghost floating above and flitted through blind nothing and re-entered flesh me. Like swimming underwater from one floating pool bar to the other.

Frozen on the floor in my flesh, I yanked ghost me down from the ceiling and positioned him for merging. Veronica and New Dwayne took a step toward me, each battling distaste thinking how best to grab and hoist me. Before they could make up their minds I shifted to my ghost to jerk flesh me seated, and from there staggered him to his feet, and had him do ghost charades at Veronica—*stay the fuck away from me.*

Then in my ghost, I turned to Samantha.

You could just vanish right now and make this easy, I ghosted at her, while flesh me tried to mimic the words and spat out *kjasf nioiushdf iu iuhr ixur.* Veronica and New Dwayne looked surprised and more confused and tried to decipher him. That was funny. Though not in a way that made me laugh.

You're making me boil back together the hard way? I demanded at her. *Really? After everything I've done for you? Which alright hasn't been <u>that</u> many things but has anyone else done more? No. No, I don't think so. A little gratitude is all I'm saying.*

Flesh me mangled all that out in a word casserole and Samantha kept ignoring me. So I bent flesh me to his knees with his hands bunched in fists, which Veronica and New Dwayne watched looking sad and a little repulsed, and I screwed his face cross-eyed and grimaced and *squeezed.*

Ghost me flipped sideways to glide in and co-inhabit my flesh body space, but were were not blended yet. Our temperatures rose. Flesh me began groaning, in our throats was the pain of burning kerosene, ghost me soul screamed, and blah blah agony while *dominion* monster-mixed my two bodies and they snapped together. It was broken bone agony in reverse. *Dominion* surged down my arm. In my fist, I had a tube of Julian's Higher paint which I'd grabbed for exactly this contingency.

As soon as the tube glowed with *dominion* I was back. One body again. I gasped and fell back on the floor.

"Thanks for nothing," I shouted at Samantha while Veronica and New Dwayne watched. "I wanna get out of here," I complained to Veronica.

"Yes," she said, probably disappointed I was awake. But she's adaptable. "Julian is clearly not here, which I think is lucky. And we have larger issues to address."

"Larger issues than a five-hundred-year-old super-powered *Fabrica* who hates me?" I asked, just to be clear. She nodded.

The gallery was hot. I stood, unsteady, but I'm practiced that way. It's natural. Veronica, tense, checked her phone and she waited for me to get verticle, while New Dwayne scanned the hall we'd come in through, taking his deep breaths and smelling threats a few seconds in our future. Or whatever. That's what they claimed. At this point there had to be so many threats, how do you really track that, considering all the people trying to kill us? Or me, anyway. Julian. Brazilian hit men. Maybe even Aeternus, assuming he was real.

I wondered if there was a scenario where I left these other two and headed off on my own to get a phone, but Veronica was waiting for that idea.

"Come," she said. "We leave together." She reached to move me out of the gallery but I dodged. "What is the problem, Mr. Gale?"

"There's more than one," I told her. Her phone chimed. Again. Billionaires.

"This is very bad," she said after a moment of scrolling.

"Stocks down?" I wondered because I'm easy to get along with.

"Tactus are canvassing the city. We must hurry you into hiding."

"Remember we talked about me hiding before and I'm not interested?"

Veronica had a history of dismissing my nonsense, and this idea too passed through her mind like clouds.

"There will be a Conclave," she insisted to me, replying to a text but talking to me. "Do you understand?"

"No, is that a serious question?"

"Listen! The leaders of all Five Families are meeting in Skysill tomorrow. A Conclave. They are filing the city. And they must not find you."

New Dwayne wheeled toward Veronica.

"Something," he said, pointing outside. "Inbound, possibly... airborne."

"We must get to my store," Veronica said to me. She dashed from the gallery, maybe expecting me to follow. "From the store, someone will take you to a safe house Asher. Come!"

"Hey," I shouted, "I said no safe house, stop making plans for me. I'll ride with you but I'm not part of your secret organization."

"What *are* you part of?" she demanded, spinning, as furious as I'd ever seen her. More than when the apprentices were killing her. She looked a little unhinged, in fact. The whites of her eyes showed for a second. "What is it you *want*, Mr. Gale?"

"Who knows," I scoffed. Then I remembered how my hair had looked lying on the floor. "I want a shower."

"A shower? There will be a *bloodbath* in Skysill unless things are managed perfectly. Your *dominion* has destabilized the entire balance, the thing that has kept the Families from destroying each other for untold eons—you are a part of *that*, I assure you. Act like it!"

New Dwayne watched us disagreeing, getting more and more unhappy.

"We need to go *now*," he said. "Something...not far ahead..."

"How soon?" snapped Veronica.

He shook his head. "Don't know. Fast."

I'm actually not super hard to influence if people really look like they know what they're doing, so when those two dashed from the room—definitely as if they had a plan—I followed from instinct. I felt I was lucky escaping Julian's hillside cabana without finding him even though that's exactly what I'd come for. The logic of it all kept bringing me to the *Gray*. Now I wanted out as fast as possible.

New Dwayne backtracked down hallways toward the front doors. My eagerness to go grew with every step, until we got to the long front hall with the door hung open from Veronica's sparkle break-in, and there New Dwayne stopped. He stood drawing breaths and waving his arms like kelp in a slow current. But I wasn't interested in waiting, which is something anyone will tell you about me.

I took a step around him toward the door. Veronica grabbed my arm. And all hell broke loose in my brain.

When she touched me, the weight of the ghost mountain fell on me again. I could see it, somehow, through the walls, towering outside, high over the world. It cast *light* shadows everywhere made of terrible ultraviolet gloom. And I felt a hole open in my skull. And pain daggered through, stabbing me in the mind. Her touch was doing it.

My knees buckled. Veronica tried to catch me. That made it worse. There wasn't anything I could do for myself. But the pain wasn't even the worst part. It was the other thing, the foreknowledge of death that came from her touch. Not my death. This time Veronica's.

This dark knowing came like electrified rot and spiked down my brain hole: I saw Veronica dead, high in the air, at the peak of a cold ghost mountain. I saw it happening in three months' time. It was the same peak as mine. The same date, too.

The rot spread through me from her grip, numbing while I gasped, "Let...go..." and then fell free and slumped against the wall. When Veronica stopped touching me my skull rupture closed.

The two of them clearly wanted me to *hurry with the episode we have to leave,* and Veronica bent to help—which you could see didn't come naturally—but I scrambled back.

"Don't touch me," I coughed, waving my arms, "nobody touch me."

"What now?" she asked, glancing to the sides, so unhappy. "More ghosts?"

"No," I said. I felt twitchy, numb in tooth and lip, like I'd put aluminum foil in my mouth or chewed a battery. "This isn't that. Not ghosts. This is something new."

"Something new." She said, "Something new in the last ten minutes?"

"Veronica," I told her, "I'll just come out and say this. I just found out I'm psychic for *sure.* What just now happened when you touched me is part of me being psychic. Probably."

"You are not psychic."

"I am so."

"Does this have something to do with Caroline?" she snapped. "With your Prime short-circuiting?"

"No! What? Look, like it or not I'm psychic. Just now when you touched me I foresaw your death. So what about that? Right? It's going to be a very weird death but those are going around. You'll die in three months on top of a mountain. Probably a ghost mountain."

I didn't say according to my information I'd be dying there at the same time because I didn't want to overwhelm her with information. It was probably just a coincidence. New Dwayne stood in the door and his breath came deeper and deeper while Veronica denied me with head shaking.

"Psychics cannot see death on the Paths," she told me. "Death is the only thing hidden from them."

"Oh, psychics don't see death? Is that your story? You don't know what you're talking about," I coughed. "This is real. I don't care if you believe me. Don't touch me."

One thing you can say about Veronica, she internalizes new

information quickly. Maybe that's why she's the billionaire and I'm the one who doesn't have a wallet or car keys or a car or a phone. You could see new information turning old ideas around in her mind.

"I die in three months?" she said. "That's when the psychics say the Paths of time will break."

"Maybe we die when the Paths break."

"We? You've seen the deaths of others?"

"I don't know what I've seen," I dissembled. "That's part of my charm."

New Dwayne was really windmilling now, sending crisscross breezes everywhere, sucking air like a dying fish.

"We have to *move*," he cried, pointing, "localized activity, definitely flying, unspecified arrival."

"Who?" Veronica asked. New Dwayne didn't know. Then they surged toward the door. I suspected "who" was "Julian." Something coming through the air, and I'd known Julian as a flier. I checked my hands for a *Gray* salute but so far nothing. I still carried my paint tube, just in case of a *storm*. So prepared. Like a boy scout.

"Let's get out of here," I yelled, hunching my shoulders and letting New Dwayne lead me through the door. He smelled us into the garden, Veronica followed and I came last. The sun was bright. I cranked my *sight* to boost the contrast, scanning hedge shadows and behind me over my shoulder. The handicap of my new psychic power was occurring to me. I wondered, was it possible to spend time in a bar without touching anyone? I was going to need a bar soon.

We reached her car. I waited while they piled in then buckled myself as far from human contact as I could get. New Dwayne spun to tilt us downhill. The windows were down so he could breathe the future through them. He punched the gas and we dropped. Down through eucalyptus switchbacks toward the beach, we whirled.

We went a few minutes going too fast saying nothing while I waited for someone else to bring it up, because why does it always have to be me? But finally, I wondered out loud, "So is anybody else worried, or concerned, about Julian? Like how can he be five hundred years old? How can he really be a Renaissance painter named Niccolo Filippi? Who's now *missing*, and a *psychopath*, and probably wants to kill us or just me?"

"We will present the information to the Families when we have the chance," Veronica said.

"He's one of you though," I accused. "Fabrica sparklers—do you *all* live five hundred years?"

"No," she snapped. She was tired of my questions, which I was just getting started with.

"So what's he doing?" I wondered. "Where'd that goblet blasting *dominion* come from? That was Samantha's goblet you know. Now her hand is empty. I don't know what that means. I feel like these are important questions. I feel like you're not—"

"*Quiet*," she insisted, watching New Dwayne drive, checking the road behind us. She looked worried as shit, but not about what I wanted her to worry about. It was frustrating.

As we took the next tire squealing curve I realized New Dwayne was driving with his eyes closed. He spun us through another corner that way. I gave him one more second to wake up then turned to Veronica with more questions. She was fixated on the road behind us.

"Is that normal?" I demanded about our blind driver, as the car swayed too fast through another curve.

"He's Sapor," she reminded me, and I shook my head, where I kept no memories, so she snarled, "Sapor! One of the Five Families. You are Aspectu. You *see*. He is Sapor, he *scents*. Through scent, Sapor build rolling models of the future, and well trained Sapor sense ten seconds or more ahead." She looked back at New Dwayne. "He knows precisely when to turn the wheel."

"It makes me uncomfortable," I told her.

"Eight seconds to contact," New Dwayne shouted, suddenly, eyes shut, "we picked up a shadow."

"Evade?" Veronica asked.

"Doesn't happen," he shook his blind eyes and whipped through another pin turn, "contact inbound, four seconds!"

"Pull over," Veronica shouted.

New Dwayne skidded us to the edge of a curve and stopped. Dust billowed. I didn't know where to look, I tried everyplace, then New Dwayne said, "Two seconds." Abruptly he pointed to the roof and opened his eyes. Veronica ripped her door wide and leaned to stare at the sky and then stepped out. New Dwayne and I followed her.

"And we're in contact," New Dwayne announced. He took impossibly deep breaths, spinning his arms, facing a point on the horizon above the water, directly toward the sun. Anything attacking from the air that way would be hard to see. Even my eyes have trouble resolving pure nuclear sun fire.

I caught an ultraviolet flash beside me. Veronica's eyes had counter crossed. Her eyeballs slipped out toward her temples and showed white, turning my stomach. Her fingers blossomed balls of *reason,* tiny galaxies of Higher *light* hooked to her hands. She circled one in the air and left a concave lens of *reason* shimmering, glassy like floating water. She stared through it with white eyes, facing New Dwayne's horizon target, while he breathed and I felt poorly prepared.

"What in the world?" she muttered, after a second. "A drone. A quadcopter."

To New Dwayne, all her ultraviolet *light* work had to be invisible, but when I looked into her Fabrica magnifier lens I saw a black drone, blades blurring, optics trained on us. Hanging in the sun the way it was, I couldn't see it without Veronica's telescope.

"*Who?*" she demanded of New Dwayne, and he shrugged.

"Let's keep moving," I urged, "and get off this ridge."

"No," Veronica snarled. "Drones? Who do they think I am?"

She looked twitchy. It reminded me of how she'd looked after the apprentices had beaten her pulpy, as she'd crawled, burned and broken to drain me of *dominion* and fight a little longer. It was a face fierce with hate. Her white eyes bulged. She bared her teeth.

With one preemptory hand she positioned her lens, then brought her other hand up, heavy with *bleed* in a throbbing ball, wavelets dripping into the air which isn't something I'd seen any kind of *light* do before. Her face hashed up fury, anguish—out of control, not at all subtle, not at all on brand for Veronica Night, sciencey mistress of irony. I guess when you've been flayed and kicked almost to death it changes you. Even billionaires.

I heard—and felt—a pressure pop, like a door closing in a sealed room, and Veronica's *bleed* beamed through her lens, lancing out into the sky. There was a flare, and pieces of drone fell from the air. I looked to the horizon and killed the opacity and just made out a puff of smoke. A long way away. A great shot.

After that I couldn't look away from her billiard ball eyes. I badly wanted them to be normal but it took a minute. While I waited I complained, which is the thing I do. "What's happening *now*?" I asked. "We're under attack?"

She hissed at me sideways. It was a hiss that said she hoped I wasn't serious because clearly, yes, we were under attack and clearly had *been* under attack for at least a week by various people and ghosts, why was I seriously asking that?

So I clarified, "Yes, snakelady, I know the obvious people have been attacking us for a week but would any of them use a *drone*? Aeternus is a ghost, supposedly, and Julian flies on his own. So who's flying drones? Do you follow my reasoning?"

"This is unbelievably clumsy," Veronica said, as her eyes finally rolled into her sockets filled with contempt. "We only have to wait. They'll make a mistake and reveal themselves. Now it is time to go."

"But why wait for them? Ask your psychic," I said at New Dwayne, whose breathing had slowed. "Are we safe now?"

"He is *Sapor*, not psychic," she snarled. I was exhausting to her. "Do you really not remember how the Families work Mr. Gale? We are about to descend into a storm of Family forces. This information could save your life."

"Or maybe I just stay out of it completely."

"You cannot. Particularly if you are, suddenly, psychic yourself, though that seems vanishingly unlikely. I doubt you know what that even means. What the psychics do on the Paths is completely different from how Auditus and Sapor use temporal data. The psychics actually travel in time, they traverse the universal continuum of time, while Sapor and Auditus use olfactory and auditory senses, physical senses. Are you following? A Sapor can gestalt odors to create predictive models of the future. Up to ten seconds ahead, though Adepts can sense much farther. Just as when the Auditus process sounds—they navigate a mental model of the past. But psychics immerse themselves in the tangible essence of time. It is the difference between a postcard of the Eiffel Tower and going to the Eiffel Tower."

"Let's do this later with a chalkboard and more vodka."

"Remember this," she told me, preparing to dumb it all down as far as possible, which is all I ever ask of anyone and why they don't just start there I do not know. "The Families are divided in two camps, toward each Prime. Some with the Tactus—those who touch —and some with us. Aspectu. These are ancient and finely balanced alliances. This has kept the peace. But now that peace is in danger. The Agreements have been breached."

"I don't like the sound of any Agreements so I'm going to pretend you didn't say that. Are you saying this drone was one of your other Families?" I asked.

"They're not mine," she snapped but glanced at New Dwayne for an answer. He had his eyes open now, though what he needed them for I didn't know. He smelled everything's future apparently. But New Dwayne just shrugged. He had no idea what was going on.

"As I said," she said to me, "we shall have to wait. They will stumble into the light. Come," she motioned, waving us toward the car, which wasn't a bad move so I started that direction, and billionaire impatience made her reach to grab my arm.

Suddenly New Dwayne was between us, deflecting her hand to keep her from touching me. He shook his head, taking deep breaths through his nose, and I wondered what future he'd just smelled. Then I remembered—my future. My brain rot.

"Ah yes," Veronica nodded, eyeing me the way they all end up doing. "Then hurry."

She pointed.

But before I could move, a sharp-cold pulse shot off the blue crystal silver-chained on my neck. It had started as a pretty simple day. But now, as they often did, it was becoming just one thing after another.

The crystal pulse spread ice through my chest, then came again. At the same time, I thought I was starting to hear things. I thought I heard a door that sounded oddly specifically like someone's front door closing behind *me*, and I turned to look while Veronica stood expressing fondness for all my delays and shenanigans.

Another freezing pulse. What was happening? I heard more footsteps and felt yet another pulse from the neutral crystal...oh! I recognized it! This was telepathy! I was eavesdropping on someone who was at that very moment thinking about calling me. But I didn't have a phone. But it was a call I really wanted to take.

"I'll take that phone you offered," I called to Veronica. "Where is it?"

"In the car," she sighed. "Why? What is *this*, now, are you having another fit?"

"It's Caroline, and right now she's thinking about calling me."

I ran to the car to fling things from the trunk to the ground, aware of someone's hand reaching into their back pocket, feeling for a phone, and I tossed out a briefcase and a hack saw and a case of water, Peter's backpack full of turtles.

Then I found Veronica's promised phone. I held it up to stare at the screen, anticipating. Someone was dialing me. My crystal pulsed harder and harder and I found myself holding it with my other hand.

"Caroline, you say?" Veronica asked, disturbed.

"Yeah...I hear...I mean not hearing...our telepathy's back! She's... she—her client's late—her phone's out—"

"What are you saying?" Veronica demanded, basically shouting. "*Telepathy?*"

"Hold it, she's calling…"

"Stop!" Veronica cried. "Asher! Are you not wearing the neutral *crystal?*"

Her eyes counter crossed as she spoke, her hands lit with *choke,* and micro bursts of *light* unraveled my shirt down the front. Exposing, around my neck on a silver chain, the brook-blue gemstone, twin to the one Caroline wore.

Then the Caroline sensation faded. Her client had come in. She couldn't call me after all. But it was exciting. She seemed to know I had a new phone.

"Never mind," I called, pocketing the phone. "False alarm."

Veronica's eyes fixed on my necklace.

"Have you taken that off?" she asked, disbelief growing. "Even once?"

"Of course not. We'll explode if I do, or whatever. I know."

Veronica came to stand very close to me. She remembered not to touch me, but she was very intense the way people who expect to be listened to because they're rich sound. It totally worked on me.

"You and Caroline will *kill* each. You will die together. That will happen. And I would simply leave you to your fate, though Amelia would be distraught, but it would be unfair to Caroline." She shook her head. "So, despite the crystals, you still feel connected to her?"

She was pointing at my chest. I looked.

"You ripped my shirt," I noticed.

"Tell me this," Veronica demanded, intense, "does your crystal ever grow *cold?*"

"Oh shit yeah, constantly. Freezing bursts, can we do anything about that? Caroline's too. Do you have another shirt for me?"

"You're in *communication* with Caroline?" Veronica increduled.

"Look, Veronica, who knows what I'm in? Or with? Let's drop the subject since it's none of your business and I don't understand it. Let's talk about, are you going to fix this shirt?"

"No," she said. "Come."

Back in the car we got, and continued pinballing downhill, me toying with the crystal like a piece of chipped ice on my chest. It felt colder, much colder than when I'd put it on a week ago in LA, and colder even than this morning. If the necklace hadn't been the only thing keeping Caroline and I safe from each other I would have thrown it off, since I'm not a jewelry person and it wasn't comfortable jewelry. But we'd formed a Prime short circuit and I believed Veronica when she said it would kill us. I'd felt it. But now, even with the crystals, our connection was returning.

Had she gotten an image of me? I suddenly feared she'd seen me in a picture, like I had her. It was a sobering thought, which is the kind I hate, since I'd recently inspected flesh me from the outside and he looked like someone's neglected dog tied to a pole. And now, on top of it all, his clothes were unraveling. Caroline deserved better, I thought. Along with ghosts, suddenly I was responsible for grooming some *body*. I'm the responsible one? It made no sense.

"Take me home," I said out loud as we came off the hill and took tree-lined avenues toward the beach. New Dwayne looked in the mirror at Veronica like all the Dwaynes before him, while Veronica looked at me.

"That is out of the way," she decided.

"Get me a little closer and I'll walk."

"You told me you lost your house key."

"I tell people a lot of things."

"Oh, of course! Amelia had a spare," she nodded to herself. "You are very lucky in her."

"You have a lot of opinions about Amelia...take me—hey my house's *that* way."

We hit Pacific Coast Highway at Pier 9 and New Dwayne went left, downcoast. But I wanted to go up the coast through downtown to my clean clothes, or whatever was in my closet.

"There is no time," Veronica said. "At the paint store we will decide where to conceal you."

"You're like a dog locked on a fender with this concealing thing—there'll be no concealing, Veronica, I need a shirt and a toothbrush. Stop at this light. I can walk."

We were going south, the beach bright and pale in fall sunlight, through a stretch where a few minor galleries lured tourists with *compulsion*. The ocean flashed on my right. The traffic was slow and steady, just the way Skysill's merchants preferred it. I was pointing New Dwayne to a curb I liked but he ignored me. His eyes were closed again, and he had one hand out the window, scooping passing air into his face. Veronica was watching.

"I want *out*," I reminded them.

"What can you tell me?" Veronica asked New Dwayne.

"Tactus," he told her, "they arrive at the store before us."

"How many?"

"There'll be three, and a Sapor. We're looped now."

I made one more try. "If you don't open this fucking door I'm going to scream," I suggested. But they didn't care.

"Quiet," Veronica said. "We have been anticipated. This is not optimal. The Tactus have their own Sapor and they know we are coming. If we stop and you get out they will know. You're destabilizing the balance, and they want you eliminated, though I don't think they know yet who you are. But they know you exist."

She counter crossed her eyes. One hand radiated *choke* and I saw a transparent strip, like ultraviolet masking tape, form in the air.

"Hold your shirt together," she told me.

I didn't. Why would I?

"Quickly," she hissed, exasperated. "The farther away we are the less they can model!"

I gave the shirt edges a halfhearted pull and Veronica flicked her *choke*. The tape *flew* and slapped onto my shirt. It was only *light*, but the way it moved, it was on a mission. When I felt bubbling on the fabric between my fingers I yelped.

The shirt was mended. Though it didn't hang right. She was no tailor.

"Only by touching you or seeing you wearing a crystal can they be sure what you are," she said. "Hopefully you will not be seen at all. If you are, we will say you are my intern."

"*Oh*," I said, juggling information, "are *these* the people flying the drone?"

"No," she scoffed, "these people do not need drones."

I tried the door on a sudden thought, though we were moving, but of course found it locked. Billionaires and their locks. These doors opened at the driver's sole discretion and New Dwayne belonged to Veronica. I was stuck.

"We're four minutes from the store," I complained since they'd reduced me to it, "so how come New Dwayne can sense anything at all? You said he smelled a few seconds into the future."

"There is a Sapor in the other party, creating an effect. A loop."

"The Tactus—it's Leander," said New Dwayne suddenly. He had his eyes closed, though by this time I'd grown completely comfortable with his blind driving style because I'm given to unreasonable adaptation and I run out of energy to worry. Maybe it'd actually be best if we crashed, I thought.

"Listen to me," Veronica said to me, like there was anything else I could do after she'd captured me. "Leander is a power among the Tactus. He may soon lead them. This will be dangerous. He will try to read me. Remain in the car."

"No! No way, I have—"

"These are Tactus you fool! Tactus—*of the body*. A purebred Tactus is immensely strong, fast, bio magnetic, among other..." she trailed off, peering through the windshield as New Dwayne, inhaling like a madman, swept our car across two lanes and pulled to the sidewalk in front of Fenestram Color. Exactly where she'd said she was going to take me. They always get their way.

The sidewalk here was crowded. A line of Fenestram artists I recognized waited in front of the store. They were squatting or they leaned against the wall single filing to the door. It looked like a strip mall nightclub for painters. What was everyone lining up to buy?

A man strolled along the line and stopped to take each painter by the hand and hold it. The question I asked myself the instant I saw him was, hello, is that a cloud of *butterflies* surrounding his head and body? Beautiful and variously colored butterflies? Flashing iridescent and churning like leashed smoke?

Yes it was. This man was surrounded by a multi-chromatic cloud of butterflies, which really highlighted his rockstar good looks. He had black skin, sexy beard shadow, lead singer cheekbones and a smile that ate all the other smiles, ravishing and hungry. And he had butterflies.

In the shade of the hipster dentist lounged two more rockstars from the same band, like backup singers but dangerous ones, clothes mostly leather. They had no butterflies or other bugs. Then there was a fourth, an ordinary one, or ordinary except her eyes were closed and she sucked oxygen and waved her arms.

"Who's *that*?" I asked, pointing at the butterfly magnet.

"Leander," she hissed. A lot of hissing from Veronica today.

The line of artists was staring at Leander just like I was. I could feel, on my chest, my neutral crystal fending off some electric kind of attraction, though a general fascination was still getting through to me. As soon as the car stopped Veronica was opening her door and sliding out, telling me things, but I wasn't listening.

"Wait," she said to me as New Dwayne got out the driver's door.

"I said no," I said and slid toward her. "I said I need clean clothes for this body and a comb, just don't get me involved in your Family bullshit, I'll slip away and no one will notice."

"You will not. Wait in the car."

She stepped out, one hand trailing behind, and the fingertips of that hand filled with *compulsion,* pointed my way. She wasn't even looking, she was that confident. Before I could say, *oh you fucking wouldn't compel me—that's shittier than...*she'd flicked the *compulsion* off her nails right at my mouth.

"Stay," she commanded as she slammed the door.

But her *compulsion* never reached me. My *dominion* sphere

flipped up like it had every other time some Fabrica probed me with *light*. The sphere caught her *compulsion* weblet and broke it into mist. I guess it doesn't protect my shirt, but my mouth is out of bounds. For a second, as the sphere glowed up, my muscles locked. Then *dominion* vanished and I was free. I remembered the truly sickening feeling when she'd *compelled* me while trying to tap me. But this time it hadn't worked. I reached for the door handle.

And something stopped me. Because, I thought, what if these people really were looking for me? Was it that outlandish? If Veronica had involved me in her Family squabble, was it the smartest thing to just jump out in full view? Even without *compulsion* she'd sort of boxed me in. I prefer coming to the attention of as few sober people as possible, even on my best days. Maybe I'd stay in the car a moment. Maybe try exercising my prudence, which I felt in some ways I'd neglected recently.

A situation was developing outside. Through tinted glass I watched Veronica and New Dwayne step onto the sidewalk, and I watched Leander turn. He stepped toward them. His butterflies came with him. His butterflies thought he was as beautiful as the rest of us did and they didn't want him getting away. My neutral crystal was working hard, battering down attraction with cold shivers, and if this knife edge horniness was what Five Family life was always like, all battling a desire to tear each other's clothes off, no wonder Veronica was such a frustrated mess.

"Leander," I heard her say, giving Leander an icy smile. She had a cloak of *wander* drawn around her body now. I had no idea what that was for.

"Veronica," Leander smiled back, "you look well."

And then, as graceful as precision jewelry, he reached for her wrist. Veronica raised her arm to grab his wrist right back. And as I watched, her *wander* shroud deformed beneath his fingers, like insulation thinning between her body and his. Leander seemed oblivious. I assumed Tactus couldn't see *light*. Tactus were...what? It was

true, what Veronica said, I should pay more attention. Tactus were…
what did *of the body* mean?

Veronica and Leander grew still, and ticking seconds passed like they do before an old west quick draw in a movie, and I saw Leander's charisma competing with whatever it was Veronica had—arrogance and derision, I decided. Slowly, though, he widened his smile. And then let go of her arm. He stepped back in his butterflies, while over in the shade by the dentist office the two backup rockstars let themselves relax, which made them even more ravishing. New Dwayne and the other lady Sapor dialed down their breathing, and suddenly they were all together having a happy sidewalk picnic. But I didn't trust it. I stayed in the car.

"This is all your doing I suppose?" Veronica asked Leander. "The Conclave tomorrow?"

"What *is* this you've got here?" he ignored her, pointing at the line of artists, then at the rest of the city, acting casually concerned though I didn't think anything he did was really casual. "A hidden city of Aspectu. Where did you Fabrica find them all?"

"Don't be an idiot," she snapped. "Aeternus did this. Ask Willametta, the Fabrica have nothing to do with it."

"Willametta," he said, shaking his head. *All the names,* I complained to myself. Willametta. Leander. Was it going to keep getting more complicated like this? Names are fucking irritating.

Leander held his pose of casual interest, in the sun, in his tight clothes, which I was happy to stare at.

"I don't think it's Willametta hiding this town of the *sighted*," he said. "I think it's *you.*"

"It is *Aeternus!*" she shouted, her face twisting. I saw her eyes counter cross, like she couldn't stop them, but then she raised a hand to her temple and shook her head, and her pupils resurfaced. She was hanging out over some raw brink today, I saw. Like with the drone, she was toying with totally losing her shit. This was a new Veronica. She was scarier than before.

Leander frowned. He'd noticed her eyes coming and going. He didn't like it.

"Aeternus again," he observed.

"Yes!" she snarled. "How long have I been saying it? He is returning, and now we find this town? Are you all *blind*?"

"We don't see what you see," he admitted, watching her face. Her eyes. "Aeternus. You see the ghost under every rock. And we all know why, of course. You poor thing. Such a tragedy. But a secret town of the untapped? Which you conveniently *discover* at the same moment we learn the Fabrica can work *light* after sunset? You expect us to believe this in a coincidence?"

He snapped and pointed, and one of his backup singers left the shadows. Running. She was *fast*. Like a blade flashing she came to the car where I waited and stopped, tilting her face toward the passenger window, trying to see through my tinted glass and steaming it up. Her breath had to be blistering to steam glass in the full sun. I had even less desire to leave the car.

She rattled the door handle and found it locked. In another blur she circled to the driver's side and tried that handle, then worked her way to my door. I leaned back in the seat, motionless. Like a rabbit.

"Unlock it?" Leander suggested to Veronica.

"It's a plague car," Veronica apologized, "it really wouldn't be wise."

"Don't be like that," Leander tsked, smiling brighter. Veronica turned casually to the line of painters watching us like cows at a salt lick.

"You should go home," she called to them. "Right now. There will be no paint today. Go home!" They didn't move. Artists are just bad at instructions, it's not only me. Veronica sighed back to Leander, and she had all her subtlety back. She smiled at him.

"Let's go inside, shall we? Fewer eyes. I don't want you children to make a mistake."

His smile went grim. A little violent. It made him even more astonishing to look at, like a black Elvis. He tossed his chin at my car and the lady outside stopped rattling the handle. A moment later the whole car heaved. I heard metal shriek and saw the door buckle, then the whole door peeled off the car and she held it out in traffic where passing cars swerved and skidded.

I scrambled away from the opening as the hot breathed beauty slipped in the back seat. She had wide green eyes and slicked hair, like she'd come from a sexy rainstorm photoshoot. She blinked, curious; she was riveting to stare at and terrifyingly strong if the door was any indication. My plan to stay inside the car had officially backfired, as my plans tend to. I faced the lady as behind me I pried the other door handle. She slid happily closer. Around her neck, I saw a blue neutral crystal.

Then the latch was open and out I fell. I stumbled, tripped on the sidewalk, and turned to get my bearings, which I'd left in my other life.

"Okay, Veronica, I'm heading home now," I called loudly, "to shower for Caroline."

"Who's *this* you're hiding?" Leander growled.

"Leave him," Veronica warned.

"I'll have what the Agreements provide," he replied, without any smile left at all.

New Dwayne and the other Sapor were huffing wolf breaths, arms wild, while the artists in line only now began noticing the tension in the air because artists are *useless*. Despite Veronica's instructions they hadn't moved.

The rainstorm beauty leapt from the car—she jumped ten feet like a gymnast—and reached me, pupils dilating, teeth exposed, and my stomach dropped. I always know when I'm being stalked. I just never know what to do about it.

My fingers began to straighten. Of course. This is exactly the situation the *Gray* suddenly likes best, where limbs get broken and blood is spilled. But the *Gray* had become too indiscriminate, it had no interest in the things I value such as not going to prison for murdering innocent artists lined up idiotically on a sidewalk. To me, they suddenly looked like nothing but playthings for the *Gray*.

Please, I thought, trying to control my fingers, *not now, no—*

But the rain shower lady was fast. She didn't give me time to go *Gray*. She split the air and came to my side and grabbed my arm, the way Leander had taken Veronica's. I saw her go puzzled when she made contact.

And a hole opened in the side of my skull.

To the east, above the coastal foothills, the ghost mountain reared up, scraping the stars and damping the sunlight, and psychic foreknowledge of this Tactus lady's death poured into me: she would die in three months, along with Veronica and me, up on the peak. Either these three deaths I'd foreseen were very coincidentally scheduled, or something was wrong with my psychic abilities or an even worse explanation.

Rot gushed into my brain through the skull hole, and a seasick weakness hit my legs, and I threw up. The sexy rainforest lady dodged that with amazing speed, but she looked dizzy and had to drop my arm. She was disoriented by whatever she'd discovered, touching me.

I collapsed to the sidewalk. Foreknowledge ended. The mountain snapped away. Sunlight returned, like a movie had stopped playing and now spooled back up to speed.

The artists were all watching me on the ground. They knew my reputation for getting up over and over again after falling over so none of them rushed to help.

"I'm good," I waved from the sidewalk, swallowing bile. "Everybody *back off*, just stay good, okay..."

The third beauty dashed in and whispered in Leander's ear and then all the beauties were looking at their Sapor and Veronica was looking at New Dwayne. The tempo of breathing and arm waving on that sidewalk was outrageous. The lined up artists frowned. They were puzzled. What was this, they wondered, like a street theater thing?

New Dwayne panted, "Willametta inbound."

"Well," Leander decided, his smile back, though it wasn't a smile that liked Veronica at all. "Apparently we'll have to take this up tomorrow. It'll be interesting."

He gave me a long, final stare, and then the whole pride of Tactus scattered. Leander was gone in an instant. The butterfly cloud hung in the air where he'd been like cartoon exit dust. I swear I saw one of the beauties literally jump up the side of Veronica's building and disappear over the roof.

"I *compelled* you to stay in the car," came Veronica's ragged complaint when they were gone. "How are you here?"

I swallowed something acidy and asked, my voice unsteady, "There's a thing happening...what's happening?"

"What?" she said, impatient, "What thing is happening?"

"The thing when people touch me, its mind poison, it's like..."

"Drink less, Mr. Gale, that is your problem. Now come! We must *hide* you."

"Do whatever you want. Leave me alone," I shouted at her, standing woozy. I felt like a boxer wobbling at the end of a round. "I've got to shower. New shirt. Go home." Short sentences are the drunkard's friend.

"You'll never make it home," she scoffed. "They are looking for you. Come with me or I will *light you up*. You will have a seizure and I will have you *carried* where I want you. I swear if I had not promised Amelia I would simply...do you *want* to be carried, Mr. Gale?"

I didn't. And Veronica had her drone killer, out of control, crazy-eye look, the whites flashing in and out. She'd beam me then touch me. Until I had a better handle on this new death foresight situation

I'd have to humor her, and maybe escape later when she wasn't looking or if someone killed her. At every step I felt myself growing less presentable and more disheveled, and now I had vomit on my shoe. It's been too long since I was home, I thought, as I followed her into Fenestram Color. Had I even locked my front door? What would I find?

Inside her store she stationed New Dwayne, who she confusedly kept calling Warren, to watch the front and hurried me out the back. We crossed the alley as the salty smell of beach hit me, then I followed her in the back of the house across the lane and remembered these houses were part of the neighborhood Veronica purchased to have *defensible space* in case of supernatural battles, which at one time I'd found laughable.

"What's up with the butterflies?" I demanded as we hurried through the empty laundry room. The butterflies had made an impression. I don't know why.

"Bio magnetism," she said. "Tactus cross species linguistics. They can speak to, or control, animals. Summon them. It's a status thing for them, it's quite intolerable."

She took us through a kitchen lacking appliances and into a dark living room, and there she stopped. Afternoon sun cast ghosty light through plastic sheets nailed over broken windows, everything boarded or sealed in a post-hurricane way. The room was a wreck. Chalky dust floated and pieces of the ceiling had fallen and the wall around the front door had a hole the size of a cannonball. Piles of glass had been swept into corners.

I recognized the room, though the wreckage was new. We'd passed through on the way to her lair, the afternoon she'd tried to tap me. Now she studied me, undecided.

"What?" I asked. "What? Are you going to beam me?"

"Stay here until I return," she said finally, pointing to the floor. "This is a safe house."

"It's filled with broken glass. How safe can it be?"

"We can protect you here—listen to me!" Even without *compul-*

sion she had one of those billionaire voices you paid attention to almost by accident. She just sounded like she knew what she was talking about. Her eyes went wide and lidless white then, spoiling the effect. She had no idea what she was talking about. She pulled her pupils back at me. She gathered a breath. She was going downhill.

"Stop and *think*," she said, and I saw it was going to be a speech. But if I tried to leave she'd beam me.

"Everything that is happening is related to *you*," she told me, unhappy. "All the pieces of the puzzle circle you. Your *sight*, altered with *chroma storms*, the purported power of the things you used to paint, and now you are seeing ghosts. The cage cups, the Kiss paintings, *dominion*—you are in the middle of everything. There is something about you..."

Suddenly she counter crossed, pitched up a beam of *compulsion*, and fired it at my face. My *dominion* ball snapped up, seizing me but blocking her *light*. A moment later she turned it off and I stumbled.

"What the *fuck*," I asked.

"You see? I should still be able to *compel* you. Only a few days have passed since the tapping ceremony, you should be in my shadow for months! But somehow you are immune. Everything about you is wrong."

Nobody was going to argue with her there. Not with eyes that looked like hers.

"You are the only Aspectu painter in Skysill who can leave this city," she demanded, "and your mother, *your mother*, was in Skysill hiding from Aeternus. So there is something about you, some clue. We cannot afford to let the Tactus find you. They are fools! Calling a Conclave, *now*? Aeternus is here. I feel him. He will open them and spread them, one by one. What the eternal ghost took from me, he will take from all of them, he will take from *everyone*, unless we stop him!"

It was pretty dramatic. I gave her a moment to get her eyes

uncrossed but then my curiosity got the better of me. I have a curiosity problem.

"What'd Aeternus take from you?" I asked.

Just before she could tell me to mind my own business a voice popped from chalky air directly in front of my face and I lurched and almost sprained my ankle.

"S'posed to tell you Veronica," the air lilted, sounding about a third sober, "Warren's in front says Willametta inbound, less'n sixty seconds, says come back to the store *fast*."

"Is that *Nella?*" I wondered, groggy, squinting through the room. "Nella?"

"S'Nella," said the air.

"She's in the Bradley Building," Veronica said, furious. "I have no time for this! Stay!" she commanded me, not at all pleased to have to hurry out the way we'd come in, slamming the door on her way.

"Okay *goodbye*," I called after she was gone. To Nella in the air I said, "Can you believe this shit?"

"You," she slurred from in front of me, "just lay low for safety."

"I don't think that sounds like me," I said. "How's Peter? Is he still with you?"

"He's here. He's'a same. No, he's worse. Fades in and out." I prowled to the boarded front door wondering if I could get out that way, and saw it was only propped closed, twisted on its hinges. Along the wall I saw the missing doorknob.

"Hey," Nella said, "stay outa that corner, you're walk through my siglium. Messes the echo."

"Your siglium?"

"Gotta network stabilized now, set of repeaters. Tryin' hear what's happen'in this town."

I stood beside her corner while I made a plan. I'd call a car and be home in ten minutes. Because yes, Tactus, but how safe could this safe house be filled with siglium and unlockable doors? I tried to remember if I had clean clothes. It'd been weeks since I'd been there. Was that right? It felt like weeks. I pulled out Veronica's gift phone.

And it was dead. Typical billionaire shit. Phone's free, you probably have to buy the charger.

"Hey Nella," I wondered, "if I asked you to call a Lyft to take me home would you do it because my phone's dead?"

"Five Families everywhere! Stay hiding *for your own good,*" she answered. It was very frustrating.

"Why can't you people keep your Five Family bullshit to yourself," I shouted, and heard a dullness in the echo which meant someone was muting my screams. Probably also for my own good.

The air sighed.

"History story," she slurred, "listenin?"

I snorted. She was inches from my face, which she knew, so of course I was listening. Auditus sigliums echolocate everything, apparently. No secrets.

"So there's Five Families," she started, while I gave the room another scan. I'd slept in crack houses that looked better. What went on here? "Right? Five? Eons and eons the Five Families'r in existence, but all'a'time violent potential between the Primes *right*? Aspectu and Tactus, love hate. Right?"

I nodded *whatever* and wondered if she'd echolocate the tone of my eyes rolling. I kept exploring while she talked. Maybe there was a safe shower in the safe house, if I had to stay maybe I could get grommed for Caroline. I knew she wouldn't care, but she'd appreciate the effort. Thinking of her sent me goose kneed for a second.

"All down those eons," Nella was repeating and repeating, it felt like, voice tracking me as I moved, "there's violence, yeah? Cause Aspectu and Tactus are violent fuckers at opposite poles. Thankfully though both the Primes's got vulnerabilities keeps'm honest: Fabrica powerless at night basically, an'Tactus easy prey for Fabrica in daylight. So it's a wipeout, whoever moves first. Slaughter. Right?"

I found no running water in the downstairs bathroom. But it looked like a two bathroom kind of place so I headed up the stairs. These old buildings by the water all were built narrow and tall, the same layout for two hundred years.

"But Prime slaughters *never happened* know why?" Nella asked, voice tracking me up the stairs like a friendly fairy. "Why is, because of alliances among in all five Families, there's confidence and trust. Alliances keeping poles balanced. Tactus with Sapor mostly, Aspectu with Auditus. A few work both sides, like Veronica's got Sapor. Sitting in the middle of everything there's family Nidor. Nuetral third party. Nidor can't do much. Taste. Pretty weak."

While she dismissed the Nidor I found the upstairs bathroom had no water, plus no soap, towels or combs. I'd never worked so hard to get clean in my life, but Caroline was worth it. In the bedroom opposite the bathroom was sunlight spread in god rays through more broken windows and glass all over the floor. A wooden beam thrust the wall from outside. Like there'd been an explosion out there. The house felt less safe the more I saw of it.

"Alliance's a funky system though," Nella droned *on and on* about alliances as I returned to the ground floor, "but they worked through history, an now *you* come with *dominion*? So Fabrica can attack anytime they want *in the dark*? Ho shit. Balances are fucked. Too powerful. Alliances breaking. It's coming apart. People're going to be killed. Veronica doesn't want'm knowing it's *you* that's responsible."

"What? Me?" I protested, waving my arms when I heard my name. Had I heard my name? "It's not me responsible! It's your five hundred-year-old Fabrica painter and it's his *goblet* and all those *apprentices*—god damnit I'm *not* a *part* of this I'm fed up you people with your Family bullshit—"

"You know *you're Family too* Aspectu boy youvvvvvzzzzzzzzz—"

Suddenly a warbling shriek of static blasted through her voice like someone smashing a police scanner in a barrel, turning to a protracted wail. I grabbed my ears. I could still hear Nella's voice, yelling, but not what she was saying.

And then silence. Normal, sudden silence. No sound baffling, no Nella. I waited, but like all silence will it compounded itself and got less welcome until I had to whisper, "Hello Nella? Is everything okay, or...?"

Had someone smashed her police scanner? Was she under attack? That's all anyone was talking about, attacks here and there. I crept back to the corner where her siglium supposedly stood whispering her name. I waved my hands through it but lacked receptors to know if it was still there. Had something attacked Nella's siglium network?

I had my *sight* dialed high, darting, but now I didn't know whether to look or listen. I pictured Veronica, wondered should I call her, pictured the people lined in front of her store, for some reason pictured a butterfly, then suddenly I was bored, which is a character flaw I am aware I have. I tiptoed to the front door, to avoid running into Veronica, and opened it to slanting, afternoon wave glare. I dialed my opacity down and stared at a shocking scene of multi-residential ruin. The ruin, I realized, that Amelia had wrought.

What was left of Veronica's seaside birdhouse was right across the street, blasted to pieces. The walls leaned away from each other like dinosaur flower petals. The back of the house was open to the sea, nothing but splinters, the roof peeled clean off. I saw it upside down in the road, still in one piece. All the houses around wore shattered windows, with clapboard debris piled in the yards. Police tape decorating things at random, because there wasn't enough police tape in the city to circle this site.

Julian had been killing Veronica. So Amelia made his goblet—Samantha's goblet—vanish, but let loose a ripple of destruction. She'd been tapped by Veronica, so she was a sparkle finger Fabrica, but maybe early in her training? A kindergartener with a grenade. I hadn't known any of that though, because no one tells me *anything*. So Amy absorbed all the *dominion* burning my body and barely controlled it and buckled the house I stared at like a play house and saved us from the apprentices. Good old Amelia.

On the street, where I'd parked it in the rain that night, Celine's car sat. A two by four dented the hood but the tires were full of air, or whatever they have, I'm no mechanic. I'd lost the keys to that car when I lost my phone and license, but I knew Celine kept half a dozen spare keys under the mat and I almost never drive with a license. A plan formed. If I was lucky I wouldn't need the Lyft no one would call for me.

Running for Celine's car as I checked the sky for drones was awkward but so is everything else I do. I reached the car and pulled the door and slammed it behind me, panting. The smell of her made me think Amelia hadn't even tried to talk to me about Celine dying, there'd been too many explosions. Too many revelations.

I reached for the mat and found a key, thrust it in—the car started—and then I was hit by a pulse from my necklace.

The gem got ten degrees colder. My mind rang with her. Wisps of her thoughts came through. She'd seen her last client and wanted to call again. I felt dreamy-excited and nervous, the way you do right after buying a stranger's cocaine. This telepathy of ours was a beautiful Ferris wheel fire—you didn't want it to stop but you knew people would be killed.

I sensed her hair lit afternoon yellow going out the front of her shop. She felt her back pocket and I dreamed I *felt* that. Another icy crystal twist and I sensed her grab her own crystal, then dreamily lift her phone, dial, waiting to connect. I waited too with the phone to my ear. It never rang because it wasn't charged. Which I'd already known but forgotten. Then Caroline dreamily rolled her eyes and left a voice message, which I couldn't listen to.

The dreaminess stopped when she went away and then it was just me and my dead phone.

They sold me a charger when I pulled into a gas station. I paid with the twenty Celine kept in the ashtray. I plugged the phone and wheeled around, scanning side streets nervously, pointed toward my house, where I'd rinse and change clothes, get money and go to the Charles to call Caroline while I drank. I'd invite her to join me though technically our instructions were avoid each other, physically, so *technically* she was supposed to tell me she couldn't meet me at the bar. But she kept revealing surprise bad judgment so maybe she'd do it, and then I could have my deepest desire and it wouldn't be my fault.

The sun had almost set by this time, and dusk was blending shadows everywhere. I had the windows open. The air cools fast this time of year. It felt damp and smelled of saltwater and eucalyptus and someone's fabric softener faded as I drove neighborhoods toward my place.

I pulled to a stop under a spread out oak, the place I park all my cars before losing them. I peered out the passenger window, up my shadowy, bush lined driveway. Cicadas chanted. I heard no night birds. A lot of times there are birds. Did that mean someone had scared them? Maybe that was only in movies. I heard a little traffic a long way down the coast. I dialed my eyes to gather extra photons. Things looked normal, though that wasn't as encouraging as it used to be.

I left the phone in the car plugged in to charge and felt in my pocket for the spare key Amelia had "loaned" me. From the same pocket I pulled the tube of Higher paint I'd infused in Julian's gallery, It glowed a slow, streaming *dominion* mist on my palm, eddying, fingering *light* around. Like a little living thing. Not as creepy as it sounds in my mind. But I threw it back into the car and slammed the door because who wants to carry that around?

Pushed deep under a shrub and overflowing with envelopes was my mailbox. It'd been two weeks since I'd been home and I seldom check my mail in the first place so it had no vacancies. I never asked for a mailbox. It came with the house. I always wanted it removed but that's illegal, plus I don't where you get a shovel. I left it in shadow, creeping carefully around a corner to get my first look at the front of my house. I felt a little ridiculous, being so cautious, because who am I trying to fool? But I froze, and hoped I'd fooled someone. Because twenty yards further up, masked behind branches, I saw my front door hanging open.

My instinct was duck, after that maybe roll, but I've learned to ignore my instincts. I thought through an organized retreat. Should I go on? I hadn't seen unfamiliar cars on the street. No movement or light from the house. Had I left that day without closing the door? Did that seem like me? It sort of seemed like me. I crept a dozen steps closer, through shadow, and from there the broken lock was impossible to miss. I hadn't broken my lock.

My cottage shared a driveway with another bungalow. There my neighbors, Tilly and Lou, had painted for as long as I'd lived here, wasting their talents on landscapes for White Cove Gallery. I saw a light in Tilly's kitchen and hurried carefully, which is not really a thing, but I'm no spy, to her landing and knocked on her screen door, softly, repeatedly.

Finally I heard her yell out, "Who is it?"

"Asher," I hissed, looking behind me at my house. "Shh. Come here please. Keep your voice down."

Tilly came into the kitchen in sweats and t-shirt. She was thin as sticks. She got sick a lot. At the moment she looked worse than usual. Strung out

"What's..." she squinted, "ohhh. Hi Ash."

I motioned to come over. She did and pushed the door open and the spring shrieked. I grabbed it. "Tilly. Hey. Have you noticed anyone around my place?"

"Like who?" she asked, looking across our driveway.

"Anyone. Someone broke my door, did you notice anything?"

"Yeah, we saw that," she nodded. "Yeah, a few days ago. Now it doesn't shut."

"A few days ago you noticed it? Did you call the police?"

Tilly eased through her door onto her landing, now wrapped in a blanket. Her hands were shaking.

"No," she said. "We thought you probably broke your own door. You know how you are."

"That's fair. But I didn't. You didn't see anyone?"

"We haven't been out. We're waiting for paint."

I thanked her and tried to ease her back through her door. She was light in the head and she'd be in the way. I have up and sidled across the drive to my own porch, cautious, wondering—would anyone wait two days in an empty house to attack me? Did people have that kind of patience? Would they stay in there with the door hanging open? As I stood figuring those odds, a mothy step sounded behind me. Tilly was off her landing, looking pale, tiptoeing behind me.

"Tilly, go *home*," I whispered.

"What difference does it make?" she shrugged.

"What?" I demanded. With eyes turned full, Highers streaming the way I *can* these days without having a *storm*, I stepped to my door. Scanning it close I saw heel strikes, black and hard, around the shattered door jamb. I roughed the door inward another foot and listened. Tilly was still behind me.

"Go away," I hissed. Veronica had *me* doing it now, hissing everything.

"We didn't go inside," she assured me, staring in. "Man your place's a mess, Ash."

I agreed. I don't own much, an electronic or two, a few books I'll never read, things Celine or Amelia thought I'd need like napkins. And my easel with my last painting. But. Those few things I did own had all been scattered and broken on the floor. Whoever'd kicked my door had spent the rest of their visit ripping all my shit apart then throwing it on the floor. What had they been looking for? I stepped in carefully, checked bedroom, bathroom, where it was all upended. Drawers in the kitchen emptied. Half a bottle of vodka, leaking onto the linoleum floor leaving half a bottle of vodka for me to drink.

When I turned back to the living room, bottle to my lips, I saw Tilly had followed me in, and now squatted amidst my chaos, carefully clearing debris off of my one canvas. I drank and watched her shake her head.

"God Ash. I forgot how good you used to be."

"Go home, Tilly," I told her through my spout.

"I'm serious, *look* at this." She held up my painting for both of us to admire. "You should enter it for Gala Lumina this year."

It was the last painting I'd ever started. The painting I'd never finished.

"I don't paint," I said, turning the bottle up.

"Oh god," Tilly mused, lost, peering at the canvas, "I remember you used to *own* Lumina. You kept changing everyone's style, everyone wanted to be like you. What you painted...it was golden. How come you stopped?"

"Self-preservation. Listen, Tilly, I have to finish this vodka, then I have to dust my house for fingerprints and ransom notes so I don't have time to reminisce. If you like the picture take it and go home. Okay?"

She stood, somehow insubstantial in shadow despite my hiked vision. She lifted the toppled easel and placed my canvas on it. In all its Higher chaos. Back in those days I'd been throwing down every fiery thought I had in twisting semi-figurative shards of Higher wild *light*, since it hurt less to paint. Though painting always led to *storming*. And those hurt most.

But people had been eager to take whatever I made and I'd been happy to get rid of it.

"You've got a *gift*," Tilly whispered. "You know that right?"

She came nearer, pointing out the canvas on its stand, almost reverent, and I wondered if we were looking at the same picture. Probably not. That never happens with me.

"You inspired us," she said. "Our generation. We were waiting for you to pick a gallery. But you refused."

I had no idea why we were talking about this. I wanted to stop her, but she came closer and went on and I could only listen.

"To me...not just me...you were like an example, Ash, like there might be a different way. To live as an artist. Something authentic..."

She touched my arm. And I thought *Oh shit.*

And foresaw her dead.

This time there was no brain rot.

I felt whatever's opposite brain rot. Whatever *that* word is. I felt whole. A luminous warmth wound up me. Tilly met my eyes. The only thing between us was between *us*. No ghost mountain. No gloom.

A landscape fissured in and stretched around us. Sunlit, with meadows, with forests, like a supernatural national park.

Tilly was going to die in one day. It would happen tomorrow night, I foreknew. The night of the Conclave.

It was going to happen right outside her house, somewhere between her porch and the street where my car was parked. I saw no hint, holding her eyes, that she was aware of my foreknowledge. We were balanced in deep equilibrium. Something in my face made her smile, which rarely happens with people and my face. Then she stepped away and dropped her hand and the landscape faded.

"You can paint again if you want, Ash," she insisted. She had no idea anything had happened. And she really liked this painting. I felt atypically fond of her.

"Whatever happened to you," she urged me, "it doesn't matter. All you can do is just *start over*. That's all an artist can ever do. Each time make it new. Just keep starting over..." She was trembling. She looked cold but worse than cold.

"Tilly are you sick?" I asked. Usually I wouldn't, but between us the warm connection of mortal doom still held.

"Nope," she shook her head. Suddenly she turned, the fastest I'd seen her move, and really scanned the mess in the room behind us.

"Hey you don't have Higher paint, do you? Ash?" she almost begged.

"I don't," I told her. "Too dangerous for me."

She sighed a little junkie sigh. As far as I knew she wasn't a user. But she was dying tomorrow, maybe she had a secret habit. Or she was terminally sick.

"Yeah," she said. "It's just, it's been weeks is all since, you know… there's no paint."

"Get your stipend at Fenestram Color—look, Tilly, please go home now."

The mortal doom party we'd been having evaporated then, as fast as all the other ecstasies in my life. Other than Caroline. Now I was jumpy again. I wanted to wrap up here. The violated room started freaking me out. Someone knew where I lived. My grooming plan changed. Showering with my front door hanging open in a city this violent seemed imprudent, even to me.

But Tilly wouldn't move.

"Tilly go home! Go! I banish you. I'd escort you but then I'd have to touch you. Go spend this time you have with Lou. You know. Real quality time. You never know what's going to happen. Who knows what'll happen tomorrow? You know what I'm saying?"

"Lou's asleep," she shrugged.

I edged past her and she pivoted and watched, holding out my canvas. I left her in my living room and ran for my car. I hadn't gotten any money for the Charles. I hadn't changed my clothes or combed my hair. I saw I was heading for another night at the Bradley, on the cushions on the floor, which wasn't all bad. The Bradley had stout doors, I remembered.

Into the car I jumped and turned the key. The engine sputtered and stalled. I turned again and got clicks and nothing else. It's just one thing after another with cars, with the breaking, melting, getting towed and booted for parking violations. I don't know why anyone likes them.

For a second I sat at the wheel, building my strength to walk to the Bradley, and saw Tilly wander down the driveway, eyes unhealthy shadows. She had my painting.

"Go home," I hissed out the window, but she came on.

"I feel like you're not coming back," she said, holding up the painting. "Don't leave this. What you did back then was real magic. Real magic, Ash. You should try again. Take this. Finish it."

"Stop following me!" I told her. "God damnit I'll take the picture. Drop it there. Step away. Go home. Go home Tilly, *please*."

She nodded and set the canvas on the concrete and stepped away but stopped. She didn't trust me to retrieve it. I snatched my phone from the charger and slid from the car, lifted the painting, showed her, and she turned, her steps so light she hardly stirred leaves. When she was gone I spun and started a furtive walk down to the coast.

The dark had settled by then. Usually I'm good in the dark and I see things before they see me. But my empty house still left me jumpy. Was it a burglary? Or maybe one of Tilly's and Lou's crazier friends? Down the street a pair of coyotes sauntered under street-lights. One of them looked back at me. Halogen made her eyes photovoltaic. She looked away, dismissing me. In one hand I had an invisible painting and with the other I explored the best way to dial a phone one handed. The coyotes of Skysill knew they had nothing to fear from me.

Then I tripped, and the coyotes jumped into the bushes, taking no chances. I kind of staggered, because my chest-crystal started throbbing glacial ice while a dream image of Caroline floated into my mind. This time it was at Three Paths, in the suite you get when you're Monarch of the Path Behind, part English-library-home-theater-gastropub, part archery range. I'd forgotten the archery.

I got her dialed, nothing even rang on her end before she answered.

"I knew you were going to call," she said, a little throaty, giving me chills.

"I'm here with some coyotes," I said. "I almost tripped when the crystal went off."

"I sort of saw. I got dizzy too. I'm at Three Paths without coyotes. A lot of psychics instead. It's a real similar crowd."

"I can sort of actually see you too," I told her.

"Me too."

I paced to a stop on the sidewalk under bugs dancing in streetlight. The night was wide and quiet and now everything felt more predictable and sane, which showcases my many delusions.

"So it's back?" I asked though I knew. "Our telepathy?"

"I guess. I get dream visions where my necklace gets freezing and I feel you. You really run around a lot."

"Do you think it's normal what's happening to us?"

"Nothing normal's happened since the first day I met you," she said.

I dreamed her sitting on her couch and heard her sigh on the phone, or felt her. In my brain I pictured her in an untucked shirt, twisting down to pull off a boot. I dreamed I knew what it would feel like holding her in both hands smelling her neck and her ear, hands on her ribs, the heat and delicacy of her bones under skin. It sped my breathing and I felt it speed hers too since we had a bubbling feedback loop going, and for just a moment I actually saw what she saw, a picture of me, and was reminded of the condition I'd fallen into physically.

"Don't worry how you *look*," she said, literally reading my mind. "You're like a beautiful cowboy who got run over in a stampede. You'll always be pretty."

"A cowboy. But I used to be your cat."

"I know honey but we can't all be cats."

The sound of her voice, a little sad, filled with trivia like cats and cowboys, added to the illusion I was going for that all this was super normal. Like two normal people flirting with telepathy in the moonlight, though one of them was inside on a couch.

"I thought Three Paths had no reception," I told her.

"Veronica put cell towers in. She says none of us can afford being unreachable right now. It's just a side benefit that when your boyfriend calls you can talk to him."

That word gave me a thrill when she used it like in high school. One of the coyotes poked a head back out of the bushes for a second, like he'd heard her say it too. I tried to remember if coyotes mated for life. I thought they did.

"I wanted to invite you to the Charles but I never got a shower," I admitted.

"I wouldn't have come. We can't get close."

"Stranger things are happening all the time. Maybe it would be fine."

I dreamed a worried frown wrinkle on her. She sighed. "I'm pretty sure we shouldn't even be doing this. Probably not any of it. Any of the things we want to do."

"I keep imagining how you smell."

"I keep imagining the way your tongue tasted. I want that."

My crystal pulsed. It was like being knifed in the spine with pure desire, which was distracting and I stopped talking. She arched too. It took a moment to get our voices back, then I cut west a block, walking fast, the air coming damper closer to the water as I followed a flood canal beachward. The distant moon bisected wave crests. The sound of beach-highway hiss never stopped.

My phone vibrated. I checked. In the red.

"Look," I said, "before my phone dies, I have to ask—"

"—about being psychic, you've been thinking you're some new kind—"

"—of psychic—right?—because now I know when and where people die but—"

"—it's weird it's not like any Pathwalking I ever heard of."

It was such a pleasure finishing sentences with someone other than myself this way. It took all the pressure off talking. After a few sentences, you forgot who'd even started the words or even which of you was talking and it didn't matter.

"I'd say you're some kind of death psychic," she told me. "since you see dead people, you send them on to wherever except psychics never see death on the Paths. Only in front and behind it. Are you sure you're really foreseeing death? Has anyone died?"

"Not yet," I said, slow, really trying to do her question justice like I wanted to do the rest of her justice. "Maybe we'll know tomorrow. My neighbor's supposed to die. The rest of us die on top of a ghost mountain in three months, which seems crowded. Maybe my psychic powers are broken."

"Psychic power's not a thing that breaks. It can break you," she said, quietly.

"That might be the explanation."

"You're not broken, you're just a little different."

"But now I'm worried, what if she doesn't die? Would that mean I'm not psychic, I'm just crazier than I thought? I'm confused what to wish for."

"I believe in you Ash, she'll totally die, poor thing. Hey." She had a thought I found myself having at the same time. She started saying our thought, "Maybe the people who die in three months—"

"—all die after time ends—"

"—and you're just foreseeing the last date reality even exists. Like a placeholder date for all our demises."

I marveled at her calm tone as I dreamed her pulling off her other boot, relaxed and happy talking to me about seeing people dead and my ideas about dead people and honestly confronting how I might be irrecoverably insane. She was perfect.

"Listen," I told her, "you said psychics know a mountain. I keep seeing a mountain. On top there's a throne. Yours came with a throne right? Is that what I'm seeing?"

I dreamed her holding up her phone and looking at me in her mind, puzzled, with another frown slow-breaking her smooth, perfect forehead, and then she brought her phone back to her mouth.

"Ash," she said. "We're cut off."

"What?"

"Look at your phone."

I pulled my phone from my ear and looked. The screen was dark. I'd run out of battery some time ago.

"Dead again," I complained, lifting it again, stopping, confused by the various deficiencies I manage. They slow my thinking. We hadn't really been talking on the phone. Not for some time.

Caroline got wavy and dreamy then, like a mirage. She smiled and her brown eyes, amazed, met mine. With her phone in one hand and her boot in the other I just appreciated the way she balanced it all. I dreamed her continuing to talk to me but now I couldn't hear her. After a moment the dreamy surf sounds rolled her completely out of my mind. Once she was gone it was just me and the sidewalk, and my dead phone and my unfinished painting.

Pacific Coast Highway winds along Skysill's beach curve, following the water, through outlying galleries and neighborhoods and houses wind weathered millionaire pale until it slides through downtown, where the Bradley Building stands, retiring, all unwavering bricks with a green glass facade. The Bradley rises on some of the most expensive real estate in the city, where by some stroke of mixed good fortune and bad luck there was an office with my name on the door.

By the time PCH wound me around to the Bradley, the tourists had mostly gone to park at their hotels and sleep. The walk had taken longer than I'd expected because just generally speaking I'm bad at predicting anything. The planet had spun the stars and Higher borealis in the western sky, suspended at the edge of the ocean in front of the rest of interstellar space. Because I still had my eyes keyed nervously wide I picked out a figure loitering on the sidewalk in front of the Bradley, near a bus bench, looking upward at the Bradley.

I recognized the small paunch and glasses, and the hand held out like it'd just lost a serving tray to strong wind. This was my former neighbor Phil in island attire. He stared at the third floor and occasionally lifted something from the palm of his serving hand to his mouth, chewing.

From nostalgia and because the bench looked inviting I headed his way. He saw me coming, watched me settle on the bench, then gave me a careful shrug. He turned to look back up. He chewed.

"What do you know Phil?" I asked after a minute.

"Nothing," he admitted. "Sunflower seed?"

From his pocket he took a half bag of seeds, poured a new pile on his palm and offered them. I was tempted, though the palm couldn't be sanitary. Had I eaten today?

"Pour a few here," I told him, holding out my own palm. He nodded like he was agreeing to do it but didn't do anything. He was deep in philosophical contemplation of the side of his old building. I scraped the pile of seeds off his serving hand and looked at the Bradley with him as I ate.

"It's such a waste," he sighed, reloading his palm and offering more. I shook my head. My mouth was full. The air was cool, the bench was calming, I was comfortable chewing and watching Phil. It was like a show.

"It's like," he continued, "do you ever think everything you once believed was true is actually *wrong*? Like everything you thought mattered was some *illusion?* And you've been fooling yourself your entire *life?*"

I held my hand out for seeds and said, "No."

"Really? Did you ever think you'd end up homeless like you are?"

"How'd you know I was homeless?" It'd just happened. He was impressing me.

"Look at you. Starving, filthy. Look at your clothes. Collecting trash, you should get a shopping cart." He pointed to the painting. Visible spectrum as he was, it appeared blank to him. "It's okay, you know," he assured me. "We'll all end up homeless in the end."

"Maybe none of us will *need* homes, I bet we'll find out in three months."

"They moved in so fast," he said, ignoring me the way I was ignoring him, a style that was companionable and easy to understand.

"Who moved where?" I asked. He pointed out a set of third floor windows where light shone. New people inside the Bradley?

"Squatters I guess?" he sighed. "They're the new Bradley Family now. The Bradley Family's dead, long live the Bradley Family. We were a beacon on a hill, a brief gleam of glory lighting the world like Camelot."

"What I like about you, Phil, is your humble self-image."

"It takes humility to be a travel agent."

"I have no idea what that means. So there are people?" I peered at the window. I didn't necessarily like the sound of that. What would it mean for me sleeping here?

He nodded. "The day we got evicted they moved in. Now we're taking shifts to keep watch."

"Who's taking shifts?"

"The old Bradley Family."

"You're keeping watch on the building you got evicted from?"

"Who else is going to do it?" he snorted. "These squatters keep leaving the heat on and yesterday I had to go turn it down *three times*. Right now there's thirteen of them. They're in your old office." He pointed again, to the third floor windows. "It's their squatter headquarters. They're not Skysill squatters. Out of towners I guess."

"You're fond of this building in an unnatural way aren't you?"

"The Bradley Family's the only family I ever had," he said, "I mean there's my brother. I have cousins on the east coast. But those people don't *get* me." He tossed the last of his seeds in his mouth with a lip pop like a dizzy champagne waiter, and after that he stood, empty hand extended, silent.

Until a sudden voice spoke, a few inches from my face.

"S'just *us* up here," Nella's voice slurred.

"Oh *fuck*," I shouted and slipped to the ground.

"Oh how the mighty have fallen," Phil whispered, eyeing me sadly. He hadn't heard Nella.

"Phil's here, he says there's thirteen of you," I told the air from the ground.

"Yeah, Auditus slippin' in town, doing whatever's possible for Pierre."

"Peter's up there? How is he?"

"No change maybe worse. Come up, got stuff for you."

While I carried on my one sided conversation with the air, Phil's concern for me deepened. But he was powerless in the face of my lunacy. So he shrugged and pushed his glasses up.

"Phil I have an idea," I told him as I stood. He looked disinterested. I didn't blame him. But I went on, "How'd you like to get the old Bradley family back together?"

"It's evicted to death," he sorrowed, making a heart with his fingers like a TikTok star. "RIP Bradley family."

"I'm thinking of taking those evictions back. Reversing them. What do you think?"

"How can you reverse them?" he snorted. "You're evicted too."

"I know but that's just paperwork. I *let* myself be evicted. I think I might let myself own this building instead. Because how bad can that be for three months? I'd be your landlord."

He froze.

"Are you kidding me with this?" His eyes were wide. He started to tremble a little. He was easy to convince of things. That was his strength and his weakness.

"Not kidding," I said. "I need someplace I own to hide out where there's a bathroom and thick doors."

"Do you mean *everybody*?" he asked, wonder in his voice. "The whole Bradley Fam?"

"Yeah. The Fam. Tell everybody. Let's get the family back. Hanging around on the sidewalk you draw too much attention. Want to be building superintendent?"

"I accept."

"Okay. Your job will be, don't let anyone inside the Bradley Building ever."

"How about customers?"

"Especially not them."

"Excellent," he said. "Wow, how amazing is this? So you're going to hide out, huh?"

"I probably am."

"From who?"

"Let's see who shows up."

"So I guess you'll be taking the penthouse?" he asked.

I looked where he was pointing, at the fourth floor. The top of the building. I knew very little about this building I was preparing to own, other than the lawyer in a wheelchair who waved paperwork at me had been cute. This was the first I'd heard about a penthouse.

"Is there a shower?" I wondered.

"Um, *yeah*," he scoffed. "Three bedrooms, three baths, thirty-one hundred square feet with ocean views, all appliances, kitchen remodeled three...wait, four years ago. Eight-foot ceilings. Fully furnished."

Someone had filled my new building superintendent with surprises. I wondered how long he could go like this. It was exhausting to be around.

"It'll be locked," I thought out loud, because I had keys on my mind these days. Car, house, heart. All the keys.

"I should hope so," he said. "You're the only one with the master."

"I'm...what is that again?"

He rolled his eyes. He smiled—he was *really* going to have to keep an *eye* on me was what his happy expression said.

"The key to your main Asher Gale office suite? That's the master key for the building," he explained. "Everybody knows that. You get in all the rooms. There's a spare in the desk drawer in your office. I was looking for some coke at the going away party, but I won't need that I guess!"

"Phil," I told him, after a few seconds, "goodbye. I guess I'll see you tomorrow."

Phil's eyes watered. He pressed his lips together and spread his arms for a hug.

"Don't touch me," I told him.

"No prob," he agreed.

"Don't ever touch me."

"Okay, and management still pays utilities and validates? Same... lease terms?"

"Everything like it used to be. We're starting again. Just no customers or any people who could touch me or kill me are allowed in the building. Call everyone."

He flicked a piece of sunflower shell off his thumb and licked his palm before rubbing it on his pants, then pulled out his phone. He was excited. His excitement faded when he looked at me.

"Hold on," he said before dialing, scampering to a sedan at the curb. He came back with a zippered satchel. I shied and waved him back, and he remembered no touching and tossed the satchel at my feet. We both looked at it.

"What's that?" I asked. The logo said *Skysill's Only Hawaiian Vacations*.

"Bradley Building dress code, *hello*," he said, "you get your act cleaned up, mister. You represent us now."

My experience with Tilly had taught me how futile it is resisting people who give you things so I took his bag. I left him dialing his phone and loped up the broad steps, and went into the lobby, wondering how quickly I'd regret all the decisions I was making. It never takes long.

I took the elevator to the third floor, and got out in the hall where the long, green carpet had a new, faint odor of bananas, and made my way to the door with the sign reading *Asher Gale: Investigation and Authentication*. Waylon Goodman had put my name on this door without asking. Without asking he'd named me trustee of a building, deeded me a list of valuables, then got murdered. It felt like some millionaire scam where your options vanish one by one leaving you one choice: living in a penthouse collecting rent from your tenants. Like in a nightmare.

"You comin'in?" asked Nella from the air in front of the Asher door.

"I don't know," I said. "Let me ask you something." You had to like talking to a door, it really lowered the stakes. "Do you own a house or any skyscrapers or anything?"

"You comin'in or *what?*"

"Does the idea of owning something make you uncomfortable or comfortable? Like what kind of commitment is that, owning a building? Do you have to pay attention to anything"

The door swung in. Nella stood facing me.

"Shit blowing up everyplace, you're worried you'll *own a building?*" she demanded, using her mouth, to communicate her extra disdain. "Inside, Aspectu boy."

She'd got new robes since I'd seen her last because being bone crushed on a sandy bluff by Julian had destroyed her first robes. She was gold and red once more, still small, round, and crew-cut. I saw flickering lights down the hall behind her and more people in Asher Gale's office. A sagey smell came wafting out. There'd been a receptionist desk before and chairs, but those were gone, along with all my forgeries off the walls, and the rugs. When I wandered in she let the door close.

Monks on mats were maybe meditating—how do you tell?—all over the place. Candles the size of torches cast light and heat at me, probably a fire code violation, not that I cared. The meditating monks all faced inward in a loose circle around a figure on the floor. A figure on his back in his favorite spot.

Peter by the Beach. They'd given him a yellow-gold belted gi, but his hair and beard they'd left wild as briar. He was all bones and skin, driftwood wrapped in onion paper holding the ceiling with castaway eyes.

Nella spread a guest mat and we folded down. Usually I'm at

home on floors and sidewalks, but I knew if I got comfortable I'd go to sleep, so I sat stiff. Like I had somewhere to go.

"What goes on in here?" I asked. "Vegetarianism? Prayers?"

"Praying? We're tryin'to call Pierre back. He's lost."

Lost in the past, she meant. Trapped there when Julian killed his Ask. Without his Ask—the only one who knew the question Peter was down to answer—he'd never find his way back to the present.

"What's he been saying?" I asked.

"He sunk too deep to talk. We hear'm in flashes *you* can't hear. Seems like there's an even worse problem, though." She spent a minute thinking about the other problem. "We think he's in the middle of some kind'a battle."

I looked at Peter, who hadn't moved, except to breathe. "I don't see it," I admitted.

She stopped moving her lips again, talking straight from the air in front of wherever she wanted me to look, which I remembered liking because it was fewer decisions for me. Now she had me look at Peter while she unraveled her theory.

"You *don't* see this," she air dropped. "You *hear* it. That's the problem. Listen. This town. This town's *too quiet.*"

She held her fingers before her face and snapped, and listened, and continued, "Somebody's masking sound in Skysill, sifting and erasing things. We can't get to the past here. Skysill's a whitewash town, no history. Someone here's *doing* that, ongoing, all the time. I put a siglium network up when I got here but somebody's unwinding'em, happened again when I was talking to you. There's one bad motherfucker Auditus hiding in Skysill Beach. An Adept. Been here all this time, under the surface, I think Pierre's down there fighting the Adept, tryin'get back. Cause he's fighting something."

"What can we do for him?"

"We can listen."

"I'm a bad listener," I admitted, looking for Nella's bottle. "What are you drinking?"

"Nothing. Too much'a do."

"But you sound drunk as shit."

"You hear what I *want* you to hear," the air informed me. "Speakin' your language for efficiency." She slid a familiar folder toward me on the floor. On the folder she put the office key I'd left with Peter back when he was my first receptionist. "The one thing Pierre did before goin' silent was give me these things for you, an' say, *receptionists have no kingdom, but they know <u>all</u> the janitors, give this to him.*"

"What kind of message is that?" I wondered. She shrugged again.

It was the folder the landlord lawyer had delivered, full of paperwork to sign. Peter had accepted it, apparently, when the lawyer had come back. He took receptionist responsibilities super seriously. I grabbed the folder and the key, lifted Phil's satchel and my canvas and I stood.

Nella watched while failing to understand something about me. Like they all do.

"Why so shitty to Veronica?" she asked. "She's tryin' help *everybody.*"

"Are you saying me? What are you talking about? I'm not shitty." I scoffed. "She does a thing, she's very condescending you know, events all around but nobody says *anything* to me about any of it? She gave my sister sparkle fingers but did she tell me? No. I'm not the shitty one."

"She's worried, Aspectu boy. You should be too. This town's full of Five Families. Veronica said remind you," and here she did the trick, the really unsettling trick of speaking a pitch-perfect impersonation of Veronica, "You must stay clear of the Conclave tomorrow night, Asher. It is not safe for you. *Do NOT go to the Conclave under any circumstances!*"

And at that moment Peter's deep rumble filled the room. I turned. He lay on his back but his voice went everywhere.

"I went the extra mile," he bassoed from his spot, "but that was miles too far, it took me off the cliff, down where they eat peanut butter flowers every day. Every day. It's too much peanut butter."

I hurried to his side. He lolled up at me, confused and woeful.

"It's too much peanut butter, man," he said.

"Peter," I said, "how are you? Sucks about peanut butter. Can I get you anything? Water?"

"I asked for flotsam but they brought jetsam, the fall lineup is so inadequate. The commercials make you cry. We should turn it off."

He shook his head, jarring the fall lineup from his mind.

"Everyone's trying to help up here," I said, gesturing useless. "Hang on."

He gave a bubbling groan like a boat engine stalling and whispered, "The death eye listens. Thread the eyes to get the prize. Brunch is coming but after that you're free. It's almost time to be free. It's almost time."

His voice was sinking deeper as he spoke, then it sank below any frequency I could hear, though from Nella's face I knew Peter went on talking for another minute. Then all the monks lost him, all at the same time. Their bodies deflated. And Peter lay, vacant, breathing shallow, lost or battling, threading dead eyes and eating peanut butter brunch.

Inside my shirt the temperature dropped a half degree. I felt my necklace pulse. Caroline was thinking of being called again. By me. I sensed it, and sort of pictured it, and pictured her resigned to the idea of me never charging my phone. I spun to Nella.

"You have a charger I can use?" I dug my phone out, juggling other items. I seemed to have a lot of items suddenly, folders, keys, phones, and wondered if that just happened when you became a landlord.

"I have a car charger," I explained, all reasonable, "but no car so that's useless."

I showed a hopeful smile, or some kind of expression, but she pretended not to hear. I knew the people in that room heard everything, so I called their bluff by waiting patiently. Finally she jerked her thumb at an outlet where a charger hung, and I piled items on my canvas like a platter and added the charger. I thanked her, which she also pretended not to hear, then I took myself away. With a last glance at Peter, I let the office door close and headed for the elevator.

"Forgot t'say," said the air so suddenly I jumped and spilled my items, but then before I could complain, Nella, went on, "since you're going'be in th'penthouse, best keep Aspectu eyes *wide*. We took a drone down today, somebody lookin'round up there windows."

"What? Who was it—hello? The drone? Nella?"

But she was gone, and the elevator came, and my crystal pulsed, and I got a picture of Caroline getting ready to go to bed. She had her phone with her like I might call at any minute which was so sweetly optimistic it almost broke my heart.

On the fourth floor, I saw a short hall and one door at the end. I juggled knickknacks and unlocked it, assessing its impregnability, and wasn't dissatisfied. So far so good, penthouse. I threw the bolt, then traversed an entry that opened in starlit darkness with three steps to a sunken living room. I dialed my *sight* wide and lit the scene.

The furniture in this room was soft in well-coordinated colors and was plentiful. There was competent impressionist art on the left wall, with a library with books on the right. The wall opposite me had floor-to-ceiling windows framing midnight, moon-hung ocean with stars. A view steeped in privilege. I should have hated it but I couldn't.

I threw my shit on a table and plugged in my phone. My crystal throbbed again and I pictured Caroline sliding into her bed in pajamas. While my phone accumulated some charge to turn on, I found a bathroom and rinsed my face of everything it'd seen. The toiletries from the Hawaiian Vacation travel bag were exactly what I needed. I took off my clothes but had nothing to change into, then found the penthouse came with towels so I wrapped one on. Getting back to my phone I found it just coming online. And ringing. I answered as I collapsed on the couch facing the star-sea windows.

"You look real nice in that towel," Caroline told me. She had a lot more energy than I did, but I was determined to keep up.

"Thanks," I said. "It came with waves and a moon."

"Where *are* you? I don't recognize that room."

"Some building I found. They're trying to give me the keys."

"Do they know your history with keys?"

"They don't really care."

"Well, it's real generous, if risky. Are they there?"

"Nope. Just me and the towels."

"Like living in a lonely bathroom." After a moment she added, "You sound fried."

"It was crazy today. Non-stop."

"How about, you just lay there in your towel looking provocative and tell me your crazy day. I'll watch."

So I started on my day, watching the moon slip under the rim of the world as I took her through the parts I could remember. Starting with Julian's gallery where I'd found he was five hundred years old. Veronica's drone and her craziness and almost going *Gray* with Leander and the Tactus. Escaping the safe house, then finding my own house ransacked. Coming here to find Phil, and Nella, and Peter.

Caroline listened and asked fascinated questions, delighted by my antics, which recalled to me her questionable judgment, and how much I liked her. I told her an Auditus was lurking in the city, erasing history, who Peter might or might not be battling. She took it in stride. And she was full of encouragement for me becoming a landlord, once she got used to the idea.

She couldn't seem to get enough of me. By the time I was done, the moon was gone. Both of us took a moment, silently imagining we were sitting in the same room and what we'd like to do to each other. Our crystals were *freezing* us. We tried to ignore them.

"And then of course," I finished, "there's the really big thing that happened."

"We had telepathy again."

"Yes. Though, right now it's a little fuzzy. Do you notice?"

I could picture her, like in a daydream, but I wasn't exactly hearing her thoughts. Mostly her voice on the phone. Which felt a lot lonelier, but was probably safer.

"So you're sure it's not because we're psychic that we have telepathy?" I asked, happy having so much in common to talk about. That hardly ever happens.

"No, telepathy's not psychic. It's our Tactus-Aspectu polarity going haywire. I saw Veronica after we talked earlier. She gave me a new crystal. Like a booster. That's probably why we're blurry. Though I got the idea the booster was supposed to cut out more than this."

I dreamed her showing me a large crystal shadowed purple, hanging on a separate chain. Part of me was irritated Veronica was in any way involved in my relationship with Caroline, and part of me thought the necklace looked pretty. I find it hard to make sense of myself.

"She's real worried," Caroline told me. "She'd be disappointed hearing I'm still daydreaming towel pictures of you."

"Let's not tell her. I see you in bed. Your pillow's crimson. You're wearing blue pajamas, your hair's...your hair makes...oh. Wow."

"What?"

"I just thought what it'd be like painting you," I admitted. It was a shock to me.

"Really?" she said. "I've never been painted before."

"It's a super bad idea. It's been ten years since I worked a canvas and it'd probably kill me. I haven't seriously considered it in a decade. But I'm picturing you sitting for me."

"What would I wear?"

"We'd both have towels on."

"That's sweet," I dreamed her saying, staring at her phone, shaking her head, her hand on her crystal. She breathed, "Ash, I swear you might be the most romantic boy I ever knew. It's so unexpected considering your appearance generally, and you being unhoused and having no job. You sure take my breath away. You're romantic by accident. Without even trying I think."

"That's true. I never try. So strap in for romance."

A series of cold prods battered me, imagining how romantic it would be to be naked with her, how we'd drift off in bed, her head on mine as she fell asleep, falling into her while watching. Then I reminded myself that falling into Caroline was the thing most likely to kill us, and I dialed my romance feelings down as far as I could.

Soon after that Caroline grew quiet.

Using dream vision I watched her fight to keep her eyes open. She was tired from Monarching, which was attractive and confusing. I wanted to ask what Monarching involved, exactly, and then her eyes closed. With her phone on her pillow an inch from her lips, I dreamed her all the way down to sleep, and when she was sleeping, her breath even, her lips parted, my dream picture faded. Whatever it was we were doing, it needed us both awake.

After that, all I had was her soft breathing on the phone. She hadn't hung up. I lay on the couch watching the sea and stars. I put my phone by my cheek. My battery died ten minutes later.

And then finally I took a shower. It felt like a victory.

Finally, I returned to the living room and plugged in my phone. I wanted to be prepared to answer more calls tomorrow. And there I saw my unfinished painting, dropped among my other knickknacks. I carried it to the couch and tilted it, watching the canvas, and past that the dark, rolling ocean. The Higher borealis traced threads of *light* through the stars. I wondered—if I did paint—and actually, why not since I no longer had crazy *chroma storms* anymore—what subject would I choose? Caroline? Or something else? Maybe something...but before I could finish the thought, I fell asleep.

CHAPTER

FOUR

Waking the next morning was a confusing mess, but not the familiar hangover kind. My lids cracked. Light hit my brain. And there was *dominion*, loping in circles beside my couch. I couldn't even sit up before my fingers curled and I ghost popped through my skull into sunrise and ghosts without a chance to so much as yawn or through up.

There Samantha hung, empty handed now, between ghost me and the penthouse windows, where thin morning sun lit the top of a deck umbrella on my balcony. The world out there was cloaked in strange gloom, but Samantha filled the living room with cascading ultraviolet radiance ribbons.

Samantha what the fuck? I ghost screamed. *"Samtha wath thuck?"* demanded flesh me from his back on the couch. This was just frustration. She'd woken me from a fantastic dream, where Caroline and I lived in a deep woods cabin with a cat, growing cherry tomatoes and reading books to each other while we screwed like forest animals. I'd been having these dreams more and more and always found them frustrating to wake from. I was even growing fond of the cat. He had a familiar face.

What are you even doing here? I demanded of the ghost. *It's too early! I thought you only showed up when something's about to go...oh. Shit.*

In an instant I spun ghost me to look behind, where no one was about to attack me. Then I shot him through the ceiling into the air above the building and circled him like a ghost periscope. Who was it—rogue Tactus? Drones? Probably Julian. When Samantha showed up it involved Julian. That was my current disposable theory. I didn't see him though. What I saw was the mountain.

It rose above Skysill behind our coastal hills, shedding translucent gloom off its flanks, blocking the sun and hazing the sea. For a moment I sat in ghost me, posted in the sky waiting for the peak to evaporate the way it had on Julian's hillside. But this time it didn't go. If anything it seemed more solid. It was a bad way to start the day.

I dropped back into the penthouse. The scene seemed ordinary enough: a ghost, an empty flesh body, a canvas representing all the bad choices I wish I could have made. But even inside the house the mountain gloom was apparent. I sat flesh me up and Samantha inched to face him, doing Higher fireworks.

I know enough to know you don't just pop in without a reason, I ghost complained at her, while flesh me mangled along. *You're like an irritating ghost alarm,* I said. *So why're you here? Something about this mountain?*

It came out a bit chaotic and screamy, I thought, hearing flesh me —naked on the couch with his towel fallen—garbling my words. He hit a few right on the nose. His verbal skills seemed to have improved. With a little effort, it might even be possible to puppet him through full sentences, though effort has never been one of my strengths and neither have sentences. I do know sentences are important. They're like camouflage. If you're forming full sentences, what can anyone really say about you?

I watched the *Samantha light* spin cocoons. If she wasn't here to warn me Julian was coming then it had to be something else. I knew there was a method to her madness. Contrary to popular opinion madness almost always has a method. That's why it's terrifying. I struggled to piece together a pattern.

She'd first haunted me when I went to her office at the Klimt, where Julian had painted the mural in *compulsion* that had driven her to kill herself. Although now that I knew more about Julian that made less sense—he preferred killing people by glowing them to death not painting them to suicide. Painting's a lot more work, and you left a murder record, but Fabrica *compulsion* was basically untraceable...

"Basketly untraceable," said flesh me.

I realized he'd been murmuring out loud the thoughts I'd been having in my brain. It had suddenly become pretty clear murmering like he'd figured out some tongue secret. It was full sentences with just enough diction like I had a leak and my words were slipping out his mouth. So now, apparently, I'd have to be careful thinking all my things or he'd just tell them to everyone. He was turning into a liability.

As an experiment I puppeted his mouth closed while I sorted thoughts of all my other Samantha meetings, and that kept him quiet: the second meeting had been in front of Psychic Touch, where our local ghosts come for release from this mortal plane. Where at that very moment, a hundred monk ghosts pressed Caroline's shop, waiting to be set free by me. It was a lot of pressure and also impossible. Who could find all the objects they had for Caroline to read? Not even someone who cared.

After my second meeting with Samantha she'd had hung above the sidewalk pretty reliably, until she'd shown up at Three Paths just as I took a picture of the Monarchs. And while her first two manifestations made some supernatural sense—the office where she'd been brain tortured, and the sidewalk where she hoped to find release, the Monarchs visitation didn't track. But I'm good ignoring things that don't track. You could call it a lifestyle.

I went through her next few visitations and they all fit a supernatural profile: she appeared when Julian attacked us in Los Angeles firing *dominion* from her goblet. Then she'd come to show me the goblet in Damely's forged version of *The Painter's Kiss*. And she appeared the night Julian had come with the goblet to kill us in Veronica's snack shack. Then just yesterday she'd appeared when we found the *non*-forged versions of the Kisses in Julian's gallery. When we'd discovered he was five hundred years old.

Other than the Monarchs, her breadcrumbs seemed to lead to Julian. Didn't they? Or the goblet? The goblet she no longer had.

I stood flesh me and walked him closer to her while she twirled to keep him centered. A foot from her I stopped him and slipped in him, frozen motionless which is the only way I'm allowed to stand in flesh me, and I stared at her empty goblet hand.

I'd never made her any promises. But here was a girl, murdered trying to free her father from a life of crime, who'd battled assault trauma for years, collected priceless period frames and put magazine advertisements in them, a doomed protest for authenticity. She was a girl you had to feel sorry for, despite being a millionaire's daughter, or maybe because of that too. I felt I owed her something. She wanted to pass on from earth. Like the other ghosts. I wanted to do that for her. But how was that supposed to happen with no object to read?

And I'm the one who told Amelia she had to *wander* the goblet Julian had been sucking on, and Amelia did—along with the roof, which is pretty typical of my sister—so it was my fault we no longer *had* the goblet. Samantha was sort of trapped. It would've felt a little heartbreaking, but I was too sober for that. Instead, I puppeted my flesh hand up and laid it on her unbreakable ghost grip, where her fingers cupped nothing.

You're here because you need your goblet, I ghosted. Flesh me said, "*Yourer cuzu nee your goblah,*" and I felt proud to look at him, all showered and semi-intelligible.

I haven't forgotten your goblet, I reminded her. *Trust me it's on my mind. Like yesterday Veronica called your goblet a diatreta, and I remem-*

bered Felicia used that word. I mean I didn't remember that yesterday. My memory's not that reliable. I just now remembered it. Diatreta. I don't think I ever asked Felicia if she knew anything about your goblet, which proves how I suck at investigation, which I've been saying for weeks but nobody listens. So I should go ask Felicia about a diatreta? Cage cups? Would that make you happy?

It might have, or maybe she didn't have a brain—ghosts never spoke or had expressions so you couldn't tell. But I had a theory to roll out now, which always makes me talkative, and I thought flesh me could use practice so I did a speech.

I don't know if it's the objects you ghosts hold that matter at all though, because when Kuparr went to heaven or stopped existing or whatever happened, he did it because I heard an address. It was me knowing the address, the information, not anythiing to do with the actual address book. Maybe if I figure out what your information is some other way, maybe I can help you. Does that make sense? Because here's the point of all this, more or less...I'm on uncertain ground here, but if it's coincidence it's crazy —I think I'm supposed to be a kind of person—like officially—who sends ghosts away. A death person. Yes I know insane but here're the arguments: one, I see ghosts. That's unusual. How come I see ghosts? Nobody else sees ghosts. Two I can become a ghost, also unusual, and three while I am a ghost flesh me can touch other ghosts, and four it turns out I foresee the moment a ghost will be created because I have death visions. I haven't mentioned that to you yet it just started, but I see when people are going to die if I touch them. So I think I'm...like I said a death person. A death guy. The opposite of a doctor. Does that make sense?

It didn't. We both knew it. But we both had reasons for keeping quiet.

So yes okay, along with the other totally bonkers crazy shit going on I'll also try to get you...evacuated to the afterlife. I need a word for that if I'm going to keep doing it. You know what I'm saying. I'll talk to Felicia. On that subject you see my hands clenched? There's nothing in my fist, that means I'm fucked unless you LEAVE, or I walk out of range... so? Are you making me pilot my naked guy out of range of you which I don't know, he could end up out on the street, or will you leave?

"*Or wilnn you leef?*" flesh me finished off. I floated, looking straight through the *light* of her and saw bluffs along beach and morning tourists claiming sea view sand through the gauze of her. The tourists didn't seem affected by the ghost gloom of the mountain dimming the world. They were happy and afraid of sunburns. For a second I worried about them but then from boredom decided I'd point flesh me to the bathroom where I'd seen a robe. He'd attract less attention on the street if his ass was covered. No way I was putting yesterday's filthy shorts back on him. I'd just gotten him cleaned.

He was surprisingly dexterous getting in the robe. Like he was eager to get his adventures started. I made him rake his hair off his face and use deodorant from Phil's satchel. On his own, he adjusted the crystal on his chest. or maybe I imagined that. I was turning him down the hall to get my phone and my other pocket junk when I felt something tug us together.

Ghost me yanked the air between us to slam stopped inside flesh me which left one or both of me whiplashed. I braced for sheets of shatter pain but no—my bodies dissolved into each other and the ghost gloom lifted, and easy as pie I was one body again. Like putting on a fresh pair of socks. Very simple and painless. From this I knew Samantha had removed herself. I took it as approval of my death guy theories, and my plan to visit her ex-girlfriend Felicia, because I'm always looking for approval. I seldom find it, so this was nice.

With a load of phone and keys in my robe pockets I thought about Caroline, but dreamed her with a client ignoring me thinking about her, and trying not to grab her necklace—her *two* necklaces, I dreamed again. We weren't talking, but I knew she was there. The crystals seemed to be doing less and less.

Before I left I looked to see if I was forgetting anything, since that's what usually happens, and noticed my painting propped on the couch gathering light off the coast. It occurred to me the light here was a painter's wet dream. So much of it. Casting no shadows on the canvas, and colors pure, and clarity. If a person were considering painting for the first time in a decade, this would be a good place to do it. The only things the room lacked were brushes and some paint. But I knew where to find those if I wanted them. Which, I had to admit to myself, I did. I wanted brushes and some paint.

I was prepared to do my Skysill business in this robe and in shoes with no socks as I went out the penthouse door. Expectations around town are pretty low for me, based on history, and as long as I wasn't staggering through traffic drink or *storming* people would be happy. But in the hall leading back to the elevator I found a fruit basket, and under that a short sleeve Hawaiian tourist outfit with a note from Phil: *To the world's best landlord!*

Scattered down the hall were other baskets, some with food, candy, a book on square dancing. One card read, *From Dale of Finances by Dale,* taped to a new, double entry accounting ledger.

So I dressed Hawaiian. It was getting to be my thing. Dale's paperwork ledger reminded me to about my landlord paperwork. Back inside I found a paperwork folder with two documents: one to sign if I wanted to own the Bradley Building, one to sign over the Bradley Building to Waylon's lawyers—my choice. It seemed like a weighty decision to make without soul searching but I did it anyway. I signed the Bradley ownership papers with the provided pen. The lawyer who met me had seen I wasn't the kind of person who'd have a pen.

And then, finally dressed and legally prepared, I took the elevator to the lobby.

When the doors opened I was confronted by a dozen people in a line. They were people waiting for me. There was Phil and Dale in Santa whiskers, and Ambrosia in medical scrubs standing with the rodeo dancers and a crew of other people who all started clapping when the elevator opened. They beamed and someone cheered. In their hands and arms the bore baskets, and wrapped packages.

Behind me the doors closed before I thought of retreat. Usually that's my first thought.

Phil stepped from the line pushing a wheeled tray stacked with bananas on sticks in beds of chrysanthemums. He flared his arms out like an orchestra conductor, and with a dramatic little frown, he cut the applause. In the silence, he cleared his throat to begin a speech.

"Get everyone out of here *Phil*," I yelled before he started, because that's how you get the advantage, I was learning, move fast and move first. Also yell.

"Okay people get the hell out of here *now!*" Phil turned and screamed instantly, staring and gesturing *go go go!* "That means you, *Dale.*"

"I don't want those," I said to the baskets and a ten speed with a bow that people showed uncertainly my direction.

"Move people *move* this crap *pronto!*" Phil knew about yelling. The line broke—confused, I thought, but not disheartened. These people had been given a new lease on Bradely family life and nothing would dishearten them today, not even me. There was something about this family's spirit you had to admire, though it was also terrifying.

"I don't ever want to see anything like this again," I complained, as everyone hurried out.

"No problem boss," Phil totally agreed and nodded.

"Don't call me boss."

"You got it Mr. Gale."

"Let's say the rule is none of you *ever* comes near me or talks to me or calls me anything. And no touching remember. Treat me like I'm on fire or I'm a ghost." He shrugged to say that wouldn't be a problem and I continued, "And to clarify—except for the squatters upstairs and you Bradley Family people, nobody comes in the Bradley Building. That's clear, right? There are people I don't want to see."

"Check," he agreed, eating a chrysanthemum. He made it look good.

"In fact, leave the front doors locked at all times," I said.

"Check," he agreed, "totally secure the building."

"And if you see drones, let me know *right away*."

"Check," he confirmed, unconcerned by anything, it seemed to me, other than homelessness, and while he listened for more instructions he approved of my outfit. "So what'd you think of my mango travel lotion and shaving oil? Creamy right?"

"All your mango shit worked great Phil—look I'm in a hurry, is there a messenger service, that—I don't know, somebody travel agents use to deliver legal documents or—"

"Suite seven!" he interrupted, pointing up. "Minnie, Skysill's Best Bike Courier. Minnie's a bulldog. She's tiny but she couriers *anything*. Last month she couriered a grand piano."

I watched him chewing flowers. I had to ask. "Someone sent a grand piano by bike courier?"

"Baby grand," he explained, holding his fingers up. "Rush job, so the bikes are faster. Want her to deliver those documents?"

I nodded and dropped the folder on the tile and slid it with my toe to Phil, who took it and stood, then gave a grand gesture to his tray as graceful as a game show host and left to care for my documents. Going out the front door I grabbed a handful of flowers around a banana and found it a sweet tropical surprise in my mouth. I was still chewing when the Lyft arrived.

We wove through modest morning traffic heading north. A few early art shoppers eyed *compulsion* parking spaces in front of second-tier galleries. I was a little nervous about Felicia. As I swept along the beach I recalled *storming* the first time I visited. She'd been wracked by grief about Samantha's death. I wasn't prone to that kind of *storm* anymore, it seemed, but I hoped she'd processed some of her sadness —that would be most convenient for me.

My driver wended us down PCH until, a mile in the distance, the upside-down *dominion* tornado appeared. Though I couldn't see the base of it yet, I knew the mouth was flattened over Caroline, where all the loose ghosts gathered.

A second later I saw one of those very ghosts, a swirling Higher monk, motionless in the center of Pacific Coast Highway. He was floating in the fast lane in front of an Italian restaurant. He'd strayed a ways from the tornado. Cars in our lane rushed straight through him. My own car was approaching him rapidly.

Of course I popped into my ghost. The towering mountain loomed. I, in my ghost, hung in one place and the car, carrying flesh me, sped on down the highway. I only move ghost me from inside flesh me, otherwise he just hangs in space.

The car was twenty feet from the ghost monk heading straight at him when I remembered how flesh me interacts with ghosts—to him they're immovable as a cliff face. Now flesh me was speeding straight at this road ghost who would pass right through the hood, the driver, and come to the back seat where, oh shit, going fifty miles an hour it would be hitting—

I'll admit it. Ghost me's no man of action. Ghost me froze. Ghost me doesn't do split-second decisions, he does complaints and theories. But in that deadly frozen second I watched flesh me through the rear window as, all on his own, he tore off his seat belt and rolled—*as the car drove through the monk*—across the seat. The ghost monk went by with inches to spare and passed out the back of the car.

Stop the car! I ghost screamed, so flesh me screamed *Stop ah car!* as I dove back into flesh me and heaved ghost me forward, going forty miles an hour, which was pure sea sickness, because up ahead I saw more ghosts, the road was filling with them, while everybody in the back seat screamed *STOP THE FUCKING CAR—STOP STOP STOP!!!*

The driver did it. He got us squealed dead motionless in the middle of the road just before plowing through the ghost gang. Why were they in the middle of the road? I heard flesh me speculate into the car, "*Why they're alln middy road?*"

The driver turned, yelling at us while I puppeted the door open and jerked us roughly from the car. I had flesh me stumble through traffic up onto the sidewalk, while my driver sped off. I'm sure to give me a terrible peer rating.

At least thirty ghosts crowded the road, all rotated toward flesh me. Cars ripped through them, back and forth, which was hard to watch. These ghosts were supposed to be at Caroline's. Were they following me?

Go away! I ghosted. *"Go away!"* flesh me yelled. A pedestrian glanced, assessing the danger we might pose, but quickly assessed flesh me to mostly be a danger to himself.

I decided walking was the safest course. There were ghosts on the sidewalk too, blocking flesh me, and those I battered out of the way swinging my ghost, like a ball on a chain. Are you really supposed to use your ghost like this? I hoped there would be no consequences, but that's what I hope about everything. Ghosts rebounded like billiard balls as flesh me forged through, the whole field of them inching around to keep oriented at him. Supernatural radar antennas.

Once I cut inland on Skysill Canyon Road, I left the monks behind. A moment later I was out of range and cohered back to one me. I felt the sun on my back and the breeze on my face. I rubbed the shoulder flesh me had bruised heroically rolling us sideways in the car.

In no way was I good enough at puppeting to have saved us the way he had, even if I'd thought to try. The only explanation was... he'd performed all the rolling and ducking on his own. Flesh me had saved us, acting entirely on his own. I decided it was disturbing, but also, I had to admit, he hadn't panicked. He'd decided he didn't want us dead, and he'd done something about it. I hoped it was a decision he never regretted. I also hoped I never saw anything like it again.

The dogs in the Canyon serenaded me as I strolled under their elms, past their picket fenced lawns, each yard drinking acre-feet of irreplaceable aquifer, though now that we only had three months til time ended, maybe our climate problems were less pressing. Soon I passed a familiar picket gate, behind which I saw the house where

Peter's Ask had been glowed to death by Julian. I saw the swing on the tree that I'd chased Peter out of. The front door hung open, days later, just the way Veronica had *choked* it. It reminded me of my own kicked-in door, un-investigated, and I thought again how Skysill PD were all hard working, citizen-centered public servants up to the point where someone broke your door or murdered you. After that point, they remembered all the parked cars they had to boot.

A few blocks further brought me to El Toro, the flammable little dead end where Felicia hid away, and turning up I saw a station wagon parked in front of her cottage, in the shade of her tree. When I got closer I saw two figures seated on her stoop under her wind chimes, one with an arm around the other. Behind them, Felicia's door swung wide open. The doorknob lay on the ground. A lot like the one at Peter's house.

I thought of the many good reasons to change my plan and leave as I came closer, but of course, good reasons alone seldom influence me. I trudged past the tree up the walk.

The figures were an older man and woman. They hadn't noticed me. Then I was close enough to see through the gaping door into the hall, where Felicia's flesh body lay on the floor looking broken. And hovering above, her ultraviolet ghost.

My fists clamped. I ghost popped. The *dominion* mountain settled above us, dimming and chilling. But flesh me rambled forward because he hadn't been given other instructions. Up the path he went, until he reached the couple on the stairs.

They had faces unglued wet, in utter shock. It wasn't an easy thing for me to see. Parents and grief, it's pretty triggery. Because obviously these were Felicia's parents. People only cry this way when their kid dies. In the news anyway. If I hadn't already been *storming* I might have gone *Gray* on the spot, just to shield myself from family trauma. My worst kind of trauma.

"Who're you?" the lady wheezed up at flesh me.

The man pointed tears up and asked, "You're the police?"

I shook flesh me's head. I wondered where the man and lady

were from that police officers had tropical shorts like flesh me, and no socks. Maybe Florida.

"Are you a friend of Felicia's?" the lady asked. They had no idea what had happened here. They craved an explanation. Anything I could offer.

I knew Samantha, I ghosted as an experiment. "I knew S'mantha," flesh me said. They weren't surprised I knew she was dead. They were irrational and griefy.

The lady's sobs redoubled and then they were spilling questions, how could this happen, where were the police, what was going to happen? I had various things to ask them, but I didn't think flesh me was up to am interrogation, though you could tell he was getting there. Instead I positioned ghost me behind flesh me where I had a view through the door, and I checked out ghost Felicia.

She faced flesh me, of course, where he slouched on what used to be her stoop. Why all the ghosts including me face flesh me I don't know, it's fucking inconvenient. When I pushed ghost me toward the crime scene, he flipped backward as he moved away from flesh me. I reversed him in, through the door into Felicia's living room and through her couch and footstools to her body on the floor in the hall.

The living room had been completely upended, paper emptied drawers, pages from books—I read Samantha's name on a magazine page. A couch leaned on its back and the grandfather clock's guts were strewn, everything turned inside out. It was chaos. I watched from ghost me now, floating backward and slowing, as flesh me took a seat beside Mr. and Mrs. Felicia. All on his own. He looked relaxed and a little bored. It was unnerving. He probably needed water. I drifted a few more feet and came to a stop on the other side of Felicia's dead body, lying twisted on the hardwood, cheek down, eyes open.

Her skull glowing *compulsion.*

Flesh me out on the stoop leapt to his feet panicked. Julian! But I calmed him, and had him sit, while I examined the scene. It had all the earmarks of Julian's work, but I didn't think Julian was here.

Despite my limited experience and historical disinterest in putting facts together in a line, it wasn't hard to guess the order of things here. It wasn't hard to picture Julian arriving, slick as wet velvet, dope filled, melting her lock, to look for something. *Compelling* Felicia, probably questioning her. Searching. She'd have given him anything he wanted but she didn't have it, so all he could do was tear the house apart. Somewhere in there, accidentally or more likely on purpose, he'd pumped so much *compulsion* through Felicia's skull, her bones had started glowing. From what I understood, people don't live long after that.

The ghost of Felicia hovered out of view behind me. In order to face her I needed flesh me standing in between us. As an experiment, because he'd been semi-autonomous recently, I gave him a simple objective instead of puppeting: *come here* I told him.

Up he jumped. Maybe a little too eager. Then he dashed into the living room. The Felicias watched, confused. It was humbling watching my flesh body so animated, with no need of me. He came with single-minded focus. A table stood between us and he jumped and walked over and jumped down because that was faster. He was unbound by the niceties.

I slowed him when I'd rotated to Felicia's ghost. He stood complacently between us. I saw ghost Felicia with a lanyard in her extended right hand, spun of Higher light. A photo ID? Admission to something? The writing wasn't English. And then, with a shock, I realized that just behind her in the hall floated another ghost: Samantha. She'd joined us I knew not when. I seem to meet a lot of ghosts in hallways like this. I wondered if they preferred hallways.

Distant sirens approached. I flashed ghost me around inside the house then, quick, looking for this lanyard she held, thinking I could bring it to Caroline, but Julian had done a great job piling one thing on top of another and I was running out of time. The sirens came closer and I suspected, with my history, maybe I shouldn't be found at the site of any more mysteriously dead bodies. Why it always goes this way, I do not know. All I'd wanted was to ask a quick question of a living girl and then leave to gather paint supplies. Now look.

Samantha hovered a little higher than Felicia. You could see something in her eyes, not an expression exactly, but maybe in how her Higher *light* coiled. It reminded me a lot of soul crushing sorrow.

We'll figure this out, I ghosted to reassure her, which I'm terrible at but somebody had to say something. Flesh me stayed silent, blinking and looking disinterested. I reached his hand up consolingly to grip Samantha's ghost arm but I'm equally terrible at consoling. The sirens were not distant.

I have to go, I ghosted Samantha, *to preserve legal deniability. We'll find Felicia's lanyard but for now*—I puppeted my flesh hand sideways, maybe to Kumbaya Felicia or something, and his hand touched her lanyard. At which point something new happened. There's always something else new.

A warm tide washed up from my ghost feet. And yes it was new, but also somehow familiar. I'd felt the same glow when I'd touched Tilly the night before. Was this *that*? No. That had been regular Asher, the one who liked vodka, with no ghosts or extra bodies touching a living girl. Here it was *flesh* me, ghosts on the side, touching a dead girl's *ghost*. But it felt similar and comfortable. Not wrong or broken, like most of my feelings. Maybe another facet of my death guy skill set. I had no one to ask but ghosts, who were keeping their ideas to themselves.

Even the gloom from the ghost mountain lifted away. A scene spread before me, similar to the one with Tilly: a scene of sunlit meadows, sylvan streams, forests, and far-off mountain ranges.

And then, through the lanyard up my flesh arm and into me, in the most natural way, like it was meant to be, flowed the death story Felicia wanted known.

A decade ago she'd been teaching English in Rrome for six months —her first time away from the United States—but she'd started feeling like she'd made the wrong choice and planned to go home early. On her last night, a friend took her to the Palazzo dei Conservatori to see a showcase of rare glasswork. The collection hadn't interested her. But when she heard a guest lecturer from America describing the sights, sounds, and artistry of ancient Roman glassmaking, it had all come alive, more alive than anything else in the museum. So after the lecture she'd left her friend and spent the next four hours rapt, in a cafe with the American girl. Samantha Goodman.

For a time after that in the city they were inseparable. Samantha had intended to return to the US herself, but they both stayed on. Felicia returned to teaching with unexpected joy, and spent the long Italian afternoons and evenings with Samantha. She was in love within the week. And Samantha had returned that love, at least at first.

But she came to understand that a mysterious burden was chained to Samantha. It dragged her from the present in a hundred tiny ways, and Felicia saw those distracted moments more and more as the months passed. Every week Samantha was a little more distant, a little more broken, and eventually Samantha had to return to the States— she felt, she said, like Italy had run out of air.

After a time Samantha told Felicia the story of the assault with the knife, years before at college. But beneath that trauma, she carried something deeper, a weight she wouldn't talk about, from early in her life. It was this secret, Felicia came to think, which lay at the root of Samantha's pain. Whatever this was, it had colored Samantha's every life decision, driven her to study ancient glasswork, to specialize in the study of cage cups.

There came a week when all Samantha's symptoms surged. She'd been spending more time in her office, away from Felicia. And then she disappeared. Soon after that Felicia discovered from me that Samantha had killed herself. And all Felicia's hours after that were spent wishing she had a memento from that day at the museum. Something she could study, remembering the beginning, remembering the brilliant girl who swept her off her feet.

The Higher *light* around Felicia arced as the story ended. The pastoral scene faded and our little hallway of ghosts got *bright*. Her *light* revolved, all seven colors, pendants ultraviolet, pulsing fast and wide, while on Felicia's face a not-expression spread, something still, calm, onward facing. Her hand was empty. The lanyard gone. She became a blinding glow, then a pinprick, then a pop of Higher sparkle. And was gone.

Samantha hung another moment facing flesh me, holding out her empty hand, as though to make a point. And then, silent as ever, she vanished. All warmth from the pastoral meadow was gone. Instantly I merged into one body. I staggered. Round and round he goes. Where he stops, nobody cares.

I went out through the kitchen, over a neighbor's fence losing a few seashell buttons, scraping an arm because what am I, a gymnast? I emerged through bushes pm the sidewalk one house away, just as a squad car fished to the curb. I was afraid that inside would be my friend Hennessy, because it's always Hennessy, and I'd be recognized. But these were unfamiliar cops. Skysill's very, very finest ignored me pretending to be someone's curious neighbor while they sprinted past, allowing me to flee the other direction.

I was feeling cold shimmers from my crystal as I ran, but I forced myself to flee the murder scene instead of stop and make a phone call, because prudence. Though there was never a bad time to talk to Caroline. Only fantastic times and slightly less fantastic times.

An ambulance roared past, then a fire truck. To remain anonymous I took the first corner, found a curb to perch with my elbows on knees, drained by the new ghost skills I'd uncovered. I don't like new skills. I don't even like my old ones.

Then I pulled out my phone to see unanswered calls and texts from Caroline, from a few minutes earlier, probably while I'd been absorbing Felicia's tale of ghost woe. I dialed and we got the thing where the other person picks up before the phone rings and we're both surprised, but not really. Dreamy pictures hit me, her in a pickup, driving from her shop up into the hills where Three Paths hid.

"Oh my god Ash, what is going *on*?" she demanded as she steered.

"I want to say nothing. But is that the wrong answer?"

"You dropped off the face of the earth! What *happened* to you?"

"What happened to me when?"

"One second you were alive, the next you were dead. Are you okay?"

"I'm okay. I am little thirsty, for sure. What do you mean dead? You seem like you're driving a little fast... "

My dreamy vision had her slicing through cliffside corners. She had one hand on the wheel while one hand held the phone to her ear. I didn't think it looked safe, but I also wasn't sure it wasn't a hallucination. Can you judge someone else's driving in a dream?

"There's a situation at Three Paths," she said. "I'm real glad you're alive. You are, right?"

"I'd never lie about that. Not to you anyway."

"So what *did* just happen if you didn't die?"

"I don't know? Let's see...I found out Julian's still in town, and still killing people," I told her helpfully. "He killed Samantha's girlfriend oh *and* I just sent a ghost to the beyond by touching a lanyard. But I'd know if I died. In fact, I happen to know I don't die for another three months, so you can rest easy."

I saw her frown tighten as she listened. She squealed her truck through another curve and then her brow cleared.

"*Oh* I see," she said, "dead in three months, that's you trying to *reassure* me? That's real sweet. It's not really one of your strengths, though, is it."

"I could probably use practice," I admitted. Suddenly I wanted to talk to her about my new theory.

"I don't have a lot of time, but yes, please tell me your new theory."

It took me a moment, then I said, "I love our telepathy."

"Though we're not supposed to have it, not with this new crystal. I like it too. It really cuts through the small talk, right?"

"It's awesome," I nodded, "I hate small talking. Okay, you please drive slower, please, because you're telepathically freaking me out, and I'll tell you the theory: I think I'm supposed to be some kind of *death guy*. Does that seem crazy? Like, a *psychic* death guy. Probably there's a better name than *death guy*, I don't know, I'm not a name guy. It's like my skill tree is the whole range of death issues: foreknowledge of death, viewing of ghosts, and now I release ghosts to the ghost beyond just touching their ghost shit."

Saying it out loud made it sound a lot crazier than saying it in my brain. Caroline steered for a moment, though she hadn't slowed down, and I daydreamed her tapping the side of her nose thoughtfully with one fingernail. It was adorable, though I'd have preferred both her hands on the wheel.

"Calm down about me on the road," she said, reading my mind again. "I was born driving a pickup."

"And was that uncomfortable for your mother?"

"It's just weird," she speculated, thinking about me. "A boy saying he's a *death guy* is normally one of my red flags. But with you, there's no effect."

"Some people think I'm crazy. But not you, because you were born in a truck, it gave you a broader perspective."

"Okay, so these psychic death abilities—what're the rules?"

"There're rules?" I hoped I didn't sound as disappointed as I felt.

"There's always clear rules to psychic visions. Who can hear our visions, where we can be, when we can do it...Anything like that?"

"No,. The only rule is I can't ever touch anybody," I said. "I get brain rot. Do you think that's normal?"

"For a psychic. Maybe you noticed when we first met, how I

never touched you? I *really* wanted to touch you. But being psychic takes discipline. Otherwise, there are consequences."

"You get brain rot."

"No that's an adorable Asher thing. I get uninvited information. I'm almost home, but say again what you found about Julian?" I loved the way her mind jumped around but still made perfect sense to me. "He's alive and killing people you said. What's he want?"

"I don't know. Maybe he's just pissed his apprentices are dead. I mean I *think* I killed them. I never saw ghosts. But at least one of them had a two-by-four through her stomach."

"That's not a story I heard," she said after a pause. "Tell it fast."

I gave her the highlights—Julian and the apprentices attacking, pinning me with beams of *light*. Me going *Gray*, being very fast and violent, tearing through the other apprentices so I could get to Julian, before all of them disappeared. It made me a queasy remembering. I wished she hadn't brought it up.

"So those people are dead? The apprentices?" she asked. I dreamed her pulling up a small driveway and dreamed Three Paths looming behind a crowd of trees. "You went *Gray* and killed people?"

"I don't know," I admitted, "not anybody good I don't think. Veronica healed Nella and Amelia, and those two were in *really* bad shape. Maybe Julian healed his apprentices. Or not. Maybe they're dead. It's easy to lose track, I guess. Maybe I should get a counter."

I wasn't super happy how blasé I seemed to be sounding.

"Ash. I want you to promise me something," Caroline said then. She'd turned her truck off but hadn't opened the door.

"Anything," I told her. "Name it. What's the thing?"

I daydreamed one hand drop to the hem of her shirt, where nails worked the stitching, scissoring, ravaging it. This was the only self-destructive habit she'd ever displayed, other than the bad relation-ship choice I already knew of. I liked it. It's nice not being the only one with issues craziness issues in a relationship.

"Promise me you won't go *Gray*," she said. "I don't want you losing control and...and murdering anyone. Don't be *that person*."

She'd shifted her intensity into high gear. Like this really was an issue. Her eyes were wide and trapped, like an escape room junkie's. "Promise," she insisted.

"Absolutely I promise," I said. All casual confidence hoping to put her mind at ease, but we had telepathy so I couldn't have been fooling her. "I honestly do not want to be murdering either, at *all*. I don't even want to be man slaughtering. Although, how do you feel about aggravated assaulting?"

"Don't joke," she warned. Her voice was soft. She let go her hem. It had come to pieces. "I'm real, real serious."

"So am I. I promise I won't go *Gray*." It was an easy promise to make. It was what I'd already decided to not do. "I'll basically do anything you want, you know. Is it okay to say that?"

"Just no murdering is all I'm asking. Now I gotta go. I'll call later."

And she hung up. If I'd wanted to I could have continued my daydream of her every move. The extra crystal from Veronica she wore was providing virtually no benefit now, it seemed to me. There was just a thin film separating our telepathic connection. I had to drag my mind out of her truck back to my sidewalk, which I only did because I remembered all the danger people kept saying I was in. Talking about murder so much had brought those warnings back.

Parked cars, to my right and left, shadowed the curb where I sat and an elm cooled me while a warm breeze blew, but none of that felt safe. And all the murder had me thinking about Julian. He could be anywhere. He'd beaten me to Felicia's when I hadn't even known we were in a race. He was too far ahead of me. I'd spent too much time sleeping on Amelia's couch. In a lot of ways this was all Amelia's fault, I knew, without bothering with the details. And now Julian's on a war footing. Thanks, *Amelia*.

I stood, casting glances, thinking of the walk I had getting to Fenestram Color. Wondering, was now really the right time to try painting again? Considering all the *other* threats to my life? And if it was the time, was it safe walking in the open from here to the paint store?

The afternoon was balmy. I took a breath of sun sweetened ocean breeze and decided the answer was probably yes, now was as good a time as any to try painting again, and no, it probably wasn't safe in the open between here and there but walking might be safer than taking a Lyft and hitting a road ghost. I had obstacles everywhere. I'd stick to shadows, get to the paint store, get supplies and after that...I didn't know what exactly, but the chances were good I'd try to paint. Paint a Higher spectrum canvas. I felt a secret shudder of delirious, eager shame. I'm an addict. It's what we do.

I stood between parked cars doing furtive surveillance, then hurried down the sidewalk to the canyon road, and headed toward the beach. I took a corner but I'd hardly gone a hundred yards when I came to a trio of ghosts on the sidewalk. Their positioning didn't appear accidental. They'd put themselves in my path.

Of course the ghost mountain rose up then, dimming the sun, spreading the gloom, blah blah blah, while ghost me shot out the top of my skull like bread from a toaster and I put aside all worries of violent attack to deal with stupid ghosts. It's just one thing after another with the ghosts. Flesh me started running to them. They gave their blank eyed stares of great expectation, which is a contradictory expression only ghosts have perfected. And now, finally, I was beginning to see what was going on. Skysill's ghost population was stalking flesh me through the town. They wanted to be released.

Flesh me yearned to touch the toy dinosaur one ghost held. His hand came up as he ran.

Hey! I shouted at him, and he stopped, and I made him put his fists in his pockets because I didn't trust him. He wanted to practice his new calling and send these ghosts to their heavenly reward by touching their objects. But we didn't have time for that. All the stories. All the whirling. I couldn't be stuck out here on the sidewalk right now. I spun ghost me all directions, nervously checking approaches. Ghost me was safe. Flesh me was vulnerable and helpless.

Hey assholes, I told the ghosts then, *or I don't know maybe you're not assholes, maybe you're trapped in those ghost bodies and just want to shuffle off this immortal coil, which if that's true I sympathize but I have to disappoint you—which is something you'll have to get used to with me—I can't send any ghosts to space right now. It takes too long. It's exhausting and I'm very busy. So go away. Okay? I want you three and all your friends to stop following us. Got it?*

They pretended to have no idea what I was saying and refused to go away, so I jumped to flesh me and I slung my ghost at them. It sent them flying, two disappeared into the hillside and the third slid halfway through a garage wall so I had to hurry flesh me two blocks more before we escaped their influences and my fingers unclenched, and the mountain gloom lifted, like an emo net drawn back from the world, and the two of me were sucked back into the one. Like a fucking circus.

It takes a moment to get your equilibrium after that. I crouched at the tail of a camper van, thinking of the much larger collection of ghosts waiting at the base of Skysill Canyon on PCH. Every time I saw a ghost I'd *storm*. I'd be a sitting duck for Julian or anyone else. If I had my own car, I could drive slow and steer around ghosts.

I knew where to get one.

I stayed off the coast road, cut across neighborhoods, turning, looking overhead. I was thinking about the way I'd been shifting back and forth between my flesh and my ghost. It was becoming such a simple thing. Like, second nature. Could that possibly be good? It almost felt like I could control both bodies at the same time, if I really concentrated, from some vantage outside both of them. Someplace where I had no body at all, though that raised profound philosophical questions about me being fucking crazy, which fortunately I'm used to.

Ten minutes more found me ducking across an alley, then I'd reached Arroyo Auto where I'd purchased my last half dozen used replacement cars. I had not seen, heard, or psychically sensed a single peril getting there. All the vigilance was exhausting, like having the flu. In the shop I emptied two cups of complimentary coffee while negotiating a price on yet another used ruin of a car. I knew I'd someday run out of money if I kept buying cars like this. Probably not in the next three months, though.

And once in a car I felt safer. And you know my life's a mess when I feel safer actually inside a car. I tanked it out of the lot onto PCH, and for a moment I breathed easier. I had the feeling I'd taken some control back into my own hands, which was both a positive and a negative considering my hands. But I still started feeling that this was the best plan I'd made in days. I took myself north up PCH, scanning for ghosts, passing coastal, post-urban mini malls in the slow lane.

When I lumbered past the Historical Society I almost stopped. I'd recently discovered things such as really, really old people that I could have used Shelby's historical perspective on. His little stucco monastery looked closed, but I knew that was just a ruse to keep the history sealed and fresh from prying eyes. But my desire for paint was growing, so I drove on. My used car had a top speed of not much faster than walking and I had no time to waste.

No further ghosts had troubled me and fifteen minutes later, I arrived at Fenestram Color.

I parked across the street and did surveillance. Yesterday Leander and Veronica had thrown some kind of fit about me right there on the sidewalk, where, funnily, so many of my dramas play out. Today the Tactus were not visible. It was possible eyes still watched from somewhere, but I didn't see any known enemies. An image of a pristine tube of Higher paint, heavy and sealed, shimmered in my mind. So many years had passed without it. Was I really about to do this now? Go off the wagon? Almost one hundred percent yes I was. I reminded myself that I no longer *chroma stormed* so everything was going to be all right. That's the thing addicts do. Remind ourselves of all the reasons this time's going to be different.

The thing about Fenestram Color is it never closes. It doesn't recognize holidays. It's open Christmas Eve. It provides an essential Skysill service, passing out free Higher paint to any stipend artist that staggers through the door. Painters in Skysill go through ultraviolet pigment the way I go through vodka—fast, and with outcomes mostly regrettable. It couldn't afford to close.

So crossing the street to find the door locked confused me.

I shook the handle. That's how I go, I'm not too proud to say, just shaking all the things that confuse me and getting nowhere. Beside me, a familiar hawk-nosed painter peered in a darkened window. I'd been in the store a few weeks ago and watched Veronica lacerate him with compliments. He pinched a desperate wrinkle above his beak.

"What gives?" I demanded, peering in with him.

He shivered. He looked extremely unfocused. It came back to me, when he didn't answer, that he wasn't a talker. Then he gulped a whole sentence out.

"They still don't have my supply," he said.

"Of what?" I asked.

He turned, wondering who I was.

"Paint," he said, "I haven't had Higher paint in a week." He rapped the window with a long, neurotic fingertip.

"You're saying they have no *paint*?" I asked, watching him. "No Higher paint at the paint store? That's all they *do* have."

"Do *you* have any?" His voice pumped when he asked. He beaded me with desperate eyes.

I gave the handle more shaking, for thoroughness. "Where's Veronica? Isn't anybody in there? This is super inconvenient."

He shrugged. After a moment he walked off, leaving the impression he wasn't going far. He was paint-deprived. He had the classic signs—just like Tilly, I realized. And now I saw other painters, loitering on curbs and in nearby shadows. Was there...some kind of Higher paint shortage? How long had this been going on?

And then, four blocks south on PCH I saw a ghost appear in the road. One second he wasn't there and the next he was flaming up a bowl of Higher *light* as a truck blasted through his chest. He was still out of range, but I guessed others were coming. Word about me was spreading.

So I abandoned the paint store and dashed across the highway, dodging the pickup that'd just smashed through the monk, and I slammed into my car and tried to start it, and it *did*—and I *love* it when that happens—then eased it into traffic. I sent it thundering slowly upcoast to put distance between me and my stalkers and tried to make a plan.

I'd need to call Veronica. I didn't like it but saw no choice. I drove one-handed while I pulled out my phone, checking everywhere for ghosts. Her number rang once before I hung up. It dawned on me suddenly that I should stop ignoring whatever it was tracking me in the air in front of my car, which was not acting like the bird that a lazy part of my brain had decided it was, which I'd been ignoring simply because as far as I knew none of my known enemies were birds. But I saw that it was a drone.

I'd picked up a drone? It paced my car, five feet ahead and five feet up.

Then a blue sedan surged up beside me. These things all tend to happen at once to me, but still, I never get used to it. The sedan did aggressive engine revving and honked, then swayed into my lane to convince me I needed to pull over if I didn't want my car smashed. A husky man was driving and I didn't recognize him. I tried accelerating, but had the wrong kind of car for that. The driver slipped a length ahead and veered over, daring me to hit him, which was the easiest dare I've ever taken since this driver had me confused with someone who valued uncrashed cars, when in fact I think of cars the way I think of paper napkins.

I slammed my wheel to the right though as I clipped him, and my tire almost stalled me on the curb then bounced me up, past the sedan which I bumper ripped, to the sound of screaming car parts. I scraped past, all the while gathering exactly zero speed due to my car not knowing how. But I got past, and then his frothing tires were smoking and the sedan came after me, so I ripped up a side street and squeezed left down an alley that you'd never know was there if you hadn't passed out in it a few times. In my rear view the sedan passed. The drone came after it but peeled into the alley behind me. Then the sedan reversed back, lost a cloud of rubber, and followed.

I put my foot to the floor and got what I expected. Out the driver's window, a brick wall flashed a foot from the door, and on the passenger side, a chain fence flashed. The drone darted above me and ahead. The sedan sped up behind like now he wanted to ram me, and I hoped he would because it might help me pick up speed, but at the last minute, he pounded his brakes.

At the far end of the alley, a second sedan appeared, skidded, and stopped. I was headed for it.

Four passengers in dark suits scrambled out as I barreled closer, undecided on braking, while the driver sat and watched me. His beard was dark around his lips and he had hair tousled in his eyes. He looked relaxed. I bore down and decided against braking. Fuck braking. Why's it always have to be me who brakes? He seemed to understand the decision. The men in suits were waving me back, but I didn't see what choice I had at this point.

Then my front tire blew, the one I'd hooked on the curb. I'm not a good enough driver to keep control under those circumstances, or really any circumstances, and my grill dipped left and hit the bricks, threw sparks, then cleared the wall and gassed out into a postage stamp parking area and ground to a halt. It rocked and steamed. I smelled fire from the engine. Or somewhere. It smelled like poison.

The sedan behind me skidded and tossed open doors. At the other end of the alley suited men who'd sprouted long knives rushed in. The group behind had knives too, and they were going to reach me first, and I thought it was familiar how they all had knives, but before I could place the feeling I felt my fingers stiffen. A greyscale cool began rising around me. The *Gray* wanted to play.

The *Gray* would go through these people like a wolf through baby birds. There were only seven of them after all, and they were running right up into range with only knives and cars. Theyu would all be murder victems if the *Gray* got out, and murders I did not need any more of, plus Caroline made such a point of me not doing murders.

Job one—stop the *Gray*. Which, the only way I know to stop the *Gray* is *storm*. Knife butts were pounding my window as I fisted the keys from the ignition—why it's always got to be car keys is another thing I don't understand—and squeezed both hands and concentrated. I had practice now. It really wasn't hard.

Pop. I *stormed* a ghost. The cold *dominion* mountain phased in, weeping gloom all over, and after that all I could do was float and watch. You're pretty helpless as a ghost. But I figured it was too public here for them to kill me. That was my bet. We'd made a lot of noise and people had to be watching. The police might even come. Too late I realized their plan might be pushing me in a trunk to kill me elsewhere.

Flesh me panicked and pawed his door but his clenched fists couldn't work his handle. Then someone yanked it from outside and he fell out. The driver of the first sedan took him by the neck and lifted him.

Shit—they're touching, I thought, and prepared for brain rot. But I felt none. And flesh me wasn't writhing in skull agony. So...maybe flesh me didn't receive psychic foreknowledge of deaths? Only my normal Asher body did?

Men and blades crowded in, pinning flesh me against the car, where he continued struggling until one of them laid a fist in his stomach, curling him. Then he kept struggling. Finally, I puppeted him still. There was no sense putting up a fight. That was only going to drag this out.

The driver who'd watched as I'd tried to ram his car stepped close, with some loose way of walking, and I saw a scar on one cheek and a tattoo of a scar like it on the other. Also familiar. Even the suits these guys wore looked familiar. The scarred one turned to spit, never taking his eyes from flesh me.

"Did you think you could escape?" His voice was thick with an accent. A Brazilian.

I decided to try out my remote talking and had flesh me tell him, "Go fuck yourself," which came out sounding great. One of his Brazilian guys—they were all his—swung and took flesh me under a rib. Flesh me doubled, sucking air he couldn't find.

"Now we have business," the Brazilian said. "You know me?"

This time when I puppeted, it came out more like a wheeze, "Did I fuck you from a dating app?" I don't think he heard me.

"I am Felipe Silva. You met my brother Marquinhos. He looks," Felipe reached for a picture, "this way. You remember?"

I swung ghost me to see the picture: broad cheek planes on a thick neck. On the cheeks, a scar and tattoo...the last time I'd seen that face it'd just stabbed me in the stomach on Mander's Beach. All that had remained of him afterward had been a couple of bloody shoe pieces.

I had flesh me shrug innocently. It looked authentic, but Felipe didn't buy it. Suddenly he had a knife in his hand and laid the point beside one of my few remaining seashell buttons.

He pressed, and not gently, though of course, flesh me felt nothing. Nothing that ghost me felt anyway. Numbness all around.

"I come into this town to find Marquinhos. And *you* know where he is."

I had flesh me protest, "What? *Me?*"

"I have a feeling. When I have a feeling, I always follow it. My magic haunches. Yes?" His men nodded, a little in awe. I guess he had great haunches. He was right about his brother. I was the last thing he saw.

"And of course," he went on, spitting again while holding flesh me with side eye, "I want my crypto back. That art bitch took it and I want it back."

"From me?" flesh me groaned out on my instructions.

"Yes."

"I don't have anybody's crypto, so how's that supposed to work?"

"That's is not my problem," Felipe shrugged. "It's yours."

"It's not my problem fuckwad," I puppeted, as a reminder of how good I am with people. "Plus *hello.* there are three months—*three months*—then we're all dead and is this the best you can do? With the rest of your life? Money's not going to save you." It was the longest speech flesh me had ever delivered and it wasn't Toastmasters, but it was pretty amazing.

Felipe pressed his knife.

"Marquinhos might be dead," he hissed, "I don't know, but that would be bad. But. Crypto does not die. In this whole piss town I know, you are the one who can find it. So."

He pressed the knife even harder. He knew exactly how hard. My shirt cut.

"I give two days," he said. "You knew them both, father and daughter. You will bring my crypto wallet. No authorities. No cops. I am watching." He pointed to the drone, hovering in a loop. He put his knife away, shook hair from his eyes, and spat yet again.

"Two. Days," he reiterated with fingers.

Then all of them reversed their sedans and went away. They were fast. As soon as they screeched off I slammed my flesh eyes crossed and made hard fists. There was no ghost to out-range here. I'd brought the *storm* on myself and I'd only escape it the hard way.

Ghost me and flesh me superimposed each other, or whatever. I squeezed harder and *dominion* pulsed from both of me in an expanding air flower. There was pain but it wasn't as bad. After a moment my bodies welded and I poured *dominion* down my arm and filled and melted the keys.

And I was back. The mountain gloom vanished. I slumped my body to my knees.

CHAPTER

SIX

The second I was down, my phone rang—Amelia calling. I ignored her, panted, explored how my rib hurt.

Ghosts, Brazilians, the end of the world, murders, thievery, it felt like a lot, which sometimes I'm known to feel, and when I do I like to drink. So ignoring my phone and the steam from my car I stood. A back door in the brick wall led into a bar I had, in the past, been thrown out of. I'd have Brazilian-sized bruises tomorrow and you can't start drinking too soon preparing for that.

"Hey! You can't leave that," called a matron from another door as I left my car.

"It doesn't move," I explained, showing my blob. "Melted keys."

"Yeah, well, it's blocking me."

"Whatever. They'll tow it in a minute."

"You called?"

"You don't *call*," I scoffed, "they just come, they take all my cars."

She remained unconvinced but powerless in the face of my civic experience. I continued ignoring Amelia's texts as I pushed into the dark tavern, stumbling a little but getting myself straight. I found this bar mostly empty. I took vodka to a stool at the end of the bar.

With *sight* twisted high, I scanned the room, looking pretty casual under the circumstances I thought, the circumstances being my shirt only had three buttons left, my ribs ached, and I wasn't drunk.

But if the bar held people I'd rather avoid I didn't see any. It wasn't The Charles, but as Higher infiltration went the place was pretty clean. There was a little Higher graffiti by the register and the couple pressed in a booth wore matching *wander* lip rings, but the median client here was visible spectrum only. Nobody watched me.

Jesus fuck the Brazilians are back, I told my glass. Unwelcome truths were the kinds I came across these days. Fortunetly experience had taught me, just proceed like nothing had changed. Often that's enough to get by. Plus the guy had given me *two days* to get his crypto—I need a much tighter schedule than tow days. Two days is beyond my event horizon.

Amelia texted. Again. *God damnit Ash answer! I know you're there!!*

I finally had vodka, so I engaged, *Oh I'm HERE?? How do you even know?*

It was childishly designed to annoy her, but also the only thing I could think of. I had more vodka and dimmed the room into shadow to make it bearable. I put my phone on the bar. It took a minute.

How do you think I know? She sent.

I think you used sparkles. Because you ARE ONE but you never told me. You're working for Veronica in secret, it's the kind of thing I should hear about.

No, she texted. I could actually hear her sigh, *I'm tracking your phone idiot.*

Amelia picked up on the first ring when I called, and demanded not very quietly, "Are you what? Tracking my actual phone?"

"Yes Asher and you're tracking mine! Location sharing is *on*. You never even looked which is just, like, *painfully* typical. You don't care!"

"You've been tracking me all this time and you *never told me?*"

"Yes, I never tell you anything, we went over this! We're tracking each other. This is what happens when you let other people handle your phone bill, and don't pay attention to details—why do you have to *argue about everything*?"

"I'm arguing? You're arguing! Seriously, you keep calling, so what do you want?"

"It's Veronica," she and paused and then said, while I drank. "I can't find her."

"Ohhhh," I told her, sounding superior, which is a habit of mine people love. "And lo, the teacher abandons the pupil. Well *you* got yourself into that sparkle tribe, don't involve me now. Go sleep in your sparkle bed."

I motioned for more vodka. I was overusing the word sparkle, I knew I had to do better. The time had come to formally level all my complaints. I wanted one more drink to get me started. Before it came I heard Amelia crying into her phone.

"Ames. What's wrong?" I asked. She cried harder. "Okay stop crying, I didn't mean what I said. Did I say something? I'm an idiot. What is it?"

"Veronica. They took her. She let them, but… "

"Who took her?"

"The Council, Asher, who do you think? The Fabrica Council. Pay attention."

"Please," I snorted, "that won't help. Take a breath and say it slow. Veronica's Fabrica Council took her somewhere?"

"They did something to her eyes."

I considered, wondering if in some way this might actually be my problem. I didn't think so. "Veronica can take care of herself," I assured her. "Believe me."

"No, they did something and she can't shape *light*." She sounded pretty desperate.

"But she went with them willingly?"

"There's willing and there's willing, Asher!"

"Okay," I sighed, unable to argue because it sounded so true. "Look. How about, come down and let me buy you a drink?"

"I don't want a *drink*," she snapped. At least she'd stopped crying. "We have to help her!"

"Why?" I wondered. "Maybe they're *promoting* her, it's some initiation. Did she ask for help?"

"Please Ash. Come over."

She was crying again. That's very uncommon. She doesn't like crying because it makes her less bossy. I suggested, very gentle, like I can do, that her coming to me was the only realistic option, because I had no car and people wanted to kill me, it wasn't safe for me wandering the streets. And she knows a fait accompli when she hears one since she took languages, and instructed me *do not move* unitl she got there. I had no car, in a city full of assasins, and she thought I was about going to leave *a bar*. She has no faith.

When she hung up I got us a booth, and her a gin and tonic, in case she decided she'd drink after all, and a basket of fries to share although I'd eaten the fries by the time she arrived.

She looked wrecked. She slipped into the booth not saying a word. She did want a the drink, though she didn't thank me for thinking of it.

"So what do you want?" I asked. Apparently I wasn't going to be gracious about anything. Amelia surveyed the bar, expression dubious.

"Why are you *here*?" she demanded, sipping.

"I said, my car broke."

"Did you forget oil again?"

"There was a *crash*—look, what do you want? Just to aggravate me?"

I heard myself get loud. But I wanted to blend in. I drained my glass to wash myself into balance, then shattered the illusion by slamming the glass down. Then there were tears in Amelia's eyes again.

"Look," I sigh-nodded, "please talk about your thing. Veronica's gone. She went with these Fabrica. I guess that's why Fenestram Color's locked?"

"There was no one to cover the shift..." she squeezed off tears, suspicious suddenly, and used my napkin on her cheeks, "...how do you know the store's closed?"

"Because I was just there."

"Wait. Why do I keep seeing you at the store? You're not *painting* are you? *Asher?*"

The conversation was going from inconvenient to uncomfortable. I called for more vodka knowing it would never come in time. There were a lot of ways I could answer her question/accusation. The easy way, the hard way, by the letter or in the spirit, or I could clam up and drink. Instead I told her the truth. I don't know why. I was tired.

"Yes," I said. "I went to the store because I'm going to try to paint again. It'll be fine."

"You're *not.*"

"I am, and did you know there's a shortage of Higher paint?"

"Asher Gale. *No you are not.* Are you crazy?"

"Is that a trick qustion? I told you it's *fine*, it's not like—"

"Not like what? Not like what? How many years did we fight to get you *stable*—oh my god you pick the worst times for *everything*!"

No one appreciates my timing. I'm used to it. For a second she held her head like it would blast away, and I'm also used to that, then she drank her remaining gin in one throw. She sat a moment.

Then she took one of her turns. The thing she does. She has a way of starting over fresh. Like the thing saints do. She reached across the table to reassure me. She knew I wanted to paint. She knew what my problem was. She was always going to help.

I reared back.

"Oh," I said, "also weird thing, from now on never touch me—*never* touch me."

She closed her eyes. Before it turned into another fight I outlined my recent problems touching people. And ghosts too. And then carefully I presented my theory of being a death guy, though I knew without a better name the *death guy* theory was never going to catch on. And Amelia, the only person who'd been with me through it all, who'd seen and made everything work, with a solution for every problem I brought her, took my theory on straight and utter faith. She knows when I'm telling the truth. It's her superpower—that and blowing roofs off houses. She didn't take my death theories with a grain of salt. She just took them.

"Oh my god Asher. You can't touch *anyone*?" she asked, and though technically flesh me *can* touch people as long as I'm not there to feel it, I knew there'd be a better time for details like that.

Her mind was circling though, and she found a flaw and frowned. "How do you know it'll happen? Your death foresight? No one's died, have they?"

"Not yet," I said "but trust me they will. We all will. Soon."

"Why's everything happening to you?" she cried. I could see she wanted to hug me.

"I don't know who cares?" I asked, because even I get tired of my problems—that's why I come to the bar. "How about you talk about your problem, whatever's with Veronica. Have another drink."

She took a breath. "I think she's being put on trial at the Conclave."

"For what?" I asked, sipping vodka like a lawyer.

Amelia had another gin and told me; she'd been at the store with Veronica when some lady called Willametta, and Leander and a couple of Sapor came in. They'd confronted Veronica. Amy overheard insinuations about the "fragile Five Family Agreements," and complaints from Leander about how dangerous all these untapped Aspectu were.

I stopped Amy. "Dangerous *why*? I heard Leander say that too. What's the big deal with untapped Aspectu?"

"Our whole town," Amelia answered slowly, "is impossible. The *Fabrica* never leave an Aspectu child untapped, It's against the Agreements. And untapped Aspect go insane as adults. Sometimes they go up in a spontaneous purgation, but they always die young. And actually tapping an adult Aspectu is super risky. The proximal energy, you know, the *surge* released when Aspectu are tapped, it gets harder to contain with older Aspectu. A weak *relino* can be killed instantly. Some of the painters in Skysill are in their nineties and a spontaneous purgation would be devastating. And tapping...only Willametta is strong enough. Maybe Veronica. All of us should be insane, Asher. We shouldn't exist, but for generations, we've been fine. Hidden here."

"What do the Tactus care if we blow ourselves up?"

"Leander thinks the untapped Aspectu are part of a plan. They know Fabrica are working *light* at night. He says Veronica's been hiding Skysill Beach from the rest of the Families, she's using it for this night casting or something, it doesn't even make sense—it's *ridiculous*. But untapped adult Aspectu are against the Agreements. So I think they're going to put her on trial at the Conclave. Ash, the Families kill anyone who breaks the Agreements. We have to go to the Conclave and tell them about *dominion*, it's not Veronica! I'll tell them too. I've felt it. We have to tell them!"

I thought it over.

"I was told pretty explicitly *do not go* exactly where you're suggesting we go. Veronica said steer clear of this Conclave."

"But that was before! And the Conclave's already started, so we have to interrupt, we have to prove she's innocent!"

"Interrupt them? Is this the best plan came up with?"

"Ash please!"

She was crying again. For the eighth time today. Because of Veronica? It made no sense. She's like a stone, usually. Once as a kid I caught her in tears after watching National Velvet and before I could run she slugged me and swore me to silence. I saw her cry when Celine died. That's about it.

"It sure sounds risky," I guessed. "Would you rather wait and see what happens?"

"We can't wait. I have to do something. I have to help her."

"Veronica's just some strange...don't let her drag...I mean... "

Something was dawning on me. I saw it in Amelia's face. I put several things together in obvious configurations. I listened. She said, "Because I love her, Ash."

I prefer ignorance, but understanding does come sometimes. And since I make everything about myself, as Nikita noted, this felt to me like yet another piece of information everyone had kept hidden. My sister and...Veronica?

"You love her," I said slowly, "as in, you're *in* love with her?"

"Yes! I love her! She...I wanted to tell you. I kept wanting to tell you but I'm terrified you'll go *Gray*, you'll *storm*, you've done it before and if I lose you, maybe this time you won't come back, but what am I supposed to do, I can't take care of everybody, all the time, it's too much—I can't! Ash, please, we have to help her!"

I did not say a long list of things at that moment that occurred to me, such as *what the fuck?* and, *she's twice your age!* and, *what the actual FUCK?* Instead, I took a breath and said of course I'll help you Amelia. That's the only thing you can do. At this point in our lives, if Amelia was committed, I was too. She'd done it for me too many times.

I wanted to grab more fries for the road but Amelia said we had no time. It never matters to her how hungry I am. Dusk had gathered by the time we got to her car. She asked me why island shorts, I admitted they were a gift and at first I hadn't preferred them, but they'd grown on me. I made her drive slow, or we'd hit ghosts, so she took side streets. She totally believed in the danger of road ghosts. Amy's my biggest fan. She's an optimist where I'm concerned, she believes that anything's possible for me. She also believes it's all going to be inconvenient for her at some point, and so far she's been right.

"Where are we going?" I asked as she drove.

"The Conclave, Ash, be quiet, let me think."

She had things to worry over in silence, which is how she's easiest to tolerate, so I let her be. She wove us higher into dark slopes until we passed the Skysill Public Park sign, and then I knew where she was headed, though still not why.

Skysill Public is our municipal rec center and arboretum. It sits atop a prime foothill ridge overlooking downtown and a sea of cottages. During the day you go for picnics and softball. At night it's closed, except on the 4th of July, and a couple of nights a year when the Wonder Faire takes it over. It couldn't be 4th of July. I would've noticed a flag. Right? Which meant that all the cars I now noticed heading the same direction we were must be going to the Faire. Shay's must be in town.

"Are we going to the *Faire?*" I complained. I wasn't in the mood for jugglers. It'd be crowded and now more than ever I hated a crowd.

"Just wait," she said.

"I do have other things to do," I pointed out.

"Yeah, like paint? I can't believe you. That's so dangerous Ash!"

"Danger's like vodka to me, I have it for breakfast and my other meals, plus you don't know what I'm—"

My necklace gave a freezing pulse. I held my finger up to her in our private sign for *I'll yell again in a minute, but now I have to take this call* and pulled my phone out. Amy squinted at my expectant smile, which is my expression that makes her the most nervous. Then just before the phone rang I pounced on the button. It was my new favorite game.

"I've been thinking about you," I told Caroline.

"I know me *too,*" she breathed. Her voice hit like a helium boxing glove.

Tonight I daydreamed her using an earbud while giving instructions to people in the background, looking sweaty in a t-shirt and jeans. She was in her Monarch suite doing...I daydreamed something I didn't understand.

I asked, "Are you doing archery?"

"Why yes I am," she said, fingering a bowstring.

"You're the most mysterious psychic I ever met," I enthused. "You're an archer?"

"I've got an archery range in my living room. What'd you think that was for?"

There were psychics coming in and out of her suite. They knew how to avoid arrows. I was picking up a sense of preparations being made. Then I dreamed her nock an arrow, draw string to cheek, and fire: bullseye.

My necklace struck ice barbs through my chest and my stomach flopped—her archery was smooth, firm, and unbelievably sexy. Those are not things I've ever thought about archery. I couldn't explain it. I felt her arrow in my crotch, or something, while we both reached for our crystals and gasped.

"Man," she breathed after a moment, "why'd you do *that*?"

"You've got *extremely* good aim," I marveled.

"That's true. I'm real accurate. Sometime I'll show you."

"You make accuracy sound *great*. Usually I can take it or leave it."

"Hold on Ash," she said, then called, "Mark tell Phyllis hurry."

We got over the hormone jolt but it's up and back with us, over and over and higher every time, it seems. That's our pattern. Eventually, it'd get us someplace, and I waited for that, daydreaming her draw a new arrow from a quiver she wore on her shoulder, like Robin Hood, then slow and even her wrist brushed her breast, kissed her cheek, and released. Bullseye.

Her accuracy was hot as fuck. I'm such a mess. It felt great but bad because there was nothing to do with the feeling.

"I'm just calling to see how you're doing," she said. "I'll be too busy to talk for a bit. Still alive?"

"When I talk to you I am. My *sister's* taking me to a Ferris wheel," I accused across the car.

I dreamed Caroline smile, "That's sweet, Ash, you're cute, tell Amy hi."

"Let's just ignore her. So what's the deal, are you a huntress?"

"That's good. A huntress."

She went nock, draw, fire, body taut, perfect, hips limber getting bullseyes—my crystal dropped ten degrees again fighting to hold something in us apart. Something I wanted together.

"What're you doing tonight?" I asked, gripping my necklace.

"Monarch business," she said, setting the bow aside to speak to someone else.

And then Amelia was parking, her headlights swinging over parked cars and trees before flicking off and leaving the trees backlit by the candy greens and blues of a county fair. Near the park entrance were soft oil lanterns in front of a wood carriage, where a line waited to buy tickets. Amy made our *wrap it up I'm really on edge* sign.

"I have to go," I told Caroline. "Veronica's captured or soemthing. I'll call you."

"Veronica?"

"I'll explain it later, it's nothing."

"I love your explanations, they're like cartoons. Be careful."

"You too."

We hung up at the exact same time. I dreamed Jorge appearing in the background, fading. Amelia watched me pocket my phone, shook her head, then pointed at the wooden wagon parked in lamplight, and the banner: *Shay's Wonder Faire.*

"Why're we here?" I started. "Where's the Conclave?"

"There are a few things you need to know," she admitted.

"Really Amy?"

People tell me "things I need to know" all the time but it has zero effect. She's perfectly aware of that. On the other hand, I really had no idea what was going on, so how bad could it be to listen?

"The Conclave *is* the Faire," she explained.

"Explain better."

"Shay's Wonder Faire...is a Nidor...thing. They own it. The Conclave's *here,* at the Faire."

It sounded improbable so I knew it had to be true, although I'd known Shay's my whole life, and there'd been no Family horseplay. Had there? Would I have noticed before this? I hardly notice anything. I spun my *sight* and took out tree shadows, remembering visits to the Faire as a kid, tasting cotton candy, the lights tilting, the goats to pet. I even had a single, simple memory of both my parents here with me. Ex-parents. Step parents? I don't know the word. As far as I could tell the Faire looked the same as it always had.

"God damnit Amelia," I told her. "So I guess now you're saying this is yet *another* thing everyone knows but me? The Faire's run by the Five Families? It's their Conclave? Is that what you're saying?"

"No one who lives in Skysill knows. Veronica told me after she tapped me. The Faire's a whole Nidor community. It travels. The Nidor are the neutral middle family. Peacekeepers or...it's complicated."

"Yeah, and hey, when *did* Veronica tap you since you bring it up?"

"Focus Ash! What do you know about the Five Families?"

Her eyes were wide, watching the crowd and disapproving of me all at the same time.

"There's *Five*," I said. "All the senses. I've had it explained."

"Shay's people are Nidor," she said. Then, "Nidor," she repeated because she knows she has to.

"Yes, *got* it, *Nidor*," I told her. "I remember."

"You remember what sense Nidor use?"

"Of course not."

"My god. Nidor's the Family of *taste*. Right? This is their way. Carnivals, traveling faires."

"They have a *way*? None of this sounds promising."

"Stop complaining for one minute! I need to figure out how to get you through the gate."

"I'll buy a ticket. Like a normal person?"

"You can't, you're wearing a neutral crystal." She reached to her chest and I realized, of course, my sister has a neutral crystal too. *Fabrica.* She showed me hers. "The Nidor *make* these crystals. At the gate, they'll know you're wearing one. But you're supposed to be *tapped* for that and you're not tapped. It'll attract attention. We can't afford attention."

"Interrupting Veronica's death trial with a dramatic speech won't attract attention?"

"It'll attract it but we'll do it *at the trial* and hopefully Veronica will get free and *save* us, but first we have to *find* her, so hello we can't attract *attention*!"

"She'll get free and—oh my god Amelia," I yelled, "this sounds like one of *my* plans, it's *terrible*!"

"Fine then get out! Hurry! Get out we have to hurry—*go*!"

She stood out of the car and slammed her door, so I did too. The night was cooling. We were going off one hundred percent half-cocked so I was perfectly comfortable. But I was surprised Amelia permitted it. She had to be desperate.

"Just follow, pretend you don't know me," she instructed, stepping out. I wondered what that strategy was supposed to accomplish, but I let a few people get between us. Amy was just making it up as she went along, I realized. I was actually proud of her. Let your chaos flag fly, sis. Let's go rescue the older girlfriend you super weirdly suddenly have.

Lights in tents winked through trees on my right like a hide-and-seek village. We hurried toward the ticket wagon. Faire smells vapored over me, steamy and primitive and I remembered how everything tasted, spun hot sugar, spice and caramel, bbq and butter. The rare tastes. Childhood tastes. Rare because of something the Nidor did? I wasn't sure what the Nidor did. What special power came with taste? Sapor told the future. Auditus made Siglium and listened to the past. Aspectu manipulated *light* and Tactus ripped doors off cars. What'd Nidor do? Make delicious pizza?

Shay's Wonder Faire was popular with everyone in Skysill, visible spectrum and *sighted*. Tonight the crowd was thick, pressing in as we neared the tail end of the line. I dodged a man, nearly touching him, and saw too late how I'd trapped myself. There'd soon be no way to avoid brain rot. Why had I agreed to this? God damnit Amelia!

But then I remembered one of my theories from earlier, that my various bodies have different disabilities, and flesh me, though clumsy and stupid, was not sensitive to death foreknowledge. I curled my hands in my pocket, fisted my key blob, and squeezed just as a skinny teen goth bumped into me.

Up and out I squirted to see the massive ghost mountain settle into place, spreading murk even in the dark. Even in the black of night, it made shadows thicker, holes deeper. I ignored it to pilot my body through the crowd, but found flesh me ambling forward on his own, bumping into people without issue. I gave him a simple instruction: go stand in line to buy tickets, and watched as he did it. He's best with simple instructions. He's a lot like me.

Amelia had already reached the window. She might have cut the line, I bet that's easy for *Fabrica,* a little *compulsion* and you get any table you want. At the wagon window a girl with flowing sleeves leaned out. There was something formal in the way Amelia put her palm on the window shelf, how the girl put her own hand glittering with crystal rings atop Amy's. After a second the girl gave Amy a silver broach and a smile. If they hadn't just done a finger dance they might have seemed to me like best friends instead of co-conspirators. Then Amy hurried through the gate without looking back, since we were pretending we didn't know each other.

And now I was worried — what the hell was I supposed to do at the gate? I don't do finger dancing. I felt underprepared, like I was about to be exposed as a fraud, like in those dreams other people have.

Someone beside flesh me was tugging his arm. He looked down. I spun ghost me and saw a little girl. She smiled up at him, trying to get his attention. She was *really* trying to pull him out of line. I told him *ignore the little girl, just keep your eyes on the gate,* while I watched from ghost me.

The girl was pointing back into the trees toward a canvas tent, deep in shadow on the skirts of the Faire. Pulling hard. I shook flesh me's head and puppeted his arm to break her hold but she'd really gripped him. Was she lost? I whipped ghost me in a circle to see—

was anyone watching?—who belonged to this girl?—but she seemed like an independent operator.

When ghost me spun back, a stooped old lady stood beside the girl. The lady wore a red and green bandanna tied over moon-white hair, with her wrinkled eyes half closed and fixed on flesh me. Where'd she come from? The tent? Behind a tree?

It seemed like the line had stopped. I badly wanted to advance flesh me past these two but couldn't. The shriveled lady stepped close, smacking her lips, sucking her teeth or something, and flesh me shied, skittish, like a wild horse. I calmed him. *Easy. There boy. She's just an old lady, let's just not look at her.*

But the old lady didn't move and the line didn't either and finally I puppeted flesh me to face her.

"Goodbye," I had him say. "We're not interested."

She nodded. She eased out her hand—a mitten of ancient skin —for flesh me to shake, but he didn't know what to do because he's missing the social graces. Plus his hands are fists. Shake her hand with your fist, I told him, maybe she goes away. So the two of them shook, palm to knuckles. It went a long time. I hung wondering what the hold up was at the wagon. Flesh me was perfectly comfortable, now that I'd told him the rules. He could shake forever. Abruptly the lady let him go and turned and tottered off, with the little girl assisting like a human walking stick.

At that moment, the line started moving.

I walked flesh me forward but kept a ghost eye on the old lady. I saw her spit something smooth and black into one palm. Then she raised the other palm, the one she'd held on my fist, and she licked it. Her tongue was long, hard, creased. She just stood in the shadows tasting her fingers and watching flesh me walk away. Finally she put whatever object she'd spit back into her mouth. Still watching.

At the ticket window, the girl with flouncing sleeves smiled and asked how many, which was a more confusing question than it used to be, but flesh me said *one* after clearing it with me. No finger dancing required. A minute later the crowd was moving us through the gate.

"What happened?" came a hiss. "Where were you?"

Amelia stepped from behind the popcorn stand where she thought she'd been hiding but hadn't been because hiding is fundamentally alien to her nature. And from her many years training in my idiosyncrasies, she instantly spotted my hands. She whispered, "Ash, are you *storming*?"

"Relax," I had flesh me explain. "So we were in line, an old lady was licking her hand, now everything's great—what do we do next?"

"I wish I'd brought a sweater," she said, turning to survey the grounds and rubbing her arms. Ghost me felt nothing, the single, never ending temperature of nothing. About sixty degrees. And flesh me, it'd been established, was just as numb. But Amelia quaked small mammalian shivers. Suddenly she seemed less eager, with lost questions collecting in her eyes. Could we even do whatever idiot plan we were trying to pull off? She was thinking probably not.

I puppeted a flesh arm to her shoulder and moved her back toward the warmth of the popcorn machine. Flesh me took it upon himself to turn this into a reassuring embrace. He had a certain innocent charm, I had to admit. Naive, but lots of heart.

"I thought you couldn't touch anyone," she said, happy for the warmth but habitually suspicious.

I had flesh me act tolerant of her.

The calliope music and lights, sights glittering from stalls, did not give me the thrill I'd once felt. It was too crowded. Paths wove people through trees into little clearings with tents and wagons arbored in warm light, but it had lost its glamour. Away on the softball field the Ferris wheel and the scream rides were making people do that. High above us, stars shone, the moon glowed, the Higher borealis shed electrons into space. And everywhere I looked the dim streams of Higher gloom ran off the flanks of the ghost mountain, which really put a damper on a carnival.

Amelia pointed beyond the softball field, to the dark behind all the rides, out toward the ridge edge of the park. I saw a huge tent, not illuminated like an attraction, and beyond that the city of Skysill Beach, a phosphorus net of streets flung up the coast. Amy took us toward that big tent.

"I think we're late," she hurried, spying on the revelers, so incredibly obvious it was almost like a disguise. "Why'd you make me drink so much gin?"

I started flesh me protesting but he looked so ridiculous, waving his arms with his mouth all open, that I stopped. Did it always look that bad?

She ran us under the super slides and out past the petting stable, and then suddenly all the lights were behind us. We'd come to a dark no-man's-land of forklifts and cables and flatbed trucks, organized and patient. I tried spinning my *sight* to see into shadow but I don't have that kind of control unless I'm in one body.

Suddenly Amelia, who was by nature more reasonably cautious than me, and had actually been paying attention to our surroundings, took a sharp breath and froze. We were in a narrow row between flatbed trucks and long stacks of pallets. She pointed to the open, far end.

"Someone's down there," she whispered. "I saw something."

"I'll check," I had flesh me say.

I flicked ghost me. I sailed backward in him, facing flesh me and Amelia, who got smaller as trucks and pallets flashed by until ghost me emerged into the open and stopped. There I saw, leaning against a truck grill, the sexy rainstorm Tactus who'd hunted me in Veronica's car the day before. She looked bored.

I had flesh me whisper an update to Amelia while I loitered near the Tactus. I was like a walky talky. I noticed my thinking spread between flesh me and ghost me, operating both, the way you'd operate both your hands, at least if you weren't drunk. I wondered if I was supposed to be doing it like that, or was I breaking something in me? Because shouldn't your mind be associated with a body, if not an actual brain?

"What's the plan?" I had flesh me ask.

"I don't know," Amy whispered, her anxiety plain, "but we have to hurry."

"The lady at the corner's looking for me. We have to go another way."

"There's no other way," she hissed.

"Can't you sparkle us invisible or something?"

"It's night, *hello!*"

"Use this," I had flesh me say, "like you did with Julian."

I puppeted up his fist where *dominion* leaked off the glob of melted keys. Amelia couldn't *see* it, of course, but she understood and shrank back. Her eyes involuntarily counter crossed bone white.

"No," she said, shaking her head, "not that. It's too much. It almost killed me."

That was news to me. Though so is everything else. "Well *what* then?" I asked.

Behind us came voices, coming near. At least two people.

"Oh god, Ash," she said, "I'm—you're not supposed to be here— they're going to see you..."

"I have an idea," I had flesh me say.

I pulled ghost me back and stopped him in front of flesh me. The voices were almost on us. *Climb up,* I instructed flesh me. *Climb on the ghost.* Simple instructions are his forte. Quick as a monkey he jumped onto ghost me, his arms wrapped around my ghost chest. Amelia stared. He was hovering in the air as far as she could see. His legs and arms wrapped around nothing.

Hold on, I told him, which made him look less comfortable and nervous, and then just as two figures turned the corner I launched ghost me skyward and rocketed up like the weight of my flesh body meant nothing. As if flesh me was nothing but moonlight on a feather.

The ground fell back *fast* and my flesh hair flattened on his skull in the wind. My flesh eyes squinted in the turbulence slipstream and for one second I thought he'd lose his grip from shock and accelera-tion. But he's a laborer. Doughty. He gripped tighter.

I stopped us hundreds of feet up. Had they seen?

Far below, two figures approached Amelia. How she did not look up where I'd just magically disappeared into the sky I have no idea. She's got iron fucking focus. I watched her join the figures, then watched the three head past the Tactus lady to cross an open field. They came to a flap in what I could now see was a mammoth, big top-style tent; the one we'd been heading for. A pennant flew at the top. Four sentries stood at the flap. I mean they looked like sentries but what do I know? Amelia was the last of her group to step through, and just as the flap closed she turned and looked up, but against the stars as high as I was she had no chance to see me. Then she was gone.

That made my new job getting into the tent undetected so she could tell me what to do.

The thing I quickly discovered about hovering three hundred feet in the air in one numb ghost body and one numb flesh body is, because between us we have such limited sensory abilities, it's a lot less exhilarating than you'd expect. No high altitude perfumes to scent, or amazing zypher soundscapes to experience. You can't taste high salt air or feel your goosebumps. It's boring. The view was okay but a view gets old fast. I saw the little dell where my own house lay, hidden between the ridge and the sea. If I spun us the other way I had a nice view of the ghost mountain glamouring out *dominion*. It looked bigger from here. Like it was closer.

I left sightseeing behind and with flesh me grappling hard I floated us south, paralleling the ridge, away from the tent, until I'd left the grounds of the Park and any potential sentries behind. Then I floated off the ridge, out toward the city, a thousand yards out into the open air, now much, *much* farther from the ground but still boring. Then finally I floated down below the top of the ridge, so I'd be hidden. From there I raced back up the way I'd come, toward the big tent, concealed. I hoped. Usually I do my hiding in plain sight, due to laziness, so this was a stretch.

My plan depended on spying a conveniently unguarded back door when I neared the tent and peeked over the ridge, but when I looked what I *actually* found was that the entire back half of the big top was open air. It was only half a big top. A half-top? Inside the half-tent rose bleachers filled with light and people. The Conclave, was my studied but knee-jerk opinion, a style of opinion that hasn't served me well enough to be my default style but I play the cards I'm dealt.

I plunged back. If there were *Fabrica* in those bleachers, they'd easily see flesh me outlined above the ridge. So I changed my plan, which I'm also practiced at because the first versions never work. I floated right up to the hillside and disembarked flesh me. I docked him beside a bush. It was steep and the ground was very loose. It was hard work for him, clinging there, but I told him *stay!* He looked betrayed, but up the air he'd be silhouetted. Ghost me's invisible though, even to *Fabrica*.

Then I ghost periscoped and surveilled.

Inside the half tent, bleachers curved circus style, and several hundred people sat facing a stage on the grass where elephants and clowns usually worked. I scanned for Amelia. You can lose a lot of things at a Faire—keys, phones, cars—but if you go to one with your sister to rescue her girlfriend you're absolutely not supposed to lose her. This particular one, *my* sister, was likely to do something idiotic since I wasn't there to offer guidance. I knew that, at this moment, wherever she was, she had no idea what to do next. And whatever she eventually did was going to be outlandish and impractical. My sister's desperately loyal but she has no fucking sense when it comes to relationships.

The crescent bleachers were divided in three sections, seating three distinct groups. The leftmost section held Tactus. Most of the Sapor sat there too. I saw a lot of gentle arm waving on that side, and animals in thrall. In the front row at ground level sat Leander, surrounded by moths. Another beautiful lady Tactus had her hand on the neck of a leopard or whatever. Not all the Tactus did animal tricks but they all did something gorgeous.

On the right-hand bleachers sat Aspectu and Auditus. There I saw Nella, other monks, and, finally, Amelia. She was near the top, on the edge of her seat. Down at ground level in this section, along with an inscrutable elderly man in a sweater sat a lady I decided to call Willametta, because I reach obvious conclusions as often as possible, for efficiency. Willametta wore the same kind of radiant Higher crown Veronica had the afternoon she'd tried to tap me. Willametta's was blasting Higher *light* like some kind of alien space probe.

Process of elimination, also just for efficiency, made the center section Nidor. They sat alone, apart from the other four Families. The ticket seller with glittering rings sat in the top row. You couldn't say what traits or features made the Nidor a group—not beauty, not Higher *decorations* or monk costumes. But the Nidor shared *something*.

For one thing, they all worked their mouths and seemed to be sucking something. In the front row of this section there were two people I recognized. The little girl who'd pulled on flesh me in the ticket line, and the stooped old lady who'd shaken his hand and licked herself. The boss crone.

All the people in all the sections watched the center ring where a chair on a platform held Veronica. She faced away from ghost me but I didn't have to see her face to feel suppressed rage flare off her. She said something toothy to a man pacing in front of her, something I couldn't hear because flesh me was too far away.

The man turned, paced back to stand before her. He was a silver-haired white guy with pacing that flowed like water from a pitcher. He was one of the rockstar Tactus, maybe as rock star as Leander himself. At his feet in the grass, green garden snakes coiled, following him in a slithering stream.

He asked Veronica another question and she snapped an answer that I still couldn't hear. I felt amazing frustration. From flesh me down below I heard nothing but crickets and rustling bushes. Then I heard a voice speak beside his ear. A voice I knew.

"The hell're you *doing* here?" said Nella.

I dropped down to flesh me to look around. She wasn't there, of course. She was airdropping from...from the bleachers. I rose back and picked her out in the stands, not moving her mouth. She looked drunk.

"I'm rescuing Veronica," I had flesh me whisper, hoping I understood what was happening and she'd hear him. He slipped, the twigs he pinched between his fists broke, he almost went backward but was able to snare a branch with his elbow. It was precarious down there.

"That's'a funniest thing I ever *heard* rescue," she scoffed. In the bleacher she took a flask, pulled at it, slipped it away, swallowing as she talked. Just showing off. "It's'a good thing I'm th'only one in Skysill can keep'a network up or they'd be allover you—so your new secret's you can *fly*? *S'that* what I just heard you do?"

"What's the snake guy saying to Veronica?" I had flesh me plead. "Nella! Tell me what's going on!"

She burped, then suddenly flesh me heard Veronica like she was standing right next to him because Nella was forwarding the messages. From there it got to me. Like five dimensional tag.

"...was the only ethical thing to do," Veronica was insisting.

"But *against the Agreements*!" the silver charmer with snakes replied, pacing. "The Agreements protecting the Families from each other and from Aeternus. You risk everything!"

"There is a time for Agreements," Veronica said, "and a time for action. How can you all fail to see it? Aeternus is coming!"

"Enough debate, let's cut to the meat!" cried a new voice, and Leander stepped forward. He drew a cloud of wings with him, gossamer wings against black skin. Some distaste passed between Leander and the snake charmer, who shrugged and sat after a moment. Leander approached Veronica, pointing her out for the audience.

"You're blinded by this Aeternus story," he declared, not really to her. "We all know you see him everywhere. Personally I think you're insane."

"Now we all know," he said to the crowd, "Aeternus drew Seamus apart. And she blames herself. Who wouldn't? The Aspectu and their children, they never bond. But we also know there have *always* been incidents. Through the eons. She's not special. Seamus wasn't special! It was *random*. And her suggestion that the eternal ghost is returning, now, to this city? A quorum, a thousand years early? It's nothing but power-hungry mania—" he spun back to face Veronica, and now he made it count, right into her face, "—under cover of your dead son you want to foment *civil war* among the Families! Do you deny it? Do you deny you've discovered some *night power*, so you and your Family can work depravity after the sun is down? I think you *want* to draw Aeternus! I think you want to drag the Five Families down in flames to atone for the mistakes you made with your son!"

I was listening pretty closely and I felt Leander had Veronica's power-hungry mania exactly right. I wasn't sure about the rest. For a moment she sat dazed.

"Nella!" I had flesh me whisper, "what's this Seamus thing?"

"Aeternus killed Veronica's son years ago pay attention!" Nella slurred.

"It is *you* who are delusional," Veronica was saying, "two hundred years ago—"

"—not this ridiculous—" Leander started.

"—I will speak!" Veronica cried. She was raw, all missing child, all missing everything and voice, body, everything about her shook with it. She was fixed in her chair, held there somehow, I now saw, but she demanded, "I will speak!"

I shoved ghost me toward her. He flipped backward so he could float away facing flesh me and for a moment I saw nothing but green sward and ridge line. Then Veronica passed under my feet and I lowered myself to her face and wished I hadn't. She had something sickly wrong with her eyes. They were all black, no whites at all. Her head hung, hair wet, exhausted—and *pissed*.

"What you do to me matters not at all," she said, "because Aeternus has *returned*. Will we accept our fate like cattle? Consumed in this quorum without a *fight*? I say no!"

"She doesn't deny she's tapping grown Aspectu," Leander said then, turning to face Willametta and shrugging. "There's nothing more to say. The punishment is clear."

"These people in Skysill are *innocents*," Veronica shouted, "who Aeternus will use, who I tap *only* to impede whatever it is Aeternus is trying to accomplish!"

"The eternal ghost *isn't here!*" Leander shouted. "He isn't pursuing anything! You're delusional! These *innocents* as you call them must be left to their fate, minds softening into death. *Anything else is an even greater contravention of the Agreements and will draw Aeternus!*"

"*Their minds will not soften!*" she yelled.

With some immense, hidden energy she straightened in her chair. She spent that energy on something I recognized—she did it to appear reasonable in front of people who thought she was batshit crazy. Oh my god did I sympathize with her right then. That's my whole life.

"Leander," Veronica started, then looked to the bleachers, "Willametta, gathered Family, you must listen. The Aspectu in this town have grown up using Higher paint. It was manufactured for them, and them alone. Using it, they are able to live normal lives—the records prove it. Generations have been born here, and died here, of *old age*, without mental decline. Painting with Higher pigment protects Aspectu. I have only recently come to see it, though I do not understand it. The population here rely on Higher paint, all unknowingly. They crave the experience of using it. And it is the *eternal ghost* who has done this. He keeps them, breeds them, expands the population—for what I do not know—exerting power I do not understand to ensure they never leave, never reveal their habits, and remain undiscovered. But whatever moment he has waited eons for has now come! His plans are finally ready. There is no more paint. Fenestram Glass and Steel, his three thousand-year-old company, has ceased operation. It will no longer provide Higher pigments to Skysill Beach. He is taking the final step."

She had them listening. She'd got her billionaire voice warmed up, rounded out her rhetorical smoothness, and they couldn't help but let her talk. It was like money. It was the most outlandish story. It was riveting.

"Everything I say can be confirmed by records—records I could never fake. Aeternus provided these people Higher pigment to *preserve* them. He clouds their minds to *keep* them. He supports them in every way, they even refer to themselves as Fenestram artists. They receive a stipend, and have, going back hundreds of years. But their end is near."

Not a pin could be heard, other than maybe by Nella and the Audituses who probably hear all the pins, which has to be distracting. Veronica's voice was weakening but she pushed.

"The untapped Aspectu in Skysill Beach will regress now, without paint. Within them, *light* will become dangerously active. But they will pass through a stage where they can be tapped. The few I have tapped myself had to be weaned off Higher paint before it was possible. You see? You cannot be tapped if your *sight* is consumed by this paint. And if no paint comes—and it will *not* come, the factory is abandoned, I have *seen* it—the minds here would soften and the people die. But *before* that happens Aeternus will use them. He will use all of them. In a quorum."

"Veronica, please, use them for what?" Willametta asked then, standing. "What will the ghost do?" Her brow circlet poured *ultraviolet* brilliance all over the scene, like hydrogen fireballs, but it didn't make anything clearer. Not for me at least. "Tell us. What will Aeternus *do*?"

"I do not know," Veronica admitted, softly. You could see she'd run out of energy. Her voice was husked. "All I know for certain is that Aeternus is preparing a quorum. There will be a slaughter. We must fight him! We must tap the Aspectu in this town so he cannot use them. He does not want them tapped!"

After a long silence, Leander scoffed.

"Does anyone believe this *fabrication?*" he asked, delicate, magnificent, full of celebrity scorn. "A quorum? It's a *thousand* years early for a quorum! And on this wild theory we're asked to overlook this outlandish breach of the Agreements? Some, *in my own Family*, are willing to overlook it. But I am not. *I've heard enough*!"

He turned toward the assembled Five Families. He looked amazing. You wanted to let him talk. He was so confident—he had a backdrop of iridescent fucking moths, you had no choice but watching.

"She and her family are preparing a war—they've discovered, some of them at least, a way to wield full Fabrica power after the sun has set, and now *none* of us are safe! This is not open to debate. The Agreements are clear. She must be put to death. Tonight!"

A plan started forming in my mind, involving flesh me saddling up on ghost me and riding over to Veronica and grabbing her and all of us shooting up into the sky before Leander killed us or the Aspectu beamed me or any of the rest of them did the things they did, whatever those were. I noticed the Sapor had begun beating their arms, eyes closed, nostrils wide, feeling for threats. I wondered if I wasn't looking at a plan with no chance of success. So often those are the ones I come up with.

I never got a chance to find out.

"Stop!" shouted Amelia, standing suddenly, like I'd predicted, because she's got no better idea of reasonable behavior than me, but unlike me she thinks she presents as persuasive and rational, "It's not *her* that's responsible for this, I'm the one who blew the top off the house after sunset. I did it—*at night.* I'm the one with *night power* —this is ridiculous—*let her go!*"

Amy started clambering down the bleachers toward the stage. People turned to watch.

"Nella stop her!" I had flesh me yell.

But we both saw there was nothing Nella could do. The Sapor were now waving and breathing like band conductors in a marathon; some of them had come off the bleachers and started walking out toward the edge of the ridge. Instinct told me they were heading for ghost me, like suddenly they could see him, and I shot him skyward, but he was always and forever invisible, not a single neck craned. I thought maybe it was flesh me they were after and I blinked my ghost over and lifted him off the hillside and spun us fifty yards down the ridge to hide, but when the Sapor got to the edge of the ridge they ignored him. More and more Sapor came to stand there, looking out over the city waving and breathing, and the other Families were starting to come off the bleachers in the same direction, not looking happy. Something in the future stirring the Sapor?

"What the hell's this?" I had flesh me ask Nella in case she'd stayed connect as I moved. She faded in, out, but I heard her.

"Don'know...Sapor sensing...event...what the shit?"

No help from Nella. I slipped up over the ridge to see Amelia by the stage, kneeling beside Veronica, pulling her chair, but the chair held tight.

And I realized nobody would notice flesh me at all. It was dark, it was chaos—I took him up, raced at ground level toward the tent and dropped him in some high grass, and *ran* him. I ran him like everyone was running and they didn't notice he was going the other direction into the tent. In ghost me I sliced ahead to spy the path of least resistance, but unfortunately flesh me doesn't know about resistance. He rolled over a hillock. He bashed through an Auditus. He jumped a barrel and *ran*. He came like Mario.

"Stay back *dumbass*!" Nella faded, but flesh me got through the back entrance, which the sentries had abandoned, while I demanded he should *get to Veronica!* If I didn't fly him I hoped he wouldn't attract attention, and maybe we'd have five seconds to organize an escape. He shouldered people aside and went under the bleachers.

"Ash!" Amelia cried, seeing him come, "no—go back!"

But flesh me had orders. He raced up to Veronica and skidded to a stop. Veronica raised black eyes to him, eyes full of no hope at all, just obsidian horror. Amelia was still pulling but Veronica was invisibly bound to the chair and the chair to the stage. My plan drew a blank at that point. How was I supposed to fly with an entire stage attached to her?

Then, from out over the city, there came a sound...

Crack...a-BOOM-M-M-M —

The Sapor froze. Just froze, arms akimbo. The Auditus in the bleachers shot to their feet. Out above the nightscape of Skysill Beach, there rose an ultraviolet cloud, a mushrooming explosion going up to bathe everything everywhere in such Higher brightness it drove off the gloom of the ghost mountain for a moment.

"A purgation," Veronica cried, as the blast echo-shattered off the hills, trying to turn, to see behind her, "that is a proximal multi-variant *purgation!*"

"But it's huge," Amelia protested, confused, "it *can't* be."

"It is," Veronica said. "An Aspectu has just been tapped. It has killed them. Along with the relino who took the *light*, almost certainly."

CHAPTER

SEVEN

For a second it seemed like no one was looking at us and maybe we'd just be able to walk out. The bleachers were emptying. Confusion was everywhere. I know a perfect opportunity when I see one since I've seen so many of the other kind.

"We should *go*," I had flesh me suggest, "you know—*right away*. This is a perfect opportunity. How do we get her loose?"

Veronica shook her head. So did Amelia. They didn't see the same opportunity I saw. Maybe Veronica saw nothing at all, her obelisk eyes didn't seem functional.

"She can't," Amelia sobbed, pointing. "They're binding her."

I saw no ropes or chains, so, "A finger sparkle thing?"

"*Nighttime* Asher," Amy unnecessarily shouted, "so *no!*"

"This is Tactus bio-magnetism," Veronica groaned at me, struggling to stand. "They have bound me to the chair."

"Really? I don't think that's how bio-magnetism works...okay, what's with your eyes?" She kept blinking inky regret at me, and I'm distractible, even during escapes, so I had to ask. "Because it's super freaking me out with the blinking—can you—"

"Asher!" Amelia yelled again.

"The block will wear off," Veronica said, "but until it does I can shape no *light*. I let Shay do this to me, so the Conclave would let me speak."

Veronica indicated the bleachers with her chin. I spun ghost me and flesh me turned too. We stood directly before the middle bleachers. The Nidor bleachers. The other sections had been abandoned but none of the Nidor had stirred from their seats. Every one of them stared at us, sucking and shifting something with their tongues. Shay had to be the old lady in front. It was her Faire, so she was the one in charge of the tongue suckers ranked behind her, and she watched us, her hand on her little girl's walking stick. Shay wasn't coming to help. She specialized in watching.

I spun flesh me back so I could complain straight into Veronica's face where it's most satisfying, and past her shoulder saw Leander stalking off the ridge toward the tent with bad violence in a grim, beautiful mouth. His moths had been left in his dust.

"Try this," I had flesh me say to Veronica and pushed the fist lit with *dominion* down against her leg, with all my limited abilities. I told it, *flow into Veronica,* because what the fuck else could I, and waaaay weirder things had already happened than some *light* going into someone's leg. But nothing happened.

"Try what, Mr. Gale?" she asked, supercilious the way she can be even stuck in a chair with no pupils.

Leander saw flesh me and his face tightened into majestic *now-I'm-enraged.* He saw we were trying to free Veronica, it wasn't hard to guess, and to put an end to that he surged, shoving people so they flew yards and yards, like—he was massively strong.

"Go, *go!*" flesh me tried shouting *dominion* into Veronica but it didn't work.

"What are you *doing?*" Amelia cried until she saw Leander too and decided Leander was a bigger problem than me being so frustrating when suddenly Veronica understood. She has a calm way in a catastrophe.

She narrowed her freak eyes and said, "*Dominion*, I must hold it, like the turtles. Make another. Quickly!"

Make another, I ghost snorted, *quickly*—who did these people think I was?—though with Leander kill stalking us, maybe it didn't matter as much who I was. I crossed my flesh eyes and pressed and *dominion* flared in racing streamers while ghost and flesh me co-habitated space. *Dominion* raked *lava flayed nuclear agony* down my arm because I did it *quick* like she wanted, then out of my flesh hand popped a new key blob. It fell on the grass.

Usually I merge into one body at that point, but I wanted my bodies separate because the crowd was thick and people were touching me. I had mind rot to worry about. The ghost mountain still loomed, portending deaths everywhere—*all* these people prob-ably died in three months, but I didn't want to find out.

With flesh fists I bobbled the blob to Veronica who somehow got it in her hand. Her head flew back. Shay's little girl was suddenly there, peering at Veronica, at my hand, the ground where the blob had fallen. Shay herself just watched.

Dominion bloomed around Veronica. She stood, pupils clear, focused, while behind us Leander *came so fast*. Veronica put hands on Amy and flesh me, counter crossed to fresh whites, then trails of *wander* surrounded those three and flesh me, Veronica, and Amelia just disappeared.

Ghost me hung right where they'd left him, though. Instantly he got yanked sideways to face flesh me, wherever he'd been taken. Out past the ridge, in the city somewhere. The angle change was a good one to watch Leander, who skidded to a stop starring at the empty chair. Shay's little girl reached for the seat where Veronica had been bio-magnetized.

Then, with no warning, ghost me blinked out of that place.

We blinked back, in a different place.

It was all completely out of my hands, all the blinking, but at least it was disorienting and made me nauseous so it was familiar. The new location I'd blinked into was also familiar. I floated at the bottom of the lane at the top of which my house hid. Celine's broken car was parked up this lane around a narrow corner unless it'd been towed, which is what usually happens. For a moment I hovered, getting my bearings, watching Veronica and Amelia standing beside flesh me yelling at him.

I felt like he was owed an explanation, so I made him demand, "What are we doing at my *house*?"

"Ash, *Ash*," Amy yelled, shaking him, "can you hear me now?"

"Very loud," I had him say in confusion. "Stop shaking him. What's your problem?"

"What? You've been standing here, saying, *hold on a minute* over and over."

"He was saying *hold on a minute*?"

"*You* were. *You* were saying it. Like a message machine. Are you all right?"

"I doubt it," I had him say.

I spun ghost me in a circle around flesh me, now that I knew where I was, but just saw shadow trees and the street to my former address. From flesh me I heard, all through the neighborhood, car alarms screaming. Something had set them off. I couldn't see what.

Flesh me appeared healthy and typically puzzled. He'd been carrying on conversations without me. Who knew what he'd do next? Maybe he'd learn to cook and we'd open a restaurant.

"Nobody touch me," I had flesh me yell, then I crossed his eyes. I did it slower than I had on the ridge, and it wasn't spa treatment but it wasn't that bad. *Dominion* flowed around my bodies, my bodies got inside each other, I fused us. I pushed *dominion* down my arm into my fist and a new blob began.

At which point I had an artistic inspiration. These are the only kind I really trust. The other inspirations tend to land me in jail or sick under the pier, but the art kind never fail me. And though normally I'm not much of a sculptor, because sculpture takes patience and I have none, as the blob in my hand became malleable I thought, wouldn't a certain person really appreciate a present?

Presents are something I have no money for, or experience buying, but what if I made her something?

So I used mental powers—or whatever it was I had, probably not mental powers, I'd have noticed those by now—to measure, to mold the *dominion* current as it went down my arm so when it hit the key blob I flowed in with it, the way I'd done with the pole in Damely's gallery, and I roughed out the shape of a cat. The cat I'd been thinking about, that I'd seen in a few dreams. I built him lean and eager, a cat you could really admire even if he had flaws. I didn't have the skill or patience to make a chain to hang him on a neck so I made, or *dominion* made, a thread of flexible steel twine threaded through his tiny collar so my cat became a necklace.

And I became one body. Mountain gloom vanished. The world got normal, the way some people like it. The charm fell from my fist when I involuntarily opened it, glowing super *dominion*. A little punchy I stooped and shoved it in my pocket.

"What was that?" Veronica wondered.

"Some people like cats," I told her, and then, back to my first-person eyes for the first time in many hours, I dialed the whole scene up as bright as day.

"What are we doing at my place?" I demanded.

"This is as close as I could bring us to the purgation," she said.

With high-tuned eyes I noticed traces of *light* in the air, motes of nothing, drifting and flexing in and out of *sight,* settling toward the earth. Up the slope behind the trees near my hidden house was where the motes seemed thickest.

"Escaping, as we just have," Veronica continued, sounding exhausted, just like she looked, "will have ugly consequences. I hope I said enough to convince Willametta. At the moment I am the only one who can translocate this far in the dark. We have only a few minutes before the other Families arrive. We must hurry."

"Hurry to *what*?" I wondered.

She pointed up my lane. "To the site of the purgation."

"But up there's where *I* lived," I told them, dubious. I'm a never-look-back kind of person. The kind who leaves his house after it's ransacked and never looks back.

But Veronica's a different kind of person. She stumbled off toward my drive with Amelia at her side, arguing that Veronica needed to get away, to rest, while I noticed, now that I was back in a single me, how crappy and beaten to shit my body felt. I felt like I was covered in nicks and cuts, road rash and welts and bruises. And one elbow was swollen like I'd hit a wall. The Brazilian bruises on my ribs I recognized, but the other pains were from flesh me crashing over concrete and falling into barrels. Flesh me was very eager but he was shockingly careless with a body.

Veronica walked with her arm over Amelia's shoulder. Amy looked back at me for a second. I faked a smile, which she took as I'd intended, as an expression of my existential doubts and of me not giving a fuck who she went out with, even if it was Veronica. She and I share a language.

We took the bend in my lane and as my driveway came into view I ghosted up and out the back of my skull. The mountain gloom shivered in. I saw a ghost thirty feet up the road. Ghosts had become pretty run of the mill by that time so this one barely registered. What did register was the ruin that only a day before had been Celine's car. I'd left it parked by the curb and it wasn't a car now. It was filigree.

A deep crater gouged twenty feet of road and sidewalk out where the car had parked. It was smoking violence like a missile strike, and it ate up the hillside into my driveway. Suspended over that hole, strung in filigree threads, Celine's car spread through the air. It arced over the rim, stretching up and out, melted and hardened in arches like water splashed from a pond and frozen.

And Higher *light* came off absolutely every single thing.

In the middle of this devastation, above the open pit, was the ghost: Tilly's ghost. My poor sick neighbor—paint sick, I knew now. Tilly was a glowing, ultraviolet showgirl. *Dominion* slid and curled all her *light* in place, shaped her as she faced flesh me, turning by quarter inches as I walked him toward the hole.

Tilly wore a gown, with hair combed in waves. She looked nothing like I'd ever seen her. In her extended right hand she held a ghost painting: the one she'd forced me to take when I'd left. She held my own painting.

"What...happened here?" I had flesh me ask. He was looking at the ghost. I was looking at Veronica. So was Amelia. Veronica shook her head.

"All I know," she said slowly, "is that this was certainly a proximal purgation. A worst case. Someone got tapped here, clearly died, and whoever tapped this poor creature also perished. But why?"

"And how come my car's like this?" I complained through flesh me.

She just kept shaking her head. I'd grown comfortable dismissing her as a person who thought she had all the answers, so this new thing wasn't welcome.

Up the hill a figure emerged to stumble down my ruined driveway, heavy in the legs and guts, light in the shoulders: Lou, Tilly's partner. My living neighbor. He wore a t-shirt and underpants and his face cycled terror and mystification.

"What the shit, man?" he said. He shook his skull like his ears were rung, and then his ankle rolled in debris and he went sliding into the blast pit. He rolled to the bottom and staggered to his feet. He stared. "Something blew up? What? Tilly was out here. Have you guys seen Tilly?"

Veronica and Amelia looked around. They looked in the hole. Under dark bushes. The only one who'd ever see Tilly again was me.

"Lou," I had flesh me say. He could barely hear. I screamed, "LOU! What was Tilly doing out here?"

"Not anything..." He shrugged, not saying something. "I mean nothing. You know."

"Was she..." I reached for the only two pieces of information I had—car and Tilly. "Did Tilly do something to my car?"

His face crumbled. "I'm sorry man. She said...you know, you left a tube of paint in your car and she...we needed to paint, man. I mean... it's been...she was gonna replace it when she could."

I saw Veronica solving equations as she took it all in, the way billionaires do, like a slot machine spinning a payout. She looked first at flesh me, then at the car in the air, then at Lou in the hole. She'd solved it. I'd solved it myself a moment earlier.

"Yesterday," she said to flesh me slowly, "at Julian's. You were holding a tube of paint."

I nodded him. "The one flesh me drained *dominion* into."

"*Flesh me?*" Amelia demanded. "What's that supposed to mean?"

"And yes, I left the tube in the car," I told Veronica, and indicated the hole where there used to be a car, remembering the events out loud for everyone's benefit, because I'm considerate like that. "Celine's car wouldn't start. Tilly followed me down. She wanted me to take a painting. I almost forgot my phone, I didn't remember the tube of paint. My hands were full. That tube was pumping *dominion,* just like all my blobs. Like the one Amelia touched. Like yours."

I pointed to the key blob Veronica still held, a little dimmer now after teleporting us here, but with plenty of freak *light* still coming. Veronica listened to me say what she already knew.

"I guess Tilly saw the tube in the car," I continued. "She came down tonight to use it, paint sick...when she touched it, what happened was..." Veronica had the answer. I could have said it, but I let her.

"*Dominion* did this," she marveled. But not in a good way.

"I had a vision," I remembered then. "I foresaw Tilly dying. But this...I didn't..."

Lou, watching, trying to listen but understanding only every fourth word, wandered the pit from one slope to the other, stunned.

"Where's Tilly?" he kept asking. "Let's find her. Let's find her."

Sirens sounded in the distance.

"Quickly," Veronica said, holding out my blob, "I must move us."

"No," I told her. I pointed flesh me at the ghost. "I can't just leave Tilly. This is my fault."

"Tilly?" Lou said, pawing to climb from the hole.

"A ghost?" Veronica asked. I nodded my flesh. She narrowed her eyes. "The Families will arrive any moment. What can you do?"

"What ghost?" Amelia said.

"Whatever you do it, must be *quick*," Veronica said.

Tilly hung over the hole where flesh me couldn't reach her. I looped ghost me behind, and as respectfully as possible bumped her toward the edge of the hole, the way a collie herds a lamb, until she floated one step from both my bodies. Flesh me reached for my painting. I let him touch it.

A deep and wonderful warmth rose while around me the world transformed. The ghost gloom burned off, the mountain faded out, and a sunlit landscape of tree shaded hills shimmered into view just as it had with Felicia. The shadow mountain was here, but far, far away, and very real—an alpine masterpiece of stone and snow and cloud. The sky above me turned a blue that didn't stop. I had a feeling of *rightness*. All very unlike me.

And from the ghost painting—my own painting—came Tilly's story. It was ugly and disappointing, like most stories featuring me or my art. That's a niche I own.

Tilly was the same age as me. We'd been peers, though I hadn't really noticed her growing up. I hadn't noticed much back then. Nothing, really. But Tilly had been drawn by some chromatic mania she saw in my work—what seemed to her the *magic* of my painting —and the things she pictured did seem like magic. In her mind, my work transformed reality.

As early as she could hold a brush, young and fierce, long before meeting me, she'd had a gift—I saw it now. She'd been extraordinary. And never satisfied, which is the curse that comes with that gift. Our paths crossed near the beginning, and my work so shocked her that she swore she'd find a way to capture the world the way she saw me capture it. My work, its commitment to a singular vision, the fact that I *never stopped working* though everyone saw it driving me insane—all of it inspired her.

The galleries wanted her but she resisted, though that's not easy, not in Skysill. Because unlike me Tilly wasn't insane. She had connections, she had friends and family and exposure to social forces. But she turned it all down, inspired by my mad vision. And then the day came when I gave up painting. I did it to save myself but she didn't know. It never occurred to me I'd affect anyone by quitting, but Tilly— and others, apparently—had seen my self-preservation as an admission of defeat. To her, I'd been a singular example of a better kind of future. Because obviously she didn't know me. For her and the others, paint-addled and searching, when I gave up, some kind of light went out.

And slowly she surrendered art, until she became nothing but a painter. A prestigious gallery accepted her. And there, for the rest of her days, she manufactured canvases, whatever they told her, whatever sold best. Until just yesterday, when she'd lifted my final painting from the wreckage in my room and felt a piece of her past come back, and remembered, wondered, wanted it again. Wanted meaning.

Her story ended there. It ended with an image of my unfinished painting.

Higher billows began turning ghost Tilly. Strings of *dominion* held her, above and below, and spinning and spraying she became a glitter ball, lighting the trees and slopes and surreal car threads in my ocean grotto, expanding like breath, all of her brightening until she reached her limit and collapsed. And pin pricked. And was no more.

My bodies came together. Cold rushed me. I fell to my knees. My ears rang with sirens and car alarms and Lou screaming and maybe me screaming.

"We must *leave*," Veronica yelled, and *wander* soaked me. I felt Veronica's hand on my back. A terrible hole opened in my head. Dark frigid rot poured into my mind. I foresaw Veronica dead on a mountain top three months from now. Then my neighborhood vanished.

CHAPTER

EIGHT

The sudden silence of wherever we appeared next was a lot more peaceful than the screaming alarms and sirens and people we'd left behind. But I didn't notice because I was dying of brain rot.

We appeared on a floor instead of a road, with me kneeling, Veronica behind me. One second after arrival she took her hand off my back and thank *god,* the ghost mountain disappeared while the ordinary dark of an empty room surrounded me. I faced a second-story window overlooking stars above dark bluffs and distant sea spray. An utterly random place to appear, I thought, but the silence was restful. I dropped my *dominion* key blob on the hardwood. I folded to lie beside it.

But as I settled I felt, or telepathed, or had a real hallucination my phone was going to ring in my pocket in four seconds. I realized that just as I fell to my side. Yes! My crystal jabbed me. Yes! I hit the floor hard on an elbow and cried at the damage flesh me had done already. Everything hurt. I groaned but daydreamed Caroline up at Three Paths, though not in her own room this time. She was afraid,

130

dialing my number, and...oh. Apparently I'd died again. I was beginning to sense a pattern. With my skills.

Amelia and Veronica stared as I yanked my pocket. My phone was pinned under me. God damnit. My coordination was bad and my brain had a speed wobble from teleportation and brain rot. Foreseeing Veronica's death again had not been pleasant.

"What is it you are doing, Mr. Gale?" she asked, watching me pocket wrestle.

"I'm fine," I waved, "just answering my phone..."

"So...what happened to Tilly?" Amelia asked the room. She's seen me on the floor enough not to care when it happened.

"Tilly was destroyed in her purgation," Veronica said, still watching me.

"So who was the relino?" Amelia asked. "Did they die?"

"There was no relino," Veronica said.

I didn't get to the phone in time. It was still in my pants when it rang. I felt like I'd failed a test I really wanted to pass, which is something I never feel about a test. But finally I pulled it out, punched it on, and answered.

"What's going on," she cried from the speaker, "you died again, disappeared..."

"I don't know what's going on, that's not my thing, but I'm not dead," I assured her, "totally not dead..." From my pocket with my phone I'd hooked the cat necklace, which now dangled from my fingers, blowing *dominion* everywhere, "...hey look, I made you this."

"Okay Ash but I've got a million problems..." she started, then trailed off. I daydreamed her daydreaming the necklace. I daydreamed her surprise, very intense, and then she said, "Oh my god that's him. That's Romeo."

"I made him for you," I assured her. "I've seen him in a few dreams where we grow tomatoes and have sex and read. I hope you like him."

"You made him for me?"

"With mind powers." I decided to call them that.

I held him up in the starlight through the window so we could both admire him. Caroline dreamed me a soft look, a wondrous look. "He's *perfect*."

"I'm glad you think so."

"Wow. Everybody always asks me what I can possibly see in you, but they have no idea. You're the best boyfriend. You make me things."

"I know, right? I feel like I'm really rounding into shape, and who are these people, exactly?"

"They don't matter. Where are you?"

I scoffed. "Who knows?"

I daydreamed her dreaming me in a dark, empty room with other people. It was like a daydream feedback loop.

"Put me on speaker," she said, so I did, and she called out, "Hi Veronica! Hi Amelia! Where's Ash right now?"

Amelia and Veronica looked at each other, then at me laying on the floor holding up a cat on a necklace, as far as they knew for a girl who couldn't see it, and Amelia was confused, but Veronica was furious.

"We're in a safe house," Veronica told Caroline. "You can see us? Your telepathy? Caroline, this is a huge risk! Every time the two of you surrender to these polarity connections the danger grows!"

Caroline frowned and only I could see it, which made it similar to a lot of things in my life but this was no hallucination. This was a girl with a secret frown. Just for me. It was intoxicating. Which, professionally speaking, isn't a term I just throw around.

"He floats through my mind in daydreams," Caroline admitted, "and I can't help how cute he is in a daydream, and just now it felt like he was dead. I can't control any of it."

"I'm not dead," I pointed out for the room.

"Like he's got nine lives," Caroline said with a secret smile.

Veronica was so unhappy hearing all this, she could hardly speak, but she managed somehow. She looked deeply confused, so at least there was that.

"Maybe it's not your polarity," she said. "Could it be something on the Path?"

"No," Caroline said, "this's like sharing someone else's senses. It's like being together in a daydream. It's tied to the neutral crystals. I feel them, every time."

"These crystals are bullshit," I offered.

Veronica paced to me on the floor, shaking her head, while Amelia had no idea what any of us were talking about, which I knew she had to hate.

"The barrier should be *cumulative*," Veronica murmured, "it makes no sense. Shay said the new crystal would buffer you. There has to be an explanation!"

I snorted—like this one thing, of all the things, had to have an explanation? Please. Veronica looked pale. Amelia hurried out through a door saying Veronica needed water. She didn't ask if *I* wanted water, of course. Apparently Amelia was familiar with Veronica's safe house sinks.

"So," I said to Caroline, all conversational, "I rescued Veronica, is your Monarch business done? Do you want to hang out?"

"No," Veronica insisted, kind of weak and bent over.

I telepathed other people around Caroline, a suit of armor...she was in Phyllis's suite.

"We haven't even started. Things keep happening...out of nowhere I keep wishing you had your hand up my dress and I'm not even wearing a dress..."

She was still on speaker but we didn't care and Veronica was sort of passing out anyway.

Then our crystals pulsed and we grabbed them, they're not *at all* comfortable, like wearing a Taser, and after we got our breath back we discovered we'd hung up, which was disappointing but probably for the best. Caroline had important things to do. As the daydream faded I saw Jorge and Phylis, her fellow Monarchs, looking impatient, probably wondering what she could possibly see in me. Then she was gone. I put the cat back in my pocket.

"We'll have to attempt more crystals," Veronica gasped. "Perhaps Shay can make..." then she swayed, and just as Amelia came back with water Veronica went over sideways. I rolled so she wouldn't land on me. Amy caught her, and helped her down, looking daggers my direction like I should risk brain rot to catch everybody's girlfriend who falls over. They ended up seated against a wall. It looked more comfortable than what I was doing. I crawled to a different wall and propped up in the dark, listening to distant surf. We wheezed for a few seconds, because of fucking *everything*.

"Whatever Caroline and I do is absolutely none of your business," I finally said when I had my energy. "How come you're so involved? It's *creepy*."

"You do remember," Veronica observed back at me, all subtle again because she knew, we both know, that I don't remember anything, "you do remember the things you and she think you feel for each other—lust, love, whatever it is—are nothing but a terrible dysfunction? You are broken. Your supposed relationship is a *disorder*. It will destroy you. So you must be careful—you should not be testing the limits of the neutral crystals with trivial contact!"

"You know what's trivial are these crystals—I don't think they're even *doing* anything," I shot back. It's her subtlety that does it to me. I get confused and I get louder. "I don't trust these crystals! At all. That Shay lady? She licks people. So... "

I pulled my slim blue shard from my shirt to see it better, my aqua nightlight catching star shine through ocean windows. I shook it, disparagingly. I hoped it was disparaging anyway—I'm never sure. "These are from those Nidor? The tongue suckers I saw at the Conclave? That Shay strikes me as a real suspicious character, and believe me, I know a suspicious character. How sure are you about her? Don't those Nidor have...you know... a vibe? To me they have a vibe. All the licking? What do they even *do*?"

It was a lot of observations at one time in no particular order without organizing principle. My usual style.

"What do they *do*?" Veronica asked. She'd been trying to follow.

"You know," I insisted. "Light powers, strength powers, hearing the past, all that shit, what's the *Nidor* thing?"

"We've covered this," Veronica sighed. "Nidor. The Alchemist."

"He doesn't remember things people cover," Amelia explained, softly, a little sad.

"It should all be in a text," I agreed. "But I mean, I know Family Nidor is *taste*. That's the only sense left so I just process-of-elimination it. But don't they have some super power or something? Like casting light spells of bio-magnetism?"

"Chemistry," Amelia explained. "Family Nidor manipulate chemical bonds."

I tried to picture it.

"Like, little laboratories in those trailers?"

"Their salivary glands," Amy said. "Biochemistry. Their mouths *are* laboratories."

"Ohhh," I nodded, because that's how you have to treat these people. "Sure. But what do they *do*?"

"They do *chemistry!*" she shouted. Like I'm some kind of professor.

"We're going round and round," I shouted back, "and I'm about to throw up. All I'm saying is, do you trust those people passing throbbing crystals out to everybody?"

"*Trust* them?" Veronica said. "The Nidor are the mediating voice that has kept the Five Families from destroying themselves for as long as the Five Families have existed. Yes. I trust them."

"So the *chemists* are the most powerful Family?" I said. "The nerds?"

"No," she said, "In most ways they are the *least* powerful, the most limited. But the Families depend on the few powers they have. They make the neutral crystals for instance." As she spoke, she stood, then almost went down again. Amelia got in fast and steadied her.

"Roni you've got to rest," Amelia pleaded, taking Veronica's hand. I let my eyes roll because *Roni*.

"Now is not the time to rest," Veronica said, "not when we have made this profound discovery. We must move *immediately*, before Aeternus realizes." Veronica looked down at me. Like she'd been doing since we met. We have our thing.

"Tell me everything you know about *dominion*," she instructed.

"I did already that."

"*What* discovery," Amelia asked. She hates being behind. She's kind of a teacher's pet.

"For the first time in history," Veronica said, "we have a tool to fight the eternal ghost."

Amelia squinted, then looked at me. "Do *you* know?" I rolled my eyes and nodded. *Roni.*

"Don't you see?" Veronica asked quietly. "We know what Aeternus wants Julian to do with the cage cup,"

I'd worked this discovery out one teleport back, but Veronica was still trying to believe any of it could possibly be true. Since I'm never troubled by those kinds of questions I was ahead of all of them.

"What are you talking about," Amelia pleaded. "The cage cup?"

"The cage cups," I told her, enjoying our role reversal, "or *diatreta*, are like little *dominion* power plants. And while any *tapped* Aspectu can handle an object glowing *dominion*—you people suck it up—apparently when an *untapped* Aspectu touches something filled with *dominion*, like a tube of paint, the Aspectu gets, like, *insta*-tapped...there's a proximal multi-variant purgation." I checked the sciencey mouthful with Veronica. "Right?"

"It appears so," she nodded. "We know the Aspectu in Skysill Beach were placed here by Aeternus, stabilized in an untapped state with ultraviolet pigment. For two hundred years he bred you. Had you pretend to be artists. Now he shutters his company, removes the stabilizing paint, and everyone here becomes vulnerable. *Everyone at the same time.* He sends Julian here with the cage cup of *dominion*..."

She lost the thread. The theory was too big for her, but no theory's too big for me. I creaked to my feet, thirsty, enjoying Amelia failing to fit pieces together.

"He wants to tap us?" Amy asked. "Why does Aeternus want to create thousands of *Fabrica*?"

"He does not," Veronica said. "He does not want *Fabrica*. There is no relino in this sick purgation, so it *cannot* create a *Fabrica*. It is the force of these purgations themselves that must be his goal. I think... he is trying to power something. Could he be trying to stop the end of time? Repair the Paths?"

"Maybe, or maybe he just likes blowing people up," I said, then regretted it. The image was pretty gruesome. Tilly was gone. I saw my image working on Amelia. One thing my sister does have is a low gruesome threshold. I tried to help her. "But it's okay, Amy—the *dominion's* gone, now that the cage cup is gone."

"The goblet..." she was finally catching up. "Yes. The goblet's gone."

Love, or whatever was going on over there, was making her dumber than she used to be. But maybe that's the secret to a successful relationship. She turned to Veronica, her eyes wide.

Veronica opened her water and took a drink. Amy remembered the other bottle she'd brought and rolled it over the floor to me. And it's true, occasionally I take her for granted and/or underestimate her.

"That purgation was *massive*," Veronica said, her voice tight. "Larger than any relino could possibly contain or reflect. Magnified by the presence of *dominion*, maybe. Aeternus must plan to create an unbelievable surge of power here. What we witnessed from the ridge was a single example. There are *thousands* in Skysill."

"That's just," Amy said, sickening. "So gruesome...oh my god..."

I watched Veronica. Even I could see this was a perfect opportunity to comfort your girlfriend. But Veronica just nodded, sage and distant. Sort of sympathetic, but mostly working on billionaire problems.

"You stopped it, Amelia," she said, distracted.

"I don't think anything's *stopped*," I said, irritated because, hello, be nice to Amy, and also I was antsy just standing around like a target. "Nobody I touch lives more than three months. If he's trying to stop time from ending he fails. And that means the end of time's still a real problem, which I feel is not getting enough attention in our conversations, maybe because it's coming from me, and no one really cares how worried I get about anything. But we can't argue I'm not psychic anymore. Tilly died, I totally called that. Sorry Ames. And I'm psychically telling you, *everything* ends in three months."

It came out sounding self-satisfied, which was probably wrong, considering everything.

"Yes," Veronica sighed, "the end of the world. That is a problem for another day."

"You wouldn't say that if you had ghost poison pouring in your ear," I told her. My water had given me the energy I needed for indignation. It doesn't really take much. "It's not a problem for another day, it's *the only problem that matters.* I'll be perfectly honest with you, I'm not convinced Aeternus even exists, I mean *I've* never seen him and I'm the only who sees ghosts. I *have* seen the end of time. *That* I know is real."

New Dwayne stuck his head through the door then and interrupted me being indignant, but I was pretty much finished.

"Hibiki's here," he told Veronica, pointing downstairs. "Willametta's coming."

Veronica nodded and New Dwayne went away. She didn't try to hide the relief she felt at New Dwayne's news.

"Before you get busy with your sparkle friends," I told Veronica, "wait. I tried to get you at your store earlier. This was the *one thing* on my list for today but all the explosions and teleportation got me distracted...look, I need Higher paint. I'll run to the store myself and get it. just give me the key."

"There is no more Higher paint," Veronica said. "Have you been listening at all?"

"Yeah, but what about your *store?*" I insisted, not listening. She gave up on me. I turned to Amelia. "How about you?" I asked. "You must have paint you can give me."

"I don't, and absolutely never! No! Why would you *consider* a risk like that?"

Because a lot of reasons, I didn't say, because she wasn't listening.

She hadn't seen ghost Tilly clinging to my canvas—I'd abandoned that painting, but Tilly had found it and she took it with her to death, to remind me of everything I'd left behind—sobriety, a work ethic, self-interest. All of which I was better off without of course, but I had a feeling growing I was going to *have* to paint. Who cared about the risk? We were all dying soon. So what if I went crazy one last time? It'd be a relief.

Amelia took a deep breath to argue more—and then all sound in the room died. The ocean, the traffic, the breathing: it was the Auditus effect. Into the room walked the man I'd seen sitting beside Willametta at the Conclave. To call him somber was unfair to somber. Whatever that means. He was old and his rounded cheeks framed narrow eyes, lidded to keep things out. His hair was silver, raked back. He wore a cardigan the way CEOs do, with authority, like business armor.

"Hibiki," Veronica said, voice soft. "Thank you. Thank you for coming."

"You gave us no choice, I'm afraid," came a voice in the air, while Hibiki's lips bent a fractional smile. He took Veronica's hand in his weathered one and airdropped, "It's good to hear you again."

"I'm sorry, Hibiki," she blurted, "so sorry about Kuparr, I can never forgive—"

Her voice got cut off, though her lips finished their sentence. Hibiki raised a finger.

"No," he had the air say. "I have been there. I heard that entire night. There was nothing you could have done. Not for Kuparr."

"I led those killers to him," she said, "all those people..."

"His sound will never die," he intoned. "No word spoken can be lost."

"I miss him."

"As do I. I'll take you to hear him sometime. His songs fill the past with glad sound."

Then Hibiki looked my way. His gaze went limpid and unsettled. "The same cannot be said of *your* songs," his air told me. I thought up a dozen snappy replies but I doubted he'd let me say any. "In fact, it cannot be said for anything in this town. There are no songs here at all."

He raised his hand to his face and snapped. There was no sound. "You hear? This town has no record. Where there should be history, and sound decaying into the distant past, there is only silence. An impenetrable sound floor rests below us, a siglium absorbing every sound occurring here before it enters the record. It is such a power-ful...this town has left no trace in the past for hundreds of years."

"Nella feels it is an Auditus," Veronica said, "planted here, long ago."

Hibiki shook his head. "I've heard. This cannot be the work of an Auditus. It's not possible. Too much wave energy has been absorbed, any Auditus trying to connect and maintain this shape would be destroyed. There are those who think it may not be a siglium at all, it may be a natural phenomenon. It may be something mechanical. Nella is right about one thing, however. Clearly, somehow, Pierre's proximity to this floor is keeping him alive. Feeding him."

He turned to me again. I remembered Kuparr examining me this way, doubtful of his interpretation. "We must trust the sound in this mystery to come clear. When the singer pauses for breath, trust alone can bridge the silence."

"Auditus," I shrugged at Veronica, pointing to him. "It's great poetry but what the hell are they really saying, am I right?"

"Hibiki Walkland, meet Asher Gale," Veronica said, because no one else was going to do it. "Asher...well, you're here. You hear him."

"Yes," Hibiki said, "I hear. And in Los Angeles. I think he's our wildcard."

"It is a terrifying thought," Veronica said while seeming to agree with him. And once again they were talking about me like I wasn't standing there listening. But I don't know. You get used to it.

"Willametta is here," voiced Hibiki's air, as he pointed below. "It is time."

Veronica took Amelia's arm and the two of them slowly exited. I wondered how long Hibiki would stand waiting for me to follow. He looked like the patient kind.

"I'm not a part of that," I told him finally. "Go ahead."

"You are a part," he said, cradling his fingers together. "Though we sing from different cathedrals, our voices rise in one choir."

"Is there a book you guys memorize or you think them up on the spot?"

He stepped closer. You don't know silence until you've known it standing a yard from the President of the Auditus, or whoever he was.

"This town may not have a past," his air told me, while nothing on his face or body moved, like having a conversation with a rainforest carving. "But *you* have a past. And, I think, for any of us to survive what is coming, you must uncover it. What is not sought is never found, Asher. You must become a seeker."

"I have bruises on my bruises," I said. "I seek vodka and acetaminophen."

"Downstairs then," said the air.

Right in front of my mouth I heard ice snapping in a glass with vodka and lime and a stir stick. It was so convincing I'd started walking before I knew what was happening. But then I stopped and retrieved my glob of car key off the floor. It was heavy with *dominion*, and warm, and curved where my fingers had melted grooves. I put it in my pocket. It wasn't safe leaving those around. As I'd discovered.

Then down the stairs I went, through a hall into a room with at least a dozen people—Auditus and Aspectu based on the robes and ultraviolet flair—debating revolution and bloodshed, which I suspected was Veronica's influence.

Everything in the room was overstuffed and curved thick with ornaments. Along with all the velvet chairs and Victorian wood, whoever had owned this place in the ancient times, JP Morgan maybe, had left a collection of canvasses by *sighted* painters on the walls, even some unknown to me, and at least two authentic Edward Hoppers. It was honest, fine work, and under normal circumstances, I'd have blocked everything else just to appreciate it. But they could've hung the Mona Lisa in that room and no one would have cared. The space belonged to Willametta.

Veronica introduced us. Willametta smiled. I told her not to touch me.

Even absent her blinding tiara everything about her was shining, tall, confident and beautiful—all the things that intimidate me. I pretended not to see her and took a bottle no one was using and eased my bruises to the floor in a corner where I'd be less likely to fall over, leaning against the chair where my sister sat. She barely acknowledged me she was so focused on the bloodshed debates. Unthinking, she reached her hand to my shoulder, fond, like we were kids watching TV, and I had to remind her no touching. Why did everyone want to touch me all of a sudden? I'd never had a problem like that before.

The group in the middle of the room was arguing a proposal Veronica had made, that Willametta and those few relinos strong enough should try to tap all of Skysill's painters, one after another, as soon as possible. This would, Veronica insisted, deprive Aeternus of whatever he planned to use them for, and that the moment to strike had come, that to do nothing was condemning Skysill's Aspectu to dementia and death. Death by the thousands, even if Aeternus never appeared again. Without Higher paint to stabilize them, they would not last.

But other people argued that the risk to the relino was too great and Veronica's plan would probably *attract* Aeternus, that it was a crime tapping adult Aspectu and Aeternus would spread them in a ring, which I didn't understand. To which Veronica replied that if a relino enacting her sole purpose in life was a crime Aeternus would punish, the Families were already doomed.

So it went, while I drank and felt my sternum where the Brazilians had been. I found myself appreciating Veronica's willingness to beat her head on a door she had no hope of opening. Even I could see she wasn't going to convince anybody this way. There was something unbalanced about her now, something I respected, strange as the realization was. As I watched, I saw her eyes start to counter cross, go full white, then get pulled back. Like she couldn't control them.

Veronica wanted to risk everything on zero evidence. That was what her arguments amounted to. It was inspiring.

"Hey," I tilted toward Amelia, "what's with Veronica's…son? Something happened with Aeternus?"

She bent to me, though her eyes stayed fixed on the controversy.

"Seamus was a teenager," she murmured. "Roni doesn't talk about it. She blames herself."

"Aeternus killed him?" Another nod. "Aeternus is a ghost, supposedly. Did they see him do it? How do they know it was Aeternus?"

"Seamus was drawn apart."

"Ames, I don't know all your cult words, what's *drawn apart*?"

"Aeternus occasionally prunes the Families," Amy said. The gruesome idea made her squeamish but she forged ahead, so I'd be less poorly informed. She made the sacrifice. "That's the word they use, prune. Sometimes it seems random, the killing, and sometimes it's punishment for breaking the Agreements. Whenever he kills—prunes—he pulls the Family member apart, spread out, into pieces. Veronica described it. Laying on their backs like snow angels. Skin and organs arranged around them…like he's looking for something… and Seamus…" She was making herself sick. She has a really active imagination.

"So Veronica blames herself," I said. "But why? Aeternus killed Seamus, not her. Right?"

Veronica was loudly scorning the case one monk was making, poised to refute him with a look I recognized. A look I finally, fully recognized. She had the look of someone whose family had been killed.

"Seamus," Amelia tried explaining, "was...they had a difficult relationship. And when he was first old enough, Veronica wouldn't tap him. She felt he wasn't ready. So Seamus went to another relino. And she blames herself for driving him away. She thinks...I guess Seamus wanted to *hunt* Aeternus, and that's why she wouldn't tap him. But whoever did tap him...let him do it."

"Let him."

"His relino could have *compelled* him. Your tapping relino has that power. Veronica would have *compelled* him."

"That power wears off in a few hours," I scoffed, thinking of my own experience, as I will when anyone lets me.

We both realized, at the same moment, that the debate floor had grown quiet. We turned and found all faces pointed at me. I lifted the bottle and drank and watched them back.

Willametta spoke. She had very bright teeth.

"Listening to these deliberations must be confusing," she said. "Is there anything I can explain?"

"No explanation required. Confusion's my sweet spot."

"Can you offer any input on these issues?"

"These are not my issues, and even if they were, no."

"I am told you see ghosts."

"I see a lot of things. I think it's the vodka."

Willametta shared a look with Veronica that I recognized, where they agreed I was a pleasure to be around and were looking forward to my bright future. Then Willametta raised an ultraviolet glow in her hand. I thought about turning to Amelia and saying <u>that's</u> the thing I was trying to get you to do, <u>night charge</u>, see?

But all the things Willametta started doing then were so fascinating I forgot to nag my sister. From Willametta's palm *farewell* flowed in sparkle waves, with visible spectrum orange stripes blurring softly around it. The whole shape began scattering reflections, and I saw shifting images. Images of Aspectu.

"We call this an inclusion," she told me. "They are not safe. They tend to draw the ghost if they are too large. But this is small, and our need is great. So watch."

In her inclusion I saw people reading books, people counter crossing their eyes, people perishing of old age or perishing being killed by Aeternus. It was like *Fabrica* Netflix. All the characters were *sighted*. She was showing me a history. Usually those bore me. But she had a little of Shelby's flair with the historical, and I found I couldn't look away.

While she played her hand movie she did the voiceover.

"Listen and I will explain why all of this matters. Since the time of the Ghost War, so long ago that all information about that time has been lost, the time when the Families themselves emerged alone on Earth, there has been no ghost but the one. The eternal ghost. For all those eons we have investigated, theorized, sought to understand, to find the truth about the Ghost War and know the reasons Aeternus persecutes us. But that knowledge has been buried, or hidden, beyond our reach. The Families had thought all other ghosts gone from the world, possibly destroyed in the War, or that perhaps there has only ever been one ghost. But whatever our theories, all through that time Aeternus has been with us, pruning us, relentless and unseen."

The hologram ripples froze on a picture of me. Not a bad picture. I wore a stained t-shirt and one of my pant legs was caught in my sock but I looked alert. Willametta spun the image slowly so we all appreciated my many angles, and continued her narration.

"But you, after all this time, have seen a ghost. Or *ghosts*. You have *felt* a ghost. Veronica believes this, she has seen proof. This is direct knowledge that untold generations of Family have sacrificed to find. This knowledge, or skill, or blessing, has been given to you.

Only you, Asher. If I could lift the weight of that gift from your shoulders I would. You did not ask for it. But that is not within my power. Our perils grow by the moment—Aeternus, the Tactus, quite possibly the ghosts themselves, closing on us. The moment has come for you to take your place. Here with your Family. Join this fight with us."

I let it wash over me. I nodded and stood, slowly, and though the vodka tilted and almost spilled I caught it, and set it upright. I'm not a barbarian.

"Willametta you're tall and intimidating," I told her, "but no. One, I do not work well in groups, people telling me what to do, it's just, you know how stupid people are in groups. And two, many other reasons, so I'll pass. I wish you all the luck. Do what your side thinks you're supposed to do, whatever, but I'm telling you—and I've told other people this and I feel like I'm not getting through to *anyone*—time ends in three months. Three. Months. Everybody dies. So whatever side you're on, it's not going to matter. And I have other things to do before then."

There were gasps here and there, from the overstuffed furniture. Willametta didn't bat an eye. She might not have known how.

"The end of time," she nodded. "Veronica mentioned this, and ancient psychics...alluded to this, I suppose? But time actually *ending*? It is a metaphor. It must be. Or a mistake, Asher. An artifact of foresight itself, perhaps. Not an actual...*event*. Do you truly believe time itself will *end*? Those words have no meaning. It cannot be true."

I shrugged, and turned, and went for the door while Amelia processed a conflicted need to help me, since my bruises were making me limp, and stay for Veronica, so I told her I was calling a car. The rest of them looked impatient. But because of Amelia, who's the finest artist I ever knew and seemed committed to this cult, I gave them one more shot.

"You people have everything twisted around."

I said *you people* in that way that makes me so delightful.

"You say the words have no *meaning,* so you decide they can't be *true.* But who the fuck cares what's *true?* Seriously. No one's ever seen a painting that was *true,* but every piece of art ever made had *meaning.* Even the worst. True's just a switch you people flip, one way or the other, mostly at your convenience as far as I see. You think you're doing something real. When the only important thing you can do is try to figure out what any of it *means.*"

"And how is an honest seeker to do that?" inquired a voice in the air, centered and curious and totally without an agenda.

Everyone looked at Hibiki, who watched me, then they turned back to me for my answer, and I knew right then they were lost. Any group waiting on any answer of mine is a group with problems they'll never solve. I pointed to their walls, the Hoppers, those isolated figures in sideways light, those simple interrogations of something infinite.

"You just keep starting over," I shrugged to Hibiki. "Like these guys. That's what everyone says."

Then I limped to the door. Amelia told me stay. No one else tried to stop me. I stepped outside and stood a minute in the dark on the landing feeling the chill and not bothering to spin the scene up or down. I let it come unfiltered. Ultraviolet, visible spectrum, shadow and highlight, planes and colors and abstraction. I took deep breaths of it. In the house I heard voices making decisions. It was better outside.

I gripped my key blob and popped a ghost and grappled flesh me up with his legs around my ghost waist while the gloom off the ultraviolet mountain weighed over the world. I took us up. Out over the water where the Higher borealis flowed, like a ghost river in the stars. I hovered a minute and watched, thinking maybe it was the borealis that I'd paint. Because I was going to paint. I knew it now. Tilly's ghost story made it a certainty. As long as Tactus, Brazilians, Julian or ghosts or the end of time didn't stop me first I was going to paint again before I died. Maybe tomorrow.

When I turned back to the shore the ghost mountain looked

bigger. Nearer. It blocked more starlight and spread more widely over the city, smothering it. The death murk weighed like a jacket of rocks. That mountain was exhausting. I flew us all home to the Bradley. I had a lot of activity planned for the next day and we all needed sleep.

CHAPTER

NINE

I came awake peering at the ceiling of a luxurious penthouse bedroom which it still felt strange remembering might soon be *my* penthouse bedroom. I was warm, the covers soft; the world felt slow and unfocused and for a moment I wondered if I was drunk. But I remembered—I'd come back from the conspiracy meeting and had a rare night of deep sleep. And I had only one thing on my list for the day: paint. Sometimes I'll sleep like that when my list for the next day has one or fewer items.

For a moment more I let my mind drift in sunshine through beach windows and thought about fruit salad in the refrigerator, and how I'd now have a fruit salad breakfast. It was a moment of absolute clarity of purpose.

But moments like that never last for me, and in the midst of a languid stretch I found myself snatched out the top of my skull into my bedroom in what was fast becoming my least favorite way to start any day. The ghost mountain shivered in, as bleak as dark coastal fog. And beside the bed Samantha vapored in, pumping star buckets through my penthouse hideaway, her eyes fixed on flesh me confused in the middle of his languid stretch.

Right away he started struggling to sit up in bed, maybe startled into action—I know *I* hadn't told him sit up. He looked like he had no idea what was going on, though it's hard to tell with him. He was able to kick our sheets past his knees and twist them, and there, since he only had fists and no real brain to solve or understand problems, he stayed, lashing around like a nature show animal waking from a dart. I puppeted him calm, then with careful remote controlling moved him to the edge of the bed where I made him sit and told him *hold still.*

Samantha! I ghost yelled then. *What a fantastic surprise. What time is it? What do you want?*

That's when I saw she'd brought another ghost. A lady. So far the ghosts had all belonged to dead bodies I'd actually seen, so I guessed this ghost had been one of the Auditus monks killed in the slaughter in Los Angeles, since she had to die someplace and I knew *I* hadn't killed her. I mean I was pretty sure.

She floated, motionless, her galaxy arms of *light* pirouetting in front of my luxury walk-in closet. *Dominion* pinned her, head and foot, and spread over her, managing her shape, which was a girl shape, my age, in a softball uniform, with a small mouth and big eyes reflecting nothing.

What am I, I complained to Samantha, *a tourist attraction? Quit coming over without asking! This place is supposed to be super-secret, fuck! I have a lot of shit to do today and I don't have time for this. I have a list of things to do. A LIST! So what? What do you want?*

But Samantha's eyes are still as doll's eyes and give no indications. I checked her friend. The softball lady held a plate of Chinese noodles in her outstretched hand, full of vegetables and fried prawns, where ultraviolet steam rose. The food looked delicious, in an ultraviolet way. On the bed flesh me held his stomach, which I could hear rumbling. He looked down at the noise, puzzled and unhappy and increasingly bemused. What he had to be bemused about, I didn't know, he wasn't responsible for any of this, he was a spectator.

I had a pretty good idea what Samantha wanted despite my rhetorical questions to her. She'd seen me send Felicia to ghost Valhalla and now she had a new candidate. And maybe it was the wrong decision. But I just thought everything would go faster if I humored her and sent the new ghost away. It was sort of the least I could do since I couldn't send Samantha herself away. And I'll almost always do the least if people will take that.

Fine, let's get this over I ghosted. I positioned myself to look over the top of flesh me at the new ghost.

I don't know how much Samantha told you, I told the lady, *hopefully this will take just a few minutes, then you'll go where you're most wanted, or whatever. Just so you know, I really do have a list of things for this morning and I'm only doing this as a favor to Samantha. Are you ready?*

I puppeted flesh me standing, and plopped his fist in the middle of her prawns.

Summery warmth rose to all sides. The bedroom disappeared and the ghost mountain and its gloom faded and a pastoral landscape of tall trees and teeming fields lit by peach-yellow sunlight stretched into the distance. Far off a structure rose on a hill, and beyond that were the mountains, range after range vanishing into mist, and beyond it all was the towering rock and snow version of my ghost mountain, unbelievably tall, rising over everything.

The one source of Higher *light* anywhere was the ghost with the plate, floating before me above meadow grass. Her name, I learned, was Tami. She was from Los Angeles. She was an Answer, like Peter. Her story was short.

It began the day she went with her Ask to eat at Super-A Chinese, where she'd had the prawns, which had made her sick. Because she'd been sick she'd been in her bunk, deep underground, going back and forth to the toilet, when the *Fabrica* attacked Kuparr's Auditus inholding.

She'd heard the first stones slam to the earth and staggered from her room, but it happened fast, she was weak and dizzy. Far above she heard her friends in agony, beset by an enemy who crushed and *compelled* them, as one by one they were silenced. Tami had no strength to run to their aid.

When the enemy found her she was kneeling, holding her stomach. There were two of them. One with red hair, one with a goatee. They laughed when they found her, sickened as she was, trying to stand. The man had thrust his arms out and grabbed her head, and she saw his eyes counter cross to white. And there was nothing she could do to stop him.

"Well fuck," he said after a moment. "I need Julian's key again."

The red haired girl laughed—in fact she'd never stopped laughing—and took Tami's head herself, counter crossing her own eyes. And the world in Tami's mind narrowed, and she felt she'd do anything this woman asked. But the woman asked nothing. Just held her. Tami's mind grew shadows. From far away she heard the man complaining.

"Julian's not even supposed to have it," he said. "Britta, if we combine forces up there we could take it and—"

"Shut up fuckhead," the girl, Britta, snarled. Tami's world was a wisp now, but she clung to consciousness, she listened while the redhead said, "Aeternus has keys for *all* of us. When I get mine, that's when the fun starts. The umbra eye's ready, all you have to..."

And then Tami knew only blackness. But she had one final thought, just as thinking ceased altogether: she thought about her Ask, and how sorry she was that she'd never be able to apologize, never be able to say, *I'm sorry I couldn't be up there with you, Nella. You were totally right about the prawns.*

Once the story was over Tami the ghost started spitting ultraviolet, and her currents ran in arcs and swelled so canopies reeled in Higher clouds around her, *lighting* the trees, blooming the sky, until she reached terminal expansion, and in a blink collapsed. Then the light of her stretched, and as through a tube into the sky, she lengthened toward the horizon. And was gone. The warm, pastoral world vanished. Ghost mountain gloom fell back on me.

And I was once more floating in a normal luxurious penthouse bedroom.

Samantha was there of course, otherwise I'd have merged into one body. Flesh me had slipped to the floor, moaning and holding his stomach, desperate for food it seemed. I wondered if he might not have a touch of hypoglycemia. I moved him to the other side of the bed to get him out of the way, and Samantha rotated to watch him.

So...this is some sort of message? I ghosted at her. *Just FYI, it works better just coming out and saying whatever I'm supposed to do. Asking me to guess at shit like this, you're just setting us both up for failure. But I'm guessing...you're trying to tell me something. Right?*

I ran back over Tami's story and got to Britta's appearance, and felt an unhappy shudder. Her appearance in my psychic vision was an unwelcome shock. But not a coincidence, I thought.

So you knew Tami was killed by Britta, I speculated. *Is that what you want me to know? Or...she said Aeternus had keys for all of them and Julian called his goblet a key. So what you're saying...your irritating ghost message...is, Julian's goblet—your goblet—wasn't the only goblet. Aeternus has goblets for all the apprentices. Four other goblets. Is that it?*

I knew that was it. She didn't have to say it. Thankfully.

So what am I supposed to do now, find these other goblets or something? Because I can't do it today, I have to go out and find someone who has paint I can use. You look like you think that's a bad idea, me painting. But what do you know? You're some ghost. How about we let the chips fall where they may? Samantha dammit please leave. Go away. Flesh me doesn't have anything in his fists so the only way I'm getting back into him is...

I sort of indicated flesh me with my ghost mind, but...I saw flesh me was gone.

I'd stored him temporarily on the side of the bed but now he wasn't there. And I noticed my orientation shifting, so I was facing a wall—clearly, flesh me had crawled off on his own. Because if it's not one thing it's another.

At least I knew how to find him. I kicked off out of ghost me, like diving off the edge of a pool, and shot underwater to the other body where flesh me waited. When I got to him, however, I stopped, stunned, before retaking him.

Flesh me stood in our penthouse kitchen, humming to himself, in nothing but underpants and a blue crystal, and he seemed to be trying to make toast. With only his fists he'd mangled a slice of bread from a bag, and he'd laid the slice carefully onto the toaster, covering the holes. I watched him depress the lever. He didn't know much about toasters. He was working fast. I saw he'd already taken eggs from the refrigerator—which surprisingly had eggs in it—and after the toast was cooking he wrestled a frying pan onto the stove upside down, because he also didn't know much about frying pans, and then, still humming, he threw several eggs onto the floor and stood back holding his stomach, hoping breakfast would soon be ready.

It was a shock how bad he was in the kitchen and by instinct I reversed course and dove back toward ghost me—or that's what I tried. When I emerged beside him, I discovered that ghost me wasn't open. I bumped around looking for an opening, but it was like trying to get into a locked car, which is very hard, which is the reason I never lock them.

I felt panic rise.

Was I caught in some kind of...space *between* bodies? Around me everything was cold and dark and full of nothing. I still had thoughts, and all my various opinions, but unattached to anything with arms or a head. It was completely disorienting. Worse than being stone cold sober. I sensed my bodies like they were limbs that'd been numbed. Like they were distant pieces of me I didn't even need. It was truly horrible. And then, through my shared senses, I detected the toaster spewing smoke, about to catch fire and burn down the kitchen.

Stop cooking anything for breakfast immediately god damnit! I ordered, and purely by instinct, I slipped toward flesh me—and into him. He froze. We did, I mean. I did. I can't move when I'm *storming* in my flesh these days. Smoke was filling the kitchen. Instinctively I jetted back to ghost me, then remembered I was locked out, but found I wasn't anymore. So I puppeted flesh me to *put the flaming toast in the sink*, which might not be the best fire management strategy but what am I, Smokey the Bear?

A loop. A body loop. Was that it? When I go from ghost me straight into flesh me, then back to ghost me, it's seamless, like a model train making stops. But apparently, you had to go in a loop from one body to the other, no stopping halfway and going back. Trying to go back left you caught in the middle, where you don't have any body at all and it's awful. It's very disappointing, discovering new rules this way, or any other way. And after all this, I still hadn't gotten pants on.

Then Samantha vanished. I knew it because I merged back into my flesh, and once there I leaned on the kitchen counter, breathing smoke, worn out, one thumb pretty badly burned. Flesh me would have to be carefully watched from now on. He liked to stay busy, I realized. But he lacked the skills to do basically any task without endangering us.

I almost slipped on the eggs he'd been trying to cook on the floor, but I got around them and into the bathroom, and once there I rinsed breakfast off myself. *After this I'll get started on my list* I thought. All I needed was clothes.

For one moment I stood critiquing hair and stubble and lack of general fitness in the mirror, and then the crystal on my neck pulsed and I wasn't critiquing anything, I was daydreaming Caroline. I liked it but it felt a little whiplashy, like getting hit by the most beautiful car on the road, since I'd just had a kitchen fire and an exorcism and was still recovering from those. One second I'm a ghost the next I'm picturing a beautiful psychic girl dialing her phone, worried I'm dead. Which...oh. The pattern.

An exciting new theory had occurred to me that I remembered now I really wanted to share with her. I dreamed her lifting the phone to her ear. But where could my phone be? I felt in my underwear—where flesh me might put things is a great unknown—then remembered the phone in the bedroom and ran, arriving out of breath. So far it had been a tiring morning. And I was disappointed all over again to find the phone dead because I hadn't plugged it in.

In my daydream Caroline was in her shop, pacing in front of her teacher's desk. My excitement and desire kept building but I had no way to use them, so in desperation, I just picked up the dead phone and held it to my ear and said *Hello?*

Hey? She replied in my mind. For a moment we were silent, stunned by the convenience.

I'm totally alive, I telepathed. *So everything's okay. I've been trying to get out of the house because I have a list of things I want to do but penthouses are hard to get out of, there's always something.*

I daydreamed her grateful to have me alive. She was going through one of her cabinets, looking for something. She put the phone in her pocket but telepathy continued.

I noticed an exciting pattern! I told her. *I have a theory about the times you think I'm dead.*

You're like a scientist in a movie.

Wait till you hear. You know how I see ghosts?

Of course. That's what brought us together. You on my sidewalk throwing up beside a ghost.

That's right, and that's something you've brought up before, I wonder if that memory's ever going to fade at all, but that's not the main thing. You know how I send these ghosts to the afterlife?

I do. And it's still real impressive, but technically aren't ghosts already in the afterlife?

I don't think they are. Or if they are...maybe there's an afterlife after this afterlife? When I'm sending them away, our world fades and I go to another world, with woods and mountains, and the pattern is, every time I go there, you feel like I'm dead. And wait'll you hear why you think I'm dead there.

I actually made her wait because as I put my theory into words in my mind before saying it I realized how batshit crazy it was. But it was all I had and I'd promised her a theory, so I plunged on.

I think that place I'm transported is…the land where the dead go. The land of death. That makes sense right? Ghosts in the land of death. So the reason you feel like <u>I'm</u> dead is, by definition, anyone in the land of death is dead. All three times I went there, Felicia, Tilly, now Tami, you feel like I'm dead. I can't believe I remembered the names.

I daydreamed her closing her cabinet and grabbing her keys off her desk to head for the door. Apparently she wasn't there to work. But she was considering my theory as she went outside and she decided she liked it. It was a rush.

It makes a kind of sense I have to admit, she telepathed. *It's hard to argue the timing. But the land of death…I hope you're being careful.*

You know me. I invented being careful.

Sure you did, hey, what happened to your thumb?

A toaster burned it.

Before or after your invention of being careful?

It's a long story. Just read my mind. In the meantime can I ask a psychic question?

Sure. She climbed into her truck and started it. *By the way I had a dream last night where you and I were waking up in a cabin. We were kissing. Oh my god your mouth was…*

I know that dream we're naked in bed and—

Yes, and our crystals iced over so we groaned, clutched chests and groins and felt weak. After it faded I could talk.

I'll just pretend that didn't happen, because what's the point? I want to ask you about this mountain, I told her. *These crystals are bullshit, I don't think they're doing anything. Listen. You said there was a mountain. A mountain for psychics.*

Not FOR psychics. But there's a mountain. Mount Tempus. She pulled her car out into traffic, heading back inland. She was thinking carefully about everything she said. It was satisfying to watch that kind of organization in my brain. Like someone shuffling perfect cards.

At the very top of Mount Tempus, the Paths of Time pass closest to our world. Every psychic vision anyone ever had started on the peak of Mount Tempus, though most psychics don't realize.

Okay! That's this mountain I keep seeing! I sweat it's getting closer. Made of dominion. It has to be Tempus right?

This thing is, Ash, I can see your mind pictures...

You see my mind pictures?

...I do, it's like puppies at a birthday party, total adorable chaos, anyway in your pictures of this mountain I see just one throne. But Mount Tempus has three thrones. Behind, Beneath, Before.

But it's got to be the same mountain. How many psychic throne mountains do you think there are?

Do you ever see anything up there?

Like what?

I don't know. People you know? Other kinds of...creatures?

No, are there supposed to be creatures?

I sure hope not. It's just, you can never be too careful.

I daydreamed her looking out her windshield. It felt like I was seeing through her eyes. Almost like I *was* her. I felt the hand that wasn't holding her steering wheel reach to her hem and begin plucking threads in her lap. In the reflection in her window I got my clearest daydream of her yet, purple tank top, hair blowing in the coastal wind. She looked tired. I felt her push back on me gently, like maybe it crossed a boundary feeling so much like I was her.

Ash, she telepathed, *we need to be real careful slipping into each other's minds like this.*

But I never have my phone charged, how are we supposed to talk?

Telepathy's one thing. But then there's getting inside each other. Like we did in Los Angeles. Remember sitting on that swing? We were inside each other then and we almost went over the edge. You just never know what you'll find inside another person. People have dark...they have unexpected places. I say we keep a little distance. Veronica keeps warning this isn't safe. She wants to give you one of these new crystals too. She says our polarity's getting worse. Stronger.

Veronica, I scoffed. *At least we're not finishing each other's sentences*

—remember on the train, how we were thinking literally the same thoughts and finishing—

—each other's sentences oh I remember the train god yes with—

—your hand—

—between—

—my legs—

The two of us were like people in that experiment with those dogs and the bell—one of us always rings that bell, we can't help it, and then both of us gasp and tremble and pull our crystals. We do it over and over, it's Pavlovian, though that might not be exactly how that experiment went, I don't know, I'm no animal psychologist.

I'm afraid we're heading for trouble, she telepathed as she pulled her truck back into her own lane. *Let's do this later.* I loved the tender way her mind sounded. She'd let go of her necklace. Now she intentionally filled her brain with Monarch ideas and appointments and things that bored me, which I'll admit did make it slightly easier to say goodbye. We hung up our minds, though in my daydream Caroline's body lingered, sunlight falling through her window across her shoulders, across her beautiful, mysterious, psychic girl body.

I went to plug in my phone and take a cold shower.

After my shower I peeked out the penthouse door and just as I'd hoped, found new food baskets and one new cellophane-wrapped set of Hawaiian clothes, sandals included. All the clothes fit me perfectly. Phil really had a talent. Anything tropical, he knew exactly how to get you into it. The whole Bradley Family seemed to be pouring it on with the gifts. Like they felt guilty about something. I appreciated it.

And finally I was ready to leave on my errand. Getting out of the Bradley Building was proving to be a constant challenge but nothing was going to stop me now. I was sure I'd find Higher paint *somewhere* in Skysill Beach, it ran here like blood, it was only a matter of time. If none of the artists I knew had any, I'd go back to Tobias' place on the beach and take his, since he was dead. Unless the police had cleaned that scene, in which case I'd go back to Julian's hillside palace and take his. I'd already taken one tube. The only problem with that plan was it came with the risk of meeting Julian, so I considered it a last resort.

Closing the penthouse door I almost whistled, enjoying the simple pleasure of the illusion of being a single person in a normal body wearing jungle flower pants walking down a hall with only one thing to do.

Once inside the elevator, though, I couldn't keep the illusion going. I now had more than one thing to do. I couldn't push the lobby. Not yet. My conscience prevented it. Typically it's procrastination that derails me, but once my conscience comes in, wet blanketing everything, all the whistling in the world won't help. I felt a kind of psychic *responsibility* come over me. Some people might call it just a regular sense of responsibility, I have no idea. But I knew I couldn't leave without relaying to Nella the story I'd heard from the softball ghost. Like some kind of messenger.

It was the *last* distraction I was going to allow, I promised myself, which meant nothing of course. After this I'd set off with my list. So I elevated one floor down and went to stand outside Asher Gale's office. Waiting. I knew she'd hear me in the hall. I thought I'd give her the story from out there, because that would mean less wasted time, and also I was guessing it would be a sad story to tell. Better to do it through a door.

"Jus'come in," Nella burst from the air in front of my face. You never get used to that. There's no way.

"I don't need to come in," I assured her, "I'm just, I have a...sort of a message. I'll say it through the door then I'll..."

But the door jerked open, and stayed that way, held by a wraith of a man who seemed made entirely of beard pinned to thin flesh, pressing himself against the wall, eyes cast to the floor: Peter by the Beach, reprising his role as my footman. A gust of warm, mammal smelling air came from the office behind him.

He seemed hardly to have the energy to stand, but something had drawn him to the door. There was nothing else I could do. I stepped through. He let the door close and slippered back into the darkened office. The windows had heavy drapes where there had never been drapes before. It was a cave now, filled with candles, smelling of sage and fried blood, looking like a campground—untidy and occupied by travelers. Five monks stood clustered near the bathroom, listening at Peter with tilted ears as he passed back in. They were the only monks I saw, though there'd been dozens the day before.

"I'm coming in," I called down the hall, "so reminder, nobody fucking touch me."

I followed Peter, saw him fold down on his back on a mat amidst a dozen candles burning low. The monks followed him. I had the sense they were echolocating my deepest secrets, which was unnerving and unwelcome and probably just paranoia. Then they arranged themselves around Peter on the floor.

Nella supervised everything from a chair, in golden robes like a Hare Krishna pumpkin. I ignored her to squat by Peter's head. Here I was getting distracted. But what else could I do? His eyes were not focused, one pupil ranged bigger than the other under eyelids dry as mummy paper. So much more of him had drained away. He was a collection of skeleton pieces bound by willpower.

Then he spoke. Deep voiced. Like whale song.

"You came just in time for the universe," he thunder whispered.

A few yards away I saw his windshield spray bottle and moved it closer to him, I don't know why, then pretended everything was just normal, like you're supposed to when people are dying. I forgot about Nella and started talking, my errand list completely forgotten, I don't know why I even bother. Who knows how much Peter heard? Everything, probably. He always used to.

I told him about the weather, and the fruit salad I'd eaten, and my mysteries—all the things I'd been plagued by, the psychics and Mount Tempus, the Nidor biochemists and the multi-variant purgations we were terrified of. I mentioned being a death guy, still unhappy with the name. One thing Peter never liked was small talk, so I kept to my central dramas. After a while I meandered into silence. When I did, he cleared his throat.

"The eye of the city is dead but no one blinks," came his dry rumble. "It is frustrating."

"I agree," I said. "Can I get you anything? Gin or whatever you like?"

"I listened for trumpets, but they played dishtowels," he said. "And dishtowels are not loud." Then, for the first time since I'd come, he lolled his head to the side and looked me in the eye. "You're a pretty sexy pole dancer," he said.

And with a massive breath, he closed his eyes and breathed no more. Or that's the way it looked. Though there was no ghost. I checked the monks. They appeared unfazed. I figured they'd hear it if Peter's heart stopped beating.

"S'been at least a day since he moved or said a'thing," Nella told me, sitting in one of Asher Gale's chairs by the window where a corner of drape was pulled back. "He likes to have you here."

"Why's he not breathing?"

"He's breathing. He's deep. Slowing down, down, down."

She looked as tired as Caroline, like it'd been a week since she'd slept. I resisted the urge to pull Peter's hair from his face, because I couldn't afford to touch him, and went navigating among the remaining monks to sit across from Nella on a chair edge where I'd be able to exit fastest. I sat staring through the sliver of window at late morning turning into noon above the foothills and heard faint tourist traffic on the street below. I wasn't sure how to begin. Messages are not my specialty, which probably makes me a bad psychic.

"So where'd all your monk friends go?" I asked, warming up.

"Hibiki took'm, an'I refused to leave," she said, gesturing at the leftover monks. "Same's them. Hibiki says' needs everybody to keep a network up, doesn't think Pierre's in danger, I said an *Adept's* in this town. Hibiki got no idea."

"He said something about Peter using the sound floor to stay alive."

"Pierre's connected for sure, I'don know, keeping himself sane somehow. Near enough the surface not to die. Doesn't matter I guess. S'almost gone. S'fightin but losing."

"I've seen him pull some amazing shit. Don't count him out."

"Why're you here, Aspectu boy?"

"Well," I sighed, "a couple reasons." I'd thought of another thing I could mention before my message. Delaying the inevitable. "My phone's dead so can you send a message to Veronica on your sigliums? It's like a radio network, right?"

"*Radio*," she snorted. She was surprised how stupid I am but she didn't mind, it was a nice distraction. "Linked up siglium there's a *lot* you do with them: tunnels into the past, snap your fingers's an blast a hole in'a building, use'm as batteries. *Radio*. What's'a message? Just say it out loud'n I'll play it when she's ready."

"Veronica," I said to the air between the seats, "this is Asher—do I need to tell her who it is?—I just found out there were actually *five* cage cups, Aeternus had one for each apprentice. So factor that into your machinations. It sounds like Julian wasn't supposed to be using the one he had, so where'd he get it? That's all, you can turn it off Nella. Do I just stop talking or what?"

"Have a drink," she pointed.

I had a drink. And finally, pretty casually, since there was no putting it off any longer, I asked, "Also by the way...did you ever know a monk named Tami?"

All the sounds around my head just switched off. Nella totally focused on me. Ambient sound drying up is a sign that your Auditus friend is paying very close attention. It's really awful.

"What about Tami?" she said without her lips.

"I guess I saw her? Like a psychic vision. Your name came up."

"Tami...was my Answer," Nella breathed. "Died at the inholding."

"She sort of had a message for you."

"You saw her ghost?"

"Yes. So you believe I see ghosts?"

"Shit yeah." Her eyes glittered. She was, in a way no one I'd ever known had been, all ears. "Say what happened."

"Well I mean, it's got unpleasant violence, you might—"

"Say it!"

So I did. I told her about the lady ghost with a plate of Chinese food named Tami. How she'd been killed by the apprentices, and at the very end, all she'd wanted to do was tell Nella she was sorry, that Nella had been right about the prawns. I said it all as fast as I thought I could get away with. After I was done I sat in silence, waiting for her to move. I badly wanted to be on my way, but I wasn't sure about the protocol. I haven't been psychic long enough.

"The prawns?" Nella whispered. "Why?"

"She was, like, sick to her stomach and couldn't help you fight, and I guess, you told her not to order the prawns for lunch? That was the gist."

"Tami...was my best friend," she said. I could feel my desire to leave growing but I just couldn't. I blamed Samantha. She'd brought Tami in the first place. Nella's eyes grew wet as she spoke and they emptied over her exhausted cheeks. The way you'd expect from a person whose friend was killed by violent psychopaths. I guess. Who knows?

"Didn't even like her at first," she said, her air voice steady despite tears. "Kuparr put us together. So mad. Such a city girl, me I grew up'n the inholding. She won you though. She gave the best advice. She was just better'n me at everything, was what I realized. My advice's always shit."

"You advised me not to be an asshole," I told her, equally soft. "That was good."

"She was my sister. Never had a sister. And inholding's pretty isolated. Hardly anybody...but Tami just...she gave up everything to study there. I only stayed because I never knew anything else. She gave up *softball*."

Then she stopped talking and her body coughed out sobs in

absolute silence. It stayed soundless on those chairs by Asher Gale's window as the moments eased away, give a little time, take a little time. How long do you stay? In a situation like this when the one monk you're starting to respect gets a message from beyond the grave? More than five minutes?

"To Tami," I heard, as Nella took a bottle, drank, and passed it to me.

"To Tami," I said, tilting it.

"To the eye of death in rice pudding," whispered Peter's basso voice all around us. "It's here. He can't hear since he's cancer. The dead eye hears though."

His voice faded out, quiet as fallen leaves, gone again.

"What is it, do you know, with his *dead eye* thing?" I asked Nella after a moment. "Does that mean anything to you?"

"What's'a dead eye thing?"

"You know. Peter brings it up. Ever since I've known him he's had, like, sort of a recurring theme, it's an eye, a dead eye or...haven't you heard him? The eye of death, the dead eye?"

"He only talks when you're here," she shrugged.

"It kind of makes you wonder," I started, though now she wasn't really listening. We both knew I was just thinking out loud so our expectations were pretty low. "I mean...what's that Aeternus siglium called? The one he leaves every fifteen hundred years? I can't remember. Britta literally just said it in my vision. I suck as a psychic. Come on, you know it, Aeternus leaves the thing. At all his quorums, what's it called?"

"Umbra eye."

"That. The umbra eye. It means ghost eye, right? I mean, just thinking out loud here's Peter lost in the past, steering his body around up in the real world...you say his messages are garbled, so let's say he's trying to talk about the umbra eye, could that come out...dead eye? Eye of death? He's been talking about it for years. Like, maybe, somewhere, in Skysill..."

She got it. We stared at each other. She'd shifted her ass out to the edge of her own chair, which gave me a lot of hope we were wrapping things up.

"He...found one," Nella whispered. "An umbra eye? Here?"

"Maybe," I said, like we were all geniuses—and mission accomplished. Psychic message forgotten.

"Yes...s'the only thing that makes...he found an umbra eye'n Skysill Beach! Maybe... maybe that's what's making the sound floor..."

The silence got thicker all of a sudden and the other monks tensed up. Nella hurried to look at Peter. No one was watching me. I pulled on Nella's bottle again a few times, just for Tami, and no one noticed me leaving. The umbra eye was not an Asher problem. Asher had other problems.

I was honestly starting to think that having a list was more trouble than it was worth and maybe I should go back to just doing the first thing I thought of. When you had a list the first thing you had to do was get out of the building where you lived which turns out to be almost impossible. I hoped I was in the home stretch. I waited impatiently for the elevator, hoping it came before my list broke down again, but when it came I changed my mind. The lobby elevator was where the Bradley Family gathered to give me gift certificates. The last thing I needed was another certificate. So I used the stairs and went quietly.

As I descended I passed the clothes I'd ruined the first time Phil dressed me in tropical flowers, the time the swimming pool fell on me. I saw boxes people had dropped and left when the Bradley family moved out of and then back into the building. On the ground floor landing, I checked through the little window into the lobby and I saw no committees or ceremonies so I dashed, got past the potted trees to the front doors, and, at long last, after prawns and telepathy and the umbra eye and various psychic messages, got outside.

The sun was straight above me. The day was clear and cool. I congratulated myself. Probably you shouldn't feel that much satisfaction just walking out of a building, but I take the victories where I find them. Almost always, as in this case, on a sidewalk.

Noon settles thin during autumn on the California coast, if you live in a town full of ghosts, and though I'd wasted all the morning hours I was confident my paint search could still be finished in time to paint today. I couldn't imagine a Skysill Beach where you weren't surrounded by tubes of pigment wherever you looked. All I needed... all I needed was a car, and as I was wondering how to call myself a car with my phone up in the penthouse charging, a hand fell on my shoulder from behind.

A blissful warmth rose up through my feet and I froze. I felt no fear, which I knew was absolutely the wrong thing not to feel. Though I couldn't see him, I knew the man touching me was both a man and a cop. A beautiful connectedness quivered between us and the entire world felt perfectly balanced as I foresaw this cop man's death. I foreknew that he'd die in about twenty-five minutes, in a building only a few blocks from the Bradley.

As I foresaw all this he took my wrist and snapped on a handcuff. Then he did the other. He yanked my shoulder. He moved fast because he didn't sense his death and had cop activities to complete. When his hands lifted, my pastoral vision did too, and then I was just a regular prisoner on a sidewalk.

I felt myself spun. The cop I faced was unfamiliar, though sized interchangeably from the other ones and a similar shape. His cop scowl said he knew what I'd say next and preferred I did not waste his time. All peace officers generally look the same to me, except this one. He had a throbbing nimbus of *compulsion* clinging to his skull, flaring like phosphorus.

He pushed me toward an open cop door at the curb. From the front of that car, in the passenger seat, Hennessy pointed back to what was my seat.

"In," he said, which the glowing cop emphasized by shoving then hunching me over and rushing me across the prison seat. When he touched me the warm death tingle returned, a little incapacitating, but what else is new? He slid in and shut the door while I leaned away from his touch—it wasn't brain rot, but it wasn't normal. And it all happened very fast before I could get any wise cracks out.

The car cut away from the curb and we went whipping down-coast. We were driven by another unfamiliar cop whose head also glowed *compulsion* and who stared, a little blank, at his speedometer. Hennessy was not glowing. He was turned to face me.

"Hello from a concerned party," he said. I nodded like he meant it friendly. "Now we'll take a drive, and you listen and do not talk. Is that clear?"

"Some parts," I nodded. "Is this about Felicia? Because I didn't do it."

"Listen and do not talk," he reminded me. He turned forward and pointed up Pelican Drive, which makes a loop around Richland Woods and back downtown. "Turn," he told the driver cop. But the driver cop didn't.

"I said *turn*," Hennessy snapped.

"Change of plans," the glowing driver said, sort of soft and weird.

"Fuck is that supposed to mean?" Hennessy growled but got no response. He then turned to me again. I watched the cop in the seat beside me, who gave off the trancey vibes cops do when thinking how much they enjoyed having prisoners, but this one was *way* more trancy. He didn't blink.

"It has come to the attention of people who are running out of patience," Hennessy had started saying, while keeping an eye out for another road where they could turn, "it has come to their attention that you continue certain investigations looking into certain missing painters. Or apprentice painters as they are sometimes called. This despite my own clear instructions to leave the cop work—okay, *turn there*," Hennessy told the driver, who didn't turn.

Hen was pissed now, all his cop team-building exercises breaking down. He seemed, for a moment, to lose his train of thought about me. He craned around as the turn he'd wanted disappeared.

"What the fuck, Tom?" he demanded. He gave the driver a long appraisal, then the other cop in the backseat. Something was dawning on him. His cop suspicions were coming up like hackles.

"You two are doing *what* here again?" he asked my chaperone. "I do not like being fucked with. I was unaware either of you even liked this freelance work." My neighbor cop said nothing. I started getting a very bad feeling. You'd think that feeling would have started before this but I'm careful to give people the benefit of my doubts, and it sometimes slows me.

Suddenly, then, our glowed-up driver *was* pulling off the road, up a side street, which Hennessy watched with surprise and increasing unhappiness.

"Hey Hen do you even know these guys?" I asked, sort of whispery even though one of them was sitting right beside me.

"Shut it Gale," Hen said.

"You should know," I explained, "these two aren't normal like you and me, someone's making them—"

The cop beside me drove his elbow into my side. For a moment I couldn't talk.

Then I gasped out, "Fuck...shithead what..."

Then he had his service revolver in his hand and that's when I felt the *Gray* rising, a cool, happy, extremely violent anticipation rising. *Oh*, I felt the *Gray* thinking, *this is going to be fun.*

Just before I lost control I remembered Caroline. She did not want me murdering any people, which I knew applied to peace officers too. Going *Gray* meant bathing in blood, at this point. All three cops would probably die. Even Hennessy, who looked almost as unhappy as I felt about the gun in my side, and the route we'd stopped taking—he would die. A *Gray* part of me already pictured how easy twisting the gun free with my cuff chain and shooting would be and then full-on murderous escape from cops who were under someone's control because of something I did. Apparently. Almost like they were innocent. How could I explain that to Caroline?

The *Gray* fought to get out but I bent my fingers inward, gripping toward a *storm*, which I knew superseded the *Gray*, and realized I needed something to palm, and felt the chain of my cuffs. These cops were positioning me for violence, bad violence, but this time at least, it wasn't their idea, so I left the *Gray* behind and *stormed*, popped a ghost, and wondered about the gun in the seat beside me.

We jerked to a stop in a small warehouse parking lot.

"What the fuck *is* this?" Hennessy was saying to the car, "Tom, hey, Earth to Tom," as Tom got out of the driver's seat without saying a word and Hen turned to the back and demanded, "Cecil? Hello?"

Cecil didn't answer either, but grabbed flesh me and ripped him over the seat and out the door with cop dexterity, then put the gun to my flesh back and walked us toward the warehouse door. I ghosted that way too. Tom came after us. He had his own gun out. It all seemed like overkill these guns with me in handcuffs. Hennessy slammed his door and came running after us.

"I will need the kind of amazing explanation," Hennessy was warning, "that I doubt you will ever be able to provide—you two dipshits are out of place here! We were to *drive* him—*I* was to drive him, give him a simple message, return him unharmed and duly warned. Unharmed was the *specific instruction*."

But Tom and Cecil had other instructions, and they shoved flesh me through the warehouse door and became two *compulsion* candles in the dark, with Hennessy scanning the street and adjacent buildings before hurrying in after them. Ghost me came last. I saw flesh me stumble and fall.

Cecil or Tom, I was already losing track, dragged flesh me across a concrete floor by his collar while the other cop flipped the weak florescent lights, carving shelves and racks in dusty warehouse rows out of shadow.

Flesh me struggled but they spun him to a wooden post running floor to ceiling near what might have been an office, and snapped his cuffs behind his back to a chain there. He howled and yanked and you could already see welts on my wrists but he never feels that kind of damage.

Hennessy stood, staring and saying nothing, still missing his explanation. The cop with the first gun pointed it at my flesh chest.

"This is what happens to talentless, cock-sucker wanna-be painters," he shouted, "and meddlers! This is your fault! And now, after *five hundred years*, Aeternus will replace me? If I die, you die too!"

He cocked the hammer and squinted my heart to fire. He was acting like a cop but screaming like a five-hundred-year-old smack addict psychopath. The situation kept getting more complicated.

"Cecil *stop!*" Hennessy shouted, pulling his own gun at Cecil, "Tom, make him stop, we're not supposed to HEY—*freeze!*"

Cecil spun and fired at Hennessy because we could all tell he was going to shoot. Hennessy went backward, hit in the side, falling against a shelf. Then Tom had his gun on flesh me again and a flash came from the muzzle but flesh me had yanked and yanked then slipped so the first bullet struck the post and flesh me hit the floor with arms stretched above him. Tom tracked for a second shot.

I had fractions of a second. I jumped to my flesh and went cross eyed and *dominion* shot my arm in *crazy-light* agony to melt my handcuff chain.

I rolled. Tom fired, concrete floor sprayed and my fingers started straightening. The *Gray* wanted *out!*

"No!" I yelled and rolled, fighting for fists. I refused to do it, I refused the *Gray,* these people were *compelled*, this was *my* problem just like all of them and I made my fists close on a shelving brace, so the *Gray went* howling in frustration and I ghost popped again.

Another gun went off—the first cop Cecil, retargetting from Hennessy but missing me and hitting the shelves with flesh me now locked in place again and and an easy target, so I crossed him, squeezed *dominion*, melted the rack in his fist into slag and rolled as the whole shelving row toppled.

Part of it toppled on me, back in one body, pinning my leg.

From shadows where Hennessy had gone a new gun cracked out and Cecil spun blood, gun flying free, while Tom fired randomly where he'd seen me last and the *Gray* rose to break Tom's neck so I *stormed*, but instantly went cross eyed again and vapored the shelf pinning my leg—more shots blasts and now a complete gunsmoke gunbattle roaring everywhere, I rolled flesh me and Tom fired at Hennessy and Hennessy screamed *everyone drop your weapons, drop them now!* at Cecil who had his gun back so both glowed cops fired at Hennessy.

I puppeted flesh me behind a stack of boxes which were not going to stop any bullets then hovered ghost me up to survey a place to hide. I heard screams and saw one glowing cop on the concrete floor with a hole in his throat while the other glower charged, gun extended, firing and bleeding and taking a final round in the groin and pitching down, sliding head first into a rack, where he stopped.

Ghost me had the perfect view of everything. Flesh me heard silence. The cop with his throat blown was gurgling what had to be his last breaths. The second cop who'd hit the shelving unit was motionless.

"Hennessy?" I had flesh me call. "Hennessy?"

"Do not move," came instructions. I did not.

The cop on the floor died. His ghost whirled up, ultraviolet everything, holding a potted plant. I saw Hennessy cop walk from the shadows, gun extended, then limp to the area filled with bodies. He kicked the gun from the dead cop, turned, staggered to the motionless cop. Hen was in pretty bad shape too.

"Are you hurt?" he called.

"No," I had flesh me assure him.

"Jesus fuck. Jesus fucking fuck what a fucking disaster," Hen was moaning.

And then I saw red all over my flesh hands. But it wasn't blood. It was...paint? Behind flesh me a pallet of stacked boxes were all labeled *Fenestram Co.* One of the nearest boxes bore a bullet hole. Paint dripped from it. Visible spectrum chromium.

I crossed my flesh eyes, bloomed *dominion,* melted the handcuff in my flesh fist and merged. As the cuff melted I shaped it and made myself a razor. With that, I started cutting boxes open

"I said do not move," Hennessy called, hearing activity, but you could tell his heart wasn't in it. He had other problems. I cut holes in more Fenestram boxes, knifing them open none too carefully, since I lack warehouse experience. It got boring but I kept going.

In the seventh box, I found a prize.

"Get out here, Gale," Hennessy yelled. "Fast. Now!"

I stood. I walked carefully through the pitched-over, semi-melted shelves, almost tripped, then saw Hennessy. Dust rose everywhere. I coughed. Behind Hennesy the ghost of the second cop revolved in Higher majesty above its body, holding headphones. The heads of both bodies still glowed—little Higher camp lanterns.

"Drop it!" Hennessy yelled at my hands, and his gun came up.

"Whoa, nothing, look, just paint junk," I said as I let the tubes spill to the floor. Every Higher shade I'd need, in one little pile. "See Hen? Nothing dangerous."

"Do *not* call me Hen," he said. He couldn't believe any of it, not *any* of it. He lowered his gun. I got my paint.

"What a massive, colossal cluster fuck," he said. Then he collapsed backward in his own pool of blood.

I hadn't been hit, I hadn't been seen, and Hennessy, maybe groggy, couldn't think of a story to account for me being there that wouldn't enrage his handlers, so he threatened me to silence and had me flee. Shoving tubes of Higher paint in my Hawaiian pockets I went panting up side streets and through alleys, not places I recognized, until I heard sirens and ducked into a neglected pocket park where a merry-go-round spun as if someone had just jumped off. I settled on a bench.

Had anyone just jumped off? The merry-go-round? Filled with cortisol and barely in control, which is how all my shootouts leave me, I dialed so wide open that *light* shook the world like reactor fire, burning everywhere, destroying nowhere, and I saw no, there wasn't anyone over by the merry-go-round.

I took meditation breaths while my mind strung questions together about what I'd escaped.

Someone had sent Hennessy to warn me away from the apprentices. The only person I'd mentioned the apprentices to had been Roman. And Hennesey himself, but he'd wanted no part of that investigation. And Hennessy did freelance work for Roman. I'd seen him.

But if Roman sent Hen to threaten me he had *not* sent the two other cops. They'd inserted themselves into Hennessy's operation. Julian—it had to be Julian—got wind of Hennessy's assignment and hijacked it to kill me because we'd come to that point. And Julian hated me because...why? Right. He was being replaced, and that was my fault. Or whatever.

But they'd taken me to a Fenestram warehouse to do it. Not a coincidence. Julian wanted my body found there, among stockpiled Higher paint and supplies. Why would Julian want that? Why not do it in the cop car? This drew a lot of attention to a paint cache someone went to a lot of trouble to conceal. Who was concealing the cache? Did Julian have something against them too?

Several different ways for the next few hours to play out ran through my mind as I sat in the park, appearing inconspicuous, probably smelling like gunpowder. Option one was I could go to the police and report being kidnapped by the other police. But Hennessy had threatened me very clearly—do not go to the police—and I'd long ago used up my presumption of innocence with the Skysill PD, being present at so many other murders. Option two was to start working backward and somehow trace the *glowed* cops to Julian, which sounded like a lot of work and not my style, plus if I found him he'd try to kill me. The third option was go straight to the *Fabrica*, or the Tactus, or maybe all of them, and complain about Julian trying to kill me in the first place. But I'd already worked so hard rejecting those people if I went there now I'd ruin the effect.

So in the end I did what I'm best at, stood, wiped red paint on my legs and proceeded home as if nothing had happened. Only one thing really mattered anyway—my ten-year *no painting* rule was about to break. Tubes in my pockets clacked softly as I walked. Other than the shootout, I was pretty happy how fast and efficient my search had been. And I honestly didn't know how big a deal the shootout really was. A few policemen shot each other. That probably happens all the time, with all the guns they have around.

From the park I looped over the hill, cutting north above the Civic Center a half mile, then angled toward the beach. Even if my phone had been with me and charged, which hardly ever happens, I'd still have walked instead of calling a car because road ghosts. I didn't see any road ghosts on the walk, but they appear suddenly and it wasn't worth the risk. I did wish I'd worn socks with my sandals. I wondered if Phil had any Hawaiian socks.

Creeping while still being nonchalant, which I think I can totally do, I went from shadow to shadow through the bistro district, and getting nearer the Bradley, felt anxiety rise. It was one part looking for skulls with *compulsion* halos, and another part the rule, I was going to break the most important rule. That was the real danger I planned to ignore.

I hit PCH, hurried right, speed walked past The Square on the Sea and Roman's forgery sales floor, and came in view of the Bradley, where there were no flashing vehicles or Tactus or other Family anywhere I could see, though I did think I spotted a drone but it turned out to be a bird. I'd lost track of what day I was on with the Brazilians. What'd they given me, two days? I handled this uncertainty by pretending the Brazilians didn't exist.

My pocket tubes weighing my pants, I scuttled, fast, across the street and through the Bradley's front doors. I felt a strange sense of security being there, panting and looking back at the world outside.

"Hey boss," Phil startled me from his seat in the shadows by the ficus.

"Don't call me that," I told him.

"Sure thing chief," he agreed. He raised a large walkie talkie from his lap and shook it like a saltshaker. "You hear about the police shootout?"

He watched me while twisting walkie-talkie knobs and ate from a Ziploc of melon in his lap.

"Was there supposedly a police shootout?" I wondered.

"Every cop in the city got killed," he marveled. "It's like a *gang war*."

"Where'd you hear this, Phil?"

"I stay informed." He shook his radio again. Suddenly it squawked. He looked me over critically, pointing to his squak box. "You have yours?"

"My...what are we talking about?"

"Bradley family police walkie. Oh jeez. Talk to Warren, first floor, Skysill's Ham Radio Repair. You've got to get a scanner. You have blood all on both your legs."

"That's red paint," I said, and he nodded and gave a wink, which was frustrating. "Has anybody been trying to get into the building?"

"Sure, tons of customers, but I say the Bradley has a firm *no customers at any time* policy. No one understands."

"Good work," I told him. He held out his bag of melons. I declined and went for the elevator, then stopped. "By any chance, did your scanner mention the address of this police shootout? If it even happened, I mean, how would I know?"

"Sure," he nodded, "these are great scanners, you hear *everything*. You have to shake them." He poured the rest of the melon into his mouth so juice covered his chin and he smacked his lips, then held the empty bag out in his palm and watched me.

"Do you remember the address you heard?" He shook his head. I nodded. "What about the other guy? Dale? You know him?"

"*Know* him?" Phil laughed. "Dale from Finances by Dale? He's a legend. First floor."

"He's smart, right? I wonder if he could find the address."

"He totally could. He's a wizard with paperwork. Not a real one, haha."

"I'd like to know who owns the building where the cops were killed."

Phil didn't miss a beat. He sprang up so fast he lost his melon bag and shook his radio until it made a noise, then pushed a button. "Finance," he called into it. "This is Hawaii, do you copy? Over."

His radio screeched and a thin voice said, "Hawaii, this is Finance. Over."

"Finance, execute a deed look-up for the site of the gang war shootout. *Pronto*. Over."

"Hawaii, I am tired, I do not want to. Over."

"Do it though Finance, it's for the *big guy*." He winked at me, his disturbing new habit.

"For the *boss*?" marveled Dale.

"Finance do not call him boss, he *will* snap at you. Over."

"Roger Hawaii. I'll pull records. Over and out."

I watched Phil click his radio off, or change the channel, then shake it, all while licking his fingers to clean the juice.

"This Bradley Family's really something, isn't it?" I asked after a moment.

"Oh yeah," he nodded. "If you want that blood off your shorts ask Caren, Skysill's Best Furniture Cleaners, floor two. She can get blood out of anything. She can get blood out of a stone."

I nodded. "Nice. You literally don't care what anything you say means, do you?"

He laughed and shrugged and tried to lick his chin juice but his tongue was too short. I left him guarding the lobby doors and took the elevator up. The paint in my pockets was getting heavy, pulling my shorts, but I ignored it. I ignore everything. On the fourth floor I kicked aside gift baskets left like offerings to a landlord god. I could see no explanation for it. The Bradley family had certain skills but were missing everything else completely. I got into the penthouse and finally emptied my pockets. I went to the bedroom to see that my phone was finally charged. There were messages from Amelia on it I didn't listen to, and one towing company telling know how to get one of my cars that I ignored too.

I dialed Caroline. She's the sweetest procrastination.

"I've been thinking about you," she said when she answered and gave me goosebumps. "I only have a minute but I had to answer. Hi."

"I'm procrastinating," I said and tried to daydream a picture of her.

"Is that so? You sound winded. How'd you get winded?"

"Just the usual dodging and totally not killing anyone." I tried daydreaming her location but drew a blank. I didn't like it. "Where *are* you?"

"You can't tell right? Isn't it nice? Veronica gave me a new crystal. She has one for you too. She's right Ash. We really have to be careful. I think it's sweet this way. Kind of like we're normal. Let's see how long it lasts. What were you dodging? What are you procrastinating?"

Even without telepathy, she knew there was more to my story than just dodging. Even without telepathy she knew me. I wondered how much better my life would be if Veronica would stop showing up with crystals or going out with my sister. Without telepathy I was forced to guess Caroline's thoughts, the way they had before social media, which Caroline could pretend to think was normal but I couldn't.

"How're things at Three Paths?" I avoided her question, which you can do when the other person can't read your mind. "Still busy?"

"It's worse and worse up here," she said. "We're packing in psychics from everywhere, more every day. Poor things are trying to hide from the break in the Path. But it's getting closer, and the walkers on Before are totally freaking out. The Monarchs can't be up here all the time. We're dealing with other problems. I actually have to go in a sec."

"What problems?"

"I don't want you worried. There's danger enough, why distract you?"

"The end of time, right? And none of these people understand. It's just the two of us. It's like we're trapped in a doomsday cult, which would be sexy if it wasn't horrible."

"This problem's too big for those people," she agreed. "Plus who knows? Maybe the end of time only affects psychics. Maybe it leaves the rest of the world unchanged—we just don't have an idea. All my Path walkers are coming into this blind." There was a momentary silence, not anything you ever had with telepathy. "I have to go. But first tell me something about your day. Something safe and ordinary."

"I'm planning to make a piece of toast," I said.

"That's safe for other people," she laughed. "Try again."

"Later I'm planning to paint for the first time in ten years which'll possibly drive me crazy, but when Tilly exploded I knew I had to."

"You don't do safe and ordinary, do you Ash?"

"I'm probably not that kind of boyfriend."

"You're the quirky kind."

"Right. And then, this painting will be a warm-up. If I live, I want to paint you."

A silent moment passed. A different kind of person might have used that time to marshal arguments or reconsider her boyfriend choices but all Caroline said was, "I can't wait to see what you make."

I didn't tell her it was going to be Higher and she wouldn't be *able* to see what I made, because that might spoil her optimism. It was something else telepathy didn't offer; protective omission. I sat on my bed, then lay on my back. Phones did create a certain mystery. Like, I had to guess what she looked like and wonder if it could possibly be that good in real life, her hips so soft, her fingers that perfect.

"I gotta go," she said. "You'll do great. You can't get much crazier than you are now so I think you're safe. But I'll like you either way."

"Because you can't help yourself."

"I don't want to help myself."

She hung up. I got a real daydream of her hanging up her phone, looking exactly how I'd guessed. Veronica and her stupid crystals. Those would never work on us. I went to the kitchen.

Very slowly and patiently I walked myself through the steps of making toast, hoping flesh me was paying attention wherever he lived. Then, because cleanliness and order are so important to me, I cleaned his eggs off the floor. Then I cleaned the refrigerator door, which had a smudge. I realized Phil or someone had stocked the refrigerator, because it was full of things I had no idea how to eat, like vegetables and something like marmalade. It seemed unusual, the amount of energy they spent feeding and clothing me. But maybe not. Maybe all tenants do this. The fruit bucket was full again. Whatever else happened to me, I wasn't going to get scurvy in the next three months.

Then for a while I distracted myself eating fruit and looking up marmalade recipes. I opened a bottle of wine from a basket and walked through more toast-making for flesh me, then thought I wanted to listen to music and spent an hour looking for the penthouse sound system. I procrastinated most of the daylight hours away. It was pretty professional. Already it had me feeling more like an artist.

Finally, late in the afternoon, I stacked three dining chairs to make an easel in the living room. Thirty minutes went by as I procrastinated putting it different places around the room. The sun was almost down by that time, but you don't need sunlight to paint with eyes like mine. Even so, I settled on a spot with the balcony doors at my back to catch the setting sun off the ocean. There I arranged the canvas Tilly had saved, and took my brush, and gessoed it empty. Out with the old. Starting over. I held a baking sheet to mix, a trick I'd learned from Celine, who'd hated baking.

And then, finally, I asked myself what the fuck I thought I was doing.

From the time I'd started painting as a baby to the hour I'd stopped, my path had run in a circle: prep a canvas, paint, *storm*, pass out. Until I turned sixteen I was deranged with it, so the wonder was I'd laid down one single coherent brush stroke. But people used to love it, and I couldn't make any of it stop.

Every Fenestram painter feels a need to paint Higher, but none like me. Canvas, paint, *storm*, pass out. Fling angst on it. Get the pain out. Gut out the ecstasy. Canvas after canvas. While all along, in the background, people I loved left, or struggled to adapt to me, to my cycle of canvas, paint, *storm*, pass out. I lived ecstasy to despair, over and over. I ate crumbs. At sixteen I was clothes hangers on a broom, ashamed because—canvas paint *storm* pass out—my dirty secret was I *liked* it. I was glad I had no choice. It was self-destructive but it was mine and no one could make me stop. Addict. Painting *was* me. Entirely.

Then at sixteen, the *Gray* came. Probably something psychic, I now thought. Somehow the *Gray* changed the way my nervous system worked. I still wanted to paint but I didn't *need* to. The first time the *Gray* took me, all my suffering went away, just for a few moments. And that was the beginning of the end for painting because suddenly I had a choice. The damage done by canvas, paint, *storm*, pass out, became something I was in control of. So, mostly to save Amelia, though not completely, I choose to stop. I went *Gray* occasionally and it kept the desperation checked. In the beginning, the *Gray* was benign. Neutral ground. A place I was relieved to go. When the *Gray* eventually got bad, all I had left was drinking.

Sitting in that darkened penthouse with a baking sheet and a stack of chairs, I admitted all the things I was feeling, because that's a form of procrastination too. Obviously I felt afraid to paint, because *crazy*, but even more I felt a fear that the ecstasy wouldn't happen. It'd been a rarefied brand of desperate ecstasy, and if that was gone, the floorboards of my life would vanish. For years, that had been my escape hatch; if everything went to shit, if I got sick or I was going to prison for one of my crimes, I could at least paint one last time and go out glorious. The addict dream.

But my *storms* were different and I no longer went crazy. There was no reason to wait for sickness, or prison, except the one lurking fear—was the escape hatch still available? Had it only been a dream, or was I still an artist? Had I used it up? With the first stroke of the brush, I'd know.

Working quickly so I wouldn't stop to think, I pooled pigment on the sheet, built a florid *reason* tinted *choke*, dipped the brush, leaned toward the canvas. Over my shoulder the sun, almost gone, threw orange fire at the surface. I dialed my *sight* maximum high. All or nothing. The universe exposed every secret color as Tip. Hit. Canvas.

And I *stormed* and popped out the top of my skull.

A ghost?

Higher gloom dumped over every surface. The ghost peak towered—now I could even see it inside the room, through the walls. Definitely closer.

I hung behind my flesh body frozen with his hand up, the brush clenched in his fist waiting for instructions, and I spun a furious half circle to confront whoever had set us off, but found no ghost behind me. There wasn't a ghost anywhere in the penthouse I saw, whipping a tour. Maybe one had floated into range on the street? On the roof? Just one thing after another.

Flesh me had his arm out, so I puppeted that down into his lap. I'd need it rested when I got back into him for painting. I waited for whatever ghost had popped me to exit the vicinity but lacking patience as I do, after ten seconds, I squeezed my flesh eyes crossed and merged down, driving *dominion* through my arm into the brush, careful not to melt it since it was my only one. I took the opportunity to shape the bristles longer and stiffer. There hadn't been a great selection at the warehouse.

The brush radiated *dominion* now, a delicate Chernobyl fuel rod glow. It fired the *choke* colored bristles into extra life. The pigment really popped. I was back. My hands were mine. The time had come.

I raised my arm to draw tip across canvas—and *stormed* to become a ghost.

Flesh me froze again of course. Ghost me floated—wait...what's happening?—was my sickening thought. Flesh me moved his arm a little and I puppeted him hard, *stop*.

Things dawn on me slow. But if I'm not hungry and enough time passes I see a pattern as well as the next drunk. Like this pattern. It made a certain sense. This was the kind of thing that would totally happen to me.

Once again I crossed my flesh eyes and shoved *dominion* out to my paintbrush and this time it started birthing a duplicate, which I reshaped, erasing bristles, building a palette knife in stainless steel. The knife fell to the floor, glowing. I returned to one flesh. Three times is the real test, I knew. That's science.

So once more I put my brush to the canvas and *stormed* and popped a ghost, and I knew.

Flesh me had the brush lodged between his curled fingers, like Captain Hook with a paintbrush attachment. It looked awkward. But I'm a problem solver at heart, and I wondered, could I puppet-paint with flesh me? With the brush in his fist like that?

I lifted his wrist and leaned him in slowly, then tried a stroke and almost punctured the canvas. I had no feel. For a moment I couldn't think what else to try. The moment stretched out and the sun set and stars came. The beach out my sliding doors got faintly phosphorescent. While waiting for inspiration I kicked out of ghost me into flesh me, and though I was frozen, suddenly the room flushed with secret colors, my eyes wide with nighttime super dazzle. Even the mountain looked great. It loomed in through the walls and ceiling like IMAX.

I was numb. Much like I'm always numb but deeper. If I hadn't expected something like this it would've been more devastating, but if there's one thing I know, it's managing expectations. I keep them low. So. Whatever. Painting's no longer on the table? All wasn't lost. I had a few remaining months of vodka.

Then, in a flash of *dominion,* a ghost swelled into the room. She floated near the library wall—Samantha, of course—and I slipped back into ghost me to greet her. I eased my ghost self over and floated beside her, watching flesh me from the side, his back to the windows.

That's one question answered, I said to her. I kept it casual.

Flesh me, left with his hand out, started waving it around. He sometimes hit the canvas, his brush leaving paint streaks. Like those elephant paintings.

I'm aware how self-centered I am, I admitted to her. She didn't look surprised. I figured she could disappear easily if she got bored listening to my self-pity, which at this point was one of the few things I had left to talk about, other than Caroline and, like I said, vodka.

Like my ideas about my parents, I explained. *So self-centered. I used to wonder why would my parents just leave me? Unless me being broken was so disappointing, and from shame just seeing me they abandoned me…super self-indulgent shit. That's what I'm like. I'm an acquired taste. You seem to have it, which is frankly weird. A few days ago I saw, maybe what happened was my parents were hiding in Skysill to get away from Aeternus who was hunting them. And it could have been, I mean, it now seems likely he found them. That they didn't abandon me at all. So, was my thought, maybe I'd had it <u>all</u> wrong. Maybe I could paint. Maybe I'm normal. But I wasn't wrong. Something's broken. I don't fit.*

Suddenly another ghost vapored into the room, doing a *dominion* shimmy, and joined Samantha and ghost me in a line against the wall facing my flesh. The new ghost was a monk. They're all mostly monks at this point. Then another came. A second later another, each appearing in silent incandescent *dominion.* Each lined up to face flesh me. I whipped ghost me around to face them from the opposite wall. What were they doing here? No one likes to see new ghost behavior. It's unsettling. I watched as three more monks appeared, and then one of the shootout cops. Tom? It was like watching people log into a video chat.

Very swiftly after that there appeared dozens more ghosts. They lined the wall, grouped two or three deep.

Scram, I ghosted. *I'm in no mood.*

But still more appeared. They weren't actually lined against the wall, I saw. They formed a curve along a periphery facing flesh me. They remained a respectful distance. Silent and motionless. And that's when I noticed—flesh me had evolved his brush style.

Maybe he'd been warming up with the elephant swings but when I looked again he was focused on his canvas like a journeyman, peering over the top of it at something in the distance, looking back down. His lips were pursed. And then as I watched, my own flesh body lowered my brush to mix paint without me. And this was nothing like the way he'd moved making toast. Here his gestures were smooth, efficient, even graceful. He'd already laid a coat of *choke* over half the canvas, tracing the axis of a shape he liked. His eyes had a critical cant. Again and again he raised them to look beyond the canvas then lowered them. Slowly solving something out of *light*.

Every stroke he lay on that canvas burst with *dominion*. His canvas was now glowing with it, it was flowing off his brush like paint. But it wasn't paint, I thought, that's impossible, I thought, there are no tubes of *dominion*.

I kicked out of ghost me and back into flesh me for a closer look. He seized up. From that vantage there was no denying it—something intentional was happening on that canvas. He was painting. He was legitimately and fairly competently mixing color, graduating tones, filling the canvas with purpose. All with his one small brush.

I kicked back out to settle into my ghost and watch. What else could I do?

It seemed safe, it's not like he was leaping barrels. His head shifted up and down every time he checked his subject, and it finally registered—he was observing the ghost mountain. Mount Tempus. Was he painting Mount Tempus? The image forming on the canvas wasn't mountain-like. I saw a hard corner, a bevel, something carved?

Samantha, I asked, sliding back to float beside her in the audience, *what's happening?*

Suddenly flesh me put his hands on his hips and shook his head and grunted. He wasn't happy. As I watched, he leapt from the canvas with a bellow and landed on a coffee table then scrambled and bounded onto a couch against the wall opposite the ghosts. He ripped the Impressionist canvases on that wall violently aside. Which, they hadn't been half bad, but okay.

Then he bounced off the couch and botched the landing and crashed sideways and all I could do was wince. There was going to be blood. I might have a concussion. But a second later he was up, a little woolly but determined, and he grabbed his canvas and bounced back to the couch

He very carefully hung that canvas on the high hook where the central piece of Impressionism had hung, and watched it critically, bouncing all the while. Then finally, with his brush in his fisted hand, he started painting the wall around it.

Myself and the rest of the ghosts were amazed. We couldn't think what to say. Flesh me turned out to be a very physically wired painter, he threw a lot of elbows, there was a lot of crouching, jumping, spinning from side to side. He was standing on a couch and that made him even bouncier. But with that style he was really covering ground. Higher pigment, enlivened by *dominion,* soon spread on the wall around the canvas, and there was no way his brush was big enough to account for it. He kept looking over his shoulder at Mount Tempus, returning to brush the wall. And it became clear, the image central to what was becoming a huge mural was the back of a throne.

I pushed ghost me very close to watch flesh me work. He'd painted such a large area so quickly it was hard to believe. He hardly seemed to use the cookie sheet, now just painting nonstop without even mixing. Every stroke he laid was some subtle grade, Higher shadows and mids and highlights and *dominion* feverish and brilliant under it all. Before long the entire wall, thirty feet, glowed. His brush work humbled me. It was fucking unbelievable. You literally couldn't tell where the bristles ended and the wall began.

I lost track of time. When the moon came up I could tell he wasn't painting just the throne atop Mount Tempus. He was painting the view looking over the back side of that peak. A landscape otherwise hidden. How he was seeing it, I had no idea. He'd covered the bottom of the wall with the throne seen from behind, and as the moon went down he was putting in detail like he was using the magic tip of Tinkerbell's wand, he just trailed color and the view of the land beyond Mount Tempus emerged. And that's when his real mastery showed.

It was frankly shocking. He was a better painter than I was or had ever been. Was that possible? He worked so fast. He rendered so deftly. I watched him built up a scene of devastated tablelands, an earth-shaken, sea flooded, tornado ravaged ghost land of snapped and shattered hills where nothing lived or even stood. Every field was broken. Stones, from structures and roads, blasted to ruin. He rendered the scene in mind-blowing Higher colors brought to life suffused with *dominion*.

The moon set about the time he began laying in the fine details. The gathered ghosts and I watched as he traced out fallen trees, wasted rivers, empty seas, cities shaken to flotsam. He painted in circles, spiraling, describing arches, basilicas, shattered columns, broad steps, everything fissured into pieces.

By that time the sun was coming back. Red and blue shadows stretched off the Bradley and out over the beach. A gull appeared and screamed. Flesh me focused on none of it, he ignored the entire world. He was feverish and sweating, covered head to foot in Higher paint and *dominion*, utterly spent. As the thin light of an autumn sunrise touched the edge of the Skysill bluff, he finished.

He slumped to the floor in front of the couch with his mouth open. And as a group, every single ghost in the room crowded forward, as near as they could get to the mural before they flipped backward on the other side of flesh me. The room was absolutely filled with ghosts. There were a hundred of them if there were five, crowding to face this wall of art.

And then the row of ghosts nearest the painting popped out. The ghosts behind shifted forward, and they vanished too. Rank on rank, like patrons at a museum being hurried past a masterpiece, they stood a moment then vanished. Finally only Samantha remained. For long minutes she hung. The sun rose higher. Until she too went away. And I was the only ghost. Since I'd paint *stormed* myself into that state I'd have to cross eye myself out. For a moment I didn't.

All I could do was stare. The painting was extraordinary. One high throne, facing away, overlooking a landscape of devastation far below. The scope was majestic. The illusion of height was dizzying. The details of even the farthest hills had life you could feel. There was balance to the work, composed but wild, warm and cool—it pulled the eye so deep you felt yourself getting lost.

Luminous *dominion* shone under every surface so the whole wall seemed lit from behind. All I could think was that I wished I'd painted it. But I'm not that good. I'm relentless, I'm searing, I'm entirely invested when I paint—painted—but I'm not this kind of draftsman. What was I supposed to think about this?

I needed to get out of the penthouse to think. Why I thought thinking would help I do not know, just optimism I guess. Squeezing to merge my bodies had become very easy and painless by that point. I birthed a new paintbrush and retook my flesh where he'd fallen on the floor beside the couch.

And he felt like shit. Or I felt like shit. My ankle hurt where flesh me had twisted it. I had a lump on my head. My arms and shoulders *ached* from working all night above my head, and I was starving. I dragged myself to the shower. There was red paint from yesterday and Higher paint all over me, it just sent the wrong message. While I was in the shower I tried not thinking about the painting but that didn't work.

Once I had on fresh Hawaiian clothes from the hall I got in the elevator, and when the elevator opened in the lobby there was Phil right in front of the lobby doors. At first I thought he was cleaning because he stood in a tub, two feet high and three around, and had his pants rolled to his knees. Then I saw his little hips swinging back and forth as he walked in place.

It was going to be exhausting but I'd have to ask. I watched him a minute, even though I was hungry.

"You're making wine," I was forced to observe.

"Nope," he said, marching, "champagne. You're not supposed to call it that. I do anyway."

"Is your champagne any good?" I wondered. There was a mystery here. Distraction.

"Probably not. Who cares? I make it for toasts and in case I have to christen a ship."

"Do you get ships very often?"

"None so far."

"I'm going to get breakfast."

"I'll watch the door to stop anyone coming in, even customers unless that's changed?"

"No. Hey. If someone does try coming in, how'll you stop them from that tub?"

He snorted. "*Reflexes*," he said.

"Nice. Are you hungry? I could get you a burrito or something."

"Oh, I don't *think* so."

He gave me a chuckle as he shook his head, then bent to scoop a palm full of crushed grapes up to his mouth and began slurping. His eyes were full of merriment. It was very strange, but somehow not at all strange. Phil had depths. Or he was the biggest idiot I'd ever met. Either way I was starting to understand him.

Down the street at La Cala I got a breakfast burrito and coffee without thinking about the painting I probably hadn't done, based on semantics. I took my burrito behind the building where surf shops face the sea and sat on a bench to watch the water, and felt totally empty. It might have been a year since I'd eaten or understood anything. I *had* to think about the painting then. So I chewed and drank coffee and pictured it. How had it happened? What did it mean? They were useless thoughts. I regretted them right away.

My surface pains eased a little in the morning sun but the deeper pains were untouched. I finished the burrito and threw the wrapper in the trash. The ocean oxygen helped make everything a little clearer. It helped me realize I needed to go to sleep.

When I pushed back into the lobby the first thing I noticed were red footprints on the floor where Phil had stepped out of his tub and then climbed back in.

"Do you worry at all about bacteria?" I asked, pointing at his feet in the grapes.

"No," he laughed. "That's disproved."

"Well, it's your tub," I agreed. I looked at his tracks. There was a lot of juice spilled but it didn't go very far. More than one trip from the tub and back. "Why'd you get out?"

"That lawyer. He needed help getting through the door."

"A lawyer? Why'd he need help?"

"The wheelchair."

"But you opened the door?"

"Yeah."

"Why?"

"To let him in."

"But I thought we had an understanding no one *came* in?"

"He's a *lawyer*. Hello, earth to boss? A lawyer? Anyway, I told him you'd be back after breakfast so he's waiting up on your floor."

I gave Phil a chance to include the rest of the story. He only scooped and slurped grape-flavored bacteria water.

"What about the rule nobody comes in," I insisted, uselessly. We were beyond rules by then. It was just a bad habit I have of trying to understand anything.

"Well, yeah, but not *lawyers*," he reminded me. "Lawyers with *paperwork?* Oh man. You get thrown in prison keeping lawyers from thier appointed rounds. That's the law, buddy."

"Where do you get your legal information?"

"Travel agent forums."

I sighed. "So you sent a lawyer to my penthouse?"

"Yeah. Then those ladies came and they went to the *third* floor. Where the squatters are."

He continued walking in place while I waited. He did not explain anything again.

"So you're saying," I habituated slowly, "that in the few minutes I was gone getting food just now, you *also* let ladies in the building?" He nodded. I got an idea. "Were they lawyers?"

He checked his memory. "You couldn't tell. The one lady wore white pants and had a foreign accent and said *Oh be silent Phil. You will let us go wherever we please*, so I did. She was pretty."

We watched each other while he crush, crush, crushed his champagne.

"So aside from lawyers," I asked, "and apparently anyone else who asks, you're still keeping people out of the Bradley building right?"

He gave me a thumbs up. He was enthusiastic. Sweat rolled off his balding head into his grapes and I wondered if sweat had been disproved with bacteria. Then on the other side of the lobby the elevator doors opened and Amelia rushed out, pissed of course because what else, and yelling as usual. I smiled really wide for her because she hates that.

"Nella says you've been *painting*," she accused as she came at me across the lobby.

"There!" Phil cried. "That's one of the ladies. See if she's a lawyer."

"Where did you get *paint*?" Amelia demanded, arriving at my side. "Asher Gale what are you *thinking*? Are you kidding?"

"*Nella* says I'm painting?" I demanded. "What's *Nella* know?"

"She hears everything in the building you..." she stopped and looked at Phil, steadily marching, closely following a conversation he did not understand. She looked at me. "Can we talk somewhere else?"

"I don't want to talk anywhere. You know, Amelia, you can't just show up and just, whatever plan you have for me I'm going to jump and do it. You're as bad as Veronica—so I guess *Veronica's* up there too? You two just go everywhere together now?"

I didn't know *exactly* why I felt so pissy but I have faith there's always some reason.

Her eyes clouded. Not because she'd noticed my scorn. She was worried.

"Something's going on with her," Amy told me. "I'm really worried. She's not sleeping, she's...over the edge."

"I don't care about any of that Amelia!" I was feeling impatient to return to look at my picture and she's infuriating. She honestly has the worst timing. "Why are you in my building?"

"We heard Peter found an umbra eye, he..." Phil was still hanging on every word. Amy sighed and raised a hand, closed her eyes, sparkled *compulsion* at Phil's face, and said, "You'll forget this conversation."

He nodded. "I totally will."

"Nice," I scoffed, "why don't you make him buy one of your paintings? Start a gallery like Roman?"

"I'd totally buy one," Phil offered. "I'd hang it in the lobby."

"Also," Amelia told me, ignoring all distractions with her usual focus, "Veronica has a new crystal for you to put on. An upgrade. From Shay. Come up with me."

"It's my building I'll go where I want."

And finally, Amy, undone by too many distractions, had to ask, "I don't understand—why's there an office with your name on it up there?"

"Because *surprise*," I said, "I have an entire life that doesn't involve you. It's that amazing? I only discovered it recently. And yeah, I'm on a door. And in fact there's a lawyer waiting for me right now with paperwork, and pretty soon I'll be on this whole *building*. The Asher Gale Building. What do you think of that?"

"If you rename the building we'll need new tenant placemats," Phil warned.

"A lawyer?" Amy said. "Who's this lawyer? Some scam artist? You know how gullible you are."

Oh my god. I gave the conversation up and started for the elevator. Amelia came after me. The doors slid closed and I waited for her to punch a number. When she punched three I punched four. We rode in slow silence. When the doors opened she stepped out and spun to instruct me.

"I'm coming up, don't sign anything about this building unless I look."

"Oh! Okay!" I nodded, and let the doors close. Oh my god. Like I'm unable to manage my own life *at all?* Which yes, that is true, but why is it her business? All my life it's been like this, no boundaries.

The doors opened again on floor four and the first thing I saw were the offerings of cheese baskets and other hallway gifts, and that someone had set a potted palm on a rug. In front of my penthouse door was the lawyer I'd met the week before in Asher Gale's office. He waited in a wheelchair with an iPad and a cup of coffee.

"Victors," I said, coming down the hall. "Of Cardsworth Victors Williamson." I'm always disappointed when my brain retains that kind of trivia.

"Asher Gale," he said. Blue eyes. Lips you liked to watch. I remembered them. Wet now from foam off his coffee and smiling. That made me think, I wish I had coffee, and then from a cup holder on his chair he lifted a second cup of coffee and held it out. I remembered...had I borrowed his coffee the first time we met? That sounded like me. So now the wet-lipped lawyer and I had a coffee thing. He raised his brows.

"Victors," I told him, "if that's for me, and I hope it is, I have to tell you I only eat from the floor."

"Like a kitten."

"I'm not supposed to touch anyone. I have a condition. Put it down and I'll grab it."

He nodded. He was very amenable for a lawyer. He put down the coffee and rolled back an extra foot for safety. Then, carrying the cup, I opened the penthouse door. The coffee had a lot of sugar, just like his other cup, and it was hot.

"I noticed you haven't evicted your tenants," he observed. "Legally speaking, they are a liability."

"All the other ways too. They're like lemmings and I'm a cliff."

"As long as you're aware," he shrugged. He wheeled in behind me. "I came to tell you the trust documents are finalized. Everything's recorded. But I wanted to deliver your copies by hand."

"You guys at Cardsworth Victors Williamson have a really personal touch."

"We're a full-service firm," he agreed. "All the services."

I wondered if we might have been flirting, which would have been nice, or if maybe I was just exhausted. I was taking him toward the living room because it seemed like the right place to receive official documents. Then I saw *dominion* blasting around the corner and remembered the painting. The *light* had grown brighter since I'd left. And suddenly, like you always do after finishing a work, I couldn't wait to see it again, the dark majesty, the devastation. I hurried forward. When I turned the corner Higher *light* came off the wall and hit like falling water. I took the steps down, realizing for Victors' sake we'd need to use the kitchen, thinking what kind of fucked up penthouse doesn't have a ramp and then I froze, amazed all over again.

The Mount Tempus mural throbbed. Like something living. Like a window. So immediate and powerful it shivered the hairs on the back of my neck, where I hadn't known I had them. It overwhelmed the room. Made it unusable for anything but fixed staring. Victors wouldn't see anything but an empty wall, of course, with an empty canvas in the middle of it. But for me it was the ultimate distraction. I'd never be able to concentrate.

I called behind me, "Let's do this in the kitchen."

I heard his tires squeak and stop at the stairs, probably watching me stare at my wall. But before I could turn and make up an explanation there came a flash of *dominion* behind me—once again a ghost had bulbed in.

Out I popped. In flowed gloom and shadow from the Mount. I ghosted around, expecting Samantha, expecting maybe *all* the ghosts, but not expecting what I saw. Just one ghost.

Ghost Victors.

His wheelchair sat at the top of the stairs, his flesh body upright in it. He faced the mural. His coffee had fallen to the floor. His hands gripped the arms of the chair. His face wore death with wild amazement.

Behind the chair he floated: ghost Victors, coiling ultraviolet wreaths. Ghost him stood two-legged, wearing English riding clothes and boots, holding a pen, all of him shaped and petted by *dominion*. Busy, busy *dominion*. My lawyer was dead—or, had he been mine? I didn't know. What am I, a judge?

You can't put the ghost back. That's one thing I know. Once they're out, that's where they stay. This death was shocking, though that feeling passed pretty fast. Because, whatever, one more ghost. But it left me with confusion. What had just happened? A heart attack, a stroke, one of those nonprofit diseases? He looked so surprised.

Flesh me bounced on his toes. He wanted to go shake the pen in Victors' hand and send his ghost to Never Never Ghostland but I backed him and sat him on a footstool. *Stay.* You had to give him very clear instructions or fucking hell, who knew what he'd do? He put his head in his hands and stared, as a sudden question occurred to me... had *we* killed Victors? Flesh Victors was staring straight at the painting. He'd died the moment he saw it, either by coincidence or...was a thing like that possible? It got very quiet in my mind. I heard the surf far, far away.

Then I thought, come on, it's totally coincidence. Paintings kill basically zero people all through history. Victors had a heart attack, I easily convinced myself—like I can whenever it's most convenient— and I was completely blameless. I tried not to think of the *other* mural, the one Julian had made, which'd killed Samantha through mental torture. Because if you included that, it meant paintings had killed at least one person. It put me on shakier ground legally I thought, though again, not a judge.

"Asher?" I heard Amy call from the front door. "It's us. Your door's open *again*."

Footsteps came down the hall.

And everything happened fast. Amelia and Veronica stepped into view—and *dominion* surged off the wall and hit them like wind through the door to hell.

Around them both, balls of seven sizzled up, though deformed under the weight of *dominion* blasting. Both stumbled, their arms out like they'd been blinded. Both screamed. *Dominion* sheared their Higher shields and started peeling *light* in every hue around the edges, raining down on them, pressing them back like animals in a wind tunnel. Veronica staggered and fell to the floor as some force flesh me and ghost me couldn't feel—an immense flow of *something* coming off the mural without affecting us—began destroying them.

Amelia went to one knee, counter crossed her eyes and slammed her palms together. I was trying to puppet flesh me toward them but without a plan. Around Amy's hands a black wall inflated into nothingness and right away its edges were fraying torn storm trails in the blast and she called to me. Flesh me tripped on a footstool. Around Amy and Veronica a Higher firestorm raged and their faces lit from inside—then both of them vanished into the black wall of nothing.

And the storm snapped off. Leaving nothing of itself behind. The room was silent other than flesh me moaning and holding his foot. He sat on the floor. At no point had I felt anything as a ghost, and flesh me was unaffected. The destructive force flaring from the mural had only affected Amy and Veronica. And they were gone. The room held only two ghosts and their respective flesh bodies; one dead, one with a stubbed toe.

From the air in front of flesh me a voice issued. "Get'own here!" Nella slur yelled. "Asher come boy *now now!*"

Flesh me jumped up and started toward the elevator. I felt like it was the right move. Nella hears everything in the building, they said. Maybe she had an idea what had just happened in the penthouse.

I'll probably be back, I told ghost Victors, *just wait here. Or whatever. Do whatever you want.*

I instructed flesh me to run and push for floor three, but he didn't know about buttons so he stood a moment prying at the doors until I puppet pushed the button myself. And as we were waiting for the car to arrive I merged into one body, one sudden blood reality, being out of ghost range from Victors. The doors opened and I stumbled in. The first flesh sensation I had was my burning hand—flesh me had squeezed Victors' hot coffee and scalded us. I dropped the empty cup. The door closed. We went down. The doors opened.

Veronica and Amelia lay on the floor on the green carpet in the hall outside the elevator like two prize fighters coming back to consciousness. Four monks I didn't know plus Nella surrounded them. The monks stood eyes closed, outward facing and humming. New Dwayne was there too, arms waving wide sweeps, heaving deep breaths. They had no idea what was happening.

"Asher," Amelia moaned, sitting up, then standing. I waved my hands in warning—no touching. Amy recovers fast in emergencies, but she appeared woozy. I thought I saw residual *light* steaming off her, but I see a lot of shit. Veronica looked less fine than Amy but she didn't look dead. Neither looked dead. Maybe everything was going to be fine—that would be nice, if unlikely.

"So everything's going to be fine?" I asked.

"I've finally seen it," Veronica whispered, staring at me from the floor. "People spoke of it but...I never imagined. I am drained. Utterly drained. It is astonishing."

"What'jst happened?" Nella demanded from her mouth.

The monks had their eyes open. Everyone watched me. I held up my hand.

"This got burned," I said, "do you have ice?"

"Your paintings," Veronica breathed, coming to her feet. "Now I finally understand."

Amy was speechless. Veronica stopped talking too.

"Yeah that was pretty weird," I admitted as they stared, knowing we were probably not talking about the same thing. We almost never are. "But everything's going to be fine."

"Your *paintings*," Veronica repeated, squinting astonishment. "It is true after all. When I came to Skysill I was seeking Aeternus. I should have paid more...when I first came, of course, I heard whispers about you."

Amy was shaking her head like she didn't want Veronica to go on. But Veronica's one of those where, once they're moving downhill with an observation they're pretty hard to stop. I stood in the car hoping the doors would close. Then I saw one of the monks had her foot in the way.

"People spoke of your work as if...the small group who saw your pieces just after you finished them all said it was as though you painted with...magic."

Now Veronica was basically talking to herself, which meant the pressure was off for paying attention, which was good because my hand really hurt.

"Each had a different story," she continued, "but they all swore what they told me was true. Your paintings had effects—reality shifting. Healing. Transportive. Big and small, near and far. These viewers struggled to put their experience into words but the *concepts* —I knew they were describing *Fabrica* powers. But I didn't believe it. All seven colors, with their effects. You remember?"

That's when I realized she'd been talking to me the whole time. It's hard to tell the difference with some people. Now she's asking me to remember things? I tried looking incredulous and indignant. Amy rolled her eyes but Veronica didn't mind, she was happy to give me a presentation. It's a boardroom thing. She likes it.

"*Choke*," she said, "for *wellness*."

And she started making a finger list, which—finally. Those are the only things that work for me. I found myself following everything she said after that, which made it all worse. It drew me out of the elevator. The doors closed behind me.

"Your paintings demonstrated the entire Higher spectrum and its effects: *compulsion*— controlling relationships, *reason*—controlling illusion," Veronica fingered, "*crush*—weight or gravity, *farewell*— knowledge, *wander*—distance, and *bleed*—manipulating entropy. As if you were somehow using *pigment* the way *Fabrica* work *light*. I had no way to verify it and many other things to do so I dropped it. You were no longer painting. It seemed a moot point. I thought you... likely a clever charlatan."

I gave Amelia our look from childhood, which meant *what is this crazy lady talking about am I in trouble?* These sibling looks are habits that never die. And she's always been awesome managing situations where people are telling me things I don't want to hear. In this case, however, she offered no help. That was weird.

"What?" I asked in the silence. "This isn't an actual thing, what Veronica's saying. Right? Paintings with...powers or whatever. Right?"

"You never knew about it," Amelia told me. She offered it slow and I could see her checking my hands, canaries in the Asher Gale coal mine. "You hardly ever *looked* at the canvases you finished, and even when you did they didn't affect you. And then you stopped painting."

"Wait. I don't get this," I said. "You're saying people were freaked out by my paintings? I guess, who cares? I was there. Fuck those people. The town's full of critics. What's the big deal?"

"People were freaking out, Mr. Gale," Veronica said, "because your paintings actually created alterations in the real world. The way this mural upstairs seems to be doing."

Finger lists and repeating your point over and over, that's what works. The point of their story occurred to me then, which is usually when I lose interest in a story, so this was an experiment.

"So you're saying I *compelled* people with my paintings?" I asked. "You're saying people...did things because my paintings made them?"

"There was hardly any *compulsion*," Amy said, quietly. A memory lane kind of quiet. "Not used in a way to control anyone's behavior. It's just...your canvases, when people saw them there were physical effects. Changes...like, transformations of time, I guess. And space, and matter, like..." She pointed up to the penthouse. "That."

"You're serious now?" I asked. She nodded. I scoffed. I tried. I didn't have a wet enough mouth. "But I've *seen* those old paintings. They're just paintings."

"You see them *now,*" she nodded, "but they always faded fast. You'd finish one and for a few minutes or hours they were more than just paintings. The Higher *color*, the way you used it..." she brain trailed, chasing words and concepts.

"So my pictures made *light* attack people, like this mural?"

"No," she shook her head, struggling to describe it, "they all..."

"Did I kill anybody?" I interrupted, thinking of the promise I'd made Caroline, hoping it wasn't retroactive. Plus the phrase *did I kill anyone* is just something that comes up in my conversations. By now it's a habit.

"No," Amy said. "People would look at a painting and...their finger would itch. Everyone who saw the picture. Or you looked at a picture and found a hundred dollar bill in your pocket. Or you're suddenly wearing a hat."

"What?" I asked. "What?"

She was watching my hands and waiting. Looking a little afraid.

"But...how would I not know this?" I demanded. "I'd know this. Or we'd talk about it, like money in people's pockets, you might ask me...I mean...you never mentioned any of this. You never told me this was going on?"

"Ashy," she groaned, "no one talks to you about *anything*. We can't. You're...you know how you are."

"I'm not like that Amelia you think..."

But she wasn't going to stop. I saw her eyes counter cross for a second and she cried, "Asher back then you were crazy, a crazy little boy, and then you were an alcoholic and then you stopped painting and practically stopped talking to me, I'd never risk setting you *Gray* or *storming*, you're too sensitive! You're too sensitive Asher and you drink too much and now you say you're not like that but are you *sure*? Because supposedly you're popping in and out as a ghost and painting and *storming*, there's this brain rot, you're worse than ever. Look at yourself!"

"Since I learned of you," Veronica said, "I've examined the few works I could locate. From one or two I felt the whisper of activated *light*. Painted. On a canvas. Like an *eminence*."

Amelia's face had shifted. She now wore our other childhood look, the warning that she was just going to say everything all at once and get it over with. The Band-Aid theory.

"Why do you think the galleries all wanted you?" she asked. "They knew about you. They wanted to control it."

As had been happening recently I experienced an assortment of information puzzle pieces sliding together in my mind: my paintings, things people had said, things they'd done, conversations with people, like with Roman a few days earlier. Pieces of my past that'd been right out in the open sitting on the table, the whole time, but only now was someone putting them together.

Silence was all I could manage, which I'm sure everyone appreciated. I processed my surprise, my fear, and my disappointment. It only took a few seconds. I could've done it even faster at the bar.

I pointed above me.

"Then I think I just killed that lawyer," I told everyone.

"Who?" Veronica asked.

"Victors, of Cardsworth Victors and Williamson. He saw my mural and now he's dead, but in my defense it was Phil who let him in the building, despite our policy."

"Wait, was Mr. Victors *sighted*?" Veronica wondered, wrapping her brain around me.

"No, visible spectrum as they come."

Nella made a snorting sound in the air.

"So you painted a thing *kills* people *not* Aspectu, an *almost* kills Aspectu?"

She kept laughing. Nella had a great appreciation for how unbelievable and ridiculous my things all were. Her drunken scoffing and the fact that Amelia had also just called me a drunk also made me wonder if Nella had any alcohal for me to drink.

And then, from the office down the hall, we all heard a thunder rumble. I could tell it was Pierre. Nella and the monks turned instantly and rushed back. Veronica, still wobbly, sent New Dwayne with them, then looked above me and frowned and I turned to see that the elevator had apparently dropped to the lobby when I'd stepped out and now was rising back to us. Because there was nothing else to do, we watched it come. For me it was a pleasant distraction from having just killed someone but I don't know what Amy and Veronica were thinking. The elevator rose to the third floor where we were and didn't stop. It rose to the penthouse and there paused.

"I wonder who that is?" I asked.

"I'm sure it's Caroline," Veronica said. She began reaching into a pocket. "I asked her to meet us. I have a new crystal for you, I need to tell Shay what happens when you both wear the upgrades. I can let Caroline know we're here..." Veronica counter crossed her eyes. On her fingers, something Higher flickered and flared, but died, and she sagged.

"It is astounding," she breathed. "Your mural has drained me."

"Ash," Amy suddenly asked, "did you lock your door? Did you close and lock your door *like I always tell you?*"

"No," I scoffed, "please, what happens if I lose my..."

But as I was saying it both Veronica and Amelia were drawing breath and Veronica was shouting and I was realizing, "The mural!"

Amelia counter-crossed her eyes but she only flickered...the mural had taken everything form both of them. And my door was open up there, with Caroline heading in to meet me.

"Stop her Asher," Veronica said, which I'd already figured out and started running to do. Amelia shouted but I heard nothing. I pounded the elevator, pounded the button. Stupid doors! I turned for the stairs.

"Take this!" Veronica yelled as I passed, fisting up a necklace, *"you must wear it!"*

CHAPTER

ELEVEN

I hit the stairwell door. I hit the stairs. Echoes of me shouting, "CAROLINE!" taking three steps three steps three steps to a landing where steps continued toward the roof and I shoved toward the penthouse and sprinted down the gift basket hall.

My front door hung open. I tried to sense her but there wasn't anything to sense. I'm not good at sensing, I told myself, it doesn't mean anything. I was yelling as I ran through the door and skidding, and turning, breathless—at the living room stairs there was a purse tipped on the floor, right beside Victors' wheelchair.

I didn't want it to be true. I didn't want it. I ghost popped when I saw Victors. I didn't want that. Flesh me continued around the corner on his own. Stagger stopped. I floated to the steps and—I saw her.

Standing in the middle of the room, staring at the mural.

When she heard flesh me she turned. She'd dressed up to visit. Her whole look was just a little curlier. A ribbon she wore on her wrist, something you put on to remind yourself of something but in her case also a beautiful soft yellow that went with her hair. Her hair with new waves. Her lips with a touch of gloss. And best of all she

204

wasn't dead. She was bursting with life. My crystal went fucking crazy and flesh me moaned and even ghost me felt it, just a tingle.

"That's unbelievable," she told him, turning back to the wall, grabbing her chest.

Flesh me went for her. He wanted to touch her. I jerked him back.

"Thanks," I had him say. She was gazing at what had to be, to her, an empty canvas hung in the middle of an empty wall, with rapt intensity.

"Your painting's like a fairy tale," she marveled, "all created out of time. How'd you *do* it?"

Flesh me reached again. He wanted to pet her. *Down*, I said, *for god's sake.*

"I'm not sure I *did* do it," I had him admit. I had a lot of things on my mind but I tried to make him sound normal, and I'm so practiced making myself sound normal, I almost pulled it off. "It's supposed to be invisible to you. It's all Higher paint."

"I see it, that's for sure," she said.

"And you feel okay?" I had flesh me ask. "Nothing weird?"

"I feel fine now you're here," she said. It was super distracting having her so close. Even as a ghost. She surveyed flesh me, the tiniest uncertainty in her eyes.

"I should tell you," I had flesh me tell her, "I'm in my ghost right now." I had him point back toward me.

"Okay," she nodded, "well I'm just going to talk to your body since he's easier to see, but know I'll be thinking of your ghost."

"I'm glad you're not dead."

"Thank you Ash, that's super sweet."

She smiled. She meant it. She wore a t-shirt and jeans, like she always does unless she's wearing a flesh-tight red dress, but these were her best jeans. They fit like magic skin. Every inch of her was casual and provocative, which are my two weaknesses. She had her beat-up boots on though, due to her deeo commitment to comfort.

She turned back to the wall; flesh me watched her, I thought, a little desperately.

"It's wild. I don't see this painting the way I see you. I see it exactly the way I see a psychic vision. I see it in *time*."

"The wall looks...old?"

"No I see *time,* the actual temporal medium—time. You painted a whole wall using *time* like paint." She almost whispered it. She went closer. Reached out, almost touched the wall. I saw her eyes close, then spring open. "I can read it like it has a real history. For one thing, this isn't Tempus. This is a different mountain. This is one called...Mount Obitus."

"This mural's a psychic vision?" I had flesh me ask, trying to actively participate because that's the feedback I always got in class and I know people prefer it. Active participation. But the curve of her shoulder and the light on the skin of her neck distracted me, and flesh me was squirming and needed attention. It was a polarity thing.

"Yes. It's like an actual psychic vision but painted on a wall," she said. "Like time flowed through your brush and made history on this wall. This is a real thing. However you painted this, *that's* what the Paths of time are made of. Time."

I had flesh me nod, really trying to participate, and thought he looked wise, like hermits who stumble from forests starving and battling hallucinations look, suffused with wisdom. Caroline wasn't fooled by him.

"And you can read this? Psychically?" I had him ask. She nodded. She's started looking honestly amazed.

"Absolutely. We're looking down here, off the top of Mount Obitus, and out beyond the throne, that's the story of the Ghost War." She was more and more entranced. "Oh my god Ash, it is a *crazy* story. Veronica always hoped I'd find the Ghost War on the Paths, but I had nothing to touch. Now you just painted it."

"So you and Veronica are working on something together?" Flesh me made it sound all peevish and pouty, he's such a child. "I wish she'd leave us alone."

"This was before I even met you," Caroline laughed. "She's nice."

"Sometimes I wish she'd find a different hobby."

"What's about the *Ghost War* now?" Nella suddenly airdropped, right in front of flesh me, who startled and slipped to the floor. "You paint'n the Ghost War up there'n don't tell anyone?"

"You all right, Ash?" Caroline asked flesh me as he rocked back up. She hadn't heard the air talking.

"Nella *please* don't do that to him," I had him say. Poor guy. He'd really had a day.

"Come down're," Nella ordered flesh me. "If this's'th Ghost War then its *unbelievably* important shit."

"I don't know what it is," I had flesh me complain. Caroline looked more and more puzzled by flesh me talking to nothing, but didn't look at all worried. Caroline had so much misplaced confidence in me, it made my heart glow.

"Be audible," flesh me yelled at Nella, "Caroline thinks I'm crazy."

"Crazy's a big part of your appeal," Caroline nodded.

Nella started broadcasting everywhere, "Good't meet you Caroline," Nella said, "I'm Nella."

Caroline's eyes widened. She looked around, and back to flesh me who was once again reaching for her hair. Back *down*, I told him. Down *down*. It's pathetic, honestly, all the reacfhing. Like an animal. But Caroline reminded us both of campfires and candle-lit dinners and a burning sun setting over a beach, and flesh me was only semi-sentient and at least a little bit afflicted by our Polarity issue. It was all just suffering for him. Thankfully he didn't care.

"Veronica's down're," Nella continued. "The Ghost War...you guys that's super important, there's people, Veronica and everybody, hearing *anything* about this's amazing."

"Is she a ghost?" Caroline asked flesh me about Nella.

"God no," he said. "Just a monk. She lives with the monks in my office."

"Veronica says come'n down fast Asher, *fast*." Nella said. Caroline absolutely loved hearing voices come from the air where nobody was, you could see it. "And Veronica says," Nella said, in Veronica's voice, *"please join us, Caroline. And PUT THE NECKLACE ON Mr. Gale."*

Flesh me, I noticed, still had Veronica's necklace in his hand, gripped like forge iron. It was going nowhere for the moment.

"Veronica you're not my mother," flesh me forwarded, "I don't need your instructions!"

I was way off balance here, the polarity thing was dinging me, and I had a decision to make and those are things I always regret later. Should I bring Caroline downstairs into this weirdness? I felt like the guard at the gate to crazy city. Did you open the gate and let your girlfriend in under these circumstances? Was that the responsible thing?

"You really think it's the Ghost War?" I had flesh me ask Caroline.

She couldn't stop studying it. "Yep. This story's full of curses, betrayals, ghosts and people, everything blasted apart, it's wild, it's... hard to believe. Do you want me to read this for you?"

"The wall?"

"The ancient history of the picture you just painted." She loved this. "Crazy, right?"

Nella airdropped Veronica's voice again, or maybe this actually was Veronica calling, "Wait, Caroline! You can read an object only once, yes?"

"That's the way it works," Caroline nodded.

"Then please. Let us all hear. We must record what you envision."

"That's okay with me," Caroline said, and she was just instantly comfortable having most of her conversations to thin air. Maybe it was a Monarch thing. Assessing the situation and commandeering it.

"But it's Ash's reading, so it's up to him," she told us all.

I made flesh me sigh, though ghost me felt no benefit. I stood him up.

"I'm sorry I got you into this," I had him tell Caroline. "After you're done reading for everyone do you want to go to the beach and find sand dollars?"

She nodded. None of my craziness had changed her ideas about me. Just confirmed them, apparently. On our first and only date I'd left her in the middle of a police yard to get interviewed about a murder, so it's not like she hadn't had warnings. But she liked it. It was hard to understand.

I flesh led us toward the front door. Flesh me, then Caroline, then ghost me bringing up the rear. So far neither of us had said a word about the dead lawyer, which was sad, but sometimes the world just goes by so fast the dead lawyers fall by the wayside.

Still she stopped and gave him a look, and shook her head. She didn't touch him but she knew he was dead.

"I have to tell you something," I made flesh me say. "I feel really bad."

She watched flesh me, waiting.

"This lawyer. I'm not trying to defend my...well here it is. I was the one who killed him." Flesh me pointed at Victors. "I know, I promised I wouldn't kill anyone. I wish it hadn't happened."

"How'd you kill him?"

"With the picture. The mural."

"Oh, Ash," she said. She had semi-sparkle eye shadow, dusted so light it hardly existed, and it caught the sun off the ocean as she faced me. "Don't get a complex for god's sake. I said don't *murder* anyone. Sometimes people die. That's not your fault."

"Well that's true. I mean I didn't *murder* him. I just killed him."

"That's what I'm saying."

"I'm not a murderer."

"No you're not, baby."

She was so encouraging and certain it made everything perfect, for just that single moment, both of us so convinced I wasn't a murderer. It was peak Asher.

I had flesh me wheel Victors out of the penthouse so I looked like I was taking responsibility, now that I knew I didn't have any. Caroline followed. Ghost me came last. Feeling very conscientious and adult I had flesh me lock the door behind him to prevent further killing. Flesh me and flesh Victors and flesh Caroline reached the elevator and I hung waiting in ghost me while flesh me pushed the button he'd learned about.

Like an afterthought, Caroline said, "You're not one, but please be careful don't *become* a murderer."

I had flesh me say, "Got it. All the murder advice is super useful, by the way."

"You'd be surprised how fast murders happen is all I'm saying. Especially for someone impulsive the way you are."

I nodded him again. I was impulsive, that was true. The elevator opened. Flesh Victors and flesh me and ghost me and Caroline all rolled in.

When the doors closed I was suddenly out of range of Victors' ghost and my two bodies collected back into one. Snap. The first thing I felt was shock, and my flesh body twisting like a supernatural force bending me. I thought *Oh shit I'm standing one foot from Caroline*, and I realized, holy fuck, flesh me had been showing *incredible restraint* if this was what it'd been like because *all I wanted to do* was touch her hair. And the rest of her.

I reached.

She gasped, grabbing her chest, her crystal.

"Caroline," I rasped, turning, "oh god."

My own crystal froze the skin on my chest but it wasn't enough to stop me. The fondness and curiosity in Caroline's eyes became open heat, drove into me as she watched my hands coming, hands she wanted on her, we were lovers in an elevator at the end of the world about to touch, at last. Her eyes closed. Her breath caught.

"Ash," she whispered, "Ash your necklace," as she reached to hold me.

I don't know how or why I did it but it was mostly for her, I wrenched, dropped the necklace in my fist over my head and it stopped us. So we didn't touch. The terrible, fatal act averted. Postponed. Caroline grabbed her stomach and slid against the wall. I went the other way, bumping the wheelchair and toppling, gasping to the floor.

When the door opened, monks and my sister looked in on us on the ground. The monks rushed to help me but Amelia shouted, *no touching*, so they helped Caroline instead. The same thing had happened to Caroline in Los Angeles. Being pulled away from each other out of elevators seemed like one of our things. That and not touching.

Amelia stepped into the car and bent next to me. She looked very sorry for me. Probably not as sorry as I was. I can be pretty sorry. The doors closed.

The elevator went down and neither of us stopped it. Amelia was too tired and I didn't care. I found myself riding inside a metaphor for my life with all the up and down and over and over and it's never me who chooses the floor. Amelia spent a moment looking at Victors in his wheelchair, then turned to me.

"What are we going to do with you Ash?" she sorrowed.

She wanted to do something. I could see it, something normal, like put her arm around me, but she couldn't. We rode until the doors opened in the lobby. And there was Phil, pants rolled up, a trail of grape juice behind him, waiting outside the doors, drying his feet with a towel. We watched him bend to his tub to pull it into the car then stop when he noticed the car had people.

"Hey boss...bossanova," he said, then tried to distract me with a salute.

"Phil," I shouted, pointing up, "you let *another* person in the building!"

"Well yeah, I let *Caroline* in, but she's psychic."

"Yeah, but she's totally a *person* isn't she?"

"Yeah but not a *customer*. Plus I know her because she once psychically found my mixing bowl. Are you getting out?"

"No," I said, sad. "I'm here for good."

"Hey! There's that lawyer," he told me, pointing at Victors. I nodded.

"He needs to go to the hospital," I told Phil. "Who's that Skysill messenger lady?"

"Skysill's Best Courier! Minnie could *totally* run the lawyer to the hospital! Rush job?"

"Probably not," I said. "Hey. Who's best in the Bradley Family at following instructions? Better than you, let's say?"

"What kind of instructions?"

"For instance, *keep people out of the building.* Are you the best?"

"God no. Haha! No, the best is Saanvi," he said. "Floor two, Best Beach Architects."

"Would Saanvi watch the front door for us?"

"She'd *love* to!"

"Remind me, what's the reason we can't just lock the front door?"

"You lost the keys."

"Right. Then call Saanvi. Tell her if she keeps people out I'll give her a break on rent."

Phil thought my rent idea was hilarious. He was laughing as he reached into the elevator to ease Victors out, and after that, he shook his head and kept laughing. His eyes watered. Amelia was confused. I wondered if Phil's grapes had fermented early. He was still chuckling as the doors started closing.

"Oh wait," he yelped, and using his hand he stopped the doors, "Dale got the lowdown on your shootout house."

"Shootout house?" Amelia asked. She prefers a different pace than this.

"Keep up," I told her. "Dale, from Finances with Dale, on the second floor. He knows all the paperwork and addresses, he's a wizard."

"Not a real one," Phil assured her. I motioned that he should tell me everything. He grabbed the radio clipped to his pants and shook and hit it against the elevator until it sprang into action and then pushed its button.

"Finance," he said. "This is Hawaii, do you copy?"

"I do copy, Finance are we going to brunch now? Over?" Dale's voice was thin. He sounded hungry.

"Negative Finance I ate grapes but the big guy's here and wants your report, over."

"Roger Finance hey big guy are you really there? Over?" Dale asked.

I said yes I was. Phil thrust the radio through the elevator doors so I could hear, which wasn't necessary and made Amelia uncomfortable, while Dale squawked his report.

"The warehouse in question is leased through a shell company," Dale informed us, like he was reading documents, "and *that* lease flows through four other shell companies, goes around a few times... *but*. At the end there's Skysill Holdings, and the trustee is someone... here in town... ah, named Roman Sutherland. He owns the company that leases the warehouse. He owns a gallery in the Square on the Sea and some other properties, but no other shootouts I could find. That's my report. Is it okay? Over?"

I gave a thumbs up, and Phil jerked his hand out just as the doors closed. We heard Phil signing off as the elevator started rising. Amelia had pushed the button this time. I was slouched in my corner. Her look said, I'm a complete mystery to her. She raised an eyebrow in our childhood sign for WTF?

"Roman's hiding Higher paint," I explained to her. "It's in a warehouse."

"How do you know?"

"I stole some. I think he's involved in all of this. Could he be *Fabrica*, like his apprentices?"

She shook her head. "Veronica suspected him since he's in the middle of all the money. But we know he's not wearing a neutral crystal—people see him sunbathing—which means he can't be tapped."

"I don't trust him."

"All he cares about is money. He bailed you out of jail half a dozen times. He likes you."

"Like I said I don't trust him."

The elevator squeaked its way upward, so slow it left time for many conversational branches. The elevator was probably slower than the stairs. I cleared my throat.

"All...everything you said about my paintings," I said. "Is that real?"

"It's real, Ash."

I found it possible to believe that my paintings had done tricks, because I'd seen with my own eyes a picture I'd painted—by proxy—with the power to kill a lawyer. But belief is the starving stepchild of understanding. You have to keep feeding it.

"*How?*" I demanded, weak. "*How* did I do what you're saying?"

"No one could ever say. You hardly believed it was real, since the effect was always different. Anyone who saw your work though...we went places, found things...I remember one painting. An apple. When we looked at it, all our clothes turned red. *Permanently.* Another one of a train, when we got close we instantly reappeared five feet away. Over and over. But the effects would fade, and you wondered...could that even have been real? Ash, listen, how could you...is this really the Ghost War you painted?"

"I have no idea. Caroline thinks so."

"She's not *sighted.* How can she even *see* it?"

I shrugged. "I'm going to show her some paintings later and maybe find out."

The elevator stopped. Amelia held the doors while I struggled up off the floor, then she urged me the direction of New Dwayne, standing guard outside Asher Gale's office, pretending I didn't exist. My relationship with New Dwayne was my most stable one. I needed someone like New Dwayne for the front lobby of the Bradley.

He let us into the office, a little grudging in my case, and once inside I was surprised to see they'd redecorated. *Again.* A brand new theme organized the space: *Fabrica* metaverse.

Instead of walls and a ceiling there spread only deepest, inkiest space, or the world's thickest blackout curtains, like mattresses of anti-matter blacking out reality. Glow balls of *farewell* hung, casting gas lamp circles every few feet on a rectangular perimeter where I thought there was—used to be?—an office, with visible spectrum orange lines vibrating out beneath our feet to bend up non-existent walls past where there'd been a ceiling, to intertwine in a mesh high above our heads. Like ribbons around a package of nothing. In the farthest corner monks squatted around Peter, who was agitated, rocking, sitting up, laying back down.

In the middle of the room—I decided to call it a room because of my limited imagination, but it wasn't a room—Caroline sat in Asher Gale's reception chair. There was no desk, just a chair. And all the orange light strips originated below that chair, and a perfect half-globe of *farewell* was suspended over her head. Like she was the bullseye on a target.

Amelia froze, bewildered when she saw it all, but bewilderment never affects me. Veronica was saying something to Caroline and had *farewell* streaming off her palms, and her eyes were fully counter crossed, and my stomach just dropped.

"No," I yelled, rushing in, "hey!"

Caroline, calm and intrigued, was gazing at the visible spectrum orange stripping through the ceiling. Veronica heard me, and turned, and looked used up and loose at the same time, like unspooled yarn. Her eyes were white and wide and it wasn't clear if she realized she had them open. Her clothes askew. Like she had a button missing, or she'd just been tossed in a judo throw.

"Stop!" I demanded. "No glowing Caroline are you fucking kidding me? What do you think you're *doing*?"

Veronica blinked, no pupils, then turned away and added more *farewell* to the crown. Every move she made was fast and short. Her breath was fast and short. She looked flushed and sweat filmed her neck. She looked like a person working furiously at something and barely pulling it off.

"I have not *compelled* Caroline," she told me absently, "if that is what you are yelling about."

I waved my hand through the *light* bowl hanging over Caroline and asked, "Oh *yeah*? What's *this*?" because I'm adept at words.

"This," she said, gesturing everywhere, "is an inclusion."

"No Veronica," Amelia said. She'd come to stand with us, her bewilderment become concern. "Wait for Willametta."

"I cannot reach Willametta," Veronica said without interrupting her preparations. Her full-on white eye look was just wrong, we all saw it. But Caroline took Veronica's behavior right in stride. I wondered, was my girlfriend a little bit of a thrill seeker? I was increasingly concerned about her judgment, while at the same time realizing her judgment formed the basis of our relationship. I was conflicted.

"It's okay," Caroline told me. "She says there's no danger."

"But that's not true!" Amy insisted.

"There is no danger to *Caroline*," Veronica insisted back. For just a moment she stopped and her pupils flipped into view, but a second later disappeared again. "I cannot reach any of the five leaders. They may be closeted in negotiations. But it does not matter. Any information on the Ghost War must be made available immediately, to every member of every Family, regardless of what the *administrators* are doing. With this inclusion, whatever Caroline knows can be captured, parsed, expanded and relayed to the Families. Everywhere. People must be told—Aeternus is *here*."

Now that I knew what to look for, I saw it in every move Veronica made—the missing family twist. The million mile stare. The denial. This wasn't about Aeternus. This was about the empty picture frame you carry around after someone's gone forever too soon. I wondered how Veronica's empty memory compared to mine. I thought hers might be as bad. That's pretty rare.

"Caroline," Amelia said, turning from Veronica with a spit of anger, "do you mind, I'd like to talk to Veronica for a second."

"This is *important*," Veronica snapped, "Amelia, stop!"

Caroline rose from the chair, her head piercing the *farewell* crown without effect. "No worries. You two talk."

"Can I show you a few paintings?" I sotto voiced to Caroline. "Out in the hall?"

"Good idea, out in the hall," Caroline agreed.

Amelia started arguing with Veronica as Caroline left. I told her I'd be right out then ducked into the admiral's office. The monks had stuffed everything that could distract a person from meditation into that little room. These monks had no respect for art—it was awesome. My forgeries were tossed around, on top of and underneath other junk, like keyboards and chairs. Behind a rolled carpet I found the Gale family collection, the paintings Celine had delivered to me the week before. I grabbed three specific ones. As I left I saw Veronica ignoring Amelia, and Amelia losing her shit.

In the hall Caroline waited, talking to New Dwayne. He looked very friendly until he saw me and clammed up. All because I couldn't remember his name? I mean what am I a card catalog? There're too many names. I encouraged Caroline to follow me with my paintings toward the elevator where we could have the illusion of privacy, which is the best you could hope for in this building.

"What are we doing?" she wondered. It was distracting how she walked beside me. Her eyes and the freckles between her eyes were distracting, her teeth distracted me when I saw them, I felt like I might be obsessing on her face. Her face was slightly asymmetrical. I couldn't get enough of it.

"Let's go over by the elevator," I explained, "to look at these."

"I thought paintings was an excuse so they could fight," Caroline complimented me, "but you've got real paintings! This is so nice. With these new necklaces I have no idea what's on in your mind. I like it."

"I like how you appreciate me for my mind. It's a refreshing change."

"Well just so you know, I also appreciate how you fill out those Hawaiian short pants. It's hard not to stare."

"I noticed. I like how you say *short pants*, where some girls just say *shorts*, which obviously leaves too much open to interpretation."

As I stopped us at the elevator, I appreciated the way, thanks to the new crystals, I could imagine us having no clothes on right there by the ashcan and really fill in the details and there was no ice bomb on my chest. I pulled it out, the new crystal I'd put on in the elevator, darker and rougher laying in my palm alongside the first. It was more primitive.

I looked back to Caroline. She let me watch her. She knew what I was thinking. She was expecting something.

"We still can't touch, right?" I double-checked.

"According to Veronica that'll kill us. But at least we can talk in person now. And when I think about you naked I don't get lust nausea." She sighed. "Maybe that's all we'll *ever* have, talk and imagine each other naked. I still like it though. Do you?"

"It's the highlight of my every single day," I told her.

I set the canvases against the wall, facing away from us.

"Here's my plan," I started. "I want to show you these paintings and maybe figure out how you're *seeing* the mural up there. Then I want to imagine you're naked while we talk some more."

"Okay," she sighed, and smiled. "I'll make it easy to imagine."

I didn't know how it could get any easier, but I had faith in her. So I turned the first picture to face us.

It was a work by Marlon Gale, my nominal father. In visible spectrum oil paint, a view of the city of Skysill Beach looking east from the boardwalk. From the way the pigment had oxidized I estimated it was finished forty-five years earlier. He'd painted a row of downtown buildings. unchanged from the way they looked today, a study of sunset refracted off west facing windows. Dusk in a California beach town. All the light transparent in broad, pale sheets, astonishingly present, day fading to evening. He'd been playing with subshade crimsons in the deep shadows.

For a moment it shook me. I'd never really looked at my parents' paintings. After they'd left I'd pretended I didn't care. Like I didn't have parents. I hadn't really known the kind of brilliance my father had been capable of. It was hard to talk. Thankfully that never lasts with me.

"What do you see?" I asked Caroline.

"It's Skysill, by Lili's cafe. It's beautiful. Did you paint this?"

"No, this was my, you know...my dad."

"I love it."

"And what do you see in...this area? You see the dog here?"

My dad, Marlon or whoever, had placed a dog in one purple shadow, a beach stray, shaggy, in bone-magenta sub-shades. Something only the *sighted* had enough resolution to detect. Caroline squinted where I pointed. She shook her head.

"I see a shadow on the side of the building. Sort of purple?"

"That's good. That's normal. It's a dog in sub shades."

"Sub shades?"

"Like, differences in color so small, your eyes don't even see it, but to me it's as clear as black and white."

She peered closer. I flipped the second picture.

"Try this one."

This painting was Katerina Gale's. My mom or whoever. It was a painting of a single wave, cresting near the main beach, flecks of sand and kelp suspended in water, luminous viridian with sunlight glowing from one side to the other. The palette was sage greens and steel blues and they broke solar energy in sub-shade patterns that whirled and repeated on the water. The wave tore you, bore down on you, like it'd drown you. I started wishing I hadn't put off appreciating these for so many years. Carolyn gasped.

"Wow," she said.

I nodded. "It's Katerina, you know, the lady who used to be my mom."

"She's not?"

"Now we don't know who my mom was."

"Katerina sure *felt* like she was your mom in my vision with Celine."

I stared at the picture with a strange sense that something was wrong. I tried to shake the sense as I pointed out the repeating sub-shade patterns on the waves, and asked Caroline about them. They were all invisible to her, the way they were supposed to be.

And then, bending close, I saw what was wrong with the painting—it was a forgery.

Or a half forgery? The bulk of it, the water, the gesture, the sky, those were all in Katerina's hand. But the sub-shades were done in a second hand. My father's. It was an extraordinary forgery. You'd never have noticed without my congenital suspicion and hyperactive rods and cones. Marlon Gale, disguising his own hand, had overlaid sub-shades onto a finished painting of Katerina's. None of the sub-shades anywhere in the picture were hers. Had it been a collaboration of some kind? No. Hers was the only signature.

I was determined to conclude my current mystery-in-progress before starting any new mystery having to do with my ex-father forging my ex-mother's paintings, so I left the wave painting and flipped the last canvas. I stepped back. This one was mine. Maybe I'd been thirteen. It was mostly figurative, a man with a book that seemed to be decomposing in his hands, all in tones of *choke* and *bleed*. It was deft and so, so certain. And supposedly, right after it had been painted, it'd exerted some kind of effect.

When I looked at it with Caroline, it might have been someone else's work. I couldn't remember doing it. But this was the same hand flesh me had used on the penthouse mural. So. Some version of me had painted both.

"What do you see here?" I asked, pointing.

"Nothing," she told me. "Is there supposed to be something?"

"This one's all ultraviolet. You're not *sighted,* you can't see ultra-violet. So that's normal too. But the one upstairs is ultraviolet. The Ghost War. I don't get it. How come you see that?"

"Whatever you did up there's totally different. You painted that with *time.*"

I waited a minute to think of a better explanation. Then I sighed.

"So I guess it's *dominion,*" I admitted—the conclusion I'd

expected but not the one I'd wanted. The one I wanted was that this was all a dream and I was going to wake up owning a bar.

"*Dominion?*"

"You're calling it time. When that mural up there was painted, by whoever painted it, *dominion* was pumping through the brush. Whatever other color was used, every inch of it's mixed with *dominion.* So I guess you see *dominion.*"

All the talk of *dominion*—it reminded me of the gift I'd sculpted for her. I reached into my pocket, felt around the melted key blob and the phone, and I pulled out the glowing necklace.

Caroline's eyes went wide and very still. Long seconds passed before she spoke.

"Ash," she breathed, "you made me a *time cat?*"

Dominion blasted off the figurine swinging between my fingers. I held the cat out, dropped him in her palm. She was more tentative than I'd ever seen her. She stared, hardly moving, then looked back up with tears in her eyes. Her free hand began picking the hem of her good t-shirt. She was actually shaking a little, shaking her head.

"What'd I do?" I asked, like I'm trained to.

"It's just..." she almost sobbed. It was very sudden. Oh how I wished for telepathy right then. Because she was a total mystery.

"I'm sorry," I said.

"Sometimes I miss him, I guess. I have issues, Ash. I told you I'm crazy. Don't worry," she wiped a tear and tried a smile. The cat on the necklace was a lodestone she couldn't look away from. "He didn't look like this when I saw him with telepathy. In person...it's like you broke a piece off the Paths of Time, just so I could wear it."

"We're talking about *dominion,* right? You can see it glowing? Like you see time? So does that mean that *dominion...is* time?"

She hung the cat around her throat. It was her third or fourth necklace, I was losing track. I probably should have made her an anklet. She didn't seem to mind. She stared down at it. "It's incredible," she whispered. "Glowing with *time.* Do you always see time like this? Is it something you can just...?" she looked at me, there was something new in her eyes, "... just hold in your hand?"

"All I know," I tried explaining, which is a known shortcoming of mine but I had to try, for Caroline's sake, "is that this whole town's lousy with whatever that is, I call it *dominion* but I'm open to other names. It's everywhere, it's in the ghosts, the mountains, sometimes clouds of it melt my keys, sometimes—I've seen it just washing around. Aimless. Like it's feeling out the place. Does any of that make sense to you?"

There's just no way to overstate how electrifying it is being taken seriously by a girl like Caroline. I watched her organize all the pieces of all my ideas in her mind.

"All I'm sure of," she replied, "is you painted the Ghost War like a psychic vision—a real object with a real story to read. To me it looks like something painted the—color I guess?—of time. But that's crazy. What is going on with us, Ash?"

"Everybody back to'th office," slurred Nella in the air. "Story time."

I'd lost track of where we even were, listening to Caroline take me seriously was that distracting, plus I have the attention span issue. I glanced down the hall toward the office where New Dwayne stood, gesturing us to hurry. Apparently the moment had come to hear whatever crazy story I'd somehow painted myself into the middle of. It's just endless, this shit.

I left the canvases on the floor. I'd let the janitor deal with them after I asked Phil if we had a janitor. I tried walking slower with Caroline. I had a feeling we were getting closer to crossing the kind of line you can't un-cross.

"This feels normal right?" I asked hopefully, as got near New Dwayne. "Like two normal people walking in a hallway? I know that's what you want."

"Imagine if we could hold hands?" she said. "Shay made these crystals just for us, just for close up. Veronica says they might get unstable when we're farther apart. But that's okay. This is perfect.

You know what I keep thinking about? Your mom's painting. That wave. It's so beautiful."

"I don't think she's my mom," I shrugged. I also didn't think she'd painted it, whoever she was. In any case it was clear she'd only painted some of it. The visible spectrum parts. Why had Marlon Gale forged parts of his wife's painting?

We reached the office door just as New Dwayne began deep breathing, arm waving, and then Peter's voice came rolling out deep as underground trains, rattling the floor.

"He's here," we heard Peter lamenting. "He's here now, here to sample us. The ghost. The ghost is finally here."

CHAPTER

TWELVE

Peter burst through the door and without stopping turned toward the stairwell—I stumbled sideways to avoid touching him. Nella and the monks boiled out after him as I yelled, "What is it now?"

"He hears something," Nella told me as she went past, and for once she didn't sound loaded. I hardly recognized her. "We don't hear it but if it's...the ghost..."

"Where's he going?" I called as Peter's skinny frame scampered down the hall. All the monks followed. He seemed full of energy, like an electrified cadaver.

"Don't know," she called back, "but I'm not letting him go alone."

"I'll come," I decided.

But Nella stopped and pointed inside.

"No," she said, "stay, help Veronica."

"Help her *what*?" By this time Nella was all the way down the hall, though her voice hadn't moved.

"They're arguing," her voice said, "go figure it out."

I shook my head. Figure it out? Did she think she was talking to someone else? Before I could protest more she'd disappeared, diving through the stairwell door after Peter, the rest of the monks trailing.

Suddenly the office door jerked wide. Veronica faced us, white eyed. Not stable.

"Come," she said, stepping back inside. I caught the door before it closed and led Caroline through. It was my job to go first, since it was my name on the door and they were all probably my problems, all happening in what had officially become my building right about the time I killed my legal counsel.

The office had been transformed again. Caroline's breath caught.

"It's Nevada," she whispered.

Evening landscape vanished to all sides of us. It was an incredible illusion. I looked at stars in a midnight sky, then dark horizon hills, at a land thick with sage, riven by shallow gullies. I wasn't just seeing it. I was experiencing the *knowledge* of it. *farewell* was creating this scene. In my head. I smelled sage, but it wasn't just smell. I heard wind, dry and chilled, but I wasn't only hearing. It was knowledge of wind. Like I had a chip in my brain feeding me experience. It was a druggy feeling.

The floor of the office was strewn with hard stones. We walked among them and I had knowledge of them, a phrase I was getting tired of thinking, knowledge of rough desert pebbles crunching under my feet. A campfire crackled to the right on a rise. In the middle of what had been Asher Gale's office stood the swivel chair from reception. Above that was the *farewell* half globe, shimmering.

Amelia waited on a slab of stone to the left, fists balled, tears on her face. Furious. Caroline turned, staring.

"This is out behind my old house..." Caroline whispered, "...where I grew up. My house was that way...down there's the river, the road where..."

"Ash," Amelia said, still staring at Veronica, "don't let her do it."

"I'm not the boss of anybody," I said. "Shouldn't we talk about Peter for a second?"

"Yes!" Amelia said. "Peter's out looking for the ghost. If Aeternus is here this is the *worst possible time* to risk an inclusion this big. She's not thinking straight. Look at her! Look at her eyes!"

Amy was pointing to Veronica, who stood by the chair with flickers of *farewell* running up her arms in glowing vines, lighting the dark, in a white smock, with white eyes, white hair disheveled, like a crazy nurse who'd just been struck by lightning.

"Yeah," I said, "the eyes are off-putting."

"Caroline," Veronica said, "please sit. We should begin the reading as soon as possible."

"Caroline," Amelia said, looking at her, "don't do it, help me stop this."

"It's Asher's reading," Caroline said, sorrowful but certain, like a surgeon passing on the bad news, "I can only do this once. There are rules and I'm not in charge. When and where's his decision."

"Aeternus could come after her," Amy said to me. "Don't you... "

"Amelia stop," Veronica interrupted, "the cage cup was a setback to his power—"

"Yes!" Amelia interjected, "and now there are other cups and we don't know—"

"—yes *exactly*! We must press our advantage while we can!"

"I'm not letting you do this," Amelia cried, "Seamus would—"

"It is *not your decision*!" Veronica screamed. Absolutely screamed.

It stunned Amelia. It stunned us all. Up to this point Veronica's whole deal had been how she was subtler than the rest of us. I'd been through bloody, terrifying battles with her where she hardly raised her voice.

After she screamed Veronica ignored Amy and came for me. Amy's fury stalled and I saw dread grow in its place. I backed away as Veronica came closer.

"This may be your reading," Veronica said to me, egg whites blinking, "but this is *everyone's fight*. Yes. There *is* some chance I will draw Aeternus. To *me*. But only a chance. It is impossible to know. What we *do* know is that Aeternus has worked tirelessly, across eons, to keep information about the Ghost War hidden. He used Auditus to obscure the quorums, gathered psychics so the Paths cannot be walked where his secrets are buried. We have a chance, here and now, to *see* the thing the Five Families have searched through history to find. Everything..." Veronica's voice caught, she swallowed, went on, "...everything I have done... I had a son Asher. He died...because... the ghost rules us through *fear*. Someone must stand up! It cannot only be the ones we have lost. It must be all of us!"

By the end she wasn't looking at me at all and I'd pretty much decided she'd lost her mind, and that Amelia was right, when a sudden wash of *dominion* colored the high stars, falling onto the hills and the brush, and I popped out the top of my skull.

Several ghosts shimmered into place in our desert landscape illusion. Samantha was there, and some dead monks. They circled the fire, their right hands out, facing flesh me. Flesh me put his own arm out and stepped toward the nearest monk, a skinny one holding a sock, because all flesh me wanted was to send the skinny monk to ghost retirement. I had to jerk him back. I'd been treating him a little rough, I knew, but this was not the time for exorcisms. One disorienting crisis at a time is all I can handle.

Suddenly Samantha disappeared from beside the fire. A second later she appeared beside Caroline. I swung ghost me behind flesh me to watch. Samantha floated, slightly overlapping Caroline's shoe, then disappeared—and this time she appeared beside the swivel chair, slightly overlapping one roller. A second later she came back to Caroline. Then back to the chair. She did it once more, to make her point clear, then flickered to rejoin the other ghosts around the fire. It was a ghost message: Caroline. Chair.

Caroline was looking at flesh me, biting her lip.

"Thoughts?" She asked.

"The ghosts have opinions," I had him admit. I knew what we had to do, and at that moment I saw flesh me—all on his own— shoot Amelia a guilty look. He has *zero* poker face. Amelia grew still. She'd been relying on me, she was realizing, which is a horrible thing for a person to realize.

"You're sure this isn't dangerous for Caroline?" I had flesh me ask Veronica.

"Yes," Veronica assured me. "Not for her."

"Then," I had flesh me say, "I guess, if someone was asking my opinion—even though why anyone would do that with my history I have no idea—it seems like we're supposed to do Veronica's thing. I'm sorry Ames. The ghosts are pretty clear. I owe this one ghost something."

"Okay then," Caroline said. She had complete faith in me, which was part of the horror.

Amelia's jaw pressed her lips bloodless. She nodded one time, like she was putting me in a new category. Not one of the good categories. Our unspoken rule had always been she'd give up having a reasonable life in order to keep me alive, and in return I'd let her make all our important decisions. But that'd been before the world got so full of ghosts and people trying to kill me and commitments pulling me different directions. I owed Samantha. Didn't I? Plus Veronica was an adult, and people always say that's an important distinction. Shouldn't she be allowed to take whatever risks she wanted?

Veronica moved Caroline to the seat.

"This environment was sourced from your mind," Veronica was telling Caroline, gesturing into the desert night. "In some ways you may think of this as your default internal state, projected outward. Once you begin your reading, the inclusion will begin imprinting, and the scene will change. Sit."

I kept flesh me quiet while Veronica got Caroline positioned, lowering the *light* headpiece over her skull. I swung ghost me up close to Samantha by the marshmallow cookout and ghosted: *This better not turn to shit Samantha. This better not be one of the things I regret doing. If anything happens to Veronica, Amelia's not going to forgive me. You understand? If I got your cryptic message wrong do something—flicker around. You hear me? I'm on a limb here. Don't fuck with me.*

Samantha didn't flicker.

"Are you ready?" Veronica asked Caroline.

"I am," Caroline said. "I just want to say...the reading from that painting's pretty wild. It isn't...normal. It's like some kind of fairy tale, with fantasy lands and, I don't know, mystic battles...but every word of it's reality, as the Paths of time have it written."

"Whatever you tell us will be more than any human has ever known before. Begin when you are ready."

Caroline nodded and closed her eyes, got in a few deep psychic breaths, while Veronica spread her arms. *Farewell*, the Higher *light* of knowledge, spread around her like a swarm of magic bees, in motes and flecks, surging to fill the room and obscure the people. If the inclusion Willametta had shown me was a candle, this was a forest burning.

Nevada vanished. A few hundred yards away and coming closer I saw the top of Mount Obitus as the painting showed it, sweeping closer like a helicopter tracking shot. The back of the throne grew as the shot brought us in and then the whole mountain top was flashing past and a landscape spread below, and I was diving from the sky. The ground rose toward me, the ground flesh me had painted, and I recognized features, hills, a riverbed, a structure. But this was the landscape altered. Instead of destruction, here there spread green forests, multihued cities, rivers and meadows, a land that glowed with color—visible spectrum and Higher.

I felt myself speeding above that land, over roads and fields. I glimpsed people in opalescent clothes, buildings of fantastical stone. And ghosts. Transparent ghosts, moving everywhere, interacting with people in cities, in villages. Cooperating.

A voice spoke that was like Caroline's, but which echoed softly with a note of ages past. The voice itself gave me a thrill. It was another of my girlfriend's undiscovered abilities. She was in her element here. Confident as a voice-over artist.

Once there was a world, like ours in some ways, that ended with a curse, said her voice, while the viewpoint sped, seemingly at random, through buildings, past island townships, over coliseums, into houses deep within forests. Everywhere you looked there was art. Painting, music, carving, exotic forms with no equivalent to art I knew, which the *inclusion* was interpreting for me as Art. And over everything there was Caroline. She was our captain in her cockpit.

In this world, creative power was the ultimate power. It was a world shared equally by people and ghosts, in peace and community. Until there came a time when people and ghosts fought a war, and then this land—which we can call the Undying Land, a land with no death, but <u>made</u> of death, in a way we cannot understand today—this world broke, and was transformed. And became our own world.

The people of the Undying Land perceived their world with the senses we know today, the five, but not individually. The people here did not even have names for sound, sight, taste, touch, or smell. For them, there was only one sense, the sum of all senses: Agape. Through Agape they perceived things incomprehensible to us today: ghosts, for one, and worlds beyond worlds. Through Agape, death and time were themselves only sensations, only sensory experiences, and the people manipulated both death and time to create extraordinary works.

People and ghosts lived together in the Undying Land, their lifecycles dependent upon each other, but they perceived the world very differently. Ghosts had supremely limited senses. They heard only distant echoes, saw nothing but foggy visions. But there is always balance, so where ghosts lacked Agape, they possessed another power: the power to curse.

A ghost curse was not intrinsically good or bad, just a powerful, flexible tool. While ghosts did hurl curses against the shape-shifting creatures who prowled their borders, those battles were not considered the highest or the best use of this power. There was nothing a ghost could not achieve with a curse; ghosts used curses to build, to create their own magnificent works of art. Though a curse was a double-edged blade—as the Ghost War so tragically proved—because every curse came with a re-curse. A side effect. An unpredictable, concurrent result. Most re-curses were so small they were never felt. Some were even desirable. But some could be dramatic and destructive.

The curse that ended the world was so powerful, the re-curse from it holds our own universe trapped to this very day.

But one thing remains the same in both the vanished Undying Land and our own world: the entwined nature of ghosts and people. It is this; that a ghost is not the result of a person dying, or an artifact of the death of living bodies. Ghosts are living creatures entirely separate from people. People and ghosts are symbiotically dependent races, and every time a person is born, a ghost is drawn into that living body, until the body dies and the ghost is released again. Ghosts provide the spark that lights human consciousness. People empower ghosts with sensory experience. One life form cannot exist without the other. It was true in the Undying Land and it is true in ours. Though this truth is hidden.

As I listened to Caroline the scene focused tightly on a single home, filled with art of all kinds created by the family living there, parents, grandparents, children. I saw one of the eldest people in a bed, attended by the rest of the family. A deathbed. And when the predictable happened I saw a ghost emerge from his body.

Frozen, one arm extended, holding a wooden carving.

Death was known only as a transition of forms. This transition was celebrated, and after the transition family and friends gathered to recount stories, and one story would set the ghost free, to dive once more into the great sea of ghosts, to be cleansed and then return to the world.

I watched as this spirit unfroze, became fully mobile, still a ghost but moving like a human, and just carried on interacting with the family. And at fast forward speed we followed the same ghost through generations, back and forth, because time was just a sense for them, and the ghost was many places at one time, newborn after newborn. And all of it almost made sense to me, mostly I think because Caroline was so good at telling it.

Sometimes, though, no family or friend came forward to celebrate the transition, because the dead person didn't have family, or sometimes they existed but didn't care—this was not a land free of spite, loneliness, or fear, in those ways it was exactly like our world. Sometimes people simply refused to recount the ghost's story, and in the Undying Land, this usually happened because of a clash of artistic ideas. When it did happen, the ghost lingered in the world, becoming a haunt. Out of place, disruptive, and filled with longing.

And then an Inmortalis would be called.

At the top of a distant hill, I saw a man in a cloak with a staff. The *inclusion* followed him as he journeyed through the Undying Land, through forests and mountain ranges, vast metropolises and temple cities. He cycled between five separate locations. Sacred places of some kind. At each of the five sacred spots was a glowing stone.

Inmortalis used shards of the five Keystones to commune with haunts, learn their stories, and release them. A similar group existed among ghosts, the Viaticus, because sometimes a ghost got stuck transitioning into a baby or became lost, a poltergeist, and the Viaticus summoned them back. Everything in the Undying Land was dependent on this transformative cycle between the species.

Inmortalis all shared a certain flexible and indomitable spirit and were often outsiders. They were like priests, and also like plumbers since an Inmortalis was only summoned if people had a problem. The Inmortalis practice tainted them in some way. Their Agape was thought of as distasteful, almost shameful. Inmortalis had their own arts and seldom shared them.

In the last days of the Undying Land there lived an Inmortalis called Nolear Fa. Nolear Fa dreamed of being more than Inmortalis. His art was performative. Theatrical. Among the Inmortalis he was considered a great Agape playwright. But Nolear Fa dreamed of respect and recognition from the wider world, and of the power that would come with it. Ghosts were drawn to successful Agape artists and cursed them even more powerfully. There was one ghost in particular he craved attention from.

The world, however, was never interested in Nolear Fa as a playwright. Only as an Inmortalis. And so, slowly, he grew bitter. Through all his years he offered play after play, placing them out like shards of himself, but failed to find success. His youth passed, his middle years, and recognition never came. His work grew darker and angrier and his rancor swelled as his own transition approached. He neglected his Inmortalis duties. He began to blame the ghosts themselves for not cursing him to success. Finally, he stopped releasing haunts at all. It was easier, and more darkly satisfying, to hide them, imprison them, and abandon them.

Caroline's voice faded for a moment as I watched Nolear Fa, bearded, heavy eyed, wielding staff and stone to shepherd haunts away from the world, into the hills where a deep cave slowly filled with them.

Spirit after spirit he imprisoned. As he came closer to his transition and his bitterness deepened, and his hate for them grew, that hate turned to madness. Or maybe it had always been madness. He viewed his art as a failed project, and he blamed the world for that. He blamed the ghosts.

And then, near Nolear Fa's final day, a world-renowned Agape artist transitioned, and ghosts and people gathered to release him with a story. Nolear Fa was drawn to this celebration. He was not welcome. He had not been asked. He would not be needed; but he appeared. Celebrants puzzled to see him, thinking surely at least one person among the great artist's friends would know the story that would bring release. How could an Inmortalis ever be needed? They began to drive him away.

And Nolear Fa, bitterness and pain outgrowing reason, used a long nursed, dark arcane power to destroy the spirit of this artist. To absorb it. His rage and hate had created such a hole inside him, the only thing that could fill it was a ghost.

This was a thing that had never been done. It was an atrocity, something so unthinkable it did not even have a name. It was not even a crime. And as it happened, no one noticed that Nolear Fa's own ghost grew larger. Stronger. Younger.

Nolear Fa noticed though. And saw what he could do. To prevent his body from transitioning, all he had to do was strengthen the ghost inside him. And why should he die? What had the cycle of the world ever done for him? If he was to be an outsider, he would become the ultimate outsider.

So he went back to his imprisoned haunts and one after the other he destroyed and consumed them. He ate them. And emerged from this cave, changed. He had become somehow <u>more</u>. Somehow great. More than Inmortalis.

The recognition he had sought from the people of the Undying Land did come then. As admiration for his art, but even more as fear of his power. So he ate more. And grew younger and more powerful.

And soon the ghosts of the world saw what was happening, a new kind of threat. It seemed at first to be a threat they could deal with through curses, as they did with everything. But Nolear Fa had already become so powerful that no individual curse was enough to affect him.

So the ghosts of the Undying Land began combining curses. They slowed him. The conflict spread. Nolear Fa convinced other Inmortalis that ghosts themselves were to blame for this conflict, that curses were actually a scourge and that he was cleansing the world. They joined him. The New Inmortalis emerged, and a slaughter of ghosts began. The world did not need so many ghosts, Nolear Fa assured the people. The world required only a few, only the proper number.

Then, among the ghosts, a champion emerged, wet from the great ocean of ghosts, a ghost maiden named Ti'eirl, who fought the New Inmortalis wielding curses of extraordinary power in ways no ghost had ever done before. She had achieved control of her re-curses. And when she led the ghosts, they defended and counterattacked, and the conflict spread to every inch of the Undying Land.

But two species so intertwined, so bent on destroying each other, could only end by destroying themselves.

Their battles shook the land. Forests burned and mountains fell. Cities crumbled. The very sea of ghosts drained. No one could stand before Nolear Fa. He demanded every ghost be killed, and with all his Agape powers, his powers as artist and Inmortalis, he ground the ghosts down. He brought their race to the very brink of extinction.

In the final days Ti'eirl and Nolear Fa met, alone, on a high hill above a shattered plain. And though Ti'eirl had called the meeting under a banner of peace, she knew no peace was possible, and she came prepared with a final curse, a curse so massive she could barely contain it. If Nolear Fa betrayed her, tried to consume her, the curse would be released. This curse would remove Nolear Fa from the Undying Land, and separate ghosts and people. It would stop the war, but there would be a period of chaos. It was a curse so powerful it could only be a last resort because she did not know if she would be able to control the re-curse.

And Nolear Fa did betray her. So Ti'eirl's curse was freed.

A curse like that has a re-curse of unimaginable potential. Unpredictable, asynchronous, unknowable. This one changed the very fabric of reality; it shook the world and reformed it.

And Nolear Fa <u>was</u> removed from the world—but so were all the other living people.

People and ghosts were separated from each other—but also from themselves.

And Agape was broken into pieces. The very foundation of the Undying Land was broken. Ti'eirl's curse ended the war but at the cost of ending the world.

Reality was rent, a new reality formed: ours. A place where time and death and the five senses were not parts of one whole—Agape was gone—but separate, walled-off domains, weak reflections of past greatness. In our world, Ti'eirl's re-curse locked ghosts away forever, with no life of their own. And here people are shattered into pieces, locked in an earthly prison, shadows of what they had been, without real art. With no memory of what had once been.

The only scenes remaining of the Undying Land now were scenes of emptiness. Broken scenes. It was the landscape painted on the wall of my penthouse, seen from high atop the mountain. Miles of devastation. Lifeless leagues of vacant space, unpopulated and ruined. It was the bleakest thing I'd ever seen.

Caroline's voice returned.

Every curse has terms, of course—to sleep until you are kissed by a prince, for instance—and so every re-curse has terms. Contained in the destructive totality of Ti'eirl's re-curse were the terms that could, someday, restore the lands, the people, and the ghosts who had all been victims of the Ghost War, and put everything back together in peace. These terms: the Undying Land will come together again only when both Nolear Fa and Ti'eirl have died, or when Agape reappears in the world. Until that day, everything will be broken.

And the world has been broken ever since.

As Caroline's *vision* concluded, the final scene—the scene on which the whole superstructure of *farewell* lingered as it faded—depicted the Undying Land just as it ended. A world shifted off its foundation. Everything fallen. Nothing but ash, empty roads, fallen forests, broken hills.

Caroline's narrator voice fell silent. Her eyes flickered but stayed closed a few seconds, as she returned from where she'd been. And when her eyes did open, the scenes of devastation around us winked out, and Nevada returned, revealing Veronica, arms spread, gathering *farewell* in sheets. Even as I watched, the Higher *light* retreated to her fingertips and she lowered her head. Then it was just normal people in Nevada by firelight with a handful of ghosts and a swivel chair. Amelia was the first to speak.

"I hope this was worth it," she rasped at Veronica, who did not look at her. "What they say about you is true. You're just proving it. You're *trying* to get his attention."

Veronica seemed to notice Amelia after a moment and turned white cue balls her way, face taut. "The Families can only defeat Aeternus with knowledge," she tight voiced.

"You don't care if he kills you," Amelia was sobbing now, "but Seamus would want—"

"Do not presume to tell me what Seamus would want!"

"Let someone *help* you, let other people sacrifice too!"

"They are idiots who will *never* sacrifice, and the ghost will win! Is that what you want?"

"What I want is to *matter to you*!" Amelia shouted. "If Aeternus draws you apart in a hundred pieces and I know you *chose* that instead of—do I matter to you at all? Am I just a project?"

They confronted each other near the campfire, where the ghosts were disinterested in anything but watching flesh me. Veronica turned away from Amelia in a clear dismissal.

"I have things I must do, as quickly as possible," Veronica said.

Amy's face fell. None of this was a surprise to me of course.

Amelia's history with relationships is at least as bad as mine, it's hilarious that she ever tries to give me relationship advice, but she doesn't see it. Her heart's always getting broken. None of us ever learns. She went for the door, coming past flesh me. I put his hands behind his back, so she wouldn't see his fists, which would just make her madder. She stopped anyway to shake her head at him.

"You are *so selfish*," she hissed. He looked like he agreed. "If Aeternus kills her..."

She didn't finish. She went out the door, it closed, and there was nothing but campfire crackle and a faraway coyote. A meteor sliced across the wide, totally fake night sky. I heard a bat. And then, with absolutely no warning, the ghosts vanished and I snapped back into one body. My fists relaxed. Caroline was standing near the chair, stretching, and I watched her for a moment before I spoke.

"I'm sorry you're in the middle here," I told her. "I know you don't drink while you're working, but I know there's a mini bar back there somewhere in case that would help."

"I'm all right Ash, this's just being psychic," she shrugged. "You're always caught in the middle. Knowing secrets people don't admit, even to themselves. But it's like Jorge says, information wants to be free. In the long run you have to let it out. Stand in the way and you go crazy."

Veronica was staring at the swirl of Milky Way rising near the horizon.

"There has to be more to the story," she suddenly protested.

She gestured, and *farewell* sprang from her palms. For a moment it felt like we were having Caroline's reading all over again, but at double speed, all the images and thoughts and voices flashing past. Caroline herself was fascinated, staring everywhere, but it made me nauseous that fast, like a rollercoaster. I wanted to get off.

Veronica turned to Caroline, looking lost.

"And what then?" she asked. "What happened *after* the curse?"

"After?" Caroline asked.

"Where is *Aeternus* in all of this?" she demanded. "This is just half a story. He makes no appearance at all. In fact, according to this new information, there should be no ghosts *anywhere*, ghosts were all locked away. Yet the eternal ghost torments us through the ages. We need to know what happened in the moments *after* the curse. When our world first came into being. Where did Aeternus come from?"

"I don't know," Caroline shrugged, "this's all there was. It stops where it stops." Her phone rang. She checked it, then said, "I have to take this. And you know what, Ash? I will have something from your mini bar. Surprise me."

Caroline took her call while I slipped into the inner office to excavate the bar. I found the door just by feel. The monks had pushed the liquor deep into an inconvenient corner. And when I did uncover the bar I saw it had been emptied. Probably Nella.

I couldn't help noticing the rest of the Gale family canvases stacked though, and in that way I'm known for, I let them distract me. There were a dozen of my mother's—Katrina's—paintings. All in the same powerful, deep, uniquely composed hand, all visible spectrum, and every one of them had been doctored by my father, disguising his hand and adding sub-shades. One painting he'd forged entirely, in her hand, and this was the only one with any Higher color. The frame had a sticker on the side from the Gala Lumina—Marlon had painted one of Katerina's entries for our yearly Higher showcase. I was holding that canvas sideways, trying to make sense of it, when I heard Caroline behind me.

"That was Phyllis," she called from the Admiral's door, "I have to go. All hell's breaking loose up there. I'll have to skip the drink." She must have seen how I was watching the canvas. "You okay?"

"Distracted by all the paint weirdness. I can't figure it out." I looked at her then. Where I'm supposed to look, I thought. Like, in a destined way. But only to look. So tiresome. "Even my mural seems... is all that, your visions, really inside that wall?"

"Every word."

"I don't know how that's possible."

"You're just a real talented painter."

"Nolear Fa. Does he remind you of anyone? Like, sending ghosts off…"

"There's no resemblance! That playwright? Totally different from you. You're a way better person. He's a killer. You're a pussy cat."

"Is that your unbiased opinion?"

"No it's super biased." The faintest pulse hit me in my blue crystal. Not enough to clutch it. But the fact that it got through at all had to mean she was *very* biased. "I'm going. Want to talk later?"

"Is that a trick question?" I put Katerina's canvas down to fully face her. "Talking to you feels like all I have left."

"Ah, bless your heart. You're a little bit ridiculously dramatic but real sweet and hot as hell," she smiled. Sad, suddenly. "Ash, thanks for the time cat. Honestly. You can't know…what he means to me."

Then we didn't embrace or kiss or shake hands. We nodded at each other like business acquaintances. For just a second, out of nowhere, I found myself wondering, without a reason; *what if this is the last time I ever see her alive*, and if that were true, shouldn't I try to keep her here? Because who cared what would happen after we touched? The world was ending. I wanted her in my arms.

But instead I let her turn, and followed as far as the door, and she left. Right after that, midnight in Nevada went away, replaced by deep black nothing striped with lines of orange and *farewell*, crossing the floor and rising past the ceiling.

Veronica was folded in the swivel chair, elbows on knees, slouched like a surgeon regretting an operation. The Higher *light* wreathing her had drained to only a few glowing fingernails. I wondered what time it was outside. Near sunset? Her pupils had even reappeared. They kept trying to slide back into hiding, but she kept hauling them back into the light. It looked like a lot of effort.

"You should go after Amelia," she told me, her voice soft.

"Yeah, well, *one* of us should," I agreed, "but if you think it's me you're worse at this shit than I am." She shook her head. She wasn't going after anyone. Honestly, I didn't blame her. Amelia's impossible.

"So now Aeternus comes to kill you?" I asked.

"Possibly," she shrugged. "The Agreements, which more and more I believe the ghost himself created, prohibit the use of any *eminence* to investigate the Ghost War, or probe deeply into Family history. What I just did was an egregious transgression. We shall see."

She lit one of her *farewell* fingertips and pointed at the metaverse where Asher Gale used to have an office. Pieces of the Ghost War reading flashed by, disjointed, the whole Undying Land a nonlinear jumble.

"We did learn one important piece of the puzzle," she said, pausing the scene on Nolear Fa.

"Did we? I didn't notice."

"We learned about you."

"Whatever we think we learned about me will end up being wrong. That's just what happens."

"We know at least what to call you. Not *death guy*. Inmortalis. Yes?"

"The ghost murderers," I shook my head, "yeah, I noticed some similarities, but Caroline says no. She has a thing about murderers. She'd know."

"Know what?"

"There's no similarity."

"But like you, the people of that world were all artists."

"What are you saying? Just because I'm—what about Julian, he's an artist, maybe *he's* the Inmortalis."

"Julian cannot see *dominion*. He cannot see ghosts. The one thing we know about Nolear Fa is he saw ghosts. Saw them, released them —it truly sounds like you."

Her pupils counter crossed, and she lit her hands with a sputtering fingertip to go reviewing the Inmortalis scenes. The Undying Land spun and froze and rewound while she tried to connect me with some genocidal cult. Just because I shared most of their defining characteristics.

"Julian might not be an Inmortalis but he's *something*," I insisted. "He's five hundred years old!"

"We have only your scholarly opinion that Julian is five hundred years old. Focus on something useful. Focus on painting. Paint us something that will help stop Aeternus."

"Oh, sure! Okay, I'll paint that. That's your suggestion? Listen to me. I just waited ten years, afraid to paint, only to find out I *can't* paint. I split apart. Who knows what flesh me would paint? Not Aeternus, I'm pretty sure. He does have a thing for toast. Maybe a kitchen still life."

Veronica had stopped tracking my complaints halfway through.

"Did you say you split apart? Your body? It *splits*, is that the way you envision it?"

"I've explained this Veronica. Pay attention." Oh my god was it satisfying to say *pay attention* to someone else. I had no idea if I was even using it the right way but it gave me so much satisfaction I did it again. "Pay attention. I *chroma storm*, I split into ghost me and flesh me, and later I come back together."

"Yes. I remember. You split into different bodies..." she trailed off, remembering, "Shay. What did she say?"

With a *farewell* flick she wiped the Inmortalis vision from the room and the scene jerked longways.

Suddenly I was watching, *knowing*, the interior of a stuffy, wood-paneled wagon, candle lit and full of musky spice. Here Shay swung, ancient, bundled in a creaking hammock. In a corner of the wagon the girl Shay used as a walking stick curled, asleep on the floor.

Veronica ran this scene backward focused on Shay, then stopped to play it in real time.

Shay's cabin was silent except for her hammock. She held things in her mouth, working her tongue. Two thin chains dropped between her lips, past her chin. I watched her draw the chains free so the new, dark, primitive crystals Caroline and I now wore hung, dripping. She handed them to Veronica.

"The original crystals for those two, hm, they grow *cold*, you say? Pulse?" Shay asked. Her voice a gnarled hiss.

"Yes," Veronica said from behind, like a police interrogation video. "What does it mean?"

"I can't tell, no, but oh I *tasted* him," Shay cackled. "At that moment, his neutral buffer was gone. Completely. I felt his crystal. It discharges, accumulates, discharges, over and over."

"But why?" Veronica asked. Shay pressed her lips. Shadows danced in the cabin.

"It's as though..." Shay thought. "Hm, as though his chemistry's being reset. He keeps sliding back to his baseline. His body resets, again and again so, hm? You said just after tapping him you could compel him, but later could not? It is as though he keeps, hm, returning to a native state. A default."

The image froze. Real life Veronica looked at me.

"Your body chemistry resets. That is what Shay is saying. And that is why the crystals do not work to keep you and Caroline apart. You keep purging the neutral buffer from your body chemistry. You purged it after our tapping ceremony. You are..."

"What, Veronica?" I demanded.

"Somehow, Aeternus keeps all the Aspectu in Skysill Beach from leaving, but whatever mechanism he uses fails with you. You can leave. What if...you reset your body when you *storm*. You split in two. When you return you're chemically restored. What if Aeternus is doing something chemical?"

Something in her theory rang true though I couldn't say what. I had too many bodies, that was one point I couldn't argue, though maybe not the point she was making. If only there'd been liquor in the mini bar I could have smoothed out the inky creep I was starting to feel.

"How does one *supposed* ghost, even an eternal one, change the chemistry of a town?" I asked.

She shrugged. Around us, orange lines defined the edges of nothing. And then we both heard a knock from the office door. I jumped, since the conversation had gotten me tense and goose pimpled. Both of us heard a radio crackle outside the door, then the door swung open. Phil's head popped through.

"Hey have any of you homeless squatters seen—oh!" He saw me, and then his eyes got wide, and he took in the orange stripes on the floor and the walls where there were no walls and the vast black spread of the seemingly limitless ceiling. He nodded.

"Nice," he bounced a little. "Hey, big guy I've been trying to find you, Saanvi won't watch the front door officially until she gets instructions from you. She's a stickler. She's in the lobby. I have to pee. What should I do?"

"I don't know, Phil," I told him. "Why's it my...you ever have a day that's all, epiphany this, discovery that and you can't even get a drink?"

"Sure, totally," he said, bouncing and holding his crotch. "What should I do?"

"Pee," I told him. "I'll go downstairs, I'm going out anyway."

Phil hurried away and the door closed. Veronica lost interest in both Phil and me the second neither of us was Aeternus, or talking about Aeternus. She sat, bent on the swivel chair, *farewell* beading and popping on her knuckles. Her mouth hung open. Her pupils were hibernating in snow.

"I'm taking off," I told her. She didn't look up. "I'm going to go ask Roman some questions about the warehouse I just discovered he has. Will you be, what's the word...okay?" She still wouldn't look up at me. She was in a pretty empty place. All her big moves kept coming up short.

"I'm going to say something to you that people have said to me," I offered, "though it never makes any difference but Veronica, you look like shit, you should consider dialing it back. All of it. I think you need some perspective and some sleep."

Then I left her, ignoring me on the chair, replaying the entire Ghost War alone in her brain cave.

THIRTEEN

Whoever the lady was Phil had selected to guard the lobby doors had to be a better choice than he was. It stood to reason. So I hurried from Asher Gale's office to wait by the elevator, thinking how Veronica had been half right and half wrong, wondering why I hadn't wanted to tell her: my biochemistry *was* getting reset. Her facts lined up with my experience. But it wasn't my *chroma storms* resetting anything. The moment everything opened up for me had been in my sixteenth year. The day I started going *Gray*. It's the *Gray*. The creepy, alternative body I slip into.

It even has its own personality. It changes everything about me, brain chemistry, body chemistry, all the chemistries. The *Gray's* obsessed with the way everything feels, things I normally hardly notice. The *Gray's* also sociopathic, which some people might say isn't a change, but this is a clinical condition. So the *Gray* has always felt like a liability. But now I wondered if it wasn't the only thing protecting me from Aeternus. Looked at like that, it became a crazy, super powerful, murderously violent *good* thing.

My *chroma storms* and the *Gray* are such opposites, they had no business even existing in the same body. Like *I* shouldn't exist. Other people had suggested that as well, over the years. But I did exist and more and more I felt there had to be an explanation, which is a feeling I'd always drunk my way around in the past. Explanations are never the answer, in my experience. There's always some new explanation.

Still, I thought, riding toward the lobby, if my *storms* are my Aspectu body malfunctioning—because I'm just lucky that way— then the *Gray*...was what? The *Gray* is basically one entire half of me. It's more than just a state of mind. I have no sense of humor, I can jump forty feet in the air, when I flip into my *Gray* body I can't see Higher. Other than *dominion*. My *storms* and the *Gray* are polar opposites.

Semi-familiar bells began ringing inside me then. Investigator bells. A dawning realization was building, I knew, which would probably be as inconvenient and poorly timed as the all rest had been. I regretted all my thinking things up. I was in no condition to be realizing anything new.

The elevator doors opened and I scanned the lobby, which was dark. I saw a heavy desk and chair and an army cot situated by the entrance, but no person. I called and no one answered. I crossed the lobby to the desk, on which an architectural drawing had been spread. On the army cot were a pillow and a blanket from Yosemite Park.

The desk was a great idea. Saanvi was already ahead of the game. You could push a desk in front of the lobby doors if a mob was brewing. You could flip it on its side if there was a gun battle. Other strategic advantages occurred to me, and then suddenly I realized— what the fuck was I asking these people to do, guarding this door where violent mobs and gun battles were so easy to imagine? I did want customers kept out, so there'd be fewer people to touch me. But what if Leander showed up looking for me? Veronica kept warning of all the dangers the Family posed to me. What if Phil tried to stop Leander? With his salad tongs or a toothpick? Or what if

Julian came? Julian would glow Phil to a husk—or the Brazilians, who I'd actually forgotten again among my abundance of antago-nists—the Brazilians knew where Asher Gale's office was.

Guarding the lobby of the Bradley Building was like a death sentence. Counting up my enemies like I kept doing was a shocking exercise—and if you threw Aeternus in the mix, assuming he existed, it was a little ridiculous. Now I saw what I actually needed was to keep the Bradley family *away* from these doors, at all costs. It was humbling—which I hate—how as a landlord, your smallest deci-sions can set your tenants up for slaughter.

I left a note on the desk: *Phil and Saanvi stay out of the lobby at all costs.* Then I pushed out the doors, down the broad steps to the side-walk, breathing deep in the cool dark. Hours had passed in Veroni-ca's chamber of sparkles and evening had come. Fog streamers held the air. Fog never thins our tourist traffic though. Once you've been *compelled* into a gallery you become a return customer for life, fog be damned. I ran across PCH when the traffic let me. Foot traffic was light. I hoped no one bumped me.

Roman's gallery—*Roman Sutherland - Master of Light and Shadow*—was tucked off PCH, up the cobbled alley emptying into The Square on the Sea. The alley was three blocks from me, but I was hearing music from two blocks off. I knew the beat. Techno club pop. I knew what it meant: it was going to be hard getting to Roman now. There were Fenestram dancers in town, holding an impromptu dance orgy. The Square would be full. This was the second time in weeks. They were starting early this year. Usually it wasn't until the end of November, a month before Gala Lumina that dancers descended. Then the parties started, getting raunchier and raunchier until the night of the Gala, when no holds were barred, which was the high point of the year if you liked that sort of thing. Which, why wouldn't you?

When I got to the alley I found it closed with a velvet rope. *Sighted* attendants manned the entrance. To enter, painters had to match a *choke* handprint painted on a spinning wheel; this was a

Fenestram only party. The crowd would be pure Skysill artist, it'd be dense and hot despite the fog. Down the alley I saw lights and bodies surging, more manic than usual. Much more, in fact. Was it the Fenestram artists all lacking Higher paint, needing an extra outlet? The whole town was super twitchy.

For a moment I stood watching as dancers passed *sighted* artists around, tonguing them, feeling them, and knew there was no way I could puppet flesh me through that, and if I found Roman I knew he'd never leave. I needed to get him alone. I wanted an explanation for the paint in his warehouse. I wanted an explanation for Julian, and to confront Roman with my theory that Julian was trying to set him up. But now that I couldn't burst into his gallery to confront him, which is how I usually conduct my business, I decided to leave him a message full of innuendo and dangerous half-knowledge, though Roman knew me well enough to be suspicious if I claimed any knowledge in particular.

I called but got his machine. I left a veiled warning about things I knew and what I'd do, though veiled was probably the wrong word. Maybe garbled. I was hanging up when I heard laughter from the end of the block and saw a group of revelers come around the corner. Dancers. I knew it because Fenestram dancers produce a certain feeling in your stomach. Awe. Every muscle in their bodies is wired for power and delight. This group had accosted a painter I knew, and were gracing her with their attentions. Then they saw me. They dropped her.

They made a beeline for me. I felt my brain slipping lusty as they got closer.

And my crystal started pumping ice. What?

I tried backing away, but you can't outrun Dancers. The closer they came the harder my crystal pumped until I realized they were going to touch me and nightmare brain rot would flash straight through me and it wouldn't stop, because the Dancers don't stop once they get you.

So as the first reached me I was squeezing my phone and

popping. Mount Obitus loomed in. Gloom shadows spread. Ghost me watched four of them pour themselves around flesh me, exhilarated by him. Flesh me stood, apprehensive, not sure what his best move was, pawing his fists at his crystal through his shirt, grimacing in shock. I tried to move him back but the Dancers formed a cage of silk-draped arms and legs and torsos, pushed up against him, hands everywhere, lips and bodies in instant, intimate contact.

He went down. He flailed an arm. They laughed, delighted by him, kissing and fondling while he writhed. He spun to the side and the phone in his hand hit one dancer in the chest, and I saw a flash of blue. The dancer cried out, and blood welled, but it didn't slow her down. She was ravenous.

But I recognized the blue. Neutral crystal blue—a crystal? I ghosted in among them, where Dancer bodies shifted through me, positioning to get a clear...yes. A neutral crystal, planted under her skin. I spun backward.

The Dancers were *Tactus*. They had neutral crystals, not worn on a necklace, some special variety Veronica had never heard of. And the Dancers were pulsing my own crystal—only Tactus ever had that effect. If the Dancers were Family, it'd explain a lot of things. Their strength. Their beauty. The polar lust they drew out of every Aspectu painter they met.

As always they were in perfect control and *very* curious about other people's erogenous zones. I watched flesh me getting killed by his crystal and trying to yank it over his head and told him *Stop! Leave it on! It's protecting you!* He believed me but he didn't like it. He rolled on the ground. The Dancers didn't care. They ate him up.

Finally they'd had enough and they twirled up the alley toward the rave and left him. They leapt both the rope and the *sighted* attendants guarding it, no need to spin the Higher color wheel, just fly a dozen feet and land posed like a group of fallen gods, to applause. Then they fell into the crowd, hungry for more.

I stood flesh me off the sidewalk. He was panting and his Hawaiian clothes were mostly pulled off. I got him dressed. I didn't mind the nudity but I was worried he'd catch cold—people got stripped down by Dancers, it's just what happened. Ravished. Every Lumina. When it happened to you it felt amazing, it felt like a gift of grace. But *watching* it happen to you from outside...there'd been very questionable consent involved. No consent, in fact.

The bells in my mind rang louder. Fenestram dancers...Tactus? The Fenestram stipend supported us. The Fenestram Company manufactured paint for us. And the Fenestram Company was Aeternus.

It meant he was here. It meant he'd always been here, that he was everywhere, pulling strings, this so-called eternal ghost. Running me up and down my own town, a rat in a maze. And all while Skysill's painters waited, an ingredient in some master plan, until Aeternus was ready to blow them up. For what? What was the purpose of this? Fuck this fucking ghost, I thought. Where is he? Watching right now? *Aeternus!* I ghost screamed, spinning in a circle. Right at that moment I wanted him to appear. Just such a bad idea.

"*ATRUNS*," flesh me mimicked, kind of plaintive. Then I noticed something come to a stop at the curb at the end of the block. A figure. A single figure. Flapping his arms. His few fronds of beard swinging like a string net, balanced on the pedals of a motionless bike like a circus acrobat. Peter by the Beach.

He'd taken off the yellow robe the monks had put him in and climbed back into shreds of beachwear. He'd slipped Nella's dragnet, which, no surprise, he'd done the same to me, he had a knowledge of Skysill's secret underbelly that surpassed anyone's. But right at that moment he didn't want to disappear, he wanted my attention. So I had flesh me wave back, really friendly, to say *Hello Peter don't ride away why're you pointing at the sky?*

He was pointing at the sky and then pointing at himself. I saw nothing up there. I had flesh me yell, *I see nothing up there* down the sidewalk, then remembered you don't need to shout for Peter. He can hear you two hundred miles up the coast.

His mouth opened. His voice lumbered down the sidewalk, "The crowd ran out of the stadium, and everyone left their bags, it's the bags," he moaned, "look in the bags!"

He kept pointing to himself and peering at the sky, just fog in tendrils curtaining a quarter moon. I wondered if he meant I should go up into the air. Did he know I could fly? And while I was wondering that, he turned and peddled back inland out of sight.

Get up, I commanded flesh me, scooting my ghost right beside him. He jumped. He'd become a very confident ghost passenger with the casual way he hung off my neck, braced atop my ghost feet. It was a commuter pose. I took us up.

The first twenty feet rising was all fog in baffling spools and then I broke into the clear. Flesh me had water on his lashes from condensation. I skirted the top of the murk, turned inland at the end of the block, and it wasn't hard to pick Peter out after that. Pedaling like mad but going not at all fast, he headed into the hills. He'd geared down for the slope. Flesh me and I drifted forward, staying above him.

Mount Obitus dominated the scene, over topping stars, sloping down over Skysill Beach. Coming in off the water, the ocean fog muted Skysill's streetlight glow, giving the neighborhood grids a good-night, tucked-in feel, like a place you'd come back to in a fairy tale, where nothing bad happened and endings were simple. The more I considered the ending in this town, though, looking down on the bobbing head of my only friend, the less simple they seemed. One ending had everyone everywhere dead in three months when time ended. In another, Aeternus set us all on fire in deadly *lightstorms.*

What could you do about a ghost like Aeternus, if he actually was a ghost? If I found him could I send him to ghost paradise by touching his object? My death guy power?

This thought reminded me of the Inmortalis, who *ate* ghosts, and I felt a little sick. Was I going to have to eat Aeternus? What the fuck?

But there was no denying he was everywhere and *something* had to be done. He'd built the entire town, was probably responsible for the cage cups—his company was Fenestram *Glass* and Steel, after all —so maybe Aeternus was responsible for time ending. Could that be possible? Because he'd pulled a lot of strings, why not strings of time?

He'd been shaping my life since I'd been born. Since before. Since Katerina, my mother or whatever I was supposed to call that lady, who had known him, feared him. She'd hidden here from him. And then I thought, *is Aeternus my real father?* Because my confusion was so heightened I was considering the possibility that I was the child of a ghost. There was no doubt he'd known my mother somehow: *If Aeternus finds me, protect the kids,* she'd told Celine. And she'd given Celine a neutral crystal.

Bells. Ringing. Like...the night of Celine's ghost goodbye cere-mony, Caroline...something else about her vision...something about Katerina...Katerina wanted to paint. But she'd been a dancer. A dancer who wanted to paint.

The alarm bells turned to screaming firetruck sirens. A realiza-tion forming, an empty, cold realization. A dancer who'd wanted to paint. A dancer. A dancer familiar with Aeternus, hiding from him. And where would my father, who'd painted the streets of Skysill Beach his entire life, who'd never left the city, meet a dancer?

Gala Lumina.

All the ringing stopped. The weight of the realization shattered the bells to pieces—forever I hoped. Fucking bells. I saw it all. The *Gray.* Marlon brushing sub-shades into Katrina's paintings. *Protect the kids.* A new theory blossomed fully formed in an instant which usually means *disregard this theory you are drunk.* But I went through, step by step, and couldn't find a flaw.

Katerina had been a Fenestram Dancer. Tactus. It explained *everything* that was broken about me. The crystal she'd given Celine had originally been something she got for Marlon, it had never been Katerina's. Katerina had one implanted, just like the other Dancers.

I pictured the Gala Lumina, a pit of sensuality, dark and hot with dancer/painter sex, Skysill's painters almost mad: where my father and my mother met. A Fenestram painter and a Fenestram dancer. She Tactus, he Aspectu. Where somehow...they'd fallen in love. I knew they loved each other. Celine had described it to me.

But that had to be rare. Right? Aeternus worked hard to keep the groups separated except at specific times of the year, under controlled circumstances. Once a year actually, when he brought the Dancers to town for our bacchanalia. Did he want us all lust crazed, but also knew the danger?

And those two, from polar opposite Families, had been crazed. Crazed enough to try hiding from their eternal overseer. Which left only one possibility I could see. A Prime polarity. What else could overpower Katerina's neutral crystal barrier? Polarity did it to Caroline's and mine, and Marlon hadn't even had one.

I could see it. Drawn together by forces beyond their control. Katerina could have...must have left the Dancers and hidden with Marlon in the hills. Hidden from Aeternus.

And though she'd been an extraordinary painter, she'd needed Marlon's help to pass as *sighted*. And once here she'd sunk into the shadows, just another Higher painter—her canvases proved it. She passed as *sighted* but she wasn't Aspectu—*that's* why Veronica couldn't find a file for her in her cardboard boxes. Those files went back generations but held nothing on Katerina. She wasn't Aspectu. But she was a painter.

I'd stopped floating forward. I hung in the sky, barely aware of what was happening below. Peter had pedaled us up out of the fog. He'd stopped at a three-way intersection. A metal arm closed one of the roads. He was motionless for a second like he couldn't decide which way to go. But everything else seemed to be moving. Everything inside me was moving. Moving and reforming to fit my theory. Fit the implications.

Marlon and Katerina had been unshakably in love. They'd hidden in the hills for years—I *knew* that was true. Celine had seen it. The three of them had lived some kind of love triangle. Marlon and Katerina kept trying for kids. Eventually, there'd been Amelia, when

Celine got pregnant from Marlon. But for me...somehow...Marlon and Katerina must have gotten pregnant themselves. It had to be. It explained everything.

So here was yet another thing Veronica had wrong. Aspectu and Tactus—the Primes—the combination was supposedly sterile but there was a way for them to have children. My parents had found a way. I was half Aspectu and half Tactus—half *chromatic* and half *Gray. I am Katerina's and Marlon's son.*

I pictured everything wrong with me and how it could be explained by incompatible genes. Polarized. Like oil and water in one body and all I could do was flip back and forth. I could be one or the other—Tactus or Aspectu—but not both. Never both.

The *Gray* was my Tactus mom. Super strong, fast as shit.

My *chroma storm* eyes, that was my Aspectu dad.

And both my Prime bodies distorted—made defective—by constant polarity.

Of *course* it's all broken. Everything inside me opposed in magnetic gene poles, struggling forever to escape from each other. It also, I realized, explained why I was psychic: the one kind of psychic no one's ever encountered. Because psychics are a mix—one Prime and another Family—and in my case, the other Family was the other Prime. Had my mother known? Had some Tactus bio insight shown my genes to her? Had this even been the *plan*?

My mind was filled, unasked, with a singsong rhyme, my mother's voice, the one she always sang lying in my bed, kissing me and putting me to sleep.

Mommy's got three,

Daddy's got four,

But little baby Asher,

Has got one more.

Five? Rods and cones? To see *dominion?*

Below me Peter moved. He'd decided which direction to go. He lifted his bike over the crossing arm then struggled back aboard and began pedaling a switchback hill into darkness. I drifted after him up the ridge road. I realized where we were. This was the road to Skysill Park, high above on its flattop. Where the Faire was parked. Peter geared down farther, looking more and more frantic, while I tracked him with only the tiniest corner of my attention.

Flesh me, clinging to ghost me, began to shiver, his teeth clattered, which was just so sad to watch. It had to be pretty cold where we hovered, and him wearing only his flowered short pants. I didn't see any way to help him, and he understood. He'd do the only thing anyone can, and hold on till it was over.

There's a truth that counselors never admit to you but I figured out on my own: finding out things about yourself is not the path to happiness. The more things you know about yourself, the more things you become responsible for, which isn't happiness, it's being trapped in a hole you can never get out of. What you want for happiness is forgetting, which is what you get at your bar. But I felt that at that moment I'd just become so committed to being responsible for my life that The Charles might never be able to help me again. I was half Tactus, half Aspectu, and bat shit crazy. I'd always be crazy. I was made of incompatible pieces. I knew that much about myself now. It was the most horrible thing.

Peter was peddling like Lance Armstrong into an empty parking lot now, and the Faire was gone, I saw. Or was it closed? The park was unlit and appeared deserted. With ghost eyes I could only make out shadows on the softball field. An unlit Ferris wheel? No crowds. No light or movement at all. Just Peter, arrowing straight for the entrance. Which even I could see was not the right direction because that park should not be dark and deserted.

All the paneled wagons and tents were in place, I saw as I swooped down, but they were dark. The lights strung in the trees were dark, the rides abandoned and unplugged. The whole Faire was lit by a rising moon, thin starlight, and nothing else. Peter was fifty yards from the entrance and riding hard. I shot both of me ahead of his bike and landed a few feet from the gate to head him off.

"Hey," flesh me called. I was grateful for some other crisis to manage about than my appalling journey of self-discovery. I waved my flesh arms. Peter did not slow, just barreled closer. I got a little worried, ghost me shouted things flesh me repeated, but Peter wasn't looking where he was going. He was staring down at his pumping feet, staring and heaving—and then two yards from impact flesh me decided he'd better jump but it was too late. Then suddenly Peter clamped his brakes.

He skidded at me sideways in dust, and stopped.

We were face to face, his eyes unfocused. He was lost. Somewhere deep inside, Pierre was struggling to be heard, while up here, Peter rode a bike in the dark, facing flesh me, breathing gasps, blowing beard, sweating. He was in terrible shape. His scalp showed, his hair was gone in patches. He was so thin, he couldn't weigh more than his ten speed.

I warned him through flesh lips, "Don't go in there Peter."

And Peter rumbled, "Tupperware bumblebee."

"I'll call somebody to come get us, but let's just move away from here right now," flesh me told him. But flesh me wasn't calling anybody, I realized, not with my phone squeezed in his fist. I could boil us down to a single body in order to dial it but then *dominion* would melt the phone. Probably?

Peter set his eyes to half open and pointed his face all along the fence, tilting, favoring his ears. I spun my ghost to see behind us, into the park, through the dark and vacant gate. The ticket wagon was open but no one in it. Where were all Shay's Nidor?

"What are we doing here," I had flesh me ask. "Let's go, something's wrong, let's go that way, over here, come on." I tried pulling him but Peter had no extra flesh to grab and his clothes just ripped, plus I had only fists to puppet around.

"Fair's fair, but watermelons pop out," he shivered, listening to the Faire grounds.

And then, dropping his bike, he dodged past flesh me and ran on skeleton legs through the gate.

"Peter," I hissed, "wait!"

Flesh me was a man with initiative, you had to give him that. Without instructions from me he lit out after Peter, who swiftly became only a form flitting among trees heading for the roller coasters. Once again I'd been caught with my irises pinched tight, and the dark was just dark, but flesh me seemed to gain on Peter, so I issued him instructions—*follow him, don't let anyone see you, don't let him hurt himself, don't hurt yourself*—then let him vanish in pursuit while I sent ghost me skimming the opposite way, out through the Fairgrounds, looking for life. Suddenly afraid. What had happened here?

At the far edge of the encampment where residential tents and wagons were gathered, I ghosted to a halt. All around were dying campfires and cabin doors hanging. Before one wagon was money on a tarp, abandoned. Through the wall of another was a meal, untouched, candle guttering. Laundry lay in the dirt. And not a soul to be seen, living or dead.

The maneuvering was awkward because I had to do it all while facing flesh me, wherever he was racing through the park, which, wait—what had I just sent him into, all alone? It's just one panic after another with me. I have defective decision making. In my new panic, I sent my ghost surging to close the distance between us, passing through a ring toss, a water pistol booth—signs of exodus everywhere. Stanchions down, prizes dropped.

Suddenly, for just a second, I lost track of him. I slowed my headlong plunge. How do you lose track of your flesh? Where *was* he? I pushed forward anyway in what I thought was the same direction, a little desperate—what was going on?—then picked up the trail of him, like a radio frequency had stabilized, and streaked in like a missile plowing carousels and popcorn outhouses until I found him, motionless by a kissing booth, petting some goats. The goats were butting his legs. They'd escaped the zoo. He was fascinated. Peter was nowhere to be seen.

Hey, I ghosted, irritated, *what? Where's Peter?*

He ignored me because the goats were so adorable, because I've always had a thing for goats. I'd left him explicit instructions though, hadn't I? I couldn't remember. Remembering instructions is what I'm worst at. Everything seemed to be accelerating now. And *where was Peter?*

Ghosting fifty feet up and spinning a circle I sighted him, stumbling but moving fast through the pallet trucks I'd visited with Amelia. Beyond that was the ocean-view half top tent where the Conclave had been.

"Hey Peter *wait!*" I had flesh me yell from the ground, while I watched from the air. I *knew* he could hear me. He just didn't stop.

I dropped and loaded flesh me—though he hated leaving the goats—and got us into the air, then turned on the speed. Under us went the whirly rides and we slashed through the air toward the half-tent. Peter slipped through the back flap and disappeared. I lofted up, overtopped the pennant on the central pole, and as I crested, I was already seeing columns of *dominion*. Active threads rising. The kind that pinched ghosts into existence.

Near the ridge edge stood Peter, waiting, I thought. Looking up with his head back. He stood within a circle of ghosts.

Five ghosts pitching out Higher canopies, a combined, miniature ultraviolet pressure zone of swelling *light*. And at the foot of each ghost, a body. Or the remains of a body. Out beyond the ridge I saw Samantha floating. Of course. Just here spectating. And I recognized the ghosts below me. There was no way you could recognize the flesh bodies though. Too much damage. I floated down slow, and again, because ghosts can't feel like throwing up, I didn't.

The flesh bodies were basically disassembled. That's the word I decided to use as I hovered, horrified but light as a snowflake, to land flesh me beside Peter so the ghosts spun in a circle and faced inwards.

Peter and I stood on a grassy field of blood.

The bodies lay on their backs at our feet, skulls inward in a circle, perfectly spaced, each posed the same way. And parts of each body had been...rearranged. Limbs, organs, blood vessels, other parts I didn't recognize because I'm not a veteran of a trench war.

And the heads…that's where the really delicate disassembling had been done. From shoulders up the heads were drawn apart, piece by piece. It was gruesome. I'd never been so glad to be a ghost. But there was clearly a pattern here, some inscrutable plan, so I looked, and tried to understand.

All the sensory organs had been displaced, very precisely. Ears, tongues, eyes, noses, skin, all with attendant nerve tissue, spread like a medical exhibit in the grass, swapped into the bodies to either side. Crisscrossed. Mixed and matched. They make you study anatomy illustration in Skysill when they still think you're sane enough to make them money, and this was like that. So gruesome it stopped meaning anything. Only it had to mean something. Because these bodies…these were the leaders of the Five Families.

Their ghosts stared as flesh me stepped off his own ghost to stand in thier blood. Willametta, Shay, Hibiki, Leander, and one other, holding objects and facing him. Flesh me moaned and raised an arm toward Leander, but I held him back. Peter still faced the sky. I looked up but only saw the Higher borealis churning electrons into space dust. Peter couldn't see that.

"You can't hear it when a river dies," Peter boomed from his basement at the stars, "nobody hears a sky fall. You can't hear but it happens. No one hears the end but it happens. Not the falcons. Not the fish." His body twitched, his mouth a bowl swallowing moonlight. He tipped sideways, caught himself, groaned.

"Let's get out of here," I had flesh me say. His voice trembled. He didn't feel as confident as I tried to make him sound.

"The more you go the more you come, lip balm frozen teeth, cavities in history."

"Here," flesh me called. "Peter come *on*."

He looked down from the stars then, very suddenly, and grabbed flesh me by his shoulders to lean close and worked his mouth like a bee was caught in it.

"Te…" Peter spat, panting with something he wanted to say. Something urgent. With jerking throat, he heaved, "te…te… te…" like it was the most important sound man had ever made, then closed his eyes, stilled his body with calming breaths so deep for a moment I thought he'd pass out. That's what I would have done.

Then his eyes flashed open and for the first time ever, Peter himself looked at me. Lucid brown eyes clear. They were doe eyes, long lashed and endless with deep-knowing, and they held me—and I found myself looking at Pierre, surfacing. Pierre had my shoulders. He spoke with a broken voice as sad as civil war.

"Tell Nella," he airdropped, without moving his lips, "that I'm falling through the umbra eye," and then his own eyes closed. He slumped to the ground. As he fell, I heard, just the barest whisper, "It started at Gala Lumina Asher…"

From his chest rose earthquake moans that shook the hill so the bleachers rattled, and made the big top sway. Then he collapsed sideways in blood, loose as a bag of cutlery.

"Peter!" flesh me yelled. "Peter?"

Not dead. Not yet. No ghost. What was I supposed to do?

At that moment a figure emerged from the tent shadows where it had been hidden under the bleachers. A small, uncertain figure, in blood-streaked clothes and hands and face. Shay's little girl. Wide-eyed.

She came in shock so deep she looked bored. She stumbled as she walked. She stopped beside Shay, staring.

"Don't look, little girl," flesh me told her. He had good instincts, if an awkward way with children. "Are you okay? Are you hurt?"

She took a step into the circle of bodies to stand beside flesh me, her face filled with a kind of…something you never escape. Her arms came up and wrapped flesh me and she clung. Flesh me had no idea what to do. None of us did.

We stood like that for a really long time it seemed to me, but ghosts don't feel time the way other people do. And when figures did start appearing through the tent, none of us really reacted. Peter was unconscious and I was busy holding flesh me back from exorcising a ring of ghosts while the girl hugged him. None of us moved as Nella and a handful of other Auditus ran from the back of the tent into hearing of us, and froze like they'd just echolocated something they'd never be able to forget.

"What...?" Nella air whispered in front of flesh me.

He shrugged. "I just got here," I had him say. "We followed Peter."

"Jesus fuck'n...it's Hibiki..." she murmured, her sonar picking up details.

"Get Peter out of here," I flesh demanded. "He's alive, in bad shape."

Nella very slowly waded forward. Several monks followed. One turned back, bent, and vomited. Nella looked like she could do the same at any moment. All I felt was dismay and horrible confusion.

"You should call Veronica," I had my flesh say. I'm not proud. I know there are some problems only rich people can solve. Like fields of bodies.

"Told'r already," Nella said. "Came when we heard, Veronica's almost..." Nella waved behind her as Veronica emerged through the bleachers.

She assessed the scene fast, like an investment gone bad—she summarized it all at one time. New Dwayne came after her, gently stirring the air, as Veronica puzzled herself up and stopped, looking down at Willametta, or what was left. Then body by body she checked them all. For a second I saw her waver, like she'd pass out, when she came to Hibiki. But she did a billionaire trick and overcame all qualms. They share many similarities, ghosts and billionaires. Good stomachs.

"The ghost is announcing himself," Veronica said when she'd finally committed it all to memory. "Now the Tactus will come. We must move quickly."

"What's that mean, announcing himself?" I had flesh me complain.

Her eyes fell on the girl. "Where did you find her?" she asked.

"I guess she was under the bleachers and saw everything.

Where's everybody else? The Nidor from the Faire? What's going on?"

"This is his sign. Aeternus spreads us apart. We do not know... why. Punishment? Culling bloodlines? Sometimes singly, sometimes in groups. It is the only communication we ever have from him."

"But...what? These people had *powers*." I tried to imagine anyone sneaking up on Hibiki—he'd hear it a million miles off. "And all at one time? Or...maybe he picked them off and brought them here dead..." I'm bad with timelines. I really struggle with problems like this.

"No, he keeps them alive. They are always alive until the very last second. He values that."

Veronica's voice was like glacier water.

"When Seamus...when we found Seamus in his dorm, Oxford you know, he...his heart had stopped only seconds...his building was entirely empty. Like this camp. Once it was done, the students returned without even knowing why they'd left. Aeternus... "

"It seems like what he's doing here," I forced flesh me to say because she'd passed me the conversational baton, pointing at the bodies, "is he's combining these people."

"Yes. It has always been the ghost's obsession."

"Why?" She shrugged. "But listen, if he can control *all this,* like... what *can't* he do?"

"That is the puzzle. His limits, yet his unimaginable power."

Nella and the monks got Peter lifted and carried from that ring of darkness. His clothes dripped blood. His beard did too. It ran off his fingertips. It was a lot.

"What was he doing here?" Veronica asked.

"I don't know. He found me and made me follow him—oh—hey Nella! Wait!" I called, forgetting again that I didn't need to shout. It's a really hard idea to get used to.

The monks were carrying Peter through the bleachers.

"What?" Nella voiced out in front of me, walking without turning.

"Peter said to tell you…he's falling through the umbra eye."

The monks all froze. Nella spun. "H'said *what?*"

"*Tell Nella I'm falling through the umbra eye.*"

"Falling *through* it?" Veronica asked.

It was a complicated remote talking setup for flesh me, but we managed it all pretty clearly. "Yeah, also something about Gala Lumina…it started at Gala Lumina. Then he passed out."

"Gala Lumina? What started? What did he mean?" Veronica demanded.

"No idea. But just for a second I swear…Pierre was there. The first one. Lucid."

"That's' not possible," Nella said. "Can only come back when his question's asked."

"It looked like the hardest thing anyone's ever done. It only lasted a few seconds. Then he was gone. Did it break him?"

Nella spun back to the monks with something like wonder on her face. Something like hope. Then, as the monks scuttled off, all around the tent came Nidor, back from wherever they'd been driven, all of them sucking, sucking and silent. They stopped at the edge of the blood. An older man came forward, to the very edge of the ring of bodies, and bent to Shay, what you could see of her, to shake his head.

His tears fell as he raised one palm to his mouth and licked it. Then he placed his palm on Shay's chest, and in a reedy voice he said, "You added savor to the banquet, Gailene Romalda Shay. From the mouth of the world you came. To the mouth return. What the ghost has taken, we will remember."

Then he stood, and he held his hand to the girl. She let go of flesh me and took the other offer. The man nodded to Veronica, then walked away. The other Nidor were already working ropes, preparing the big top for travel.

From behind us a group of Tactus bounded up the ridge—they came pouring straight over the edge because hills are nothing to them, they came in lopping, impossible strides, skidding to stop where the blood and bodies got obvious. They were snarling disbelief and rage. One stood away from the rest. He gave Leander's remains a contemptuous glance, then fixed his eyes on Veronica. Faintly, through flesh me, I felt my crystal turn to ice. He was great looking, this guy. It makes me feel so shallow being polarized. No one else has this problem.

"This is your doing," he snarled at her. I recognized him—he was the Tactus from the Conclave who'd had snakes at his feet. "You drew the ghost here. You did this to us."

Veronica laughed, and faced him. She waited. New Dwayne came to stand beside her. More Tactus arrived, some with animals. I saw a tiger and some bats and they all started pressing in.

"I'm going to kill you now," the Tactus assured Veronica. The others spread in a semi-circle.

"I do not doubt you would like to try," Veronica shrugged. "But."

"Your night charge and your traitor Sapor can't save you, *relino*."

"You think I want to be saved? I do not! But I will burn you where you stand, Hardmar Brone!" She raised her voice, so all the Tactus could hear. "You have heard what an Aspectu can do *at night*. You will all die. Do not try this. I do not want it. The Families must *unite*. Go home. Tell your people...Aeternus has come. This is a sign. The quorum is upon us."

When they still didn't move, Veronica counter crossed her eyes, bent her knees, and held her hands extended, palms cocked. Very aggressive. But she wasn't holding any *light*. Something only she and I could see, She was empty. She braced one foot and raised a curious eyebrow at the group, as if wondering who'd like to be first to die. It was a stone-cold bluff. From behind I saw her braced calf trembling.

A moment passed and then Hardmar flicked his hands behind him, and the Tactus turned and dispersed. So fast. So coordinated. Hardmar himself took a few extra seconds to stare down Veronica.

Then he looked at flesh me. He pointed. "You have been marked."

And he turned with strides so long he only needed three to vanish back over the ridge. I watched him out of sight because I'd been marked and I take that kind of thing seriously, though seldom seriously enough to make any difference.

New Dwayne stepped forward to stand above the body of the one man I didn't know and did something fast with a knife, and then he'd cut a swath from the man's shirt. He held this to his nose, then to the sky.

"To your endless future, Charles Redhorse," he said, then turned his back to the body. He stood without moving, holding his cupped hands to his face, breathing. Flesh me looked at Veronica. What now? WTF now?

"Oh, here's something," I had flesh me announce. Getting jabbed by my crystal had reminded me, and we all wanted something other than dismembered bodies to talk about. "These Fenestram Dancers all over? They're *Tactus*. How come you never mentioned they were Family?"

"They are not," Veronica said, staring at Willametta, not listening. Her pupils, I saw, hadn't rolled back into view, and the whites reflected like full moons. She swayed. "The Dancers wear no crystals. They would be unable to operate in a city full of Aspectu if they were un-neutered Tactus."

"I saw one. They wear it under their skin."

"No. No Nidor could make such a thing. The neutral crystal must be worn exposed, or it is ineffective."

"Well *some* Nidor *somewhere* makes them because I saw it, and remember, I'm not fucking blind. Plus I *know* they're Tactus, because they set off my crystal the way Leander does, and all the other rock-stars." She stared like she didn't get it.

"Your crystal did *what* around Leander?" she asked.

"They jab you when you're around Tactus. You don't get that?"

"I do not," she said. "But you and Caroline are hyper-polarized, maybe over sensitized."

"Well, take my word for it, the Dancers are Tactus. Plus here's *another* question."

"Yes. So many questions. Can it wait?" She turned from me and got out her phone.

"No," flesh me told her, "it can't wait. Is there some way a Tactus mom could...could an Aspectu and a Tactus ever have a kid? I thought you said no."

"That union is infertile."

"Yeah, but *how* infertile?"

"Utterly. It has been studied, trust me. Tactus can deep sense living tissue."

"What exactly do they deep sense?"

"The polarized gametes destroy each other in utero." I'd got her attention at least, though now I was sorry. "They are utterly incompatible. Why are you asking, Mr. Gale?"

"My mom," I said. "She knew what being born half Tactus and half Aspectu meant. I have five rods and cones. That's why I see *dominion.* The union's not utterly sterile. My parents found a way to... have me."

Veronica wasn't following. Behind her, one corner of the big top folded over. The Nidor called to each other, heaving. As Veronica turned to watch, she fell. One of her legs just went. But New Dwayne was beside her before she hit the ground, which, of course. Veronica leaned on him. She'd reached the end of the bluff she'd been playing. New Dwayne had his arm under her, and when she couldn't walk he lifted her, then looked at flesh me.

"Get off this ridge," he said. "Everyone's coming."

And then he carried her from the field and it was only the five Family ghosts and Samantha plus my ghost and my flesh standing ankle-deep in ritual murder left there on the edge of that ridge. The Family ghosts seemed eager for flesh me to do his trick, *set us free,* you could see that's what they wanted. They faced him *dead on* and it was intense. And he definitely wanted to oblige, straining a hand up, but I was holding him back. Because all the death guy work was suddenly feeling very...Inmortalis. I wasn't sure I wanted to align myself with those people. Whoever they were. Considering the things they ate.

Out beyond the ridge top of ghosts was the gloom shadow of Mount Obitus, darkening the coast. Where it fell on the city the lights were dimmed like fairyland embattled, which made the scene extra sickening. And for the first time, I was absolutely certain—the mountain was closer. The peak was lower. The throne, previously so high I'd only seen it because I've got these eyes, could now be seen by anyone with good binoculars. Assuming they could *see* it at all.

As I rose into the sky carrying flesh me I saw Samantha blink out. The five remaining ghosts all pivoted, swirling galaxies in their blood bath, tracking flesh me off the mesa out over the city. Not happy to see him go. I assumed we'd all meet again. Probably in my living room.

CHAPTER

FOURTEEN

’d seen a lot of dead bodies the previous few weeks. Some dead by knife work and some in shootouts, at least a hundred killed by Fabrica turning their brains off. I’d seen razor blade suicides and miscellaneous homicides and at least one natural death, and I admit I’d grown blasé about dead bodies. But you couldn’t be blasé about the ridge top blood bowl I’d just left. Even my well developed dissociative skills have limits. It might actually be chemically impossible to disassociate from butchery like that.

I’d continue trying, of course, but I’m a visual person and my brain kept recalling new things for me to imagine seeing: Aeternus (according to Veronica) dissecting the living bodies, the leaders of the Families in a circle of gore, sensory organs swapping and criss-crossing in moire patterns. Very purposeful, inscrutable, and hideous things to imagine.

I was streaking across Skysill’s night sky with my flesh body clubbed onto my ghost body, ham fisted in his way, torn by the wind from our passage. Every few seconds I spun backward to make sure the ghosts weren’t coming after me. They just dwindled, ultraviolet on their ridge top above flesh bodies they’d once been in.

268

Usually when I'm freaked out like this I go to my bar. Often the only reason I'm freaked out to begin with is because I'm not already at my bar. But The Charles was out of the question at the moment. Flesh me, cinched tight in the crook of my right ghost arm, was covered with murder blood. His legs dripped like slaughterhouse stir sticks and all his Hawaiian clothes were ruined. He must've fallen among the bodies or kneeled when I wasn't looking. Maybe he just scooped it up and rubbed it on, these days you didn't know what he'd do. They had no formal dress code at The Charles, but if you came in looking like a Stephen King prom queen, it'd attract attention you didn't want.

I went in circles for a few minutes which is, along with the bar, the other thing I do when I'm freaked out for any reason, such as, for instance, being covered in blood so I can't go to my bar. Five of the most powerful people on earth—five people empowered with car bending strength, and future sight and slicing swimming pools with *light* beams—these five had been overwhelmed, as a group, and arranged in a murder mosaic. Which meant I myself would have no chance at all. Yes, I personally was going to die in three months. But I did not want to die like that. I actually didn't want anyone to die like that.

Flying in circles is boring though, and so my anxiety faded and my natural tendency to lose interest in things reasserted itself. Fog was banking in along the beach and I found I'd drifted to a stop in the air above the Civic Center Auditorium, probably subconsciously drawn by all the spotlights because in Skysill a spotlight means free booze.

Below me the dome of the Auditorium was colored with visible spectrum lasers, and in front of that was a black-tie social event in progress as an audience flowed from the theatre doors onto a plaza. Little tuxedoes escorted little ball gowns, pairs wandering here and there pretending to laugh. Some people like that kind of party. They wanted to get their money's worth out of their annual donations and didn't have much time left because donation season was almost over. Soon the Auditorium and the rest of the Civic would close to begin preparations for Gala Lumina. And I thought, *Oh yeah, Gala Lumina,* since my brain historically just darts around, and I remembered Peter and his message about Gala Lumina.

Something had started at Gala Lumina.

Flesh me had lost his sandals in the slaughter circus, and blood dripped off his toes toward the guests below. I knew I couldn't just float up there and watch people drink all night. The question was, where else to go?

Some of my anxiety came back. A bat flew past and at first I thought it was a drone, which reminded me of the Brazilians implicitly marking me the same way the Tactus had *explicitly* marked me, for all of which, I totally blamed Veronica. Where could I go where I'd be safe? When I thought of being safe I instantly thought of Caroline. Because mind darting.

Suddenly I wanted to call to share the story of what had happened just now. It was exactly the kind of story she loved, I'd started to realize—kind of gruesome with lots of action and filled with mysteries. Since telling that exact kind of story is one of the few things I can offer in any relationship, it's pure luck she's that kind of girl.

My phone was clenched in my flesh fist however, and would it still make calls if I shot a bolt of *dominion* into it? I didn't know. I hesitated ruining another phone since it just played into people's idea of me being a person who ruins his phones, which I eventually do of course if I don't lose them first. But no one likes to be pigeonholed.

If I tried telepathy it wouldn't work I knew; a ghost doesn't have the telepathy organ or whatever you need. Ghosts are useless, romanticly.

It was probably a bad idea floating back down the coast a few miles and then angling into the hills to loiter in the air above Three Paths the way I decided to. For one thing, because it was kind of stalker-y. And for another, I'd been told by Monarchs Jorge and Phyllis that I was unwelcome on those grounds. Still, I thought there was a chance I'd coincidentally see Caroline outside walking around, maybe getting firewood or something psychic, and I'd land beside her and she could be delighted. Sometimes things like that happen.

Flesh me seemed to know who we were going to see and started nodding. The sky cleared. Stars flared above foothills black with oaken undergrowth. The ghost mountain towered inland, damping any hope I nurtured that the future was less bleak than I pictured it.

Then the triple wings of her stone estate were coming into view, nested between steep and wooded escarpments. A fenced perimeter surrounded the building. Gates and thick hedge gardens discouraged visitors who weren't psychic.

But I was psychic. Plus I was flying, so none of it slowed me. I dropped toward the round, four-story turret with its castle door, where the three wings attached. Not a light shone in any window, but I'd started thinking they were painted black. The psychics liked their illusion of privacy. One or two of the back doors did shed light onto stoops.

I winged back and forth slowly but saw no one who was conveniently Caroline taking a walk. And I'd seen enough guns on the premises, I hesitated returning without an invitation. So in moonlight and mountain gloom I floated, hoping she'd just *sense* me—maybe there was some way *that* could happen?—and come out, but that didn't happen. I found I really wanted a drink. Flesh me was shivering from the cold. Did I really want Caroline to see him basted in blood? She might not have cared. She did seem to have some blind spots. But why stress test the relationship like that?

It would have to be the Bradley. There I'd rely on the Auditus—who apparently heard everything—to sound the alarm if any of the people who'd marked me mounted an attack. So I left Caroline's psychic boarding house and swept back up the coast, low over the fog. As downtown came closer I turned and went a hundred yards out to sea. I wanted to approach the Bradley over the waves, low and in fog because that was less conspicuous than dropping out of the sky in the middle of downtown Skysill on a sidewalk, and being inconspicuous was a skill I was trying to learn.

I swept closer, and then I saw an inverted funnel of *dominion* churning above the Bradley. It just appeared, in an instant, as I got into range, vanishing up towsard the Higher borealis. A ghost tornado. It looked exactly like the one Caroline had, above Psychic Touch—because it probably was that one. Did I now have new ghost tenants? They seemed to come with a tornado. And they knew where I lived.

We landed in surf. Flesh me waded ashore. I kept him in the water—which he detested—long enough to wash some of the blood off. His Hawaiian short pants were holding up surprisingly well considering everything they'd been through. The blood kind of blended with the flowers.

He emerged dripping onto hard sand. I struggled him across the beach and past the dark snack shops, out onto the sidewalk where Pacific Coast Highway curves through downtown, a block from the Bradley. The *dominion* funnel grew thicker with every step I took. Shadows were everywhere. And I mistrust every shadow, I suddenly found.

Snapping back into one body had become a lot like shaving for me, like routine self-care. *Dominion* poofed down into the phone in my fist. There was no other way. It glowed, and then the screen came on. It seemed unaltered by *dominion*. I would have tested it, but there were still shadows. One of my legs was bruised and achy. Flesh me was numb as a post with no idea what his body felt like. But I whimpered.

He'd left my shoulders spasmed from clinging in the air all night, and I discovered a sprained finger and some cuts on one shoulder, and shivering and confusion and starvation and thirst. This body was just very badly in need of maintenance. I felt like an absentee landlord.

When I dialed the brightness up I saw the drone drifting from one Bradley window to the next. But as I hyper-focused I saw a line of steam strike from the building and shatter it into pieces. It dropped like reverse fireworks. Monk defense, I figured. They worked sound bolts the way the *Fabrica* tossed *light* around. The Brazilians were probably going crazy it was such a very bad town for drones. I tried to remember how much time I had with them...to do something they'd wanted...but I couldn't. I keep telling people write that kind of stuff in a text. The only kind of details I retain are a kind I have not yet encountered.

Holding the key blob in one hand, in case of ghosts, I dashed for the entrance, my thigh throbbing every step, scanning street and traffic for adversaries. I crushed drone pieces going up the steps and then I was in the lobby, panting, the city noise fading as the doors closed behind me. No one from the Bradley Family guarded the entrance. I wondered if they'd gotten my note or just forgotten.

Nursing my shoulders and leg I pulled the desk to block the front door, knowing it wasn't going to stop anyone, just hoping it gave the right impression. Then I took the elevator to the penthouse.

When the elevator opened on the fourth floor my fists curled and I popped. Immediately in front of me, like a doorman, floated a ghost monk holding a bag of peanuts, bedazzling me with *light*. Just as I'd feared. The ghosts had tracked me. Why congregate at Psychic Touch when the star attraction was me? Well, flesh me.

Ghosts were everywhere in the hallway; halfway through walls, tucked behind my potted plants, and I ghost bounced a few out of the way as I steered flesh me up to the penthouse door. Even though (I think) I tried to lock it, I found I'd failed, which was lucky because my keys were a melted blob. Locks. All the locks everywhere, all the names everywhere, I guess that's a world some people enjoy.

In the living room it was more ghosts. Many many more. They lined the walls, and there I saw Willametta, near the back. She'd beaten me home from the ridge top. I had all the ghosts in Skysill in my living room. They did try to position themselves out of my way, but a hundred and fifty ghosts in a house is just inconvenient. And every ghost in the place rotated to face flesh me. Though I had the feeling before I arrived they'd been watching the mural.

Dominion slammed from it, power washing the room. The ghosts just loved that. They were soaking in *light* like day trippers at a ghost spa. Samantha had prime position, nearest to the mural.

I steered flesh me to the kitchen. There a few stray ghosts gathered. I bounced one of the recently killed cops so flesh me could get in the refrigerator. I made him drink a liter of filtered water and fist up awkward scoops from Phil's tub of fruit, which was dwindling. Now that I lacked keys again I'd have to remind Phil to not come in with any more fruit, since it will kill him. My mural, deadly to everyone but psychics and ghosts. And me, whatever I am. Both.

I found flesh me some crackers in a Bradley basket. By himself he'd found a different basket with vodka and kept reaching but I had to tell him no. Because yes it was absolutely true *I'd* be better off drunk, but he was a different story. Pouring liquor into flesh me was a waste. He was too numb for my own good already.

When he was full of food—or when he started gagging every time I had him swallow—I got him to the bathroom and put him on the toilet, and when he was done there I hosed him down in the shower to get the rest of the blood off him, dried him, and walked us all back to the living room naked which I assumed wouldn't faze the ghosts, and fuck them if it did it was my penthouse.

So this is how it's going to be? I ghosted at Samantha. She spun Higher brilliance, ignoring ghost me to face flesh me, who I'd laid on the couch.

Are you ghosts living here now? I hope all these ghosts don't expect to be touched to the great beyond because, for one thing, look at flesh me he's exhausted. Also, I've started thinking that touching you ghosts that way, that's an Inmortalis thing. Ever hear of the Inmortalis? Like priests and like plumbers is what I'm told, and ate ghosts and started the Ghost War, so I need more information before I lay hands again.

Since no one was paying any attention to him I positioned ghost me so I could stare at the blasting mural of the Undying Land. According to Caroline—who I still couldn't call because I couldn't retake my body because ghosts—the mural was more than just a mural. It was a real thing, with eons of history, real stories or at least *a* real story. Which could be read by psychics on the Path Behind. Reading the past.

Combined with what I'd found out from Amelia—more essential information no one told me, so frustrating—my Higher paintings always had special powers, at least the mural fit a pattern. My earlier works had teleported people, or changed their hats or whatever. So in a way it was inevitable, with my history, eventually I'd make a painting that killed people. And here it was. The Undying Land of the Ghost War. Homeland of Aeternus? I assumed so, without any evidence, because gathering evidence is inconvenient.

Let me ask you something, I ghosted absently at Samantha, *do you know anything about Aeternus?*

She said nothing, nor did she blink into a chair or make any other sign. She was very inconsistently helpful. Maybe she was just inconsistently *here*. Cognitively. Was that the right word for a ghost? But like Peter, maybe she was lost somewhere in some ghost hole. One way or another she served her own agenda and not mine. And yet she was the ghost I seemed bound to.

I had doubts about Aeternus before this, maybe he was a myth, I continued as she paid me even less attention, *but tonight in the Park… he's psychotic but I don't think he's a myth. I think he's got a two hundred year plan for Skysill Beach and anyone in the way of that plan gets killed. He built the town and made Higher paint and keeps us secret, he pays the Fenestram Stipend, sends the Fenestram Dancers—nothing happens here he doesn't plan. And every year it's probably Aeternus organizing…the—*

Gala. Gala Lumina. The most *Fenestram* of events, the hub of our civic and artistic life. We revolved around the Gala. Once a year on the solstice it came, our wild festival, and the rest of the year we anticipated it. The parties of Dancers, the abandon, the relief. All on the solstice. The day of the least *light*…everything in our lives circled the Gala. And *this* year in not-a-coincidence Lumina happened in three months, at the precise point when the Paths of time were going to break. And what would Gala Lumina even look like, if no one was making Higher art? Would it be canceled?

Another puzzle piece snapped in. So tiresome. I can't make it stop. Ask any addict, they'll tell you, some things are out of our control.

It was Roman Sutherland. He was in the middle everywhere—he headed every Gala Lumina committee. I'd been trying to reach him for days but he'd gone missing. The Gala took on a whole new meaning with Aeternus in charge, with Roman looking ever less innocent. All my Roman Sutherland questions appeared more sinister. He had his own supply of Higher paint. Where did that come from?

Actually, what did we really know about Roman *at all*? I knew he ran at least one cop as personal law enforcement. Veronica was convinced he wasn't Fabrica, but now you didn't need a crystal on a necklace to be tapped, so her conclusions were outdated. And then I thought, on the other hand, did we know for sure that Roman was *sighted at all?*

It was a destabilizing thought. Roman *judged* at Gala Lumina so he'd never submitted a painting. He appeared to be *sighted* but if a person had helpers—like, say, *sighted* apprentices—it wouldn't be hard to fake. No one in town ever talked about *sight,* so who was there to really keep track? We just assumed. He was Skysill's spider, his hands on all our webs, and Gala Lumina was his favorite time.

There was something about Lumina that Peter wanted me to know. All I knew were the tourist things from the banners. I found myself wishing for an objective third party I could consult. A book. We didn't even have a website. If only someone had ever kept track of Skysill's weird history—and yes. Yes there was an objective third party who knew all the city's secrets back to its founding. The realization would've made me smile but ghosts can't. And just like that I had a plan for the next day.

Ocean starlight through the window fell, soft and uncomplicated. I knew flesh me was exhausted. I'd *been* him only an hour before. So for good stewardship and having energy to execute my tomorrow plans, I had him two fist my phone and then moved him toward the bedroom to sleep him.

No ghosts in the bedroom. We were still in ghost range but had some privacy. Did that mean I wouldn't be sleeping in my own body? What was that going to be like? I sat him on the mattress. The phone fell to the floor sizzling *dominion*. I wondered if it even worked, and had him get it and knuckle text. It took forever.

How peter? I knuckled Veronica.

Alive, she replied. *He is with Nella. Do NOT leave the building tomorrow without talking to Nella!*

Whatever, I texted, cryptic and petulant the way I can't help being.

Next I had him text Amelia.

We have talk abt mom dad, he tapped. I didn't wait for her reply. She'd assume I was drunk since it was after nine. She'd leave it for tomorrow. And she was still mad at me, I was pretty sure, for not stopping Caroline from reading my psychic vision into Veronica's *inclusion*. Or for something related to that? Who knows. She's the one who usually keeps track of that stuff for me.

Finally, I had him knuckle Caroline.

Are you up? I wrote. *It's just ghosts at my place it's boring.*

I didn't wait for her reply but texted, *can't do telepathy I'm a ghost how r you?*

But she was sleeping, or her phone was out of charge—it had to happen to other people too—so I tried another experiment. I laid flesh me on the bed, his head on the pillow, and I closed his eyes, and I watched him. Would he go to sleep? We needed rest. He was beat to shit. He looked very peaceful. But it was impossible to say—was he sleeping?

Ghost bodies I discovered do *not* sleep. They float beside beds for hours through the night with nothing to do, which I've been told isn't my strength. For a while I continued wondering about the Gala Lumina and whether there really were any facts for me to find, and thinking of five dark bodies spread apart on wet grass and a little girl stumbling from bleachers, bloody and blank with shock. I couldn't get her out of my mind.

Then almost instantly it was morning. Thank god.

Flesh me sat up, then stood. Ghost me pivoted. And a new day began.

In the bathroom I rinsed my flesh again. He still had red under his fingernails. He had stubble but I wasn't comfortable handing him a razor. I did let him style our hair, pinning the brush betwen two fists. He'd gotten pretty good at that kind of maneuver, better than any puppeting I could do. In the kitchen I fed him fruit and crackers and gave him a raw egg—he was amazed by it—and had him drink as much water as he'd hold, like preparing him for a trip into the outback.

When I walked him past the living room I saw ghosts in all the same spots. And I thought, if the ghosts are all in my penthouse and not out on the road maybe it's safe to take a car. I liked flying all right but it still felt a little showy. I checked in the hall for fresh island wear because I'm easy to train and yes, there was a new set. These people were really taking care of me and I had no idea why. Phil seemed to have a never ending supply of clean shorts. He was a godsend to a person like me who had a penthouse but didn't own any clothes. I let flesh me half dress himself, then got us into the elevator.

The doors closed, and snip-snap I was back in one body.

Instantly I felt bloated, like maybe I'd throw up, and regretted the egg. Also, flesh me had put my shorts on backward, and combing my hair he'd scraped a painful groove on my scalp. All things considered, I felt pretty good.

"Don'go anyplace'n *come 'ere*," the air said to me.

"That scares the *shit* out of me Nella!"

"Come'n the office," she insisted. "S'important."

"Fine," I sighed. It felt nice. I did it again. "But I have a lot to do today so it'll have to be fast."

My backward shorts chaffed when I stepped out on the third floor, so I stopped and pulled them off, to turn them, and noticed the large tags stapled inside. Someone needed to pay more attention dressing me.

Then Phil came out of his office into the hall. He carried an ice sculpture of an eagle. He saw me with my pants in my hands. I've spent too much time naked at parties and in life drawing class and in alleys to care about not having underwear. I nodded at him as I pulled a staple out.

His sculpture looked slippery. He made a tight face, breathing through his teeth to show me ice is cold, but he didn't come any closer. He watched me holding my pants and his eyes fell to my crotch.

"Hey big guy," he said.

"You got my message? Stop guarding the front door?" I asked, ripping tags.

"Sure," he nodded, "I get all your big messages."

"Also stop going into my penthouse or you'll die."

He nodded and continued studying me while his eagle melted. The eagle was getting colder and colder, you could see, but Phil didn't move.

"So the Bradley's now clothing optional?" he wondered.

"If you want," I said.

"Because I have no problem with penises."

"Awesome, hey let me ask you a question. A lawyer called you a legal liability the other day. All you Bradley family tenants. Does that ring any bells with you?"

"Jeez, could be anything," Phil shrugged, though I thought he looked worried. Like maybe he knew something I didn't. Which said at least as much about me as it did Phil.

I finally got my shorts pulled on and Phil waddled to the elevator, and when the doors spread he stepped in and braced his ice sculpture. It continued to slip. He tried several strategies but couldn't get the button pushed.

"Where're you going?" I asked.

"Lobby," he said, so I pressed the lobby for him.

"Thanks big guy," he said, eyes wandering back to my crotch. He had no idea he was doing it. It was kind of sweet.

"What's with the eagle?" I asked.

As the doors closed Phil was saying, "Bradley mascot of course, goes with the Bradley motto *Death From Above*! Caw! Caw! Ca..."

He made the sculpture dive as the elevator took him away. How he'd manage any future buttons I didn't know. I turned toward my former office and wondered if this was going to be one of those days where it's impossible to get out of your Building, or was this just what happened when you lived in a building?

Asher Gale's was an office I'd started thinking of as mine but immediately had to surrender. Now it was more like a public restroom or a mall parking lot, claimed by whoever got there first. This time when I came through the door I found Veronica's midnight madness metaverse gone and the walls familiar eggshell blond, and friendly morning sunlight coming through the windows.

Peter by the Beach stretched at his usual end of the room, suspended in the air. His heels were a few inches off the floor and the rest of him tilted up like he lay in an invisible display case. Five pairs of monks sat on the floor, posted in two lines ending at Peter's feet. All were humming a chord that never stopped.

Between the monk pairs five glimmering, increasingly large toruses floated, the smallest ring near Peter's feet, the largest near me, so he appeared to be hanging at the small end of a science fiction speaking tube. The toruses wavered, fractionally distorting light from the windows though mostly transparent. Some kind of *siglium*, I assumed, because I like using words I don't know the meaning of. Nella sat in a waiting room chair, watching Peter.

"Are you healing him?" I asked, taking a stab.

"No," she said in the air.

"What am I doing here?" I wanted to know.

She turned to me and spoke with her lips, just to make sure I got the gravity.

"After slaughter last night," she said, "everything's shit, Five Family peace falling apart."

"Okay, but those are not my problems."

"Hey asshole don't be an asshole remember? Listen. Pierre can't have an interruption a'this point. S'delicate. Got to hide him, from Families, from this Adept somewhere. So that's you."

"Me what? Not speaking as an asshole but what the fuck are you talking about?"

"This's your building Mr. landlord these're your people, so's all your problem, you either clear 'em out or keep'm quiet. Or I will. No one can know Peter's here are we agreed?"

"Agreed on what? What's even happening here?"

"The umbra eye. Pierre's falling through all the umbra eyes, back to the beginning." She was still talking with her mouth but the funny thing was it made her seem more distant and less normal. "Pierre's coming back to us. Back to the present."

"I'm not drunk enough to make sense of this. Hold on."

I looked for a bottle—one of what might have been considered *my* bottles but which were now public property—and found gin on the floor. I opened it and gestured *continue*, listening while I swallowed compensation.

"Like this," she sighed. "I'm explain one time. *Sigliums.* You know them?"

"Eh," I shrugged. "That's your radio network. Your sound sculptures."

"Siglium's for all kinda things," she said, her hand out for the bottle. I relayed it. "Art n'all yeah. Weapons too. Hook'em up you can network sound. Sense to you so far?"

"Like you're a drunken, talking encyclopedia. Get to how it involves Peter."

"Siglium network takes sound in th'present, like radio whatever, but'also sound in the past. Right? Networked siglium let you travel further back to older sound. Much farther. Lensing back and back and back to when the first node built."

"Like a telescope," I said, taking the bottle, "for sound."

"You're'little smarter'n you look," she marveled. "S'called a *traversal*. Use any group networked siglium created at different times. Listen all the way back. Guess the world's deepest siglium network?"

"Always a test with you people," I complained. "Just say it. What's the deepest?"

"Umbra eyes," she answered. She said it soft, amazed. "Aeternus leaves'm every quorum going back...we don't know how far. And Pierre found'an umbra eye here. Skysill *Beach*. He got through this one now's going down. It's a traversal. Back to th'beginning." Her amazement grew as she talked. She shook her head. "Using *umbra eyes* for traversal. He's the best of us."

"Got it. Totally. What happens when he gets to the beginning of time?"

She turned to me. She gave me her full, open lidded, wonder filled attention.

"Trampoline mother*fucker*!" she said, for the first time gesturing at the floating toruses and the monk pairs. "He comes shooting back! An we catch'm in that. Once he bounces on the bottom he'll come *fast*. Might be some earthquakes."

"Earthquakes?"

She held up her fingers to show how little they might be. I found myself watching Peter. Watching as he invisibly fought off hidden Adepts, traversed sound-time, discovered butchery—he got more done in a few days than a lot of people in five hundred years. I took the bottle again.

"So he's already going down, toward the first quorum?"

"Started on the ridge last night."

"The umbra eye's up there?"

"No. Somewhere'n Skysill though."

"What about this Adept he's battling? How's he involved?"

"Adept's tryin' stop' Pierre. Maybe Adept *made* this umbra eye."

I tried mental math. It was just addition so I was confident.

"The umbra eye's been in Skysill two hundred years so this Adept's..."

"Very old who knows? All we'cn do now's wait. Pierre's in trance, heart beats every ten seconds. Could bounce back any time. *Trampoline.*"

I handed her the bottle. I'd forgotten how satisfying it was, drinking on a stomach full of undigested breakfast. I pointed at Peter.

"Okay, when he starts coming back call me. Or whatever. Use your network. I want to be here. I'll remind the Bradley family to keep their mouths shut. Not that they're credible witnesses to anything, no one would listen. And you take care of Peter."

"Hey, Spectu," she aired as I was exiting the office, "las'night blasted couple'a drones. Watch your back."

I gave her a thumbs up and let the door shut behind me. People love the thumbs up, it absolves them of responsibility. The vodka had calmed my stomach. While I waited for the elevators I examined the three Gale canvases still leaning on the floor. Of those I found I preferred my mother's. My father's canvas was brilliant, very formal —except for the sub-shade dog—but the piece seemed mildly critical, to which I'm sensitive. My own painting totally discarded criticality. It had never heard of criticality. It was unmoored.

But Katerina's wave was just pure, almost overwhelming love for waves. Just because you can't see Higher *light* doesn't mean you can't see meaning. In fact Higher *light* may be an impediment. I loved the way my father's hand and hers had combined on that canvas. They'd been utterly synched. The painting was like a conversation in pigment, like they'd been reading each other's minds.

As I got in the elevator I was thinking about telepathy. Caroline had said it—Katerina and Marlon had felt a lot like Caroline and I. Polarized. Just the fact of Katerina hiding from Aeternus so she could be with Marlon showed how obsessed they were. Considering what Aeternus was capable of, that risk was insane. But they'd pulled it off for years, living together...which meant, I realized, they'd somehow controlled their polarity. Even without the crystals—Katerina had given away Marlon's neutral crystal, she'd given it to Celine—and they'd been able to share a life. They'd *touched* each other. How had they done it?

In the elevator I noticed an eagle talon melting in the corner, and then the doors opened. Late morning sun eased over the floor, tinted green by our windows, giving the lobby a quiet, aquarium feeling. The desk still blocked the door. I went and stood on it, and watched through the glass for glowing cops or drone pilots or dancers, and seeing nothing up in the sky or in any shadows I called a Lyft. Three minutes later I pushed the lobby doors open, jumped to the sidewalk, and scampered into the car, checking above as I ran.

The driver was a midlife Skysill surfer. He'd coconut-scented the air. Sometimes I like that because it reminds me of Kalua, but this morning it started my stomach queasing. I started feeling light-headed the minute I sat. Because of course it's always something.

We sliced out into traffic. Even sitting, my balance was bad. I had a moment of neck twisting dizziness. It wasn't the coconut. Was I getting sick? From Phil's fruit? I moaned. I tried laying on the back seat but it was worse. I sat up just as a cop car raced by.

My driver shook his puka bracelets in disbelief.

"Can you believe this man?" he asked, glancing in the rearview.

"No," I said, " I don't even try."

Another cop whipped by, sirens blasting. My head pulsed.

"That's fifteen," the driver muttered. "Fifteen murders. What's going on, man?"

"Fifteen murders?" I asked, confused, watching both cop cars turn inland. A pendulum turned my stomach and the rest of me tilted the opposite way. I moaned again.

My driver counted murders out loud for my benefit.

"Plus five murders last night," he counted, "up in the Park, so that's *more* than fifteen, man."

"You're saying...murders?" I said, feeling I might throw up.

"Dude, there's been like dozens of murders in just *this week*. I sell grass to a janitor at the sheriff's and they think it's a gang war. Hey are you going to throw up? If you're going to throw up drop the window and pitch it that way."

"*Dozens* of murders?" I said, thinking of the handful I was familiar with, "I think I would've heard..."

When my dizzy confusion expanded to sway my head side to side I gripped the edge of the seat, speechless, while my driver rolled out murder math.

"Dude just *count*. I love crime so I totally count, it's like second nature now. First was that art collector dude stabbed in The Seacliffs. Then that artist stabbed on the beach—those two were *stabbed*, man. So hardcore. Then those five homeless dudes supposedly murdered, according to my janitor, and also five painters dying in that arson murder, then that car bomb the other day where that chick was killed and those two cops in that shootout, and now *five more murders* in the park? That's like, how many was I? In *two weeks*. It's like Armageddon, I hope someone's making a podcast."

Another sheriff went the other direction, turning up toward the Park. I wasn't sure about his murder totals, but even half those struck me as a lot of murders for Skysill Beach. Plus, even nauseous, I could think of others he hadn't listed.

But it was too late to correct him. My vertigo came to a head popping crescendo and from the collection of crystals I now had on my chest I felt a deep, dark throb. Not icy. Not sharp. It was a purple bone throb. The new crystal—*thump*—making my muscles twitch, radiating out.

And I was swinging on a pendulum.

Caroline was trying to work her phone but riding a similar pendulum the opposite direction. I recognized this: we'd felt the same thing on the train to Los Angeles. The day Caroline and I almost short-circuited each other to death.

Ash what's...? Caroline's dream voice blurred as the scene in my back seat faded, like shortwave in a tropical storm, fading and swinging back...*do you know what's...*

I'm in ...I thought while plunging toward her, meeting, rushing past...*car I'm...Gala Lumina...*

Her voice swept away, returned dragging a scene behind it. The scene unfurling was the inside of Psychic Touch. I fell into it. Saw what she was seeing.

Her own view lurched and she staggered into a chair. Were we in trouble here, I wondered? Me seeing what she's seeing? But then that faded too. Shay's new crystal pounded me deeper, my bones rang... *throw up...*

We stopped talking or thinking to control our stomachs and the pendulum slowed. After a time its motion stilled.

And we were sitting on a wooden swing at the edge of a forest. Before us a small greensward ran to the edge of a cliff. It was the spot we'd come to the first time we discovered our telepathy. I could sense her beside me but couldn't see her. I was locked in position, face forward. Facing the show.

The last time, this show had been our two massive, lust addled flesh bodies tearing each other's clothes off in an Amtrak car. This time, past the cliff edge, I saw a perfectly manicured garden, flower beds in squares, trees in rows, neatly formed paths moving toward a mansion painted poppy yellow with lavender trim. The door of the mansion was open.

It was just the most natural thing to fall off the swing and through the door. I found myself going down a long hall. I stepped into a room with doors on four sides showing more halls, like the set of a game show about doors and halls. This house I'd entered was large. Maybe endless. Chairs faced each other in some rooms, comfortable looking, perfectly spaced. Dormer chests stood, closed, against walls. Above each chest hung a shelf with little boxes.

It was so well organized I knew instantly what I was looking at. I'd pendulumed in and now I was looking at Caroline. This was her. *Inside.* Not telepathy, but something more.

I think I'm inside you, I thought out loud. *Can you hear me?*

I think I'm inside you. Oh my god.

It's amazing here.

My god Ash. What <u>is</u> all this?

All what exactly?

Inside...you're... she took a moment, clearly stunned, then said, *it's a crazy theme park where I am. Is this what your brain's like every day? How do you get anything done?*

I never know, I admitted. *I wish I was like you. Over here it's...*

What do you see? She asked, sounding suddenly tense.

You're very, how do I say...organized.

Okay, well I'm sure it looks that way to you. God lord Ash, is this a boy thing? Are you all like this?

No, I'm different. That's what I tell myself.

It's amazing!

I felt her laughing. She was extremely fascinated by whatever mess she'd found. I wondered if I shouldn't be freaking out, since one of my bodies was at this very moment being driven by a surfer with limited math skills down a busy coastal highway with absolutely no oversight. But the place I was astounded me, being in Caroline's halls and doors and seeing her chests and shelves. Everything in its place. Nothing could get lost here. You could breathe.

It was a revelation.

Oh my <u>god</u>, she laughed, delighted, *there's a dragon with feet made of tea kettles! He's going up a staircase of playground dreams and eating a coyote.*

Over here it's doors and halls and shelves. It's super restful.

I love him! He changed into a rock band. I love it inside you!

The Caroline room was warm, soft, and smelled like chocolate and rain and the back of her neck. Not scrubbed and washed but a work smell. Musky, delirious, dirty hot, sensuous.

Something new caught my attention—strolling away down one corridor was a small black animal. Padding softly, waving a tail like a wand. A cat. A black cat. He stopped and looked back, then continued walking. I found myself drifting down the hall after him. A tour guide?

Then, somewhere, I heard a voice. Something poked my chest.

"Hey," cried the voice, echoing in the halls of Caroline. "Dude, yo! Snap out of it, yo! It's your stop. Skysill Beach Historical Society."

As though rising from a well of dreams I surfaced and found myself back in my ride share. The sound of Caroline's laughing amazement faded. I emerged dripping confusion, in my regular body, thinking about a cat. The crystal throbbing faded.

My driver was leaning into the back seat with a water bottle to poke me. Focus, I said to myself, though I knew how likely that was to help. The car was idling at a curb. Out the window I saw the terra-cotta dollhouse where they kept Skysill Beach's Historical Society museum.

"Dude, have some water," my driver said, "come back to Earth. Hey. You okay?"

I grabbed the bottle, grateful he hadn't touched me. I'd been out like a light, he could've filled me with brain poison and I would've been defenseless. What'd just happened? A new Caroline thing? What an astounding, super dangerous mystery she was.

The driver watched, worried.

"Was I freaking you out?" he asked. "About the murders?"

"No, no, it's a thing with my girlfriend," I explained. "She's amazing."

"Awesome. A dude left a one star review yesterday from me supposedly talking about all these murders but I think people *like* hearing about murders. I know I do. Keep the water but you gotta get out, ride's over."

My crystal gave a final pulse and lay still. The driver was pointing at the history headquarters but I needed a moment before heaving out on a new sidewalk. I wanted to think about this escalation with Caroline.

But from my back seat I saw the thick oak of the Historical Society door open and let out a tiny man in cranberry and sunflower garments, his shaved skull polished like obsidian. He carried a shopping bag. He closed the door and turned to lock it, then shook the handle gently. After that he stepped from the landing and took the little path through succulents toward the back of the building. Shelby. My favorite historian. Going home early?

CHAPTER

FIFTEEN

I came out of the car like something from a cat's mouth and my surf driver sped off. Shelby had almost made the corner before I'd staggered into the cactus garden and cut him off. I tried looking harmless and happy, just someone really eager for history. I didn't know if he would remember me. His face was old bird bones under ancient skin, eyes a little cloudy.

"You probably don't remember me," I started.

"You came on the 19th," he said. He chuckled. It was wind chimes.

"Yes, that might have been me, you would know, you never forget a date," I gushed, just trying to charm him. Failing but trying. I nodded at the locked front door. "So the past is closed for the day?"

"I'm afraid so."

"Ah, man. I was hoping we could talk. You know. About history."

He sighed. "I'm afraid the museum is now closed *permanently.* Yesterday was my last day. I only came back because I remembered some things I'd left in the fridge." He showed me his bag.

"You quit?" I protested.

"Oh no," he shook his head. "No, the entire Historical Society has been shut down I'm afraid. By the arts council. I've been told it was a funding issue. Isn't it always a funding issue?" He found that a little funny but I didn't.

"But you're Skysill's only historian. They closed you *down*?" I heard the desperation. I hoped it wouldn't scare him off.

"I'm afraid so. It is a sad day," he said. "Inevitable, perhaps."

We watched each other standing in his succulents, and after a moment he looked at his watch.

"Okay, Shelby," I said. "I'm just going to lay it all out. I need your help. For history."

"For history?"

"It's these murders."

"Oh. Yes, it's been terrible, hasn't it?" he agreed, with a grim head shake.

"And I think my own parents might have been murdered in Skysill in the *past*." I was trying to hook him with a mystery. Also it was true. I wondered if it'd be enough.

"Oh dear!" he said. "What do the police say?"

"This was years ago. I used to think they abandoned me but now I think they were murdered."

"How horrible. How truly horrible. By whom? Do you know?"

It was a historian's kind of question. Names and dates, that's what they liked. I didn't know what to tell him. I spun my *sight* up to check for Higher talismans, pins or buttons, but saw none. He wasn't one of us. He liked colored clothes but he was pure visible spectrum. It wasn't going to help, getting into details about Aeternus. There was no sense mentioning Peter. I shoved off in a different direction, purely on instinct.

"I didn't really know my mom but I'm pretty sure she was a Fenestram dancer," I started, "so I'm trying to find where the dancers are from. And I know they come every year for Gala Lumina. Do you know about Gala Lumina?"

I knew he knew. It was a leading question, the kind historians probably see right through, but I was desperate. He watched me not acting as desperate as I felt and titled his head.

"We do have our Gala Lumina *wing*," he observed. I saw a gleam in his eye, the one he seemed slightly blind in. "Perhaps...shall we get our hands dirty in the annals? One last time? No guarantees, of course." He smiled. "Please don't tell the arts council."

"Shelby, you're my new best friend."

He laughed. This time I let it relax me just to put him at ease. He deserved that much. He unlocked and opened his speakeasy gate and took me into his sanctum, setting his paper bag by the guest registry and flipping lights on. The entrance hall split off in three arched galleries. I'd seen them before: *The Fenestram Legacy* to the left, *Skysill Beach - A Planned Community* at the end of the hall, and *The Gala Lumina* to the right. All in solid adobe, like it'd been here since the dinosaurs.

Shelby guided me into the Gala Lumina wing, though calling it a wing was just doing him and his Society a favor. It was one room, dense with documentation—shit I'd never be interested in under any other circumstances, and which I had no idea how to make sense of. Shelby didn't need any help from me, thankfully. I gave him my mother's name. He dove in happily, opening drawers, rifling documents, making fascinated connections between disparate facts as he recalled anecdotes. For several hours I watched him infer shadows of truth from scanty data.

He was some historian. But by the end of his search I knew as little as ever. Every winter solstice Skysill Beach has a big party. That was the gist. None of his documents touched on the Dancers at all. Which seemed strange to me. I felt my hopes flagging. They always do.

"It's rather *peculiar*," Shelby agreed when I mentioned it. "No original sources on the Dancers."

"You think there might be some in the other wings?" I asked. "*The Fenestram Legacy*? They're called Fenestram dancers. Maybe they're part of the Legacy."

His enthusiasm for our project still seemed high. He nodded. I followed him to the second room. In the Legacy room it was all pictures of Rome, and examples of glasswork in small enclosures. Shelby dove back into history and this time I actually learned a little, which sometimes happens if I'm not paying enough attention.

The Fenestram Company was old, early Rome old, possibly the oldest continuously operating company in history. Pretty much what Veronica had said. Historically, Fenestram was credited with seminal advances in glassmaking. Over time the company became a commercial behemoth with holdings in science, agriculture, steel, philanthropy—the list went on. The whole Legacy. Ownership was passed through one family, the Fenestrams. None of it had anything to do with my parents. And history didn't say why the Fenestram Company had recently completely stopped functioning.

I presumed Veronica had fully investigated this Fenestram family. She'd chased down all these leads already—if there's one thing billionaires are good at it's opposition research. So I was happy to ignore them. But I couldn't ignore the fact that nowhere in dissecting the Fenestram Legacy did we find reference to the Dancers, or their connection to Gala Lumina.

"I have a friend," I told Shelby as we stood lacking any insights. "He said something started at Gala Lumina. Do you have any idea what that could be?"

"Even a historian needs more to go on than that," he said, with a sad smile.

"Why are they called Fenestram dancers if the company's not even associated with them?" I complained. "There has to be a missing record...I'm not sure this Society of yours really even knows what it's doing, really, I mean..."

It came out pretty surly and I was sorry for that, but I was running out of what historians call *any slim chance of finding what I was looking for* and Shelby saw what was happening.

"It's a matter of available texts," he consoled me. He himself had begun looking strained by this time, like it'd been almost enough history even for him. I felt bad pushing my elderly historian friend around his museum like a metal detector, desperate for a ping, since I was here on nothing but a hunch—but Shelby himself had said historians follow their hunches.

"One room left," I suggested. "Is it worth a look?"

He sighed, peering at me a little dubious, but finally nodded. "You have a historian's persistence, young man."

"Yeah. I want to learn history so I'm not doomed to repeat it. Repeating it would suck."

"I'll tell you a secret," he said, flipping on lights so we could view the last gallery, *Skysill Beach - A Planned Community*. "We're all doomed to repeat history."

"Then what's the point of learning it?"

"The point is very simple: while history endlessly repeats, *meaning* evolves. We learn, and learning, we evolve the meaning of history. And advance."

"Shelby. You should write a book."

"Oh no," he chuckled. "I'm much too busy reading. Shall we?"

The third room was the one I'd already spent time in. It was all photographs and maps and models of Skysill Beach. In that room you learned how Skysill had been built on a scheme created over two hundred years earlier—though I now knew the scheme was actually at least five hundred years old, schemed in the Renaissance when Aeternus discovered that the Paths were about to break. I knew Skysill hadn't actually been built according to the scheme; it looked today the way it was always going to look. The scheme had been modeled on *it*.

The photos, thick on the walls, went left to right in chronological order, showing the city swelling into existence through the decades, spreading up and down the coast. The earliest photos showed a scion of the Fenestram family, Cosimo Fenestram, a glum man holding rolled up plans under one arm, with a group of other glum men in high-waisted breeches and tight vests behind him. Something about one of those photos caught my eye. Something familiar. It was the view. I knew the hilltop where those men stood.

At that moment Samantha came shimmering in with her *dominion* carnival dance, and my fists balled, and I popped. Mount Obitus gloomed in. I hung behind my flesh body, facing the photo of Cosimo Fenestram.

But before I could lay out my first choice word, she disappeared again.

I snapped back to one body. My fists limbered. I think I gasped. Shelby glanced my way. Fucking Samantha. What was that, like a wrong number?

I was about to offer Shelby a shrug and no explanation when Samantha came back and I fist clamped and ghost popped again. I hung facing the wall while her ultraviolet super saturation swirled and Mount Obitus swooned up—and then she disappeared.

"Gagh!" I grunted, and now Shelby looked concerned, but before I could move, Samantha came *again*, and out I popped, then she vanished, and back I merged—and suddenly she was flickering in and out, faster and faster, over and over, like nothing she'd ever done before. Shelby stared at me. It was obvious I was insane. And probably a danger to myself or others.

I don't know how many cycles we went like that, pop, hang, merge, before I started to see what she was trying to tell me, but it was too many cycles. It must be frustrating to people. Ghosts. Whatever. Eventually I noticed—the photo of Cosimo Fenestram changed every time I popped, and changed back when I merged.

Every time I was a ghost a new figure appeared behind Cosimo and his men on the hill.

The figure was male. I couldn't see him when I looked from flesh eyes but as a ghost I saw him standing there taller than the others, naked but for a loincloth, with wide Mediterranean eyes and curling black hair in ringlets. The Cosimo tintype was blurry, details hard to make out, but I saw it clearly enough—over this figure's heart was a mark. A tattoo. A familiar, dark tattoo. Of an eye with five pupils inside a triangle. The umbra eye.

I raised my arms, over the course of seven or eight transitions, and pointed with my fist.

Then Samantha flashed out, stayed out, and I gave myself a seat on the floor, just for security. I was weak, my breath ragged. I was sweating. Shelby was so concerned he asked if he should call an ambulance. I told him I needed food, which was actually true.

And when my wits were back I stood and stepped close.

When I looked at the photo now, with my regular Aspectu flesh eyes, there was no figure. All I saw was blurred ocean background. I splayed the ultraviolet spectrum wide but saw nothing. Cosimo and his men stood on a high ridge where bougainvillea grew in bunches. It was the bougainvillea that had tipped me—first I recognized the bushes, then the rest was obvious. The sweep of the coast, the hillside falling away, Point Marshal just visible to the north. This picture had been taken two hundred years ago on the ridge where Waylon Goodman's estate would one day be built. One of the most beautiful views in the city. A hilltop spectacle that had regularly *stormed* me whenever Waylon badgered me up to talk to him.

"Whaa..." I asked Shelby, pointing at the photo, "hooo..."

"What is it?" he asked, peering at the picture. "Nothing to do with Dancers, surely?"

"What do...you know about this photo?" I managed. He peered. For a historian his eyes really kind of sucked. Maybe he made up for that with his other sense—of history. He shook his head.

"Not much is known. These are some of the earliest documents in the collection," he told me. "Unattributed photographer. This shows Cosimo Fenestram and his planning committee, the year Skysill was founded. Taken when our city was literally nothing but a tangle of buckthorn and manzanita, without a road or building. They came in by boat."

I pointed to the empty spot where the semi-naked, tattooed man was not, at that moment, visible. "Do you see anything right there?"

He squinted. He looked at me. "The ocean behind them?"

"I don't...know. Do you think the arts committee would mind if I borrowed this from the collection?" Shelby smiled, shook his head, and we both laughed at my joke. I got my phone. "How about a photo?"

"Usually discouraged," he said. "But for a fellow historian, an exception can be made."

I copied each of the five Cosimo photos, though this was the only one that had changed. I was filled with new confusion. I sighed, then did it again, then turned to Shelby, who was paying very close attention to all my sighing and wondering if he'd made a mistake letting me into his clubhouse. Or maybe I was just like all the other historians now. Just hopelessly lost.

"I should go," I told him. He thought so too, much as he'd enjoyed our time together finding nothing. He led me toward the front door. He turned off lights as he went. His eyes lingered in corners, on this display or that, and I remembered he was leaving for the last time. We got to his shopping bag by the door. We'd been there most of the day.

"So I guess this is the end for you here?" I asked, by the guest registry. He nodded, taking out his keys and opening the door.

"Everything ends," he said.

"What'll you do? Can you go to another Society? Are historians in demand?"

"The job market's a little dry," he admitted with a smile. "No, I've been in Skysill more years than I care to count, so whatever time I have left I'll spend here. I am where history has brought me." He held out his hand. "Make the best of whatever life you're permitted, young man. Control what you can, appreciate the rest. Live a good life."

And then, because I was feeling a little choked up, and also I just don't pay any attention to what I'm doing, I reached and shook the hand he held out. Just as our fingers closed I realized what I'd done. I braced for brain rot.

But instead I got a warm tide of energy rising around me, up my ankles, over my chest, up past my head. I found myself smiling down on Shelby's wizened face. Just the two of us in all the world. Shelby smiled back, dark and thin and intrigued to the end. Shelby was going to die tomorrow, I saw. He'd die in downtown Skysill Beach, on a sidewalk in the middle of the day. Just like that. He'd die in the city he'd studied all his life.

All the while I shook his hand the knowledge was very comforting.

But then I let him go and the warm tide ebbed. And I felt cheated. Cheated by it all. Shelby gets fired one day before he dies? It wasn't fair. I was sure he'd rather die opening a drawer or fixing a chart. Better at a desk, surrounded by useless old knowledge, than on a city sidewalk.

"Maybe you should...stay here another day," I croaked out. "Catch up on research. Order food. What's another day matter to the Arts Council?"

"A pleasant thought," he smiled, "but that simply delays the inevitable."

"People don't always know what's inevitable."

"Oh, but I do," he said, peering at me as though just now realizing how little attention I'd been paying. "The study of history is nothing but the study the inevitable. I'm afraid I'm an expert."

What can you say to that? Hardly anything, if you're a person like me who's been paying very little attention. Shelby turned, passed through his Historical door, and I followed him out, where late afternoon sun was lengthening into shadow. He locked everything.

"Shelby," I said, "it's been fantastic to know you. I mean really. You're great."

"Here," he said, holding out his bag. "This will go bad if it's not eaten. I'm not hungry."

I gestured to say *thanks, just put it on the ground, I don't think I can stand to touch you again,* which amazingly, he understood. I'd found myself more and more reliant on charades recently. I wondered if maybe I should have been a mime, if my life would have made more sense that way.

"Goodbye young man," he said. "I'm sorry about your mother. It is a difficult thing when the people we value slip into the past. Perhaps we'll meet again." I nodded *sure that might happen.* And then, with a wave, he disappeared around the building.

People die all the time, I consoled myself. It's got nothing to do with me. I'm just a person in a cactus garden who's hungry and needs a ride, not a ghost-eating Inmortalis responsible for everybody dead and all their ghost problems. It wasn't very convincing though.

I phoned myself a car and while I waited I looked in Shelby's bag, where I found two cellophane grocery sandwiches, which I ate. It was better this way since Shelby might not've had a chance to eat them, and thinking that, I found his sandwiches harder to swallow. I forced them down though.

What I really wanted to do, I realized, was talk it over with Caroline, an impulse I was having more and more. She was the only person I knew with problems like mine, or that were at least as hard to understand as mine. As hard to believe. I was aching for someone to tell me there wasn't anything to be responsible for, though that seemed like a lot of responsibility to put on her. I just wanted her voice-echo in my brain. I wanted to lay in her garden. So restful and well organized. I sent out a telepathic invitation. Come on in.

But my car got there before I felt anything. As the driver pulled into traffic I settled deeper in the back, digesting sandwiches, preparing for the pendulum disorientation of Caroline. It was a twenty-minute drive to the Seacliffs. I was wondering if that would be long enough, when suddenly Nella was air voicing in front of me.

I sat up and yelled. The driver didn't notice. She'd put me in a cone of silence.

"You'shd come back to the office," Nella said. "Come *now.*"

"God damnit wear a bell or something!" I shouted, prepared with other complaints, then stopped short. "Is it Peter? Is he doing his trampoline back?"

"No," she said, "told you there'd be earthquakes. It's th'other Auditus, the Adept, blanketing everything. On the move suddenly. Something's goin'happen."

"That's it?" I protested. "Some Auditus someplace is moving around? You scared the shit out of me—maybe he's taking a walk! Leave me alone. Actually wait. I want to throw something out. This Adept you can't find, who's *moving*—you know who's *also* out of touch right now, moving somewhere? And also a mystery? Roman Sutherland. And let me ask you, do we *really* know Roman's even Aspectu? I don't think so. I don't think we know shit about him."

Suddenly Veronica's voice barbed from the air

"Are you suggesting Roman is the Auditus Adept? Do not be absurd," she snapped.

"Fine. Did you people just call to berate me or is there something?"

"You should be with Peter," Veronica—or Nella pretending to be Veronica—insisted.

"Peter doesn't need me," I assured them. "I'll come when he's bouncing. What's the real reason?"

A moment of silence passed which I did not appreciate because I recognized it as the silence other people fill talking behind your back. Then Nella returned.

"We need you here," she admitted. "You're handy'n a fight. Killin' people. A battle's comin', you killin' everybody, that'd let me concentrate on keepin'Pierre safe."

It took a moment. Then I realized she was talking about the *Gray*.

"No!" I shouted. "Absolutely not. You have no idea what you're asking. You can't let that loose, that guy, he doesn't have just bad judgment, he has *no* judgment. Too dangerous. Anyway I have important errands."

"What could possibly be more important than Pierre, Mr. Gale?" Veronica asked.

"Oh, *what's more important?*" I asked, and heard myself saddling my high horse and climbing up. People love me up there. They appreciate all the effort it takes. "Well I'll *tell* you *what's more impor-tant*—umbra eye stuff, *that's* more important." I found myself putting a lot of awkward emphasis on words I didn't understand because I'm terrible riding a horse.

"What *stuff?* What have you found?" Veronica asked.

"I just found a photo," I explained. I paused a moment to get the theory assembled. I had so many these days, and details are not my forte.

"There's a two-hundred-year-old photo with a hidden image of a half-naked man with an umbra eye tattoo on his chest. Sound familiar? Yes it sounds familiar. It sounds like the guy in all the Kiss paintings. The one being kissed on the ground. We never see his face. Only in this photo we see his face. I do anyway. I'm the only one who can see the face."

"Mr. Gale," Veronica suggested after a pause, "saying that so often—this or that is conveniently only visible you—does your credibility no good."

"Credibility's useless to me. Listen. I know the place this picture was taken, up at Waylon's estate in the Seacliffs. Right where Samantha grew up. And who was obsessed with paintings of the tattoo man? Samantha, Waylon's daughter. She had Damely buy the last one. You see a connection? I want to know what the tattoo guy was doing two hundred years ago before Skysill Beach even *existed*, getting his picture taken where Samantha would one day live."

Another pause. More talking about me. It was actually kind of restful.

Then Veronica was back. "How can I see this hidden figure?"

"You see him if you're in a ghost body."

"Are you saying the photo is *haunted?*" she sighed. "There is a ghost in the photograph?"

"I'm saying, for whatever reason, you can't see the tattoo guy with flesh eyes." I waited. I heard nothing. I waved my hands in front of my face. "Are we done?"

"If you discover anything in the Seacliffs report immediately," Veronica aired out finally.

"Okay I'll report *immediately*," I agreed wholeheartedly, "for *sure*. Hey, you know, you using that arrogant condescending tone all the time does your likability no good, plus..." I caught my driver staring in the rearview, eyes wide. Apparently the cone of silence was gone. The car had stopped. He was the only one listening.

"We're here," he said.

We were idling in Waylon's bougainvillea cul-de-sac. The driver was unnerved by me. He'd seen me waving my arms and arguing with people who did not exist. The way mimes do. I took it as food for thought, though I didn't need more of that food. As I shut the door the car was u-turning away, off down the hill.

The view. The view that used to *storm* me, almost every time. The sky was pure red and orange ignition and Waylon's forged compound gates framed trumpets of sunset cloud. In a few minutes the show would be over, so I took it in, full spectrum, Higher all the way down, amazed that I could. Until the colors desaturated and a wisp of breeze pushed up from the sea far below, and then I turned back to the serious work of investigating things without a license or any qualifications.

I swiped the picture up on the phone: Cosimo Fenestram and his landing party stared at me, Victorian and impatient, unhappy about their heavy sideburns. Two hundred years ago—before there'd been so much as a trail to this high hilltop—Cosimo and crew had climbed here to document something. I knew they hadn't come for the view. People with whiskers and rolls of documents like these, they didn't care about a view. They had empires to run.

Where I now stood the photo didn't exactly match. The men had posed a little north, toward the other end of Waylon's estate. Balancing the phone on the back of one hand I fisted my key blob from my other pocket and ghost popped. It was all totally second nature now, like putting on clothes or pouring alcohol. I puppeted my flesh fists together and squirted *dominion* out the blob to fuse the keys to the bottom of the phone, as an experiment. I'm like a scientist. Then I had the phone mounted on top of one fist like a cell phone lollipop, so I could look at the photo and fly around matching the view. It shows how practical I can be when no one's paying attention.

Then I flew.

Rising over the fence, photo for reference, felt a bit showy, though it's unusual for me to feel any kind of judgment about my behavior. I guess I'd just become the kind of person who flew around anytime he wanted like it was nothing. But I hadn't gone up three yards in the air before I checked my phone and right away, with ghost eyes, noticed the tattoo man in the picture.

What kind of crazy photographic ink or developing chemicals would translate hidden information from a two hundred-year-old tintype into the pixels of a smart phone? Smart phone cameras only reproduce what's present. They don't do invisible ink, digital photos aren't magic, they're just pixels. I know they can't capture a ghost. I'd seen that at Caroline's the time Samantha photo bombed the Monarchs. Did that mean the tattoo man's image was captured in the photo but hidden some other way? Maybe it *was* some kind of magic. I really hoped I wasn't going to discover there were magic spells along with fucking everything else.

It was something I only saw using my ghost eyes. I just accepted it and moved on.

Waylon's bougainvillea fell away below me as I cut north, up the coast. The sun was slipping under the horizon. I kept checking, picture versus view. Waylon's convertibles passed below me, one with a windshield I'd shattered. I floated on, overtopping his sandcastle mansion, his whole estate now dark. Dark as the dead. There was police tape on his front door.

I'd considered the idea that Waylon himself was connected to Cosimo, or the tattoo man, except Waylon'd never betrayed the slightest knowledge of Higher paint or *sight* or any of the other Fenestram influences percolating in Skysill Beach. Waylon had been rich and criminal minded, had come to Skysill for buying and stealing, and he'd settled high on a hillside, the way the rich always do. But his only interests had been laundering money and raising a daughter. He was the multi-millionaire I felt least conflicted about.

It must have been a great place for a daughter to grow up though, even with your father a crook. I floated over swimming pools. Stables. There'd been servants, gardeners, chefs. Any distraction money could buy. A father who loved you but could only express it with money was still better than no father. And at least Waylon hated forgeries. Not many people can say that about their parent.

I really hadn't done enough investigating, I thought, for Samantha. For Waylon I'd confirmed that she'd killed herself and I'd moved on. I felt some guilt about it—a feeling I'm seldom sober enough to notice. Samantha, the ghost driven to suicide by Julian's mural, forever locked in Skysill Beach because we'd thrown away her key, had gotten the shortest stick of them all and nobody knew or cared. Not even me. It was kind of shitty. Had there even been a funeral? Waylon himself had been killed just a few days after Samantha, so I doubted he'd made her arrangements. All I knew about her past was Felicia's ghost story of meeting her in Italy. Who had her friends been?

And how had she stumbled onto her obsession with cage cups?

Downslope of Waylon's mansion were dark, manicured gardens, a vineyard, an arboretum, and then I reached the wall ringing the whole estate. I still hadn't found the spot matching the photo. On the other side of Waylon's wall the change in foliage was stark. Waylon's side was colonized, domesticated, but the other was wild and Mediterranean and sheer. A gate stood in the wall there, but overgrown. It couldn't have been used in many years.

Over the gate I floated and up the back break ridge, checking my phone, closer and closer to a match—until view and picture mirrored each other. A pair of reflections separated by two hundred years.

I lowered us to the dirt among tall, stiff shrubs, and turned my ghost off. *Dominion* belled down my arm and my phone broke free as a new blob formed and fell. I grabbed the phone and kicked the new blob down the hillside like you do when something's dangerously toxic.

Cool wind stirred my hair. I heard night birds. Overhead were stars and the Higher borealis. I spun my *sight* wide and surveyed Cosimo's perch. Tall plants crowded me. I saw nothing to mark the spot at all. Why take a picture here? They'd forced a path all the way here from the shore. For what?

In front of me the Pacific thinned toward the horizon, reflecting UV star wash and brightening my undergrowth. The ridge continued rising beyond my landing spot, tangles of vegetation on steep stone. I saw no paths.

Downslope an outcrop of stone sent a finger up through buckthorn at the sky. It was the only feature. I pushed under a branch to get a view down the hill—when behind me leaves cracked. Even as I spun I knew it was a possum or rabbit. That's how jumpy I'd grown.

When I pointed my eyes back to the stone finger, a gleam of *dominion* broke from the outcrop.

I stumble back and the gleam flicked out. My heart went fast, which is not how I do my best work, I know. I eased my breathing. I swallowed, but without vodka that never helps. And then I inched forward again to peer downslope, through semi darkness, to *see* a brilliant sheen, many times brighter than my key blobs. A *dominion* arc light burning on the high, dark hillside. Someone with a cage cup?

Despite my better judgment—which just got weaker and less effective as time went by—I started down the hillside. I moved in absolute silence until the second step I took when a rock flood of debris cascaded out under my foot and I slid, on my back, out of control—the way I'm apt to—watching *dominion* come and go through branches and trunks. One Hawaiian sleeve ripped, my hip raked submerged granite, and then I hit a piece of solid footing and grabbed a branch and stopped myself.

I panted and held my breath, a combination I was surprised existed, with my *sight* spun up. Whatever element of surprise I might have had was gone. I don't know what people expect, though. What am I, a ninja?

I found myself standing at the top of a stairway of stone dropping toward the outcrop, weaving through bramble toward a handful of large stones standing in a crescent, walling off the sea. They looked naturally occurring, but also like a movie set.

And I wondered, had Samantha seen this? Wandering up through her garden gate?

I eased down the steps. They led down onto a flagstone dais raised among the standing stones. And in front of those stones stood a plinth of concrete, with a jagged hole at its peak. A hole right at head height. From the hole *dominion* blasted. The entire top of the plinth glowed, wavery, like sunlight slamming off a lake. Was this what Cosimo and crew had come for? To build this?

In for a penny in for a pound, I thought, and stepped onto the dais.

I crossed the pavers in starlight, silent despite my recent land-slide because the place demanded it. There did not seem to be anyone here. I stepped up to the hole in the column, glowing so bright I had to twist my *sight* down, and even then had trouble looking in. From three feet off the cavity in the top of the monolith made me think of a piñata broken open. Definitely broken open.

One more step and I was peering into a little chamber with a skillfully carved recess in the base. The perfect shape for a half bowl, a thick stem, and a round foot. A place a cage cup, now vanished, had rested. How long had that cup lain there, radiating *dominion*, to satu-rate the plinth like this?

At my feet were the broken shards, also glowing. Those pieces had been years in sun and rain. Their jagged edges had rounded but still they glowed. The plinth had no other marks. The standing stones behind it were unmarked. What had happened here?

I looked back up the hillside to get my bearings, which, I don't know why I even try. This time, though I failed with bearings I did see a sleeping bag discarded beneath the scrub oaks on the other side of flagstones. Around it were empty food containers, a shirt and other homeless flotsam. There was also a small paper box where bullets glinted, and beside that a little junkie kit, needle, strap, spoon and lighter.

A sound from behind spun me. And then my body froze. My *dominion* ball of seven curved up around me. A figure stepped from behind the standing stones, beaming me with *bleed*. I didn't recognize the figure for a second. But his voice gave him away. Sharp, sarcastic, and gentled with smack.

"Asher Gale," Julian said, "could there possibly be anyone I'd rather see?"

I wasn't sure who the question was meant for. Maybe me, maybe him, maybe Santa Claus—with his eyes cue balled and his head lolling it was hard to tell.

And he looked...*old*. His face had deep lines, his hair was steel and snow, his shoulders hunched thin. Over it all he still wore matador black.

He took a step closer, his one hand trembling and beaming me so my joints ground in spasm, his other hand holding a pistol. He waved it like a person who doesn't care where his pistol is pointed when it goes off.

"So...you found me...what difference will it make, you shitfuck, you shitfuck, you shit on *everything*, it's not my fault...he *won't believe me*, and now... look..."

I couldn't talk. I couldn't breathe. I watched Julian tottering closer. For long seconds at a time he seemed to forget I was there at all. I was listening to a conversation he'd been having with himself for hours. Or centuries.

"What did he expect me...to *do*? How else..." he brought the gun up. He remembered me, tried to sight my brains with eyes of polished chalk. I had a flashback to Li Wei doing this and remembered how much I hadn't liked that either.

Julian had no cage cup. No *dominion*. So what he was doing here was all night charge. Just a massive reserve, from what I'd come to understand. Massive.

"The *girl*," he rasped, forgetting the gun again, looking at the sky, to the broken plinth, "the little slut, the little...look...she broke the cenotaph—*broken*—well *I* didn't do it, she took the key...how could she find it *how*?"

Then he looked back to me. It was getting harder to recognize him, he seemed to be folding as I watched. He was slurred and disjointed and teetered to a stop where his *bleed* beamed out against my *dominion* shell. I hadn't taken a breath in a long time. I felt a rib cracking.

"And you came asking questions," he snarled, "so you *know*, you must *know*, and it disappeared and...*ahhhh*—" He sobbed, turned to the shattered chamber and broke into another language, Italian maybe or Latin, something old and full of threats and hatred.

"Tell it!" he shouted at me. "What'd I *do*? Why let me *paint* him if it's going to end like this for me? I've always been his favored...he *described* himself to me! To *me*! And now...now he *replaces* me, his most devoted...*you* destroyed the key, but he protects *you*! I'm *ten thousand times the painter* you'll ever be you simpering child but he replaces *me*?" he sobbed, holding his arms out, showing me track marks and aged, sagging skin. "Why won't he let me die? I keep trying...I love him..."

His veiny, arthritic hand put the barrel to his temple. He cocked the gun. "He kisses me alive for five centuries then leaves me to suffer without him...this is all I have. Before *my* bullet though...yours, I think. That's justice. That's justice."

He thrust his gun through my *dominion* shell and held it a foot from my face, his hand shaking but that wasn't going to matter at this range. And I felt myself start going *Gray*. I fought it back. The *Gray* wouldn't help here. He'd be frozen too. I didn't want to die transformed. Because fuck all my different bodies, the one thing a person should control is the body he *dies* in. Like Shelby said. Control the things you can. No *Gray*, no ghost *storm*. Just me and a gun.

But suddenly a new source of *dominion* flared up and a ghost shimmered in and then I popped from my flesh despite my best intentions. *Storming*. I couldn't even control that. God damnit Samantha. I hung behind flesh me and saw her, Samantha, facing us, and ghosted disappointment at her while Julian's finger tightened. I didn't want to die a ghost.

So I squeezed ghost me and flesh me together. And *dominion* gathered. It heated, my bodies almost merged, and...nothing... nothing in my hand. I remembered too late—no place to channel *dominion*—

—it started to hollow me—

—consumptive heat razor—

—no place to push—

—but—

—I felt a channel; there was one place *dominion* could go, it could go out—

I pushed.

Dominion flowed between my bodies out to my ball and flashed down Julian's *bleed* beam. Straight into his *bleed* fingertips down his arm and across his chest, Julian uncomprehending, sensing something while *dominion* ran up his *other* arm toward the gun. In his hand. Hit the gun. And melted it.

And I was an open circuit, *dominion* a wild torrent flooding down his beam to bind us; it just kept flowing.

Julian screamed. He threw the pistol blob down, staring at it. It lay glowing *light* he couldn't see. At first I assumed it would end there. That I'd merge into one body and *dominion* dissipate. But my ghost was unable to rejoin my flesh because *dominion* hadn't dispersed, it was still flowing through me into another living Aspectu. *Dominion* had to disperse before I could retake my flesh. And I couldn't stop the flow. It wasn't mine to control.

"*What is this?*" Julian raged fear, beaming me still, "what *are you?*"

My seizure was crushing me, shoulders dislocated from pressure. I wanted to scream but couldn't. I gave up merging my bodies and clawed back to my ghost, a refuge from pain at least, and watched Julian's seventy-year-old body shake. His white eyes blinked, his dry tongue lashed and he screamed.

"My night charge is *five hundred years old* and I will *kill—*"

Then suddenly—very suddenly—he stopped screaming and stood absolutely still, looking at his beaming hand. Gently he shook it. His *bleed* beam went side to side but held me, and then he jerked that hand as if trying to get away, and I saw he was locked to me, like I was locked to him. My *dominion* flew down his beam. It held him.

"Why can't..." he whispered.

His confusion was total. Mine was too. I crouched—metaphorically—in my ghost and watched as something was pulled from Julian: he wasn't beaming *bleed*, I realized, sickened. *I was sucking bleed from him.*

I was pulling out his *light.* I couldn't stop it.

He wrenched, twisting like a rabbit, ripping his arm to break it free but he couldn't, *dominion* had him chained. And his face was aging as I watched. He felt it. He touched his skin, eyes sinking deeper under his brow, now bending with scoliosis, neck stiffening.

"Please," he begged, weakening, "not my *light...*"

But *dominion* was a straw and through it I emptied him, so he fell, his beaming arm pinned, pointed at me, and in horror stared as that beam thinned, grew timorous, faltered, and fizzled out.

He'd aged a mummy. His lips a rictus. Teeth missing.

My *dominion* shield vanished when his beam died. But flesh me still couldn't move. I couldn't retake my body; a thread of *dominion* still tied flesh me to Julian. From ghost me I tried to puppet flesh me but he couldn't move. We had a circuit stuck open and *dominion* pouring out, or sucking in, who could tell?

Samantha flicker-shifted to float behind Julian. There she and flesh me faced off, Julian crumpled between them. I knew my circuit wouldn't close until I was one body. But I couldn't be one body until Samantha left.

She was holding the circuit open. She was staying on purpose. For Julian. On *purpose*.

Dominion sucked everything out of him—that was the direction I'd decided on—until it drank his final spark of *light*. But it didn't stop there because Samantha wouldn't leave. *Dominion* wiped his cells, zeroed out his very capacity for *light*. Zeroed him. I felt it and watched as his face collapsed and his hair vanished and bones broke beneath the weight of his few pounds of flesh. It was fucking horrifying.

Samantha, I ghosted, *please, enough! Just—stop—Samantha, enough, just leave!*

Samantha ignored me. They always do. As Julian fell inward, like time lapse decay, Samantha just hung, watching. Finally Julian had but a few seconds to live. Only then did she shimmer away. Maybe so Julian could experience a few extra seconds of loss before he was gone.

Something like what he'd done to her.

My bodies snapped together. I stumbled and crept in the dark to Julian's side, but didn't touch him. I had one question. Only one. I'd realized something just a second earlier. And Samantha'd almost killed him before I could ask.

"Julian," I said, crouching, the night around us deep and still, the foliage and stars pressing down, "you killed Samantha after she came here and took your cage cup. You drove her insane with a painting she couldn't see. But all the other people you kill, you glow them. So why not glow Samantha? Did you try?"

He was whispering. I leaned in. I didn't need to hear. I'd figured it out. He had just a few breaths left. He was a bad person, he'd done grotesque things, so why I felt unhappy seeing him this way I do not know. The smell of him was terrible. Dead animal.

His pupils, visible at last, searched for me. But he was blind.

"I wanted his love again," he whispered. "I collected his paintings...to show him..."

"Samantha," I insisted, "why kill her with a mural? Why not *light* her up?"

"...she was immune..." he breathed, hardly aware I was there. "...don't know why..."

Then he sighed. And a ghost seethed up in the dark behind him, and hung spinning a Higher superstorm. While I, of course, popped a ghost myself. It's all very tiresome. Just endless trivial obstacles.

Julian's ghost held a book, a tiny, rough leather volume with twine for a bookmark. He wore leggings and a codpiece, under a very short, belted tunic. I backed flesh me away. I wanted no Inmortalis operations on this ominous hillside. Or any other, I had about decided. I wanted flesh me out of range of Julian. I pointed him toward the stone stairway. I needed to make a phone call.

Flesh me looked exhausted. He was impervious to inconveniences like pain or hunger, but you *could* exhaust him if you kept pushing. I was happy to see he had sense enough to want to get away from these stones in their ghost-henge. I sent him clambering back to the top of the ridge on his own.

The last I saw of Julian, his ghost spun the night in unbound Higher multitudes hanging over a pile of rags. And beyond him, above, a silhouette against the luminous Higher borealis: Mount Obitus, with its throne, creeping ever closer.

The End of Book Three

Enjoy a sneak peak inside Book Four: *The Sacrifice the Dead Will Make*

❧

CHAPTER ONE

THE RIDGE TOP, when flesh me crawled up onto it, was out of ghost range. My bodies snapped together and I fell, panting, my shoulder killed me where my spasms had wrenched it. I groaned, grabbed it, wondering if I shouldn't just pop again and leave all this discomfort for someone else to feel, but I had phone calls to make so I stayed. Shivering. The air was cold now. It was maybe midnight. The breeze had grown and now it rattled the branches.

I took a moment to rest, which is what people do when they don't know what to do next.

Julian's death worried me. To an outside observer—which invisible Higher *light* made impossible but this was just hypothetical—it might have looked like whatever had happened to him was my fault. But this was another case where I *knew* I hadn't murdered anyone, despite all the evidence. Still I was worried the image—Julian on the ground, just marionette bones in the dark, withered inside a sharp pile of black clothes—might never leave me.

Two times tonight Samantha had invited herself to a party I was already having on my own and both times she'd turned events to her own purposes. First flickering in and out at Shelby's, showing me the figure in the picture, then refusing to flicker out at all, killing Julian once I got where her photo lured me. She had a lot of nerve the way she obviously continued using me. Being annoyed with Samantha made me think about Samantha and I remembered my question to Julian. He hadn't glowed her. He'd played on her tortured subconscious, and she'd killed herself.

I got my phone and dialed the billionaire number.

"Finally," Veronica answered, "and what did you find?"

"Thanks! I'm totally fine," I told her. "Almost murdered in the face a little bit that's all."

She wasn't listening. I heard muted conversation in her background. I wondered if she'd heard my sarcasm, which I'd probably have to do again. What a lot of work. She came back and demanded, "Where are you?"

"Look I told you I'm near Waylon's, what diff—"

She palm muted me once more but I still heard drunken complaining.

"Nella can't hear you," Veronica said. "As though you are beneath a sound dome."

I looked up. That's how suggestible I get when I'm overstimulated. I was under nothing but branches and constellations.

"Who cares, listen," I said, "Julian's dead, years ago Samantha broke his plinth and found his cage cup and I think left it behind, and then Julian took it, but he wasn't supposed to, and now Aeternus's replacing him. And he's dead. Did I say that?"

"What does that mean? Aeternus is replacing Julian?" she asked. She goes on tangents.

"That's what he said. And guess what."

"Please, Mr. Gale, can you...?"

"Julian *painted* Samantha crazy because he couldn't glow her. He couldn't glow her. You know what that means." I gave her a second. I heard her catching up. "Here's my reconstruction. Pay attention I only do one of these a day. Samantha saw *dominion,* she *saw* this plinth glowing with that one Higher *light.* She had to be pretty young, but still she hammered the concrete open and found this goblet. And then she just left it behind, I think because when she touched it, she had a vision of everything there was to know about it. And for the rest of her life she was obsessed with cage cups. See?"

She did. She's not a slow thinker. "Samantha was psychic ... "

CLICK TO BUY BOOK FOUR!

The Sacrifice the Dead will Make: The Book of Taste

AFTERWORD

This ends The History of Light, Book Three: *The Shadow Waiting on its Throne: The Book of Scent*. The History of Light series continues with Book Four, *The Sacrifice the Dead Will Make: The Book of Taste*.

Sacrifice the Dead Will Make begins on a ridgetop, just seconds after the end of Book Three. As Asher becomes more and more fearful of Samantha, and Aeternus tightens his grip on Skysill Beach, the eternal ghost's long-sought prize comes at last into his reach. When Peter's past is finally revealed, Asher finds he is central to the eternal ghost's plans, and as Asher's family, friends, and lovers begin to die, he must become the thing he fears most to save them. To keep the broken Path from ending the world, he'll make any sacrifice he has too, even *The Sacrifice the Dead Will Make*.

THE HISTORY OF LIGHT
BOOKS 1 THROUGH 5

~

— THE GHOST WITH A KNIFE AT HER THROAT: The Book of Sight

— THE QUESTION IN THE DANCER'S KISS: The Book of Sound

— THE SHADOW WAITING ON ITS THRONE: The Book of Scent

— THE SACRIFICE THE DEAD WILL MAKE: The Book of Taste

— THE CURSE AT THE END OF THE WORLD: The Book of Touch

ALSO BY KEVIN HINCKER

The Little Queen

The Einstein Object

A Debt to the Stars

ABOUT THE AUTHOR

Kevin Hincker writes speculative fiction for curious readers. If you'd like to join his mailing list, or find extra information about his books, you can signup, or just explore, at https://kevinhincker.com/

If you want Amazon to deliver you information about his future releases, such as Book Five of this series, go to his Amazon page, https://www.amazon.com/author/kevinhincker and click the "Follow" button in the upper left next to his picture.